WATCH
HER
VANISH

WATCH HER VANISH

ELLERY KANE

bookouture

Published by Bookouture in 2020

An imprint of Storyfire Ltd.
Carmelite House
50 Victoria Embankment
London EC4Y 0DZ

www.bookouture.com

ISBN: 978-1-83888-857-2
eBook ISBN: 978-1-83888-856-5

For Gar
My partner in crime

I have never known birds of different species to flock together. The very concept is unimaginable. Why, if that happened, we wouldn't stand a chance! How could we possibly hope to fight them?
—Alfred Hitchcock, *The Birds*

PROLOGUE

Bonnie McMillan sat alone in the theater, relishing the anonymity of the dark. Tonight, she didn't have to be anybody's mommy, or wife, or teacher. No sticky little hands grabbed for her popcorn. No one whispered to pass the soda. Her cell phone stayed tucked in her purse, mercifully silent.

She hunkered down in her seat, her face lit by the screen. Behind her, the old-school film reel whirred. Here, she could simply be Bonnie, the same breathless, eager teenaged girl who'd first watched *Vertigo* at a Hitchcock marathon in San Francisco fifteen years ago. Back then, she'd dreamed of writing scripts and directing films herself.

That girl with big city ambitions seemed light-years away from Fog Harbor, with its bone-cold ocean and dreary winters. For a long five months a year, the tourists vanished like migrant birds, taking their rental cars and fat pocketbooks with them. Many of the locals worked at Crescent Bay State Prison, like her and James. The others lived behind its walls. Permanently.

Bonnie couldn't remember the last time she'd caught a Wednesday midnight showing at Fog City Cinema, the one-feature relic on the outskirts of town, and it had been ages since she'd been to a movie alone. Certainly not since Noah was born. It felt deliciously strange, indulgent even, to be here, and on a weeknight no less. But when James had offered to take the boys on an overnight trip whale-watching at Ecola State Park, she'd known exactly how to spend her first free evening.

Leaning forward, Bonnie tensed; on the screen, a middle-aged Jimmy Stewart chased Kim Novak up the stairs of the bell tower, where he stopped short, disoriented and perspiring. The woman screamed as her body hurtled toward the ground. Bonnie couldn't look, so she shoveled another bite of popcorn instead, licking the salt from her lips.

A thin blade of light sliced the theater's shadowy entrance and Bonnie heard the soft thud of approaching footsteps. The man didn't look up as he rounded the divider, his face obscured by the hood of his coat. He lumbered up the aisle, dripping rainwater and tracking mud with his boots, and took a seat somewhere in the darkness behind her. Worry prickled at the back of her neck.

She focused her mind back on *Vertigo*'s spiraling soundtrack. The trills, the brass crescendo, the shuddering dissonance. Pitch-perfect for a cinematic study on obsession. Hitch did crazy better than anybody. And she knew crazy. She'd taught creative writing in the prison's education department for eight years running.

Squinting at her watch and anticipating the final, fatal scene, she planned to bolt for the door as soon as the film was over. James would've laughed at her for her skittishness. The boys too. *Silly Mommy.* Nevertheless, as the credits rolled, Bonnie quickly gathered her things—purse, umbrella, jacket—and headed for the EXIT sign, its blood-colored letters eerie in the dark. She pushed through the swinging door and into the empty lobby, clumsily putting on her jacket as she crossed the dingy red carpet. Though she heard no one behind her, her heartbeat quickened. Beyond the lobby, she couldn't see past the rain-streaked outer doors, but she knew the parking lot would be wet and deserted. It was well after two in the morning in a town that fell asleep by nine. Only the liquor store and the Hickory Pit stayed open past midnight.

Bonnie didn't bother with the umbrella, though she hated the thought of her designer boots getting wet. James had spent way too much on them last Christmas, which had started everybody at the prison whispering behind her back. These boots made her feel like the vivacious San Francisco Bonnie. Not the gray Fog Harbor girl she'd turned into. So, she didn't care where that money had come from. After ten years of marriage, she'd perfected the art of looking the other way.

The cold rain stung her skin as she ran. Her hair whipped and lashed about her face, covering her eyes, but she pressed on, her car beckoning like a lighthouse, a safe harbor in the storm.

It might've been the rain, or the wind, or her writer's imagination, but the man seemed to loom in and out of her periphery. Working at the prison, she knew what men could do to women on their own for a night. That knowledge had buried itself in her brain, a dormant seed just waiting for the right moment to burst open.

When Bonnie reached the car, she felt the heat of him behind her, heard the hungry splash of his boots. She didn't turn around, certain she would freeze like a rabbit if she saw him there.

She flung open the car door and collapsed into the seat, locking herself in. The rain beat its tiny fists against the windows, but she was safe now in a world familiar to her. James' favorite baseball cap sat on the passenger seat—he'd be furious he'd left it behind. Two booster seats in the back, and Cheerios scattered like confetti on the floorboard.

Bonnie turned the key, cranked the heat, and listened to the sweep of the wipers on the glass, the static on the radio. By the time she could see clearly, the man had vanished. As if a seam had split open in the predawn quiet and simply swallowed him whole. If he'd ever been there at all.

Fog Harbor Gazette

"Search for Missing Fog Harbor Mother Intensifies"
by Heather Hoffman

Authorities in Fog Harbor, California, are intensifying their search for Bonnie McMillan, the married mother of two who went missing three days ago. According to Fog Harbor police, thirty-two-year-old Bonnie McMillan was last seen in the early morning hours of Thursday, December 12th, when security footage captured her leaving Fog City Cinema around 2:30 a.m. The following day, her Toyota Corolla was found abandoned with a flat tire on Pine Grove Road, just one mile south of the entrance to Crescent Bay State Prison (CBSP). Both McMillan's wallet and her cell were found in the vehicle, leading authorities to suspect she may have been a victim of foul play. Local authorities have partnered with the state police in the investigation and have deployed K-9 units to search for the missing woman, but their efforts have been hampered by poor weather conditions, with one inch of rain falling in Fog Harbor on the night of McMillan's disappearance and another winter rainstorm forecasted for this week.

Police confirmed McMillan's husband, James, was traveling with their two young children at the time. Sources close to the family say that the couple seemed happy and enjoyed working together in the adult education department at CBSP, where James manages the GED program. Bonnie had been employed there as a creative writing teacher.

Lester Blevins, Warden of CBSP, issued the following statement regarding their missing employee: "Bonnie is a highly valued member of our staff and is well respected by her colleagues and students. We are doing everything we can to assist in the search and pray for her safe and speedy return."

Police Chief Sheila Flack also issued a statement Sunday morning urging anyone who may have seen McMillan on the evening of December 11th or who may have information regarding her disappearance to contact the Fog Harbor Police Department. McMillan is described as five feet, four inches tall, with an average build, blonde hair, and blue eyes and was last seen wearing blue jeans and a beige raincoat. A public vigil for McMillan is planned for Sunday, December 15th at 4 p.m. at Grateful Heart Chapel in Fog Harbor.

CHAPTER ONE

Olivia hesitated outside the door of the chapel. No one should be afraid to set foot in a church, but Olivia was terrified, frankly, and with good reason. Every time she'd pushed open those heavy oak doors, crossed the threshold, and seated herself in a pew, something terrible had happened. It started on the day her mother had forced her into a dress and itchy white tights and dragged her into a church near their apartment in the Double Rock Projects, where they'd dropped to their knees to pray. That very night, the jury had returned with a decision—*guilty*—and the police carted her father away to the place he still called home. Prison.

"Going inside?"

The voice, a man's, belonged to the hand on the bronze door pull. The door pull that stood between her and the curse which had begun with her mother at Holy Name's in San Francisco, but hadn't ended there. Not even close. The man's nails were clean and cut short. His grip, strong and capable. The middle knuckle bore a faded bruise and a small knife scar marred the skin between his thumb and forefinger.

The man opened the door without effort, and held it there expectantly, while she gaped at the somber crowd already gathered inside.

"You expecting a formal invitation?"

Olivia bristled at his tone. She could go toe to toe with any smartass even on her worst day. But when her eyes left his hand, she went mute, swallowing the razor-sharp comeback on her tongue. Not because he carried a gun and wore a Fog Harbor police badge on his waistband, but because she didn't recognize his face. And in Fog Harbor—population 6,532—that was something of a miracle.

"Thank you," Olivia managed, taking a quick breath as she breached the doorway. *Done*. No turning back now. At least it was warm inside.

She took a vigil candle from the basket at the entrance and lingered near the back of the church, assessing her options while Mr. Wise Guy Detective settled himself into the last row of pews. A few up, she spotted a smattering of familiar faces, some of the fifteen or so staff members she supervised as chief psychologist at Crescent Bay State Prison. Leah waved her over, but Olivia couldn't bear to walk down the aisle.

The moment she'd start that walk she'd be eighteen again, with the trumpet announcing her arrival, the organ playing Mendelssohn's "Wedding March". The congregation would stand and Erik Ziegler, not Bonnie McMillan's family, would be waiting for her at the end of the aisle the way he had seventeen years earlier, his eyes brimming with the kind of love she'd hoped would fill the dad-sized hole in her heart. But they hadn't even cut the wedding cake before she'd caught Erik in a broom closet with one of her bridesmaids. And the worst part? She'd been so desperate to leave Fog Harbor that she'd given him five hundred and fifteen more days of her life before she'd sent him packing. Him and his last name.

So there you go. She leaned against the wall, claiming this spot as her own, the sting of betrayal as sharp as ever. *Cursed.*

Anyway, she liked it better back here where she could make a quick getaway. As she watched Bonnie's husband drag himself up to the podium, their two boys clinging to either hand, she suspected her position close to the exit would come in handy. She already felt hot, stripping off her coat and lifting her hair from the nape of her neck.

Olivia scanned the crowd for her sister. Emily had promised to be here. Granted, she'd been half asleep and still hungover when she'd mumbled *yeah, yeah, yeah* to stave off Olivia's nagging. But Emily had known Bonnie, too, even better than Olivia. Since the state cutbacks a few years earlier, Crescent Bay's education department had shared space with the dental clinic, where Emily worked as a hygienist. She'd even babysat the boys a few times. Yesterday afternoon they'd both joined the search outside the prison grounds and beyond, tromping around with the other volunteers. Looking for the tiniest clue that might tell them where Bonnie had gone. What had become of her.

Olivia checked her phone again. No new messages. She did another sweep of the crowd. No Em. Plenty of cops though, everywhere, in plain clothes and uniform. She understood it, but the unease that had been swirling in her stomach since Bonnie disappeared ratcheted up a notch. Cops meant something bad had definitely happened. Cops also meant she might see Graham. Which meant she might have to explain why she'd never called him back. Why seven perfectly adequate dates and one semi-awkward night were enough.

When the church bells marked 4 p.m., the doleful peals thrummed straight through her and resurrected another long-dead memory: her mother lying cold and still in a cherrywood coffin in this very church two years ago, Emily falling apart at her side. Little sisters could do that, while big sisters had to prove their mettle, had to put up prison-worthy walls around their hearts. Big sisters got stuff done. Big sisters showed up, curses be damned. And little sisters, well—Olivia searched once more for Em's strawberry-blonde curls—they arrived late or not at all, leaving big sisters alone and fretting.

James McMillan tapped the microphone, bringing everyone's focus to the front of the church. She squinted up at him, trying to recognize him as the boy she'd gone to Fog Harbor High with years ago. Somehow, in the last four days, he'd grown smaller. His frame shrunken, his cheeks sunken in. Grief and worry could do that to a body. She'd seen it in her father. In the inmates who sat across from her every day. In her mother too, and then, for a time, in herself.

James lit the candle in his hand and dipped the flame toward the vacant-eyed woman on his right who looked a lot like Bonnie. Her mother, Olivia guessed. The woman did the same, reaching up toward a somber Warden Blevins. One by one, the candles began to glow in the dim room, casting shadows and light that reflected in the stained glass.

"Hello, everyone. Thank you for being here tonight. I'm not sure I'll be able to get through this, but I'll give it my best shot. As you all know, Bonnie has been missing since early Thursday morning, and the boys and I…"

He wrapped his arms around the two of them, pulling them to his sides and squishing their little faces against his hips. Holding them close or holding himself upright, Olivia couldn't tell which.

"Well, the boys and I have been a total wreck. Bonnie is the light of our family. She never complained. So many of you probably don't realize all the things she gave up to move here with me eight years ago when I was reassigned to Crescent Bay State Prison. Before that, Bonnie studied film at UC Berkeley, and she'd won awards for her screenwriting. But she's been even more impressive as a wife, a mother, and a teacher. We asked some of her inmate students to put down their thoughts to share with you so you'd understand, if you don't already, just how special Bonnie is…"

Is. Such a small word brimming with hope. Olivia's throat ached.

The flame had traveled through the room like a whispered secret, finally reaching her, full and bright and perfect. She extended her unlit candle to the woman next to her, who she recognized as Jane Seely, a bartender at the Hickory Pit, and the wick slowly began to flicker. Then, she leaned over, carefully offering the flame to the mohawked teen on her left. He juggled his candle and his cell phone, trying to capture the exchange on video.

"…and how much we miss her and need her home with us. The first poem was written by Drake Devere, one of Bonnie's most accomplished students. With Bonnie's help, Drake self-published his own novel last year, donating all the proceeds to a domestic violence shelter."

A disapproving grunt from the back row startled Olivia, and the candle dropped from her hand, landing like a fallen angel at her feet. It hardly made a sound as she extinguished the flame with the toe of her boot.

"Damn, lady." The teen viewed her through the apathetic eye of the camera, still rolling, and his exaggerated whisper turned heads. "You almost set the whole place on fire."

But Olivia had already spun away, seething. Because she knew who to blame. Mr. Wise Guy with his handsome face and his disapproving noises. She concentrated on the back of his head, his hair a perfect match for the mahogany pews, willing him to look at her. When he finally glanced over his shoulder and shrugged, one corner of his mouth turned up.

At the podium, James continued his speech, plodding ahead with the steady persistence of a zombie, and Olivia cursed herself for making it harder on him. She should've known better than to cross the threshold into the church. She slipped back into her coat and slunk toward the exit, suddenly craving the burn of cold air in her lungs.

"Drake titled this tribute, 'A Student's Haiku'. 'All our eyes on her. Classroom of second chances. She treats us as men.'" James paused, and Olivia waited, her hand on the door. If she left now, in the utter quiet, everyone would realize.

But standing there, another memory bowled her over, inescapable now as an oncoming train. The last time she'd been in a church, just two weeks earlier. The prison chapel, with its straight-backed chairs, simple wooden crosses and hidden spaces to do very unholy things. What she'd seen there. What she'd run from. It all flooded in, welling up in her throat, thick as cotton.

To hell with it.

She nudged the door ajar, imagining them all looking at her, including that smug detective. For a moment, she froze under the weight of their judgment. Until a scream, sharp as a blade, slit the white-bellied silence wide open.

CHAPTER TWO

Olivia ran in the direction of the screaming. Though it had stopped now, the absence of it chilled her. Down the steps of Grateful Heart, up the stone path that wound around the back and into the grove of ancient redwoods. Here, the path turned to dirt and led to the Earl River that flowed into the bay.

"Doctor Rockwell!"

Olivia heard one of the Murdock twins calling her name before she saw her, bone-white and trembling, near the large drainpipe at the river's edge. A dog whined and circled her, its leash trailing behind, forgotten. Olivia knew then, it was Maryann and her poodle, Luna.

Just behind Maryann, plain as day, Olivia saw the feet. The soles, booted and unmoving. The legs, still as driftwood. They protruded from the pipe and rested on the mossy rocks below. Whatever else remained lay inside the tunnel, shrouded in the endless dark.

"It's *her*," Maryann said, her voice one-note. Hollow as a dead piano key.

Olivia hurried down the embankment to the river, careful not to slip, and past Maryann toward the pipe's entrance. In the summer, the river beneath the bridge slowed to a trickle here, and kids smoked cigarettes and weed, and immortalized their names in spray paint under the shelter of the drainpipe. Other things happened too. Bad things. Like the rape of the Simmons girl a few summers back. But now, the water hit Olivia, ice-cold, at mid-calf. She sloshed across the river and toward that pair of feet, extending her arms to keep her balance on the shifting rocks.

"It's her," Maryann said again. "It's her."

Olivia heard voices behind her. A panicked jumble of them. One, in particular, rose above the others, announcing himself as an officer of the law, telling her to get back. To wait.

She ignored them all. All her life she'd run toward trouble. How else could she explain her chosen profession? Em called it her savior complex. But in truth, Olivia had only ever wanted to save one person. But her dad didn't want saving. So, she had to settle for saving somebody else. A whole lot of somebodies.

Bonnie, though, was beyond saving.

Olivia had known it from the moment she'd heard Luna whimpering, seen her wandering free, her fur slick with river water. Luna, the kind of dog who had outfits for every holiday and rode around town in a baby carriage and had her hair groomed more often than Olivia. Luna, who Maryann loved so much she had a life-sized stuffed replica in her office at the library.

Maybe, in some dark crevice of Olivia's heart, she'd known all along. Mothers don't go missing voluntarily. Not mothers like Bonnie.

When Olivia reached the drainpipe and could finally see inside, it hit her like pounding waves breaking against the sheer cliffs that bordered Fog Harbor.

First, the hands, partially submerged and bloated as oven mitts. Olivia braced herself against the tunnel's rim.

Then, the blouse strewn open; the jeans undone. Olivia's legs anchored her to the spot like the roots of the centuries-old trees that watched, unaffected by it all.

The eyes open but opaque and unseeing; the lips slightly parted. Olivia intended to scream, but the sound got stuck, and she only managed a shallow gasp.

Finally, the ligature around the neck. The head, oddly angled. Olivia bent over, dry-heaving, and felt her knees buckle beneath her, just as a hand cleaved to her elbow to hold her upright. She knew that hand. It belonged to the smartass detective.

"What the hell are you thinking?" he asked. "You can't just go charging into a crime scene."

Olivia couldn't tell him she blamed herself for this; it sounded ridiculous. But she'd knowingly gone into Grateful Heart, and now Maryann and Bonnie had to suffer the consequences of her curse. She also couldn't tell him the other thing: that it wasn't her first dead body. Not even Em knew that. Only her father knew, and he'd made her swear to take it to the grave.

She couldn't explain any of that, so she simply nodded, her head bobbing like a child's balloon as he guided her to the rocks nearby. With his help, she lowered herself onto a dry spot next to Maryann. She focused on her breathing and Luna's lolling pink tongue until she felt halfway human again.

At the top of the embankment, James pushed his way through the crowd, but he didn't make it far. His face twisted. Animal sounds escaped his mouth. Someone grabbed him, and he collapsed to the ground, sobbing. Olivia knew it was a moment she'd live again and again in the worst of her nightmares.

"It's her, right?" Maryann sounded better now. Less like the undead and more like the Maryann who worked as the prison librarian, her nose stuck in a book and everybody else's business.

There was no one else but Olivia to answer.

"Yes."

"Tell me your name, ma'am."

The detective stood with his back to Olivia, notepad in hand, while the other cops milled around the drainpipe. They'd already dispersed the shell-shocked crowd and extended yellow tape around a wide perimeter of the river, marking it as the scene of a crime. Clad in a hooded, disposable jumpsuit, a person—man or woman, Olivia couldn't tell—captured the whole scene with a camera. Why would you want a job like that? A job that required you to stare, unblinking, into the vilest parts of our animal nature. She'd been asked the same herself.

"Maryann Murdock."

"Ms. Murdock, my name is Detective Will Decker, Fog Harbor Homicide. I know it's been a difficult afternoon but I need to ask you a few questions."

"Of course. I'll do my best. I'm very observant. I watch *Forensic Files*. My sister always says I'd make a great witness."

So Mr. Wise Guy had a name. *Will Decker*. Olivia mulled it over, certain she'd heard it before.

"This is your dog?"

"Luna. Isn't she precious? Poor little thing got the scare of her life. I did too." Maryann hugged the dog to her, a wet spot forming on her ample chest where Luna's paws rested.

"Can you tell me what happened this afternoon?"

"I intended on coming up here to the vigil but Melody—that's my twin sister—she had to pull a double up at Crescent Bay. She's a CO. That's stands for correctional officer, in case you didn't know."

Olivia couldn't see Detective Decker's face but she could picture it. Lips pressed together in an unforgiving line. A faint eye roll, perhaps. "I'm aware," he answered flatly.

"So, I didn't want to leave Mama alone at home for too long. She's pretty out of it these days. But Luna… I guess you might say nature was calling. I walked her down the block, and she did her business. Then, she spots one of those pesky gray squirrels, and she's off to the races and into the woods. Now, you can probably tell I'm no runner, Detective."

Maryann gestured down the length of her body. She and Melody were shaped just the same, from their short bowl haircuts to their stout, tree-trunk legs. The only difference, Maryann wore floral blouses and Crocs to work, while Melody squeezed herself into a standard green officer's uniform.

"Before I caught up, Luna was already in the water getting her paws all filthy. I just had her groomed. I was so worried about Luna, I wasn't really looking around until I got down here and saw... well, you know what I saw."

As Maryann talked, Olivia's phone vibrated in her coat pocket. Finally, a text from Em.

U ok? Got here late. Up at the church. Heard what happened. Please tell me it's not really her.

Olivia closed the message without responding—let her worry for a change—and typed *William Decker police* into the search bar, gawking as hundreds of results populated her screen. So, this was *the* Will Decker. No wonder he acted like someone had spit on his shoe. They probably had.

"Did you go inside the tunnel?" he asked Maryann.

"Heck no. But I knew it was Bonnie on account of the boots. They're designer. She got those last Christmas from James. All the girls at Crescent Bay turned into green-eyed monsters. Ask Doc over there. She remembers."

Olivia wondered at how pathetic her life had become since she'd returned to Fog Harbor three years ago, because she did remember the boots. They were Marc Jacobs, black leather and ankle-high, and looked too good to wear to work in a place that smelled of bleach and bodily fluids. When Bonnie had shown up in them the week after Christmas, the rumor mill had begun its brutal churning.

James is selling cell phones to inmates. How else did he get that kind of money?

He had an affair with a CO and had to buy her something special to make up for it.

The Vulture gave her those boots. James is just saving face.

Bonnie thinks she's so special, prancing around here. They're knockoffs anyway.

Olivia sorted through the rumors she'd heard, preparing the perfect answer. One that involved none of them. But Detective Decker didn't glance in her direction.

"Go on," he encouraged Maryann.

"As soon as I saw those boots, I screamed bloody murder." Maryann clamped her hand over her mouth, her eyes wide behind her thick glasses. "I didn't mean to say it that way. It's just that I was real upset. I thought I might pass out, kind of like a heroine in a Brontë novel. Thank God, Doc came running when she did."

At least someone appreciated her responsiveness.

Detective Decker jotted Maryann's contact information into his notepad. "You're free to leave, Ms. Murdock. If we have any other questions, we'll be in touch."

He turned toward Olivia but his gaze traveled past her, to the drainpipe. To the boots. The fine leather had already turned a dirty gray and Olivia imagined them in their final resting place: a sealed cardboard box in a stuffy evidence room.

The detective cleared his throat. His broad shoulders tensed. Olivia wondered why he wouldn't look at her.

"If you don't have any questions for me, Detective, I'd like to go. My sister's waiting at the church. It's getting pretty cold out here, and my clothes are wet."

She stood up, brushing off her backside, the legs of her pants clinging to her skin. A gust of wind stirred the crime scene tape, raising the fine hairs on her arms. She shivered.

"Actually—*Doctor, is it?*—you're not free to leave." When she finally met his eyes, they'd hardened into stones of amber. "You're under arrest for obstruction."

CHAPTER THREE

That same damn look. Dr. Smarty Pants—*of course, she would be a doctor*—had been giving Will that look, or some variation of it, since he'd held the door for her outside the church. He'd seen it before, too. Women were always giving him that look, though it happened less since he'd fled from San Francisco four months ago and moved here, where the cover of the fog and the redwoods seemed to keep the real world at bay. Equal parts pity, confusion, and judgment, that look meant one thing. She knew. Somehow, she knew.

That's why he'd said it, told her she was under arrest. Total bullshit. But he had to say something. Anything to wipe that look from her face. And it worked. Only problem, the new look wasn't much better. Fierce green eyes and a scowl that cut him off at the knees.

Smooth, Deck. Real smooth. No wonder he hadn't been laid in two years.

"Seriously? On what grounds?"

"I identified myself as an officer of the law. I told you to stop. Several times. And you blatantly, willfully, ignored my commands."

Will waited for her to argue. He welcomed it, actually. That way he could justify being an asshole.

"I just thought—well, I don't know why I did it. I guess I hoped there was a chance... I know it sounds silly."

He couldn't bear seeing her eyes fill. But he'd started it, and he couldn't back down now. "What if the perp had been hiding out in there? What if you'd stepped on some crucial piece of evidence? Blown our chance at catching this guy? That's obstruction in my book."

She took a step toward him, teetering on the rocks, until she was close enough to touch, but he resisted the urge to steady her. She extended both her hands, goosebumps visible on her skin. The tears in her eyes had vanished. "Fine. Arrest me then. Let's get it over with."

Heat crept up his neck. She'd boxed him into a corner. Nothing could save him now. Except—

"Hey, Deck. JB's on his way. Said to start without him on account of the rain coming. I'll see ya in there."

Chet Clancy, Fog Harbor Medical Examiner and last-minute savior of total lost causes. Will nodded at him and held up a finger.

"Duty calls, Doctor. But consider this a stern warning. Listen to the police. Next time you won't be so lucky."

"*Lucky*. Right."

"And give your contact info to the officer up there, in case we need it."

Will stood motionless as she trudged up the embankment and back in the direction of the church, her auburn hair whipping in the wind like a kite tail. Chet had been right to hurry him. The sky had turned the color of a tombstone. The air felt heavy, ready to burst.

Will traversed the silty river bottom, as a few stray raindrops broke the water's surface. When he reached the pipe's opening, the victim came into full view again, and the tightly coiled muscles in his shoulders unwound. Lately, he'd been more comfortable with the dead bodies than the live ones. The dead had no expectations. They made no demands. Most of all, they didn't let you down or screw you over. They gave up all their secrets in time if you knew where and how to look.

Chet knelt over the body, carefully studying the dark bruising around the neck with his gloved hands. He looked up as

Will sloshed inside. Then he rose to his feet, groaning with the effort. Fog Harbor was lucky to have him. Most of the smaller counties couldn't afford MEs and employed coroners instead, wannabes who spent two weeks at coroners' college and called themselves experts.

"Looks like you managed to piss off the second-smartest doctor in this town."

Will chuckled. "You know her?"

"Sure do." Chet moved around the body—Will mirrored him—examining the hands, the boots. Marc Jacobs, according to the logo stamped on the wet soles. "Most folks around here know Olivia Rockwell. She's kind of a big deal. Local girl. Moved back a couple years ago to take care of her mom. She's chief psychologist over at Crescent Bay."

Will nodded as if he didn't care. As if he didn't loathe the idea that a shrink had unearthed the skeletons in his closet, probably via the Internet, the place where old bones never stayed buried.

"So, what do you think?" he asked, eager to change the subject. Besides, he wanted to get a head start before JB, his know-it-all partner, showed up to put his boot on Will's neck like usual. "Killed somewhere else and dumped here?"

"Looks that way. She's well past rigor mortis. I'd say she was probably asphyxiated shortly after she went missing. But I'd expect a few more critters would've got to her if she'd been down here since early Thursday morning. Also, the skin back here..." He gently lifted the exposed right shoulder, where the shirt had been pulled away. "It's intact. Not much maceration or softening like you'd see with a long period of immersion in water. I'd venture a guess she was moved here today."

"Sexual assault?"

"It's possible. But the undergarments appear intact. Maybe he started to and was interrupted. Killed her in a panic. We'll have to wait for the autopsy and the labs to be sure. I've gotta warn you, though, a lot of the evidence is probably a wash. Literally."

Will pointed his flashlight down the pipe. Past the first twenty or so feet, the leaves and graffiti and cigarette butts ended. Beyond that, the darkness consumed everything, even the shadows.

"I didn't see any drag marks or tracks," Will told Chet. "Except for Maryann Murdock's—she found the body. And your 'big deal' doctor. Why is she such a big deal anyway?"

Chet shrugged, moving back toward Bonnie's head. "I'll let her tell you."

"What makes you think I plan on speaking to her again?" He asked himself another question. *Why do I want to?*

"Have a look at this, will ya?" Chet shined his penlight onto the victim's neck. The ligature, denim blue. Near the back, underneath the clumps of her matted hair, the color changed to a sunshine yellow that seemed all wrong down here.

"What is it made of?"

"Can't say for absolute sure, but it seems to be fabric. This yellow could be a stamp of some sort. To me, it looks a helluva lot like prison blues."

The drainpipe glowed from within, lit by a fleet of high-powered utility lamps, as the officers combed the length of it for evidence. Will looked on from the top of the embankment while they bagged Bonnie's hands and carted her off in a bag of her own. Chief Flack had insisted on delivering the official news to James and Bonnie's mother herself, which saved Will from his least favorite part of dealing with dead bodies.

"Want to start with the husband in the morning?" Will asked, while JB glowered and lit another cigarette. That man's chest was empty as a steel drum, and he had the four ex-wives to prove it.

"We can get more background on the vic while we wait for the autopsy. What do you say?"

JB took a long drag and exhaled in his direction. Will would've rather passed out than give him the satisfaction of a single cough. He wished the rain would start up again and extinguish that cigarette with a single fat drop.

"I'd say *you* should've waited for your partner to do the walk-through with Chet. I'd also say you don't call the shots around here, City Boy."

City Boy. Will liked it better than what they'd called him in San Francisco. *Rat. Traitor. Snitch.*

"Alright, JB. Whatever you want. You tell me where you'd like to start."

"Now you're talking. How 'bout we start with the husband?"

Will had gritted his teeth and nodded. Nothing that a few hard right hooks couldn't fix. And now that he'd made it home, to the cabin he'd rented outside of town, he planned to make good on his promise to take it out on the heavy bag.

He changed quickly, stripping off his mud-spattered vigil-wear and tossing on an SFPD T-shirt and shorts—working out was the only thing they were good for these days—and headed into the one-car garage he called a gym. Or his salvation. Depending on the day.

Will waved at a darting shadow in the corner. "Hey, get outta here!"

That damn one-eyed cat had been weaseling its way into the garage every rainstorm for the last few weeks. Probably because he'd broken once and left out a can of tuna. The cat slipped out the way it came through a feline-sized hole in the garage door siding. The whole cabin was a fixer-upper he didn't have the time or energy to fix up. So, he couldn't hold it against the poor fella.

Truth be told, he felt a kinship with that orange tabby; permanently damaged with nobody to claim him.

Outside, the rain sounded indignant. Beating against the roof like it channeled his outrage.

Will didn't bother with boxing gloves. Just wrapped his hands like he'd learned at King's in Oakland. He cranked the music he always played for these sessions. His 1980s hard rock mix that started with Bon Jovi and ended with Guns N' Roses.

First, a left jab to the face. That's for JB. The bag swayed right to left and back again. Not bad for a guy on the wrong side of forty.

Followed up with a heavy right cross. That's for whatever sicko had ended Bonnie and dumped her body like a sack of trash in a sewer drainpipe.

Then, a couple right hooks to the body. For the old bones of his past. The whole goddamned skeleton.

Last, he delivered the knockout. A fierce uppercut that juddered his whole arm but still wasn't hard enough. One more. And another. His knuckles stung as he pictured his brother's face.

CHAPTER FOUR

Olivia rubbed her aching temples and took another scalding sip of coffee, wincing as it hit the back of her throat. Across from her, Emily pushed her eggs from one side of her plate to the other. Her fork made the music of Olivia's soul, a vicious, rhythmic scraping against the bone china. The plates had been a wedding gift from Erik's mother, and Olivia had thought of smashing them more than once. But here they were, the last artifacts of her ruined marriage.

"Want a coffee for the road?" Olivia tried to sound normal. To pretend the thought of it—leaving the house, driving to the prison, going through the day—didn't exhaust her. Didn't worsen the dull throb at the base of her skull.

Emily gave no answer. The rain-soaked newspaper sat between them like an uninvited guest, stoic despite its gut-punch headline. **Fog Harbor Mother Found Dead.**

Olivia didn't bother to unfold it. It had landed in a puddle on their front porch, the pages melded together. What more could it tell them anyway? She'd already spent the entire night staring at the ceiling, replaying the whole garish scene. The scream. The boots, the ligature, the anguish on James' face. Finally, she'd surrendered and laced up her running shoes to hit the dirt trail behind the house, eager to outpace yesterday. Even if it meant her best sneakers were squishy and caked with mud. She'd left them on the front step to dry in the sun. If it ever showed its face again.

"Em? Coffee?"

Emily lifted her eyes. Mossy green, those eyes belonged first to their mother, then to Olivia. And ten years later, to Emily as well. *Green as the grass in the Yankee Stadium*, their father had teased, pinching baby Emily's chubby cheek. *But you've never been to Yankee Stadium*, Olivia would remind him, the bench in the Crescent Bay visiting room cold and hard beneath her legs. By then, she'd feared he would never see anything beyond those barbed wire fences.

Emily sniffled and pushed her plate away, finally laying the fork to rest. "I still can't believe she's really gone. I keep thinking about the boys, you know?"

"Me too." Olivia wondered what James had told Nathan and Noah about their mother. How he'd managed to get words out at all.

"They're so young. Those poor kids going through something like that. They're gonna be royally screwed up."

Olivia stood abruptly, bumping the table with her hip. Her coffee sloshed over the lip of the cup, leaving a mud-colored puddle on the checkered tablecloth. "Shit."

"I'm sorry, Liv. I didn't mean it that way."

Olivia waved off her sister's apology and soaked up the stain, tossing the dishrag in the sink. Em didn't know any better. She hadn't even been born yet. A prison baby, conceived back when lifers still had conjugal visits, she'd gotten to know their father in small doses. Twice-a-week, hour-long doses. "It's okay. At least Dad's still alive. Come to think of it, that's probably the only reason why I'm not royally screwed up."

Typically Em would've jumped on that one, cracking a joke and making them both laugh. In fact, that's exactly why Olivia had said it. Instead, Emily joined Olivia at the sink, wrapping an arm around her. Olivia let her pretend to be the big sister, leaning into her shoulder and laying her head against the fleece sweatshirt that covered Emily's dental scrubs.

When they broke apart, Emily's gray face brightened. Maybe the sun would peek through the fog today. Even in the middle of December. "Not royally screwed up, huh? Are you sure about that?"

Olivia sidestepped a brown pool of standing water as she showed her ID at the prison entrance. Every winter, like clockwork, the older lower buildings flooded, leaving the whole place slick with mildew and smelling like laundry left too long in the washer.

Olivia and Emily parted ways at the control booth, Olivia heading east to the Mental Health Unit and her sister heading west to the combined Education Department and Dental Services. Usually, Olivia watched Em until she reached the door, but today she waited until her sister had pressed the buzzer—twice for staff—and disappeared inside.

Then, she began the runway walk. She'd heard Melody Murdock call it that once, snickering, and that's how she'd thought of it ever since. Down the long concrete corridor marked with lines of red paint. If the inmates stepped inside those lines, they'd be out of bounds, so they lingered on the outskirts, leaning up against the walls, watching and occasionally calling out. Olivia would've rather they simply crossed the red lines. Because their eyes did just that, following her as if they'd never seen a woman before.

Today, as she passed the first group of inmates, she realized the runway walk felt more like a funeral procession. The inmates appeared somber, averting their eyes and talking quietly, if at all. Somehow, stupidly, she hadn't considered it. The way the news of Bonnie's murder would reach them, through the dense forest that surrounded the prison on three sides. Through the walls and bars and regrets. That it would hit them just as hard, maybe harder. Because Bonnie had been one of the few who really saw them. Who, like Drake had written in his poem, treated them as men.

"Hey, Doctor Rockwell, can I have a minute?"

Olivia's stomach flipped when she spotted Melody outside the door to the chapel, her eyes as tired as Olivia's.

"Of course. How's your sister?"

Melody sighed. "She's holding up alright. Luckily, she had the day off. She was snuggled up with Luna when I left her. Anyway, she told me you were there too. By the river. Where they found the body. Maryann said to thank you. That you made her feel a little better."

"I'm glad to hear that. She had quite a shock. We both did. The whole prison seems to be reeling."

When Melody spoke again, Olivia strained to hear her. "So is what they're saying true?"

"What are they saying?"

Melody scanned the corridor, her pale eyes darting. "Not out here."

Olivia stifled a gasp as Melody opened the chapel door—one of the few in the prison that didn't require a key—and tried to pull her inside. She felt the cold first. Inhaled a gulp of the stale air. Finally, when her head stopped swimming, she turned to look out at the sea of gray plastic chairs that faced a simple wooden altar with a door on either side. One, where the chaplain kept his office. The other, the confessional.

"I—I can't go in there," Olivia told her, freeing her arm from Melody's grip. She floundered, searching for a reasonable explanation, but she couldn't think straight. Not through the white noise of panic in her brain.

With a quick glance over her shoulder, Melody moved in so close Olivia could smell her peppermint toothpaste. Her breath warm against Olivia's ear, her words startling and bright as a spot of blood. Still, as Olivia walked away she'd replay them again and again, certain she'd misheard.

"They're saying that Bonnie was strangled by an inmate."

*

Olivia kept her head down until she reached the Mental Health Unit at the end of the runway. After an inmate had jumped from the tier a few years back and his family had sued Crescent Bay for negligence, the MHU had undergone a complete facelift. The unfinished concrete floors had been replaced by tile that the inmate porters buffed once a week. It shined so bright beneath the fluorescent light panels she could almost see her own reflection. On the far wall, the patients had hung the holiday mural they'd created in their art therapy group. The bright red acrylic of Santa's suit drew Olivia's eyes, quickening her breath, until she realized: just paint.

Through the small rectangular window at the center of the door, Olivia spotted Leah at the officers' station squirming away from Sergeant Hank Wickersham. Even through the metal door, she heard him cackling. His bald head thrown back. His mouth, a gash.

Olivia removed the oversized key from her pocket, the one she'd exchanged for a chit at the control booth, and turned the heavy lock. She stepped inside, immediately shedding her coat. Unlike most of the prison, the MHU had central heating and air conditioning, but it never seemed to work quite right, leaving her sweating or shivering most days.

"Mornin', Doctor Rockwell." Hank's face lit up when he saw her. He left Leah alone at the desk, her hands resting on her pregnant belly. But she didn't wait long, widening her eyes at Olivia and escaping to her office before he noticed. "Maybe *you'll* like my joke. Not like Doctor Party-Pooper Chapman over here."

Hank gestured with his thumb to where Leah had been standing. "Hey, where'd she go?"

Leave it to Handsy Hank to tell jokes the day after a vigil. The day after they'd found Bonnie dead. He never could keep his jokes—or his hands—to himself. Rumor had it, he'd been transferred from the Los Angeles Women's Institution a few months back after they'd caught him in a compromising position with an inmate. Yet somehow, he'd ended up here. The benefits of being a state employee. Never fired, just relocated. Exiled to gloomy Crescent Bay, the prison nobody volunteered for, and to the MHU no less.

"Alright, let's hear it, Hank."

He rubbed his hands together and grinned, showing Olivia the chipped front tooth where he'd taken a lick from a delusional inmate armed with a chair and a bad temper. "What do prisoners use to call each other?"

Olivia had heard Hank tell this one before, but she played along, shrugging at him as she chose a clip-on alarm from the box on the desk. She affixed it to the waistband of her slacks like she did every morning, trying not to focus on that cheap red push button. It looked like a child's toy. A child's toy that was supposed to keep her alive.

Anticipating his punchline delivery, Hank drummed his hands on the desk. Afterward, he'd punctuate it with his own cymbal crash too. He always did. But, before Hank could speak, someone beat him to it. A voice, deep and smooth as honey. Olivia knew it well.

"*Cell* phones. Good one, Handsy. Only problem, you told that joke last week. And it wasn't that funny the first time."

Hank glowered as if a dark cloud had passed over him.

"Where'd you come from, Devere? Unlock ain't till nine. You're supposed to be outside that door, waiting like a good little boy."

Drake sat on the bench nearest Olivia's office, running a casual hand through his slick black hair, before he covered his ears with a set of headphones. He fixed his eager eyes on Hank. The way a vulture would sight its next meal. "Door was open."

Olivia's stomach clenched, and she squeezed the key in her palm. *How could I be so stupid?* "It's my fault, Hank. I must've forgotten to lock it behind me."

Hank shook his head at her and sighed, and Olivia wriggled out from beneath the arm he'd set around her shoulders. "Don't beat yourself up, Doc. You've got a lot on your mind. We all do. I'm sure you were distracted."

Then he approached Drake. He stood over him, jabbing a finger down into the center of his denim blue prison jumpsuit. Drake didn't flinch when Hank yanked off his headphones. Just smirked like he enjoyed it. "And you. Next time, I'm writing you up for being out of bounds."

"Suit yourself, Handsy."

Hank's whole head turned splotchy, and he fled back to the desk, retrieving his keys, while Drake preened. Olivia looked on with guilt as Hank waved the other inmate patients through and locked the door with an authoritative click.

"Hey," Drake said, once all the benches had filled with a warm audience of men in blue like himself. "What d'ya call chow hall duty at a women's prison?"

Leah's nine o'clock—Greg Petowski, schizophrenic—guffawed. Even the quiet inmates twittered in anticipation. Drake never disappointed his fans.

"Handsy Hank's last date."

Olivia had just turned eight years old the first time she'd sat face to face with a murderer. The man had towered over her like a mythical giant, his hands the size of bear paws. Though she'd grown a full two inches since they'd taken him away, he'd easily lifted her above his head, and she'd squealed with delight. When he'd laughed along with her—a deep chortle that shook his belly—she'd felt both scared and electrified. He'd told her he couldn't leave with her and her mother that day. He had to stay there, in the middle of the redwood forest, in the old stone building that looked like a castle, until he'd finished his work. More than anything, Olivia had wanted to believe him. Because her mother told her to. Because she still thought grownups told the truth. But above all else, because he was her father.

"Look at me." Drake wiped at his eyes, cast down on his lap. A lucky break for Olivia, because he didn't seem to notice her jump at the sound of his voice just then. "Crying like a little girl."

"Take your time, Drake. It's okay to be vulnerable in here." Olivia studied his cheeks for tear tracks. Dry as a bone.

"I'm devastated, Doc. Devastated. Nobody's ever believed in me the way Ms. McMillan did. She recognized my talent. Everybody else just sees the Vulture. Not Ms. McMillan. She saw me as a writer, a poet, an artist. A man."

Olivia heard James' voice, reciting Drake's haiku. *She treats us as men.* And the sharp scream—Maryann's—that left a gaping wound in the silence that followed. When she thought of the scream, she thought of Bonnie, and when she thought of Bonnie she thought of her father. Of that other body she'd been carrying around for the last twenty-seven years, the heaviest kind of baggage. The mental kind. "Would it be fair to say Ms. McMillan was one of the few women you trusted?"

With a faraway look, Drake rubbed his chin. As if after three years of therapizing him, Olivia had stumped him. Had finally asked a question for which he didn't have a ready answer.

"The only woman," he said, finally. He paused for a beat, then grinned. "Well, present company excluded, of course."

Olivia knew better than to return his smile. Drake wielded flattery like a weapon. Best to duck and cover. To return fire.

"Is that why you were rude to Sergeant Wickersham? Making jokes at his expense."

"You mean, Handsy? That guy is a prick. Always hitting on you and Doctor Chapman and the rest of the lady psych doctors. I even heard him flirting with Ms. McMillan a few times right under her husband's nose. So, I don't see what me putting him in his place has to do with anything. You're overthinking this one, Doc."

"Well, I'm worried about you. If there are only two women you trust in the whole world, and you've just lost one of them, that seems significant. It seems like something that might cause you to lash out."

"Lash out? *Puh-lease*. You think that was me lashing out?"

Drake flopped back in his chair, his hair falling in his face like a petulant teenager. Seeing him pout like that, it would have been easy to forget the reason he'd ended up in prison serving a sentence of life without parole. Five reasons, actually.

"I do. We've talked about the losses you've experienced in your life, big and small. Your mom, for starters. Abandoning you in foster care. Choosing heroin over her only child. You didn't cope well with that, did you?"

Drake's head tipped back, exposing his long, pale neck. His laugh reminded Olivia of his nickname. Because it sounded like the cry of a vulture. Shrill and wild and unnerving.

"I guess you're right about that. I ended up in this hellhole talking to you. No offense."

"And when they took your yard privileges a few years back? That was a loss, albeit a temporary one."

"C'mon, Doc. That's not fair. You know I had to make a statement. Drake Devere needs his fresh air. I'm like Walt Whitman, drawing my inspiration from nature."

"You broke that CO's hand."

"Technically, the door fractured her index metacarpal." On any other day, Olivia would've stopped Drake right there and put an official label on his bullshit. Minimization. Justification. Externalization of blame. "But, you've made your point. I don't react well to stress. And you're right. This thing with Ms. McMillan has got me strung out. I couldn't even focus on my audiobook. Do you know what bothers me the most? What's been keeping me up every night since she went missing?"

Today, he steamrolled her, dragging Olivia along for the ride. "Who else is gonna help me finish the series? My readers are expecting the sequel in February. And she was supposed to talk to the Classification Committee about my working as a teacher's assistant. Now, I'll be stuck working for Ms. Ricci, slinging that chow hall slop for fifteen cents an hour. She hates me. She's always writing me up for being late when she knows good and well it takes at least ten minutes to walk to the kitchen from here."

"Stop." Olivia suddenly wished she'd stayed home today. Pulled the covers over her head and postponed returning to the real world with its cruel lessons, its sharp edges. None sharper than Drake.

"I'd like you to take a step back. Work on your perspective-taking. Your empathy, remember? Next session, I want an answer to my question. To this question."

Drake raised his hands in surrender to an invisible gun. "Fire away. You're the best psych doctor in this joint."

"You cared for Ms. McMillan. You valued her. She helped you achieve a long-held dream of publishing your manuscript and gave you confidence when others doubted you. Then, someone took her away. Ended her life. Violently."

Olivia thought of her father. Of his eyes. Which weren't green like hers and Em's, but blue and seemed to fade out the longer he'd been locked up, like a photograph left too long in the sun. By the time they'd transferred him to the minimum security facility at Valley View ten years ago, they'd dimmed to a soft gray mist.

But Drake's eyes glinted with life as they followed her. As golden brown as a hawk's feather and bright as the day they'd taken his first prison photo. The one tacked onto the front of his file on Olivia's desk and immortalized on the last page of his self-published novel, *Bird of Prey*.

Though it left her inexplicably angry, she stared into them, unafraid. "What is it like knowing you did that very same thing to the families of your victims five times over?"

*

Olivia watched Drake through her office window as he strolled past the officers' desk and toward the locked outer door of the MHU. Hank didn't look up. Not even when Drake called out to him.

"C'mon, Sarge. Help me out. Ms. Ricci's gonna ride my ass if I'm late for lunch prep again."

Leah's patient, Greg, emerged from her door across the hall, his mouth moving strangely as he talked to the voices in his head. The same ones that had told him to drive a stake—which turned out to be a steak knife—through his mother's vampire heart.

Leah came out behind him and stood in the doorway. She made a face at Olivia, equal parts eye roll and exasperation.

"You know I was just pulling your chain, Sarge. You're alright."

Hank remained stone-faced at his computer while, one by one, all the 9 a.m. patients gathered at the locked door, waiting for him and his precious key. Olivia could've put an end to the standoff and simply opened it herself, but after the incident in the chapel she'd been trying to stick to the unwritten rules: *Keep your head down. Don't get involved.*

Hank pushed back in his chair and kicked his boots up on the desk, humming, as Drake made one more effort.

"I didn't mean it, Sarge. Ask Doctor Rockwell. She'll tell you. I've been real upset about Ms. McMillan. I probably took it out on you."

Hank began singing Johnny Cash's "Folsom Prison Blues", and Drake kicked the door, the hollow sound ringing like a gunshot.

At the sound, the other doctors emerged from their offices and looked on from their own doorways, the whole MHU poised on a knife's edge. When Olivia spotted Drake whispering to Greg, a cold dread crept up her spine and stood her hair on end.

Her finger hovered over the red push button at her waist.

"Let me out!" Greg screamed, flailing at the door with his fists. "He's going to damn me to a life of eternal ruin! He's a vampire!"

Another inmate tried to hold him back and took an elbow shot to the nose, blood dripping down his chin and spreading onto his prison blues. The blood only ratcheted up Greg's terror. He stretched his hand out in front of him and made the sign of the cross before he returned to thrashing the door, desperate to get out.

Olivia launched herself straight into the fray, pressing the button as she ran. The alarms blasted, flashing red, until all the inmates hit the ground per prison protocol. Only Greg remained upright, cowering in the corner, his knuckles bruised and already swollen from the pounding.

"It's okay," Olivia told him, steadying the quiver in her own voice. "There are no vampires in the MHU. Sergeant Wickersham is here to help you, and so am I. So is Doctor Chapman."

Hank's hands shook as he unlocked the door and the rest of the officers stormed in to restore order.

Secured in handcuffs and pinned to the wall, Greg began to cry as Leah tried to soothe him. "Keep him away from me," he sobbed. "Please. He's going to bite me. He told me so."

"Sergeant Wickersham isn't a vampire," Olivia said again.

"Not Sarge." Greg pointed at the ground, where Drake lay on his belly. Olivia swore she heard him laughing. "*Him.*"

Except for the soft swish of the porter's mop across the tiles near the door, the MHU had quieted again. Leah collapsed into the chair opposite Olivia. With a frustrated sigh, she blew her blonde bangs from her face. "Girl, tell me again why we can't bring booze to work?"

Olivia laughed but it didn't quiet her nerves which had frayed down to the last wire. "For one, I don't think Baby Chapman would appreciate you drinking."

"It's really not fair. I'm big as a house. My hormones are raging. I've got two more months until I get this kid out of me. Then, I come to work and have to put up with these lunatics. And it's not just the inmates. I'm telling you, I could use a strong shot of pruno right now." Leah stuck her thumb in Hank's direction. He hadn't spoken a word since Warden Blevins stormed out ten minutes ago. "That guy is a riot just waiting to happen."

"I should've unlocked the door myself."

"That's not your job."

"Yeah, but I knew Drake was in a mood today."

"You mean the part where he acted like a psychopath? That's not a mood. That's a lifestyle."

Olivia had to hand it to Leah. She'd been lightening the glum atmosphere of the MHU with her wide smile for the last two years, when she'd relocated to Fog Harbor with her husband, Jake, who'd quit his nine-to-five in San Francisco and bought Shells-by-the-Sea, the fixer-upper B&B he'd repaired with the entirety of his retirement fund. Even last summer, the slowest tourist season on record, Leah hadn't complained once. She reminded Olivia of her own mother, always putting on a brave face, the way she had the day they'd moved to Fog Harbor, turning her back on the Oaktown Boys—at their hideout, no less—when they'd offered her help. *I don't want to owe them a damn thing*, she'd said. *They've already taken enough from me.*

"I really thought he'd made some progress. One step forward, ten steps back, I suppose."

"You know, I still don't understand why you even bother. You're the chief. The head honcho. You don't have to waste your time doing therapy with these guys. Especially Drake. He's a lost cause. Kick up your feet like Jake does every fall when the tourists disappear. Do some paperwork."

"Bor-ing." The truth was she needed guys like Drake to hold up against her father, measuring him and what he'd done. Trying to make the pieces fit.

But Olivia had learned the hard way that people treated you differently when they discovered a convicted murderer in your family tree. That's why she hadn't told Leah—or anyone at Crescent

Bay—about Martin Reilly. Why she and her sister used their mother's maiden name. Olivia figured the warden knew though, since she'd answered the questions on the personnel form honestly, filling in her father's name beside the blank that required her to identify any inmates with whom she had a family or personal relationship. The guards who might have still recognized her as the spirited teenager she'd been when she'd left Fog Harbor had either died or retired.

"Girl, you need a life, ASAP. Whatever happened with Graham Bauer?"

"Over before it started." Olivia sighed, glancing at her computer screen, where she'd already begun typing the incident report. Her cursor flashed at the end of the word 'vampire'. She should've never accepted a first date with Officer Bauer to begin with. Dating a cop is hard enough without a murderer for a dad. "Hey, speaking of paperwork, want to do our incident reports over lunch?"

"You know we're always hungry," Leah said, patting Baby Chapman. "But it's only ten thirty."

Olivia gaped at the oversized clock on the wall. Surely, it had stopped. But the second hand ticked on, steady as a beating heart, reminding her of the tattoo her father had inked on his own forearm in county jail after he'd received a life sentence. A distorted clock face that had always scared her a little. He'd told her once, *You don't do time in the joint. Time does you.*

CHAPTER FIVE

Will glanced at the watch his dad had given him the day he'd taken his sworn oath as an officer of the law. Just like his father and his father's father before him. His brother, Ben, too. Though Ben's oath had been shot to hell two years ago. Literally.

"You got somewhere else to be, City Boy?" JB redirected the beam of his flashlight from the muck of the drainpipe to Will's face. Will squinted into the harsh glare, feeling like a sewer rat blinded by the light. They'd been down here long enough, covering the same ground the officers had searched last night, looking for tracks that didn't exist. For evidence that had washed away. For a smoking gun to tell them exactly how Bonnie had ended up here.

"Just making sure we don't miss the autopsy. I want to get a better look at that garrote." He swore his partner had horns beneath his salt-and-pepper buzz cut.

JB shifted the beam down the tunnel toward the faint hint of daylight at the end. The pipe had only two other main exits—the one by Earl River and another midway. A ladder leading to a manhole in the center of town. "Keep your eyes on the prize, alright?"

Will kept trudging ahead, tracking his own flashlight across the muddy cement bottom. Last night's rain had already erased the officers' footprints and left a good two inches of standing water in some places. "So, what did you think of the husband?"

JB cleared his throat, delivering a message about as subtle as a sledgehammer. They walked the rest of the way with only the sloshing of their boots between them.

The pipe opened at the beach overlooking the coast of Crescent Bay, exactly where the city map showed it would. Will followed JB down onto the rocky shore, cursing the cold as he zipped up his windbreaker.

The beach parking lot sat empty up the hill behind them, a small wooden staircase guiding the way down to the sand and the stone path that bordered it. About a half mile out, the Little Gull lighthouse rose up like a towering angel through the fog. Will let the wind run its rough fingers through his hair and inhaled the brine of Crescent Bay. Fog Harbor may have been three hundred miles from San Francisco, but out here, Will felt at home. He had to admit this place had its moments.

"Well, that was a goddamned waste of time." JB puckered a cigarette between his lips. He flicked his lighter once, twice, three times, each meager flame extinguished by another brutal gust. Finally, the wind quieted long enough.

"Do you think our perp could've carried the body from here?" Will asked.

"It would take one hell of an effort. We walked a good three-quarters of a mile down that pipe. And I don't know about you, but I'm plumb out of breath."

Will left that one alone. "Maybe he had help."

"Nah. Don't think so. My gut's telling me this is a one-man job." JB patted his beer belly which was no doubt telling him something, either reminding him of the approaching lunch hour or reviewing the menu of snack options he kept stashed in the glove box. "Frankly, I like the husband for it. He's conveniently out of town with the kiddos, knows exactly where she'll be and when. He hires a guy. Tells him to slit the tire and stage the scene to look like a rape. Bingo."

"But why?"

JB shrugged, chuckled. "You ain't ever been married. Am I right, City Boy?"

Will gritted his teeth—he'd have to go another nine rounds on the heavy bag tonight—and shook his head. "Nope. Still single." JB never missed a chance to rub it in. Will had been close once. Close enough to know he'd never get that close again.

"Well, there you go," JB said. "They'd been married for ten years. Who the hell needs more of a motive than that?"

He wouldn't bet against JB. The stats didn't lie. It's usually the husband. But Will didn't see it. Not this time. When they'd stopped by the McMillan house that morning, James had the look of a man who'd just had his life blown up, Hiroshima-style. Still, he agreed with JB about two things: The McMillan house looked too nice, too fancy for two state employees; and James hadn't told them the whole truth. Beads of sweat had broken out on his forehead before they'd asked him a single question, most of which he'd answered with curt one-word replies.

"Should we head back?" Will asked, taking a mental snapshot of the whitecaps crashing against the shoreline, the gulls diving through the mist. A little guided imagery for the return trek through the pipe with JB.

At the entrance, JB sucked in the last drag from his cigarette before tossing the butt onto a pile of kelp. As he stepped into the pipe, he grimaced. "Dammit. The old knee's actin' up again. You get the car. I'll wait here."

Will rolled his eyes, reaching down to retrieve JB's trash. It's no wonder JB had been without a partner for a year. Until Will had shown up, with nowhere else to go, and drawn the short straw.

"Are you the litter police now, too?"

The smoldering butt had rolled onto the sand alongside the pipe. Next to it, Will noticed something peculiar. He slipped his phone from his windbreaker and snapped a few photos, before he pushed aside the sand to reveal the object, hard black rubber and paddle-shaped.

"What is it?" Will asked, as JB leaned down to get a closer look.

"I have no goddamned idea, but I'd say this litter bug might've just found you a clue."

Bonnie's body lay naked at the center of a metal table. Beneath it, a rubber block lifted the chest, though Chet hadn't done any cutting yet. The bone saw rested, clean and lustrous, on a cart behind him. It kept catching Will's eye, winking at him under the fluorescent lighting.

In the bright light, nothing could be avoided. Including the deep scratches beneath Bonnie's jawbones. Self-inflicted, according to Chet. She'd fought like hell to free herself from the garrote, even as it squeezed the life from her.

Chet carefully removed the material from her neck and placed it on a tray for closer examination. The length of blue fabric was tied between two wooden dowels, which had been hidden in the rainwater. As Chet gently pulled at the edges of the cloth, Will's chest tightened.

"Well, I'll be damned." JB pointed a gloved finger at the yellow California Department of Corrections and Rehabilitation stamp. "You were right. Prison issued."

"What about the handles, Doc? Any ideas?"

Chet nodded at Will, picking up one of the dowels so that the end was visible. "These holes were probably drilled in, and the fabric inserted with a wire and a stop knot to keep it from slipping out. Because the ends have a little weight to them, the assailant could easily toss one across the victim's throat and catch it with the other hand. Then, pull back tight. It takes considerably less effort than manual strangulation."

JB frowned at the handles the way he frowned at Will sometimes. Like a fly he couldn't quite catch to swat. He paced around the small tray, crouching to inspect it from all angles, until finally he smacked his hands together. "I've got it. I know exactly what they are."

JB preened while Chet photographed and measured the garrote, speaking into a recorder as he moved. When he finished, he placed the garrote in a clear evidence bag for further testing for fingerprints and DNA.

"So, are you gonna tell us or should we guess?" Will asked, finally.

"Get this. My third wife, Bev, she was a hell of a lousy cook. Also, a hell of a nag, but that's neither here nor there. Her grandmother had given her this antique rolling pin, and she got this wild idea that she was gonna bake her own bread from scratch. That dough was hard as a brick. So tough that one of the handles popped right off. She was always on my ass to fix it. Anyway, it looked just like that."

Will shook his head at JB. Half annoyed, half amazed, he couldn't help but smile.

"I think you might be right," Chet told him, taking another look at the dowels.

"Damn-skippy, I'm right. I'll bet you Chief Flack nominates me for Detective of the Year."

"Detective of the Year?" Will asked. "Aren't there just two of us?"

JB shrugged. "Guess you're runner-up then."

Chet met them outside the examination room having shed his gloves, his face shield and lab coat. The smell of formalin still wafted from his clothing. Will had been to enough autopsies to recognize it as the official odor of death. It seemed fitting, the way it grabbed you by the throat. The repulsive way it lingered in your nose. He'd probably still be smelling it tonight, after a long, hot shower. Death doesn't wash off easy.

"Gentlemen, you've got yourselves a homicide. That's for certain. Death by asphyxiation, likely early Thursday morning. No obvious signs of trauma to the genitals. No tearing of the cervix or vaginal cavity. But, given the state of undress, I don't think we can rule out a sexually motivated murder at this point."

"C'mon," JB said. "Tell us something we don't know."

"I'm getting there, Jimmy."

"Well, could you speed it up a bit? My stomach's been growling all morning since City Boy here had me runnin' laps through the muck in that damn tunnel."

"Alright. Remember how I showed you those reddish-purple stains on the victim's lower legs and feet? Those are the lividity stains, the lowest point on the body, where the blood pools after death. They become fixed somewhere between twelve and twenty-four hours."

JB groaned. "Give it to me in English, Clancy."

"I think what Doc is saying is that someone moved Bonnie's body at least twelve hours after her death."

"Exactly," Chet said. "Before that the blood had already pooled in the lower extremities. That tells me she was sitting. And for a while, too."

Will's phone buzzed in his pocket—"Give me one minute."—and he left Chet and JB, pushing through two sets of double doors and out into the crisp, fresh air. A welcome relief, even if it didn't quite rid his nostrils of death's perfume.

"Will Decker, Homicide."

The caller took a long, shaky breath. "Uh, Will. Detective Decker. I didn't know if you'd answer. It's James McMillan. You told me to call if I thought of anything, and, well… there is something I'd like to talk to you about."

It had been nearly two years since Will had felt it, that blood-pumping, heart-pounding, indescribable rush of chasing a lead. Of working a homicide. The last two years in San Francisco, that part of him had gone numb. Like he'd been packed in ice. Slowly, slowly, he felt himself coming alive again.

"We'll be there in ten minutes."

"Could you come alone? It's just that Detective Benson's ex-wife's grandson goes to school with Noah. And, I'd rather talk to somebody that's not so local."

"Of course. I understand."

Will understood better than anyone. Sometimes the people who knew you best didn't know you at all.

Will volunteered to swing by Fog City Cinema to speak to the manager about the security footage, while JB stayed back at the station with a sack of barbecue ribs from the Hickory Pit and a mission to identify the strange object they'd found half-buried on the beach near the entrance to the drainpipe. It might amount to nothing. Just a piece of discarded junk washed up onshore. Or not. Will flipped and flipped and flipped that mental coin as he drove down Pine Grove Road toward the McMillan house.

The route took him past the place where Bonnie's car had been discovered by a long-haul trucker, with the door gaping open to the rain-soaked seat and floorboard. If Will hadn't known the spot, he might've driven right past it. The crime scene tape had been removed; the car towed to the station. Only the vague remnants of Bonnie's tire tracks remained. Along with a single white ribbon tied to a fence post. In the spring, when it stopped raining, Will guessed they'd make a proper memorial.

James answered the door on the first knock. A television played cartoons in the background as he stood there, blank-faced and barefoot. A half-dead man walking.

"Let's talk in here." He directed Will toward a closed door just off the entryway. "The kids are watching TV with their grandma."

Will didn't need to be told the room belonged to Bonnie. The walls were decorated with framed movie posters. The classics like *Gone with the Wind*, *Casablanca*, and *Vertigo*, the last film she'd ever seen. He selected the chair opposite Bonnie's desk, so he could get a good look at the papers she'd left there.

"So, you said you thought of something that might be important?"

James slumped. "I owe you an apology. I wasn't completely honest with you and Detective Benson."

On the corner nearest him, Will scanned a piece of notebook paper. Judging by the neat block print, he figured it had been written by an inmate. Those guys had nothing better to do than perfect their penmanship. The page was marked with red ink.

"There is something you should know. Somebody you might want to take a look at."

Will slipped a small notepad from his pocket, hoping it wouldn't slow James down or shut him up entirely. But James didn't notice. Will followed his eyes to the bookshelf. The first row. The second row. The third row too. The same book on every shelf. Will had a copy just like it at home. A signed copy.

"Drake Devere." James spoke Will's worst fear aloud. "He's the *who*. And these goddamned books. They're the *why*."

"Look, I don't want to offend you, but these guys can be extremely manipulative. Was Bonnie involved with—"

"No!" James pounded the desk with his fist, scattering a few papers onto the floor. "Nothing like that. She took her job very seriously. She never crossed the line. It was me. It was my fault."

"Tell me what happened."

"Two years ago, Drake enrolled in Bonnie's class. Apparently, he had real talent. That's what she told me. He wrote this novel, a thriller he called *Bird of Prey*. Bonnie edited it and helped him self-publish online." He cast a scathing side-eye at the bookshelf. "Those are the signed promotional copies."

"All those? You've got to be kidding me."

"I wish I was. It was Bonnie's idea to donate the proceeds. I don't think either of us expected it to take off, but the guy's got a real cult following. Women love him, if you can imagine that. After a while, the whole thing started to piss me off. So, I rerouted the money into our retirement account."

"Did Bonnie know?"

"I don't think so. She always let me take care of the finances. But Drake figured it out somehow. He accused Bonnie of stealing the money."

"When?"

"Monday." James hung his head. "Are you going to arrest me?"

Will wanted to reassure him. Drake Devere could choke on his literary talent for all he cared. "Not right now. But I need you to cooperate. To tell me everything you know."

James nodded, gathering Bonnie's papers from the floor. By the time he'd finished, tears spilled over, and he buried his face in his hands. "I killed her, didn't I?"

The words startled Will, but he'd learned not to show it. Hiding your emotions so well you can't find them yourself. Classic cop job hazard. "What do you mean?"

"Maybe Drake paid somebody off."

"Do you think that's what happened?" Will thought of the garrote, as he scanned Bonnie's desk one last time. It struck him then. The familiar handwriting. All the papers had the same name in the top right corner. The same words painstakingly etched across the top, as if the title itself was art. *Hawk's Revenge, The Second Book in the Bird of Prey Series. Copyright: Drake Devere.*

"He's certainly capable. You should ask Doctor Rockwell over at the prison. Aside from Bonnie, she's the one who knows him best."

Will deposited his gun at the base of the Crescent Bay State Prison guard tower, just like the sign instructed him. The last time he'd visited a prison he hadn't brought his gun along. He'd come on a personal mission. Now, as he stared down the long concrete hallway, the old bones rattling in his head, he wished JB had come along to distract him. But he hadn't even called his partner. He had to see for himself if James' story had any merit, and he'd promised James he'd be discreet. Not to mention, if he had to deal with Dr. Smarty Pants again, he didn't want any witnesses.

Will tried the door to the Mental Health Unit. Locked. He tapped on the window, and the officer at the desk hurried over.

"You must be Detective Decker."

Will nodded and shook the sweaty hand of Sergeant Wickersham. The small black square on his uniform told him so.

"Control said you were on your way. Doctor Rockwell's office is that one, right over there. She's expecting you."

So much for the element of surprise. Each of his footfalls clacked on the tile floor, a countdown to his arrival. Will found the door open. He knocked anyway.

"Doctor Rockwell?"

Her eyes were unexpected. Greener, softer. More tired than he remembered. He wondered if she'd lain awake like him, thinking of Bonnie.

"Please, call me Olivia. Unless you're here to arrest me again, Detective."

"Deck," he said. "That's what most people call me. And, I owe you an apology."

She shook her head, waved him off. "It's okay. I shouldn't have run down there. You were right."

"I get the feeling you don't say those three little words very often, so I'll count myself among the lucky." When Olivia smiled at him, revealing a single dimple in her freckled cheek, Will considered himself just that. He'd never seen her smile before.

"How can I help you, Deck?"

"It's about the McMillan case." Dimple, erased. Smile, faded. A hard line appeared in its place.

"I spoke with the officer yesterday like you asked. He took my statement."

"Not that." Will gestured to the chair opposite her. Probably the one where her patients sat, the Vulture included. "May I?"

She didn't answer, but he sat anyway, immediately glancing at the wall to her left. From here, he could look without being obvious. Doctor of Philosophy in Psychology, Stanford University. Special Commendation, Federal Bureau of Investigation, San Francisco. Every bit the big deal Chet had warned him about.

"What, then?" she asked.

"An inmate here at Crescent Bay. Drake Devere. Someone told me you know him well."

"Have you spoken with the warden? I'm not allowed to discuss my patients outside of the institution." Olivia turned her attention to straightening a neat stack of files at the edge of her desk. "Now, if you'll excuse me, I have some paperwork to finish."

"So, he is a patient then?"

"I didn't say that. But I will need the warden's approval before I speak with you any further."

"Warden Blevins is aware." He'd spoken to Blevins on the way and told him only what he'd needed to secure entry into Crescent Bay. That he had official police business with Dr. Rockwell related to the McMillan case. Still, the half-truth left a bitter taste. "Otherwise I wouldn't be here."

"I'm sorry. I'm afraid I'll have to talk with him first. I'm sure you understand."

"I can see Devere's file right there." The way she kept fidgeting with the stack, he had a hunch. "Can't you just answer a few questions off the record? Or should I assume you're protecting him from something?"

Olivia's glare pinned him to the seat, and he knew he'd pushed too far. This must be how it felt to be one of her inmate patients. Leveled with a single look.

"Listen, Deck." She made his name sound like a dirty word. "I'm following the ethics code. And the law. Maybe you've heard of it?"

He stood up and turned to go but reconsidered. No smarty-pants doctor would make him slink out with his tail between his legs. "You know, after the way you acted yesterday, I didn't think you'd be so by-the-book."

"You're one to talk."

"What's that supposed to mean?"

Will knew exactly what it meant, and he hoped she wouldn't answer. He couldn't bear for anyone to say it out loud. Mercifully, she only shrugged at him. There it was again. That look.

He flung open Olivia's door. "Let me out."

Sergeant Wickersham flinched, nodding his head so fast Will wondered he didn't pull a muscle.

Out in the hallway, he leaned against the cold bricks, watching the inmates file past. Guilt settled on his chest, the way it always did when he thought of Ben, heavy as a millstone. He started back down the hallway toward the exit, feeling the weight of it around his neck. It wasn't just knowing Ben would spend five more years in a prison just like this one. It was knowing he'd put him there.

"Hey, I know you."

Some voices you never forget. You hear them in the dark spaces in your head. You wake up drenched in your own sweat, your heart pounding against your rib cage like the hooves of a racehorse. Drake Devere had a voice like that. Will had been hearing it for five years. Like the Vulture had pecked his way into Will's brain and taken perch there.

But this voice didn't come from inside his head. It came from behind him.

"Detective William Decker. After all those letters I wrote you, it's about time you paid me a visit."

CHAPTER SIX

"Who was that?" Leah asked, poking her head into Olivia's office.

"You mean, Mister Wise Guy?" After Will fled, Olivia had counted to ten, waiting for her frontal lobe to catch up to her amygdala. Then, she'd counted to ten again, until her blood had gone from a boil to a simmer.

"I mean the ruggedly handsome gentleman you just sent running for the exit." Leave it to Leah to notice the ruggedly handsome part.

"He's a homicide detective."

"Homicide?" Leah came inside and shut the door behind her. "Was he here about Bonnie?"

"That's what he said. But then he asked me about Drake."

Leah frowned, twirling her ponytail around her hand the way she always did when she was worried. "What did you tell him?"

"Nothing."

Olivia thought of the morning. Her walk down the runway. Melody's whispered words. *Strangled by an inmate.*

"So, why did he run out of here like he'd seen a ghost?"

Olivia didn't answer, and when Leah dressed her down with an accusatory look, she changed the subject. "Hey, have any of your patients said anything about Bonnie being strangled by an inmate?"

"What? God, no. Where did you hear that?"

"Good ole Crescent Bay rumor mill."

"Do you think that detective knew something about it?"

"His name is Will Decker." Olivia felt the sting of shame hot on her neck. She shouldn't have thrown it in his face like that, even if she hadn't said it aloud. The past should never be a weapon. She'd learned that long before she'd come to work in the prison, where all of her patients had pasts sharp as axe blades.

"Okay. Will *Ruggedly Handsome* Decker. Got it."

Olivia sighed. "Ring any bells?"

Leah shrugged, so Olivia waved her over and typed Will's name into the search bar on her computer. The same way she'd done dripping wet on the rock by the Earl River. She picked the first article on the list and waited for the gasp as Leah read over her shoulder.

"Oh. Jesus. The poor guy. No wonder he moved here."

San Francisco Post

"SFPD Officer Convicted of Voluntary Manslaughter in Tenderloin Shooting"
by Angela Nguyen

Former San Francisco police officer Benjamin Decker was sentenced to six years behind bars for the fatal shooting of an unarmed female, Rochelle Townes, who he had observed behaving suspiciously outside of the Aces High nightclub in the Tenderloin District. At the time of the shooting, Decker was employed by the San Francisco Police Department as a patrol officer. A jury convicted Decker on multiple charges, including violating the oath of office, making a false statement, and voluntary manslaughter, but rejected the more serious charge of second-degree murder.

Witnesses testified that on the night of the shooting, Decker was off duty and had left the nightclub after drinking there with several other police officers, including his brother, William Decker, when he encountered the victim loitering by his vehicle with another suspect. When confronted by the officers, the pair ran. Both Benjamin and William Decker gave chase, pursuing the suspects into the Double Rock Projects, where Benjamin fired several shots from his service weapon, fatally wounding Ms. Townes. Though Benjamin told detectives Ms. Townes had reached for a gun, no weapon was recovered at the scene.

The case gained national attention due to allegations of police misconduct in the handling of the investigation. Attorneys for the victim's family told the Post that the police had waited five hours before obtaining blood samples from the officers involved. By that time, Benjamin Decker had a BAC of .07%, just under the legal intoxication level in California. The San Francisco Coroner's Office also came under fire for ignoring crucial evidence. A private autopsy requested by the family revealed fresh bruising on the victim's face and indicated the fatal shot had been fired from close range, rather than the distance testified to by Benjamin Decker.

Earlier this week, William Decker appeared in court on behalf of the prosecution, giving testimony against his brother, including damning statements that Benjamin was intoxicated at the time of the shooting; had not followed proper police procedure before using lethal force; and that a "reasonable" officer would not have acted similarly. Benjamin Decker testified in his own defense on Friday, describing Ms. Townes as a known drug dealer who often carried a firearm and had refused to follow his commands.

The Townes family has been outspoken in their search for justice. "Rochelle wasn't perfect, but she didn't deserve the death penalty," her mother, Toni, told reporters at a press conference following the verdict. "We're just thankful that William Decker stood up and did the right thing, even if it meant going against his own brother."

CHAPTER SEVEN

Olivia pushed through the double doors into the crowded chow hall in search of Drake's work supervisor, Laura Ricci. She didn't owe Drake any favors but she suspected he was one rules infraction away from losing it. Maybe Laura could go easy on him for a few weeks. Pissing off a serial killer never did anybody any favors.

Olivia nodded at the officer stationed by the entrance and walked a straight line to the kitchen through the tables of incarcerated men. She kept her head up, confident, but moved quickly, her eyes darting like a gazelle among lions.

During the dinner shift, Laura could usually be found patrolling the line, making sure nobody doled out extras or pocketed so much as an orange. According to Drake, she ruled her domain with an iron spatula. But today, Laura's second-in-command had assumed her position on line duty.

"Where can I find Ms. Ricci?" Olivia directed her question to the young man spooning mystery meat from an oversized pan. His knuckles bore the inked words, CRIME PAYS.

"In the back. But she said not to bother her."

Olivia headed into the bowels of the kitchen anyway, listening for Laura's boisterous voice, her throaty laughter. She heard nothing above the whir of the industrial mixer and the clatter of the metal trays tossed in the dirty bin.

She stepped carefully, avoiding the vegetable parts that littered the sticky floor as she followed a few sets of wet footprints toward the back. When she neared the loading dock, the sound of hurried voices drew her into the shadows by the overhead door. Outside, a delivery truck idled.

Olivia shivered as the cold air reached her. She kept close to the wall and out of sight.

The first time she'd met Laura, at a case consultation meeting to discuss Drake's adjustment at Crescent Bay, she'd known in an instant why Drake hated her. With her silky black hair and her big brown eyes, she resembled the only picture Drake had of his mother, Serena. He'd desecrated it with a red ink pen as a boy but kept it anyway. She'd seen it taped on the wall of his cell, the word 'whore' scratched into the photo paper.

Olivia spotted Laura from behind, her long braid hanging between her shoulder blades like a hangman's noose. She started to call out to her but shut her mouth as soon as she saw Laura's arms, elbows-deep in a sack of flour.

Laura cast a furtive glance over her shoulder, and Olivia ducked back behind the corner, her heart racing. She waited, then looked again at Laura's palm prints, stark white on the dingy dishtowel she'd slung over her shoulder. At the bag of flour, gutted on the table. At her hands, still ghostly white. At what she held in them.

Olivia opened her umbrella. A light rain had begun to fall, dotting the sidewalk. At least she didn't have far to go. As chief psychologist, she had her very own parking spot between the chaplain and the lead custodian.

Most of the parking lot had emptied, and Olivia gazed across the concrete sea to the bordering redwoods, barely visible in the vanishing twilight. She admired those trees, but she feared them too. She always felt small beneath them. Like the eight-year-old girl she'd been, the first time she and her mother had made the sudden turn off Pine Grove Road and rumbled past the VISITING HOURS sign in their beat-up Buick station wagon. Her mother applying lipstick in the rearview and reminding Olivia to put on a smile for her dad.

The prison had changed since then. It had grown larger, spreading its concrete tentacles across the salt grass in every direction. But the trees, those ancient sentinels, would still be here long after she'd returned to the earth.

Emily had already arrived at the car and unlocked it with her spare key. Her face lit by her phone's tiny screen, she relaxed in the passenger's seat, cozy in her blue raincoat. The headlights beckoned to Olivia through the mist, promising to take her far away from here, at least for the night, and she hurried toward them.

"Olivia, could I have a minute?"

Warden Blevins appeared behind her, his thin frame dwarfed under a golf-sized umbrella. His glasses fogged, he lifted the frames with one hand, considering her from beneath them. Under the shadow of his umbrella, his eyes were black as currants.

Olivia let the rush of panic subside before she spoke. She worked with murderers and rapists, for God's sake. "Of course. Would you like to meet back inside the entrance?"

"That won't be necessary. I'm sure you've had a long day. What with Bonnie's death and the unfortunate melee in the MHU this morning."

The longest. But Olivia only nodded, wishing she'd left work earlier, before the sun had set. Before most of the eight-to-fivers went home. Before the trees closed in like soldiers guarding their fortress.

"You can rest assured I gave Sergeant Wickersham a good talking-to. Though, frankly, I don't blame him. Sometimes it feels like we're trying to go against nature here, expecting too much. We wouldn't ask the wolves not to bite us. Every once in a while, I feel the need to throw them a rabbit just so they won't gnaw my face off."

Olivia nodded again, anxious to be rid of him and his disturbing metaphors.

"Actually, I'm glad you stopped me," she said. "I was planning to call you first thing tomorrow morning. A homicide detective stopped by to ask some questions about Drake Devere, and I wasn't sure what to tell him."

"I'm surprised you'd even ask. Finding Bonnie's killer is our priority. Tell him he's got our full cooperation."

"Yes, sir. But I'll have to limit what I disclose. You know, the ethics code and all." Olivia knew the rules better than anybody. She gave the speech to the interns every year. *You may breach confidentiality if there is a credible threat to the safety and security of the institution.*

"There's no one more ethical than you, Doc."

The rain fell harder now, and a gust jerked Olivia's umbrella, briefly turning it inside out. The warden laughed, a thin, reedy sound that was nearly lost in the wind. His umbrella hardly budged, sturdy as an armored shell above him.

"Funny enough, Drake is exactly who I wanted to speak to you about. I'd like to ask you a favor. Just between us."

Olivia glanced over her shoulder, hoping Emily would bear witness. But to what, exactly? Em doesn't know what I know, she reminded herself. She hasn't seen what I saw. Still, when her sister lifted her hand to wave, Olivia felt an inexplicable relief.

"A favor?" That word prodded at the base of her spine with an icicle finger. "From me?"

"You've got a lifetime of experience dealing with these types. Some things you just can't learn in a classroom." So, he'd finally called it out. Her father, the murderer. She wondered if the warden had been holding it back all this time like an ace in his pocket. Waiting to shock her. Well, two could play that game.

"You're right. I can spot a con from a mile away. So, what can I do for you, Warden?"

"Keep an eye on Drake Devere. After he and Hank got into it this morning, he mouthed off to Ms. Ricci. I think he's up to something, and I don't want either of us to be caught in the middle of it."

Olivia heard herself agree. But, the moment she spotted a smudge of flour on the warden's jaw, she went somewhere else in her mind. Back to the chapel, two weeks ago. When she'd slipped into the confessional in search of a quiet place to think.

Got the goods?

Keep your voice down.

Relax, dude.

Call me dude again, and I'll make sure the only parole you get is the back door kind.

Easy, man. Ain't no need for those kind of threats. I ain't dyin' in here. You hear me?

We'll see about that. Now take it and get out.

She'd peeked out of the narrow gap between the door and the frame. What she'd seen stunned her. Not *what*. But *who*.

The tattooed hands of Tommy Rigsby, shot caller for the Oaktown Boys. And the delicate, unmarred skin of Warden Blevins. Passing in between them, a mysterious brown package exactly like the one she'd seen Laura fish from a bag of flour in the kitchen. The goods. Which Olivia knew weren't good at all.

If Emily noticed Olivia's hands shaking on the wheel, she kept it to herself. Olivia didn't want to lie, and she couldn't explain. For once, she felt grateful Em didn't look up from her cell phone.

Olivia piloted the car cautiously past the exit, flashing her ID badge once more, and made the turn onto Pine Grove Road. A fifteen-minute drive and she could put this day behind her.

"What're you looking at?" she asked Emily.

"The news. I wanted to see what they're saying about Bonnie."

"And?"

"The same." Emily tossed her phone in her purse and took a breath. "Did you hear anything today?"

"Did you?" Big sisters had earned the right to answer a question with a question.

"Maybe. But it seems far-fetched even for Crescent Bay gossip."

Olivia tried to focus on the road through the rain-soaked windshield. "Well, let's hear it."

"Bonnie was stealing Drake's book money, so he snuck out of his cell at night. You know how the cameras always fritz in the rain. He hot-wired a prison truck at the off-site lot on Pine Grove, punched a hole in her tire, and followed her. Then, when she pulled off the road, he snuck up and—Liv, stop!"

The lone light on their route flashed red, and Olivia jammed the brake. The car seemed to float for a moment, then the back wheels fishtailed as she tried to gain control, skidding to a stop just before the intersection.

Now Olivia had a good excuse for her shaky hands. She gripped the wheel as tight as she could, her knuckles whitening. "That's the most ridiculous story I've ever heard. Do not repeat it."

Emily groaned.

"I'm serious, Em."

"Duh. I'd never do that to Bonnie."

Olivia turned to her sister, needing to see her eyes. But Emily denied her the one thing she wanted, pointing her finger straight ahead.

"Green light."

CHAPTER EIGHT

"I'll give you the bad news first." JB didn't look up from his cubicle desk as Will shook the rain from his coat and slumped into the seat next to him, exhausted and hungry as hell. In the trash can they shared, JB had stacked a pile of cleaned spareribs, remnants of the Hickory Pit.

"You ran out of barbecue sauce?"

"Worse. No prints on the garrote or our UBO. Not a one."

"UBO?" Will rifled through the Pit's brown paper bag. Napkins, utensils, a grease-stained receipt. No sign of the barbecue sandwich he'd ordered.

"Unidentified buried object."

Will rolled his eyes. This was the sort of thing that happened when JB had too much time on his hands. "And the good news?"

JB grinned and patted his belly. "They threw in an extra barbecue sandwich. Pays to be a cop sometimes."

Will glared at the trash can, his sandwich wrapper visible beneath the bones. The waitress had written DECK across the butcher paper in black marker. "That was mine. Didn't you check the wrapper?"

The door opened, and Lieutenant Gary Wheeler stepped inside, holding up a clear plastic evidence bag like a trophy. "General consensus among the guys is it's a footrest. Like the kind you attach to a wheelchair. That, or the flat end of a kid's beach shovel."

"Looks like a shovel to me," JB said. "What d'ya say, City Boy?"

Lieutenant Wheeler chuckled as he laid the bag on JB's desk. Now, Will could see it. The nonslip grip and the rigging where the rubber would attach to the chair. "It's a footrest. And look."

Will took an unsatisfying bite of the stale granola bar he'd scrounged from his desk drawer while he examined the bottom of the plate. "That's a serial number. Maybe Forensics can figure out the company name and trace it back to the store where it was purchased."

"I'll leave that to you," JB told Will. "Since I already did most of the work, finding the damn thing."

"You mean littering? Yeah, you did do that. And you stole my sandwich."

JB shrugged. "We don't even know if this thing is connected to our case."

"This morning you seemed to think it was the Treasure of Lima. Our guy could've used a wheelchair to transport the body down that tunnel. It would make sense with what Chet told us about the lividity stains on her legs and feet."

"Treasure of *who?*"

"Just sort it out, you two." Lieutenant Wheeler retreated in the direction of his office. "Chief Flack wants a word. You'd both better be on the same page by then or she'll have your balls."

JB wriggled his eyebrows. "As long as she's gentle."

Chief Flack wasn't a Botox kind of woman. Every line on her face had been hard-earned, and she wore them like battle scars. Will liked that about her. Even now, when the lines gathered between her brows and soured her mouth.

"So, you're telling me we've got nothing? Our first homicide in nearly a year, and we've got nothing?"

JB shook his head. "I wouldn't say that, Chief."

Will sat back and prepared to be entertained.

"Oh really, Detective Benson. We're more than twenty-four hours into this thing, and we've got no suspects, no DNA, and no prints. In my book, that sounds a lot like nothing."

"We've got this." JB held up the evidence bag with the UBO. Two splatter spots of barbecue sauce dotted the plastic.

"Right. *That*. A real smoking gun. If that's all we've got, I'd say we're still in the starting blocks."

"Well, that's my mistake. I let City Boy here take the lead." He leaned in toward Chief Flack's desk, putting his back to Will. "You know how it is, Chief. If you want a job done right…"

It had been a solid ten years since Will had punched a face, but damn, he wanted to end that streak with a windup hook right to JB's kisser. "Actually, we do have a suspect."

"First I've heard of it." JB tried to pretend Will hadn't thrown a knockout. But his hard swallow had the sound of victory. Not as satisfying as the crunch of his bulbous nose, but it would do.

"You would've known that if you'd watched the security footage I emailed you from the theater." Will opened the link on his phone, propped it on the edge of the desk, and pressed play. "Alright, Bonnie exits the theater right at the 2:12 a.m. mark." On cue, she burst through the door. Her umbrella unopened in her hand, she shielded her face from the rain and ran through the parking lot. Will tapped the screen to pause the video. "You can tell she's in a hurry. Didn't even take the time to open her umbrella. Like she might be afraid of someone.

"Now, just a few seconds later…" He hit play. "This guy comes out. Also no umbrella. He follows her until we lose them in the rain out of camera range."

Will rewound the video, stopping when the man appeared closest to the camera.

JB guffawed. "That's our suspect? Good luck, man. With that hood on, you can't even tell if it's a guy."

Will shrugged, smug in the knowledge he had someone in mind. Even if that someone was trapped behind bars in Crescent Bay. "I say we release it to the media. See if it stirs up any leads."

Chief Flack nodded. "Looks like the gun's finally gone off, gentlemen. Start running."

She waited until JB had a firm grip on the doorknob, ready to make his getaway and find a spot to lick his wounds. "And Jimmy, keep the barbecue sauce off the evidence."

Will wiped the sweat from his face and leaned against his truck, huffing. His knuckles ached from a solid nine rounds on the bag, and his right shoulder creaked when he took a swig of water. But inside he felt new again, blown clean.

He unwound the wraps from his hands and hung them across the truck bed to dry, peeking into the far corner of the garage at the cat who'd made himself at home in the old towels Will had left out for him.

"Don't get used to it, buddy. It's only temporary." The cat stretched his front paws and laid his head atop them, closing his one good eye. The other had been stitched shut long ago, when he'd belonged to someone. "And don't scratch my truck."

Will had a plan for the rest of the evening. It involved a hot shower, a piece of cold pizza, and *Three's Company* reruns. But the shrill ringing of his phone was a death knell. His plan, doomed to crash and burn.

"Will Decker, Homicide."

"You have a collect call from Peter Decker, an inmate at San Francisco City Jail. This call may be recorded and monitored. To accept this call, please press 0. If you do not wish to—"

Will stabbed at the zero on the screen, and the line crackled. He hadn't heard from his little brother, Petey, in months. And the last time he'd seen him, slinging drinks behind the bar at Aces High, the nightclub he owned, Petey had told him he wouldn't be attending Ben's trial. *Where would I sit?* he'd asked. *I can't take sides.*

"Thank you for using Talk-net. Go ahead with your call."

"Seriously? What did you do this time, Petey?"

"I'm sorry, Deck. But you're the only one I can call. Damn pigs raided the club again. No offense. They got me for resisting."

"How much do you need?" Will asked, through gritted teeth. Technically, he was one of said pigs.

"Twenty-five hundred."

"Jesus. You do realize I'm a cop, right? In a Podunk town. Not an investment banker."

"I wouldn't ask if I had any other options. You know I'm good for it. I promise I'll pay you back."

Will had heard that before. "Plus interest."

"Yeah. Of course." The silence stretched between them, taking the shape of all that had gone unsaid after that night at Aces High. Will hadn't taken a drink since. "Hey, by the way, your Podunk town is in the news down here. You solved that lady's murder yet, big brother?"

"I'll call the bail bondsman first thing in the morning."

"*Morning?* You mean—"

Will sat there for a while, listening to the rain and staring at the phone. That's the thing about the past. You can hang up, but it always calls back.

Will couldn't breathe. He'd been running. Hard and fast. And drunk. Something terrible waited around the corner. He knew it, but he didn't stop.

His Glock felt like a viper in his hand. Alive and writhing. Hungry.

When he turned into the shadows, time stopped. His fate poised in mid-air like the toss of a quarter. Or the spin of a revolver's chamber. Then, he heard a shot.

Will sat up, gasping. He took his own inventory. Shirt, soaked through. Heart, pounding. Gun, still and cold on his nightstand. Unfired. He finally took a breath.

Outside, the rain beat on, and the clock assured him he'd only been asleep for an hour. The dream had left him shaken but focused too. He sprang up, padding into the spare bedroom where he kept the boxes he hadn't unpacked yet. Fog Harbor still felt temporary.

He knew exactly where to find it, muscling open the tape with his bare hands and tossing the other books aside as if his own life depended on it.

Will guessed Drake had designed the cover of *Bird of Prey* himself, because his name figured prominently in bold type. The design—a close-up of a hawk's golden eye—sent a chill through him every time he looked at it.

He opened the cover to the title page, where Drake had written a personal message with the same meticulous penmanship he'd used in Bonnie's class. Will had received the package, like the four letters before it, in the mail last February 3rd. No return address, postmarked Devil's Rock, Oregon.

Happy anniversary, Detective Decker! Can you believe it's been five years since we rendezvoused? I've been busy, as you can tell. So have you, I hear. Too bad about your brother, Benjamin. I do hope I'll have the chance to make his acquaintance. Remember what I promised you. We'll meet again, and this time, I'll know you even better. Inside and out. This time I'll be ready. Will you?

Fondly,
Vulture

Will propped himself against another box, turned to Chapter One, and settled in for a long night—well, an early morning—of reading. He didn't need Dr. Smarty Pants. He'd figure Drake out all by himself. Just like last time.

"Modesto Man Dubbed 'The Vulture' Arrested in San Francisco Slayings"
by Tori Sheffield

Authorities in California have arrested a man they believe is responsible for the deaths of at least five young women over the past decade. San Francisco Police apprehended Drake Mortimer Devere, 40, at his home in Modesto. He has been charged with five counts of first-degree murder and rape in the deaths of Alecia Ramirez, Constance Poole, Lana Booker, Jennifer Li, and Amelia Gutierrez. All of the victims apparently encountered Devere on Let's Get Together, a dating website where Devere maintained multiple fictitious profiles. Authorities allege Devere targeted women with low popularity scores, a controversial feature of the site which has since been disabled, and lured them to remote locations near Muir Woods, where he sexually assaulted them and strangled them with pieces of their own clothing.

Dubbed 'The Vulture' due to the predatory nature of his crimes, as well as injuries left behind on the victims' neck which resembled claw marks, Devere first came to police attention six months ago, after he submitted a short story to the *San Francisco Post* featuring details specific to the crimes. DNA evidence obtained from the victims' bodies did not result in a match on CODIS, the FBI's combined DNA index system; however, investigators obtained a sample of Devere's DNA through other means, resulting in a match.

Arresting homicide detective William Decker did not mince words at a news conference on Monday, telling reporters, "Devere is pure evil. He's the worst kind of predator. The kind who can't be reformed. There's only one place for a monster like that, and we're relieved he's finally behind bars." San Francisco Prosecutor, Mark McGovern, told reporters he plans to seek the death penalty.

CHAPTER NINE

Laura Ricci had no clue how she'd gotten here. Here being 4 a.m. in downtown Fog Harbor, the same town where she'd grown up. Though for a thirty-seven-year-old junior college dropout who supervised the dredges of society in Crescent Bay's chow hall, grownup seemed debatable.

That's why she'd fallen in love with running. You plotted a course. You followed it. You didn't get lost and end up living somebody else's life. With its sudden starts and stops, its sheer cliffs, its misdirection, life was nothing like running. Which was why she'd had to start from scratch a few years back when Ricci's Bistro burned to the ground in an electrical fire. Life was no marathon. It was a trial by literal fire.

Laura's shins ached as her sneakers pounded the sidewalk, splashing rainwater onto her leggings. But her thighs no longer rubbed together. Her breasts didn't jostle with every stride. And her stomach felt semi-taut beneath her T-shirt. Still thirty pounds from her goal weight, she felt light as air. When she passed Thrifty Dry Cleaners, with its massive windows and sparkly Christmas display, the reflection shocked her. She looked skinny. No, not skinny. *Strong*.

Take that, Devere. She couldn't believe she'd let him get to her. When he'd arrived late to work again yesterday—blaming Handsy Hank, a nickname she had to admit hit the mark—she'd sent him back to his cell. She'd written him up. She'd told him, come January he'd be reassigned, and not to the Education Department like he hoped. Not with Bonnie gone. Nobody else there wanted him.

Fat bitch, he'd muttered, just loud enough for the rest of the inmate staff to hear him. They'd hung their heads, embarrassed for her, before she'd snapped at them to get to work. At least with Devere gone, the job wouldn't be such a headache, and if she kept saving, she'd be able to reopen Ricci's within a year. Even less, with her slightly unpleasant side gig. Back on course, after all.

Laura's five-mile route took her on a loop downtown around the quaint Fog Harbor square. She never tired of it. Lost in time, the sandstone courthouse sat like a jewel in the center of the block, the frame and the tall narrow windows, outlined in twinkling white Christmas lights. She allowed herself a quick stop to gaze upward at the clock tower which read 4:05 a.m.

She'd need to pick up the pace if she intended to make it to work by five. She lengthened her stride and pumped her arms in time to the drums on her holiday workout mix. In ten minutes, she'd made it back to the dirt road that led through the redwoods toward home, her headlamp illuminating the path.

The air smelled different here. Clean and mossy and wet. The fog threaded its skeleton fingers through the tree trunks, obscuring some of them entirely. She always dreaded the final leg of her run. Even more so after Bonnie had vanished and turned up dead outside her own vigil—how's that for a kick in the teeth?—though Laura laid the blame squarely at James' feet. He hadn't done the deed himself, of course, but everybody knew the guy smuggled in cell phones. They sold for a cool grand a pop. If you're not careful things like that catch up to you. But Laura had learned to be exceedingly careful.

Laura tried to stay focused on the trail. The redwoods weren't friendly. She'd realized that a long time ago, when her best dog had chased a raccoon into the tree cover and never returned. And then again, years later, when Uncle Rick started taking her hunting every weekend. Sometimes, they'd stay out so late they had to crash in the back of his truck. He only brought one sleeping bag. Come to think of it, she could hold the redwoods responsible for the forty pounds she put on during her thirteenth year, hoping it would be enough to protect her. That maybe if she'd added enough layers between them, there'd be no way for his hands to get through.

A drop of rain splashed onto her forehead, as if the universe took joy in mocking her. Like Drake. One drop became two became ten became a hundred. Until the sky opened up again.

The trees played tricks with her. Little sounds. Furtive movements. Footsteps. Maybe just the beat of her heart. By the time she reached her mailbox, she'd hit a full-on sprint, and her lungs ached.

Laura got a few paces up her own dirt road and stopped cold. The rain attacked her now, stinging her skin, but she couldn't move. In the glow of her headlamp, a hooded figure lay on the ground, unmoving.

"Are you okay?" She sounded no different than the girl she'd been when Uncle Rick had laid his hands on her. She'd never been able to stop him, no matter how fat she'd made herself. Only God had done that, striking him dead with a rare Northern California lightning bolt in that very same forest the summer she'd turned sixteen. "I'll call an ambulance."

But she'd left her cell phone behind. She always did, despite the dangers.

Laura took one step forward, and her legs shook.

"I'm coming," she said. "It's okay. I'm coming." The words more for herself, since the figure—whoever it was—stayed still as a stump.

As she moved, the redwoods closed in around her. Until it seemed the entire world had grown as small and hateful as this forest.

Dread thickened in her throat, and she wiped the rain from her eyes. Futile, because it kept coming. She kept coming too.

Closer and closer, until she saw hands, white and clawing against the muddy ground.

Just then, a flicker of movement caught her eye, and the fog parted. The forest revealed what it had been hiding all along. A truck, like the kind they used at the prison to make the rounds, checking the fences for weak spots. The old jalopy studied her through its headlamps, a pair of dark, lifeless eyes.

Laura bent over and drew back the hood, as the figure finally stirred. The last face she'd ever see, familiar.

CHAPTER TEN

The blood-red sun woke Olivia, her mother's voice repeating that old mariner's adage. *Red sky at morning, sailors take warning.* It had always amused Olivia, how well her mother played a role. When people had gotten nosy, which they often did in Fog Harbor, her mother had told them Martin Reilly worked as a fisherman on the *Arcadia*, the biggest boat in the marina. That a wave had taken him overboard one winter and they'd never found him. No body. No bones. No trace. To Olivia, it seemed not so far from the truth, even now. Her father had sunk himself to the bottom of the sea. A rusting hull gathering barnacles.

Olivia slogged toward the kitchen, pausing at Emily's closed door at the sound of her alarm clock blaring on the other side.

"Em?"

Olivia knocked, softly at first, then louder. Nothing. She put her ear to the door. The shrill, insistent beeping drilled right through the pinewood.

"Emily. Get up."

Punishment. That's what this was. Punishment for last night. For the argument they'd been having for the last six months.

"I get it, Em. You've made your point."

Olivia tried the knob, expecting it to be locked. Instead, the door yawned open. Emily's bed empty, except for the sheets and the quilt balled carelessly at the foot. Two pillows rumpled near the headboard. The Christmas snow globe that had once belonged to their mother resting on the nightstand, the plastic flakes settled at the bottom. Emily's easel propped near the window, her painting of Little Gull half-finished.

Like a trapdoor had opened, Olivia's heart fell clear through to the pit of her stomach. She rushed inside, searching the bathroom. The closet. She wanted to yell, but she feared the sound of her own panicked voice would just make it worse.

"Stopped raining." Emily leaned against the doorframe, her cheeks whipped red from the wind. In her hand, she held a sketchpad and charcoal pencil. Olivia could see the outline of the lighthouse, the rocks, the crashing waves.

"Where were you? You scared the hell out of me."

"This is exactly what I'm talking about, Liv. You're always overreacting." Emily flopped onto the bed and groaned into her pillow. "I walked down to the beach and did a few sketches. You still act like I'm a kid sometimes."

"I worry, okay? Somebody has to. What happens when you move to San Francisco and your paintings don't sell and you've got nobody to help you? What happens then?"

"I'll figure it out. Like you did." But Olivia hadn't really figured it out. She'd taken Erik's alimony in one lump sum and put it straight to use, renting an apartment in Palo Alto, buying the BMW, and paying her way to a doctorate degree. Still, that money hadn't been free. She'd earned it the hard way.

"I don't want you to do what I did."

"Don't you want a life, too? A husband? A family? A boyfriend, at least? I know it didn't work out with Graham but…"

"Of course." Olivia didn't sound convincing. Not even to herself. She had to face facts. She'd stopped trusting men a very long time ago. Long before she met Graham or Erik. Long before she'd started getting inside the heads of the worst the male species had to offer. "I just don't understand your rush. Why now? With everything that's going on here?"

"That's exactly why. What happened to Bonnie, it made me realize how short life is. I don't want to be stuck here living with my big sister and scraping plaque forever. Do you know what it's like to look inside the mouth of a guy who hasn't brushed in six months because he's whittled his toothbrush into a shank?"

Olivia's laughter burst out of her closed mouth without her permission and refused to stop. She joined Em on the bed, bopping her with the other pillow, until they both sighed, breathless with laughter. Damn little-sister voodoo.

Olivia's stomach knotted as she approached the MHU. Drake waited out front, pacing like a caged tiger.

"Doc! Boy, am I glad to see you." He jerked out his headphones, his voice sharp as a razor. An easy smile drew up one corner of his mouth. Olivia prepared to be charmed. Or sliced in two.

"We don't have another session scheduled till next week," she reminded him, unlocking the door. Icebox-cold today. She pulled her jacket tighter as Drake followed her inside.

"Aw, c'mon. I really need to talk to you. It's important."

Drake strolled past the desk, running his hand along the counter, and Hank's whole body stiffened. Like a dog with his hackles raised.

"You alright, Doctor Rockwell?"

She nodded, and kept moving, hoping Drake would too.

"Please, Doc. I'll be so quick you'll forget I was ever here."

Impossible, but she invited him in anyway. She set her bag beneath the desk, started her computer. Opened her notebook and laid it on her lap, stalling. She should send him packing. When they'd first started therapy, he'd done this all the time, shown up on a whim issuing his demands. But now, he knew the rules. She'd worked damn hard at that. One fifty-minute session per week.

Even insatiable Drake Devere had learned to fit himself inside the therapeutic frame.

"You're the only one I can talk to about this shit. You ask the right questions. Good questions. Like the one you left me with yesterday. Spent the whole night thinkin' about that."

Olivia resisted the urge to roll her eyes. Maybe the warden had been right. Something was up. She retrieved a dial timer from her drawer. She'd bought it just for Drake but it came in handy with her other patients too. That authoritative little ding had a way of setting boundaries.

"Five minutes, Drake. Time starts now."

He pushed the door shut with his boot and dropped into the chair across from her, as if he'd known her answer all along.

"So, what is it?" she asked.

"I screwed up. I screwed up real bad."

"Is this about yesterday? The thing with Hank."

Drake cackled. "Handsy? Hell no. I don't feel one iota for that loser. It's Ms. Ricci. With all that mess yesterday morning, I got to work late. Again. And then, I said some things I didn't mean."

"What did you say, exactly?" Making Drake accountable. She'd worked damn hard at that too, for diminishing returns.

He answered in a voice so low she couldn't understand him, but his eyes peeked up at her, bright and unashamed.

"I'm sorry, Drake. I can't hear you when you mumble." In her own voice, she heard her mother, scolding her. Which worked out fine because that's what Drake needed her to be. His own mom, battling her own demons, had laid the first stone on his dark and crooked path.

"I called her a bitch. A fat bitch."

"That sounds like old Drake behavior. A lot like what happened yesterday with Hank. I thought you'd moved past petty insults."

"She said nobody wanted me. That they wouldn't give me that teaching assistant job." His fists clenched in his lap. Olivia knew exactly what those hands were capable of. The way his rage turned them into talons.

"It sounds like you're feeling sorry for yourself rather than for what you said to Ms. Ricci."

He smacked his knee, the sudden movement drawing Hank's attention. Olivia gave a little head shake, waving him off. She couldn't have Handsy interrupting now.

"Damn, Doc. You're good. I tell everybody I got the smartest shrink in the joint." He puffed his chest as if he'd pinned her there like a medal.

"Well, then you know I'm not going to tell you what to do. Part of the reason you started therapy is to figure out some of these dilemmas on your own."

"That's exactly what Shauna talked about at the Changes group this week. *Options*. You always have options."

"So, what are they?"

"Well, I figure I've got two of them. New and improved Drake knows he should apologize. But I can't. Ms. Ricci's not here today. She didn't show up to work. It's probably my fault."

"And old Drake, the Vulture?"

"The Vulture would stay pissed. Work himself into a real frenzy. The Vulture would… *nah*. I can't tell you what the Vulture would do. That's what ended me up here in the first place."

Olivia waited out a shiver before she spoke.

"What does that mean?"

"You know what it means. But I'm not gonna say it. I'm already in enough trouble. I mean, have you heard the rumors?"

"Which ones?" Playing dumb. A therapist's secret weapon.

"Somebody's trying to make me look real bad. Probably that Oaktown asshole, Riggs. The guy's had it in for me ever since he got out of the hole. He knows I told the goon squad about his little plan to shank O'Brien. They should've given me a medal for that shit."

"Riggs, huh? And what is it he's saying about you?"

Drake laid his hands on the desk and leaned in. Olivia couldn't look away from them now. As he spoke, his fingers curled in like claws against the wood veneer.

"That I murdered Ms. McMillan. From here in prison. Just like Hawk, the main character in my book. Ain't that a hoot? I mean, it's fiction. Made up. That's the whole goddamn point. Nobody's goin' around saying James Patterson is bumping off ladies."

Drake pushed away, smirking, and pointed at the egg timer which had steadily advanced to its end.

Ding.

Olivia waved at Maryann as she pulled the library door shut behind her. The soft click of her heels turned the heads of a few inmates seated at a long table in the center of the room, their legal paperwork strewn around them. White-haired Morrie Mulvaney sat at the head, overseeing them. Olivia offered a polite smile, pretended not to know him. Morrie had been a friend of her father's before they'd transferred him to Valley View. She'd sat on his lap as a little girl, played with his handlebar mustache. A lifer just like her dad. Oaktown Boy too, with the tattoo to prove it. Branches of the inked oak tree barely visible beneath his collar, a remnant of his old life. The new clean-shaven Morrie worked as a paralegal for canteen money. He'd been lucky enough to convince the parole board he deserved a second chance, and unlucky enough to have his grant rescinded by the governor.

"Hey, Maryann. I'm glad to see you back. You doing alright?"

Olivia found the answer on Maryann's face. In the fluorescent light, her skin had a pallor, a sickly glow. Her eyes like two dark holes on the surface of the moon, the loose skin beneath them magnified under her glasses.

"I haven't been sleeping well. Neither has Luna. We can't stop thinking about Bonnie. And the rumors."

"Melody told you too?" Olivia kept her voice low. When your life depends on your five senses, you hone them. Sharpen them to a point. Inmates had ears as sharp as Dobermans.

Maryann mouthed *Drake*. "He's in here all the time working on his books. I've been trying to act normal. I even agreed to edit the sequel for him. Since Bonnie's… well, you know. You don't think there's any truth to the talk, do you?"

"Remember last year? That story about the warden's secretary." *Leeza's a stripper*, Em had told her one night. Olivia wouldn't dare repeat it now. But it had made the rounds along with a thousand other tall tales cooked up behind these walls. These men could fashion ink pens into needles. Nunchucks out of chair legs. Rumors out of thin air.

"You're right. It is pretty far-fetched. How would he get out of his cell and past those fences? Crescent Bay is airtight. Even the cockroaches die here."

Depressing, but Olivia had seen the proof. The upturned bodies, the spindly legs, in the corner outside the control booth. As if they'd made it as far as they could before they'd surrendered. "Do you happen to have a copy of *Bird of Prey*?"

"Sure do. We don't keep it on the shelf. But I've got my own. Drake signed it to me." Maryann's voice carried, and Morrie raised a caterpillar eyebrow at them. "I'm in the Acknowledgments, too," she whispered, covering her mouth with her pudgy fingers. "So is Bonnie."

"I didn't realize."

"Yeah. I helped with some of the research. He wanted to get all the details right." Maryann reached behind the counter and produced the book.

"I'm sure he did." Olivia had forgotten the cover. That creepy golden eye Drake had drawn himself. It fixed on her, followed her, as she slid the book across the counter and tucked it under a magazine. Because inmates talk. The last thing she needed was a run through the rumor mill. "I'll be at the desk in the back if anybody asks."

Maryann nodded. "Happy reading."

CHAPTER ELEVEN

Will sat in his truck outside the prison, rubbing his temples. He'd sucked down one and a half doughnuts and two cups of coffee on the way. That's what it would take, minimum, to make it through today on two hours' sleep. But the JB diet had taken an axe to his skull. He peeked at his face in the rearview mirror but found no blade, no protruding handle. Just a day's worth of scruff and hair that looked like he'd skipped a shower. Which he had. Amy had never liked it mussed. *You look like a hoodlum*, she'd told him. *Not a detective.*

That right there told him he needed sleep. A solid eight hours. Because the Amy synapses never fired unless they were pickled in alcohol or high on the fumes of exhaustion.

He popped the remainder of doughnut number two in his mouth and washed it down with the last shot of coffee. Might as well do it big. Then, he locked the truck and headed inside the gates of Crescent Bay to the prison library. At least there'd be no danger of running into Dr. Smarty Pants.

Will spotted Maryann hunched over the circulation desk, cataloguing a stack of nature books. One tap of the service bell, and she jumped. A book about redwoods tumbled predictably from her hand to the floor, splitting down the center so that the cover splayed wide.

"Detective Decker, what a surprise."

Will winced at it all. The book, her pale face, the volume of her announcement. Which, as he expected, cleared the library faster than a fire alarm, the center table vacant in ten seconds flat. Granted, the badge clipped to his belt probably didn't help.

"Sorry. I forgot where I was for a moment. You startled me."

"Redwoods, huh?" He pointed to the book at her feet. "I wouldn't have figured it."

Maryann twittered. "Nature books and thrillers. Our two most popular categories."

Will placed the book he'd brought with him on the countertop. "Tell me about this thriller."

"Well, that's Drake Devere's book. But I reckon you already know that."

"His name is rather large. Pretty hard to miss."

With a simpering smile, Maryann took a seat on the stool behind the desk. Will wondered if she'd ever been a preschool teacher. She looked at him like that. Like a boy. Or her little white dog. A thing to be coddled. "It's a story about an inmate, Hawk, on death row. He digs a tunnel from his cell to the outside, so he can do what he wants to. Kill women."

"I've read it." Cover to cover.

"Oh. Then, how can I help you, Detective?"

"Your name is in the Acknowledgments. I'm wondering why."

"Drake asked me to help him with some research for the book. I suppose it was his way of thanking me. I was as surprised as anybody."

"Research on what, exactly?"

Maryann's gaze traveled past him. "Is Drake in trouble? Are you investigating him?"

"Let's just say I'm curious."

"You're not the only one, I guess."

"Someone else has been asking?"

She nodded eagerly, pointing behind him. "I loaned my signed copy within the last ten minutes."

Will spun around and followed her finger. Past the center table. Down the long shelf marked A–D. To the little desk pushed into the corner and the woman sitting there, her nose in the very same book.

The axe blade in his head began to throb again. He couldn't say what was worse. That he liked the way she tucked a strand of her auburn hair behind her ear as she read. That she looked put-together—and hell, he could admit it, beautiful—while he bore a strong resemblance to the dead mouse he'd found on his porch that morning. A gift from one stray to another, no doubt. Or that he realized he'd been hoping to see her all along.

CHAPTER TWELVE

Drake Devere could write. He could strangle women, too. But, he had a way with words that Olivia had forgotten. It had been a year since she'd read *Bird of Prey*, and it resonated differently now that she'd been poking around inside his head, wandering the endless maze of dark and winding corridors up there, certain she'd stumble upon the one thing she always wanted from her patients. To understand. To make meaning.

Deep in Chapter Three, her stomach hollowed. She gripped the book's jacket a little tighter. She felt like someone was watching her. Finally, the heat from unseen eyes forced her to look up.

"Deck? Uh—Will… I didn't see you there, Detective."

Detective. She owed him that much after she'd sent him running for the hills. She wondered if all men saw her that way; as a flood, formidable and destructive. Never satisfied. *You're too much*, Erik had told her once. Because she wanted things like fidelity and honest conversations. A husband who'd binge-watch *CSI* with her, who wouldn't refer to her job as mumbo-jumbo.

"Seems like we have the same taste in books." Will's mouth hinted at a smile. He looked like he hadn't slept. He certainly hadn't shaved. And his hair hadn't seen a comb. Some girls liked it that way though. Mussed.

Will held up the book he had tucked to his chest, and Olivia cursed herself. She'd been so focused on his damn hair she hadn't noticed the copy of *Bird of Prey* that matched her own. "I suppose we do."

"So, what did you think?" He took the seat opposite her. "I'd give it two stars at most. It's a bit theatrical for my taste. A little overwrought. I mean…" He opened the book to a dog-eared page and read aloud. "'The night sky beckoned to Hawk from the window of his airless cell like the call of a siren luring him to his doom.' Jeez."

"Theatrical and overwrought. That's Drake in a nutshell."

Will set the open book on the desk. The pages fluttered, landing where the spine had creased, on the page he'd turned to the most. He glanced over his right shoulder, then his left, before he settled his gaze back on her. "Are you sure you should be telling me that? I don't want you to violate any rules. Since we're both such *strict* rule followers."

Olivia sighed, smiled. He'd given her an out. "Fair enough. I deserved that. But in my defense, Warden Blevins gave the all-clear. I'm to cooperate fully."

"Oh. Lucky me."

"By the way, I want to apologize for my comment yesterday. It was uncalled for."

She saw it in his eyes. The past lingered there, unresolved and heavy. "I'll let it slide. Since I did threaten to arrest you."

"Should we call it even then?" She laid down her own book and extended her hand. He took it into his and held it there for a moment, as warm and strong as she'd expected. His knife scar, smooth beneath her thumb.

"Even-steven." He glanced at the notes she'd been writing, and she quickly moved the paper out of his line of sight. "Oh, so it's like that."

"Well, you haven't told me why you're so interested in Drake. Or why you're back here again. Or why your book is signed by the author."

"What? How do you—?"

She pointed at his copy. At the title page and the writing she saw there. He leaned back in the chair and ran an exasperated hand through his hair, mussing it again. Some girls liked it that way, and Olivia decided right then she was one of them.

CHAPTER THIRTEEN

Will drove toward the station in a haze of exhaustion. He'd used up the last dregs of his energy on witty banter with Olivia, and thank God he had. Because she'd agreed to give up the goods on Drake. They'd made plans to meet that night at the Hickory Pit. Will's choice. He needed to see Dr. Smarty Pants tackle a plate of spareribs before he could fully trust her. If she ordered a salad, forget about it.

Otherwise, the visit to Crescent Bay had been a bust. Warden Blevins had let him scroll through the security footage from the night of Bonnie's murder. Useless, since it had cut out around midnight when the rain hit. He'd also offered up Drake's Central file, where Will had found and photocopied rules violations for disrespect, theft, manipulation of staff, and overfamiliarity. In other words, typical Vulture. Maryann had printed Drake's library check-out log, a list of thrillers, dime store romances, and the classics, the last few in audiobook format. According to Maryann, only inmates with certain conditions were allowed audiobooks, but Drake had shown her a doctor's chrono for dry eyes. Will could think of a few diagnoses for him, starting with a fatal case of *full of shit*.

With only a couple miles to go before the turnoff for downtown, Will slammed on the brakes. Petey. He'd totally flaked on his promise to call the bail bondsman first thing this morning. He pulled off the road into the grove of redwood trees and searched his contacts for Dan the Bailout Man. He pressed call and waited.

No signal. Just the sort of thing that happened in middle-of-nowhere Fog Harbor. Times like this, he missed the big city, even if SFPD had practically exiled him, branded him a leper. Hell, they'd done better than that. They'd graffitied it on his front door in red spray paint—*Get out, snitch*—though he couldn't prove it.

Will cracked the door and hopped out, instantly awakened by the December air. It stung like a shock of cold water to his face. He walked a bit down the highway, holding his phone to the sky as he went.

"This is ridiculous." He traipsed back the other way, down the dirt road that led God knows where.

One bar. That's all he needed. Just one bar.

"Yes!" He'd been walking for a while, repeatedly pressing the call button, when the phone began to ring.

"This is Dan the Bailout Man. How can I help you?"

Will stopped moving. He didn't speak the words he'd planned to say.

In the clearing, the woman's body sat propped up against the massive trunk of a redwood, her head drooped to the side, eyes closed, as if she'd decided to take a nap. He didn't go any closer. He didn't need to.

"I'll have to call you back." His voice sounded strange out here, with only the trees to hear him. The trees and the dead woman with the denim blue garrote around her neck.

"What the hell, City Boy?" Red-faced and out of breath, JB puffed up the dirt road toward Will, making his way through a sea of blue uniforms. "Are you part bloodhound? Who stumbles on a body out here?"

"I couldn't get a cell signal."

Will led JB into the clearing, where Chet had already begun to do his work, and waited for the lightning to strike his partner.

The same strike that had riveted him to the spot. These kinds of cases didn't come along often. Once or twice in a career, maybe more, if you got really unlucky. Which he had, apparently.

"Are you shittin' me?" JB stared ahead, mouth hanging open like an old bulldog, circuits sufficiently fried. "Is that what I think it is?"

Will nodded.

"Doc, tell me he's wrong. Please. For the love of God."

Chet examined the garrote with a gloved finger. "We'll have to take a closer look in the—"

"Goddamnit, man. Just tell me. Is it the same?"

"It appears highly similar. Same fabric, same yellow stamp," Chet continued over JB's groaning. "Manner of death, strangulation, just like Bonnie. Probably posed here post-mortem. The tights are pulled down; the shirt is torn. Possibility of sexual assault. Judging by the minimal insect activity and the beginnings of rigor mortis, I'd say she's only been dead a few hours though."

"Got an ID yet?" Will asked.

"There's a couple patrol officers, Bauer and Milner, said they recognize her. I guess she runs the same route every morning. They headed back up to the road. I told them you'd want to talk."

Will pointed at the yellow evidence markers near the dirt road and on both sides of the body. "Look, partner. We got tire tracks and footprints."

JB grunted, before stomping away and parking himself on a nearby stump. He lit up a cigarette. "You know, I had a plan. Put in two more good years and retire to a condo in Florida with a fat pension. Maybe find myself a little lady. Get married again. Who knows? Then you show up, and women start droppin' like flies. And now, we've got ourselves the *s* word."

"'The *s* word'? Seriously?"

"You don't say it out loud, City Boy. It's bad juju. Like seeing your doppelgänger, or opening your umbrella inside the house, or gettin' busy with your socks on."

Will winced. That mental image would be tough to erase. It still boggled his mind that four reasonably sane women had chosen Jimmy Benson, of all the men in the world, to spend forever with. Even if forever had turned out to be seven years max. Meanwhile, Will had an engagement ring packed in a box somewhere. He didn't have the heart to pawn it. The finger it had been meant for claimed by someone else. "You had me till the last one."

JB shrugged. "You'll learn."

As they walked back to the road, Will bristled. An SFTV van had already arrived. The reporter lingered outside, tugging at the bottom of her short skirt suit, and pacing to keep warm. When she spotted them, she tottered up the ditch in their direction, her cameraman in tow. They waved her off, but she kept coming, determined to get a comment or sprain an ankle.

"What can you tell us, Detectives? Does Fog Harbor have a serial killer?"

JB unleashed a string of curse words under his breath. "I'll be in the car."

"Are you Decker?"

Will nodded at the officer leaning on the hood of a patrol car. He'd seen the guy a few times at the Hickory Pit drunk as a fish, but they'd never spoken. He couldn't take a man with a toothbrush mustache seriously. Especially a man who couldn't hold his liquor and wore those ridiculous mirrored sunglasses.

Will pointed to the nameplate on the officer's uniform. "Bauer, right?"

"That's right. Graham Bauer. Doc Clancy said you need an ID on the victim." A gust of wind swirled through the grass. Not a single blond hair on Bauer's head moved.

"Did you know her?"

"Not personally, no. Her name's Laura Ricci. She worked over at Crescent Bay as a kitchen supervisor. Before that, she owned a restaurant in town that burned down a couple years back. She lived just down that road. There's a few old cabins back there."

Will jotted the details in his notebook, already feeling uneasy. Unsettled. Like he had an itch he couldn't scratch. "She worked at the prison, huh?"

"Yeah, my girl works there. That's how I know." Bauer's chest puffed. Will figured him for the kind of guy who spent a couple hours in the gym, only working the muscles he could flex in the mirror.

"He means, *ex*-girlfriend." The ribbing came from the officer approaching alongside Will. If she hadn't been in uniform, he would've figured her for Bauer's kid sister. Her nameplate read Milner. Her exasperated face, *I need a new partner.* "Does Olivia know you're still laying claim to her like a caveman?"

Bauer directed a middle finger at his partner. "She's just been busy."

"Yeah. Busy ghosting you. I don't recall her ever saying you two were official."

"Not everything needs to be said out loud, Milner. Ever heard of body language?"

She shook her head at her partner, exasperated. Her whipping blonde ponytail and vicious scowl all the body language Will needed. He wondered who she'd crossed to wind up riding shotgun to that guy.

Bauer glared after her. "Must be that time of the month, huh?"

Will didn't answer. The name Olivia ringing in his ears.

"Alright. Thanks for the info."

Bauer didn't even acknowledge his departure. Which was fine by him. No way Dr. Smarty Pants would let that meathead within ten feet of her. And if she had, well, Will would have to face facts. There's not a shred of justice left in this world.

*

Will warmed his hands in front of the heater as JB scarfed down a blueberry muffin.

Through the windshield, Will watched Bauer, Milner, and the other officers extend the crime scene tape, wrapping it around the trunks of the bordering redwoods to form a perimeter.

JB took a swig of coffee and wiped the crumbs from his face with the sleeve of his jacket. "Okay. Much better. Now, we've gotta talk."

"Let's not overreact," Will said. "We don't know exactly what's going on yet, and—"

"Not about this."

"About what then?"

"Forensics called this morning. They found something in Bonnie's car. I guessed they'd missed it in the initial sweep. Morons." JB took his phone from his pocket and pulled up an image.

The note had been scrawled in marker on a small strip of paper, one corner ripped. Will enlarged it with his finger to make out the small print. *James better do the right thing or somebody dies. We're watching.*

"Where did they find it?"

"Between the seat and the console, half-hidden under the metal slide bar. No prints."

"Not even Bonnie's?"

"Nope. I reckon it must've dropped there before she spotted it."

Will cracked the door, letting the cold in all over again. "Send me the picture of that note, will ya?"

"And where do you think you're going?" JB asked.

"To my truck. I have to talk to James."

JB raised his eyebrows. "I see. What am I supposed to do? Sit here and twiddle my thumbs?"

"Do you trust me?" Will wanted a take-back. He'd walked himself right into a JB insult.

"About as far as I can throw you. I shot-putted in college but I reckon you're about a hundred seventy pounds heavier and I'm about thirty-five years older than I was then. Well, you do the math."

Will released an exasperated breath.

"But I know you're a good cop, so…" He gestured to the open door.

"That means a lot, JB. I promise I'll fill you in back at the station. In the meantime, go see Judge Purcell about a search warrant. We'll want to take a look inside the victim's house."

"Yeah, yeah, yeah."

Will slid out and started walking. He'd only gone a few steps before JB called him back to his open window. "If you repeat that, City Boy, I'll deny it."

"I'd expect nothing less. Hey, did you really shot-put in college?"

"Junior college record holder. Look it up."

Will wondered if he'd been born with it. That niggling feeling at the back of his brain that always seemed to be one step ahead of the rest of him. *Cop clairvoyance*, his dad used to call it. *Just like your old man.* When Will ignored it, bad things happened. Catastrophic things. Like that night with Ben. He'd never make a mistake like that again. Not if he could help it.

Right now, he wanted to fire up his truck, barrel out of the ditch, and find James McMillan. Shake him down. But first he had to scratch the itch. He opened the folder he'd taken with him from Crescent Bay and turned to the most recent of Drake's rules violations. It hit him like a rock to the face as he read. He couldn't believe he'd only just realized.

Yep, Dad. Cop clairvoyance.

RULES VIOLATION REPORT

INMATE NUMBER: 78VRT1   INMATE'S NAME: DRAKE DEVERE
FACILITY: CBSP   VIOLATION DATE: 10/3/19
VIOLATION LOCATION: MAIN KITCHEN

SPECIFIC ACT: THEFT

CIRCUMSTANCES OF VIOLATION:
On October 3, 2019, main kitchen supervisor, Laura Ricci, reported several items went missing from the galley between the hours of 7 and 11 a.m. According to Ms. Ricci, only four inmates had access to the galley at that time. A confidential source identified Drake Devere as the inmate responsible for the theft. However, a search of his cell yielded negative results. Items missing included two bags of flour, one bag of sugar, a mixing bowl, five spoons, and five rolling pins.

INMATE STATEMENT:
"I didn't steal anything. Ms. Ricci's just trying to get me in trouble like always. Go ahead and search. You ain't going to find nothing." Devere reported seeing the items in question in the galley at the time he left work in the afternoon.

FINDINGS: NOT GUILTY, INSUFFICIENT EVIDENCE

CHAPTER FOURTEEN

Olivia closed *Bird of Prey* and jotted a phrase into her notebook. *Anger at women.* Though anger didn't quite cut it. Drake's antihero, Hawk, had raped and decapitated four women all while awaiting his end on death row and plotting his escape. He'd gotten away with it so far. *To be continued*, Drake had added at the end of the last chapter.

Olivia shook her head. Scratched through the first word in her notes and wrote *Rage* instead. The rage didn't come as a revelation, though. It didn't take a shrink to feel the heat of Drake's fury or to understand its origins. But the intensity of his own blatant acknowledgment of it took her by surprise. She'd been wrong to dismiss the book as a narcissist's ploy for attention. It made a statement. It proclaimed things Drake wouldn't say aloud.

"It ends on a real cliffhanger, doesn't it?" Maryann meandered through the stacks toward Olivia. "Drake has a way of making you feel like you're right there in the story. Like you're rooting for Hawk, even though he's the devil incarnate."

Olivia nodded, gathering her things. She passed the book to Maryann, anxious to be rid of it. Her own copy buried in a drawer at home, not deep enough. "Did it scare you? When you first read it?"

"A little. But I like those kinds of stories. I own all fourteen seasons of *Forensic Files* on DVD."

"Wow."

"Yeah, Melody says I oughta have been a cop or a CO like her. I don't do well under pressure though. Like today with your detective friend. I think I screwed up. I've been playing it over and over in my mind."

Olivia understood that. She'd been replaying her own conversation with Mr. Wise Guy. Mostly the part where she'd agreed to meet him at the Hickory Pit. Graham and his cop buddies went there to unwind almost every night. "Why? What did you say?"

"It's sort of what I didn't say. He was asking a lot of questions about Drake's writing and the research I helped him with. I started telling him about the medical books I'd loaned Drake so he could understand things like rigor mortis and…" Maryann's eyes teared, and she covered them with her hands.

"I'm sure it's fine, Maryann. C'mon, sit down."

They walked together, back to the small desk, away from the inmates who had returned in Will's absence. Olivia fished a tissue from her pocket. "Unused, I promise."

Maryann started to laugh but it only made her cry harder. Finally, she lifted her head to Olivia, her cheeks splotched. Her eyes raw beneath her glasses. "I didn't think it was a big deal at the time. Now, I feel so stupid. Promise me you won't tell him."

"Detective Decker?"

Maryann nodded, sniffled. "He'd probably arrest me if he knew. Or he'd tell the warden, and then I'd be toast."

"Knew what?"

"That I helped Drake with more than just medical research. He said he was having trouble imagining the sort of implement Hawk would need to cut the heads off his victims. So, I helped him research weapons. *Homemade* weapons."

Olivia hurried from the library in a fog of unease, wondering how Maryann could be so naive. She'd worked as the prison librarian for at least twenty years. Olivia had been at the ceremony where Warden Blevins had given her the service pin she wore every day affixed to the lapel of another awful floral print. But Maryann and her sister had it rough as kids. Olivia had heard the rumors about their mother and her need to open her legs to any man within a thirty-mile radius of Fog Harbor, including their convicted sex offender stepdad, Ken. So, maybe gullibility ran in the family.

What kind of weapons? she'd asked Maryann.

Oh, all kinds. Slingshots, bows and arrows, bullwhips. He wasn't much interested in those, though. He wanted a weapon for the neck.

A weapon for the neck. Of course. Olivia could still see Bonnie, lifeless in the drainpipe. The ligature pulled so tight against her flesh, it would've broken the blood vessels beneath it, compressed the trachea. Squeezed the life from the jugular veins. A hell of a way to go. She'd assisted the Feds with a ligature cold case in San Francisco. That guy had been a lot like Drake. Disturbed, callous. So filled with rage, his hands became his weapons. His instruments of revenge.

Olivia shook her head at her own ridiculousness. Nobody walked out of Crescent Bay unless they'd earned it. The hard way—by serving the length of their sentence or receiving a coveted grant of parole. Or the harder way—by living out the rest of their days in a cell and leaving in a body bag. The infamous back door parole; Blevins had used it to threaten Riggs. The kind that awaited Drake. Probably her father too, though it ached to think of it.

"Psst."

Olivia stopped walking and listened, certain she'd imagined the sound. When it came again from over her shoulder, she turned to see Morrie Mulvaney shuffling along the wall in his wheelchair.

"Need a push?" she asked, trying to conjure him as a young man, some fifty years ago. Long before she'd known him, Morrie had ridden a Harley he called Bess and had blond hair down to the center of his back. Or at least that's what he'd told her and Em when they'd visited their father as girls. He'd also stabbed a man in a bar fight. Four wounds to the upper torso, three of them fatal. That part she'd read for herself in his C-file.

"What was that all about?" he asked Olivia, as she wheeled him up the runway toward the dining hall. "You talking to the 5-0?"

"The walls have eyes, apparently. I thought you'd left."

"Eyes *and* ears. Remember that. You know what your daddy would say."

Olivia made a face, glad he couldn't see it. Her father hadn't been around to say much of anything.

"He'd say no good comes from talking with the cops."

"Well, to a criminal, I suppose that makes sense. But that detective is trying to solve a murder." She wondered what her father would say if he knew about Graham. That she'd not only talked with a cop but slept with one. Regrettably. "Besides, Dad lost the right to give me advice a long time ago."

Morrie shook his head. "Have you written to him lately? Been down to see him? Your mama's passing was a big wakeup call. He's making changes. Big changes. And he's bound to be worried about you with that McMillan lady turned up dead."

The line for the dining hall snaked down the corridor toward them. Olivia slowed the wheelchair to a stop, ready to make her getaway. She couldn't tell Morrie the truth. That it had been a decade since she'd seen her father. That she planned to never see him again. That the day she'd gone hiding in the chapel confessional he'd left a message on her work phone. How he'd gotten her number, she didn't know. *We need to talk about that night, honey. About what you saw.*

As Olivia passed beside the wheelchair, Morrie seized her arm, pinning her into place beside him. She didn't pull away or cry out. Instead, she gave in, seeing the glint in his eyes. The way they darted sharp and fast as a knife strike. *Young Morrie.*

"You're a smart gal, Olivia. More Reilly than Rockwell. Just remember, us criminals ain't the only criminals in this joint. Watch your back."

She jerked her arm from him and kept moving. Her stride measured and exact. Her heart pounding like a wild stallion trying to outrun the wind.

*

Olivia flung open the door to hell. That's how it felt in the MHU. Hotter than Hades. Or maybe the heat came from inside her. From the ball of fire that rose in her throat, scorching it dry as a bone. She filled a cup at the water cooler and tossed it back like a shot of vodka.

"Can you believe it, Doc? That bastard 602'd me." Hank stared at the complaint form on his desk, barely looking up at her. Just as well, because he might've noticed the beads of sweat gathering at her hairline. He might've told her she didn't look well. Might've stood up and walked over, wrapping an octopus arm around her. She couldn't handle a handsy Hank right now. Even this version of Hank would take some effort.

"Drake, you mean? For what?"

"He said my unlock policy is, and I quote, 'not only unfair but potentially harmful to the stability of the patients in the MHU.' What a crock."

Leah emerged from the bathroom, pulling her wool sweater tight to her body. It barely stretched across her belly. Even Hank had covered his bald head with an army green CDCR beanie.

"Are you cold?" Olivia asked, following Leah back to her office.

"Freezing." Leah pushed up one arm of the sweater to show her goosebumps. "Girl, you look like you've seen a ghost."

Olivia shut the door behind her and leaned against it. Sure enough, the handle felt ice-cold against her back. "I read Drake's book again."

"That explains it," Leah said, taking a seat at her desk. "I wondered where you ran off to."

"And that detective came by too. Not to see me, but we ran into each other anyway."

"Oh, did you?"

"He asked me if I'd meet him tonight to talk about the case."

"The case. *Mm-hmm.*"

Olivia heard her own high, breathy voice, as if from a distance. "Seriously, Leah. I'm freaking out here. Do you think my patient is a murderer? I mean, I know he's a murderer. But, do you think he killed Bonnie? Is that even possible?"

"Whoa. Slow down, hon." But that was the problem. Olivia couldn't slow down. Her heart hadn't stopped its gallop. Now, her thoughts raced too. From Drake to Maryann to Deck to Morrie. To her father and that phone call. It all came to a hard stop right there. "You know the Vulture best. What do you think?"

"Why does everyone keep saying that?"

Leah answered with a sad smile.

"Okay, okay. Fine. I know him best." When she spoke, Olivia pictured her father's face, not Drake's. "I can't believe I'm about to say this, but I agree with him. Someone's trying to make him look guilty. He's being set up."

Olivia collapsed into the nearest chair, reeling from her own revelation. "Now, can we please change the subject?"

Leah blinked a few times before she rubbed her belly. "So, what do you think of Liam for a boy?"

Grateful, Olivia smiled. "Sounds like a heartbreaker already. Or a celebrity."

"That's what Jake said too. He told me we'd be destining him to a life of paparazzi and dating iconic child stars. That or playing a renegade vigilante in every action movie known to man."

"Could be worse. How 'bout member of a boy band?"

Olivia laughed at her own joke, but the moment she returned to her own desk, she spun up her computer again. Morrie's words, her father's too, whirled like a tornado in her brain as she typed Martin Reilly's inmate number into the database and searched his file, opening the tab marked PAROLE HEARING.

She could get in trouble for looking. But she had to know.

NOTICE OF PAROLE HEARING

INMATE NUMBER: 22CMY2   INMATE'S NAME: MARTIN REILLY

FACILITY: VVSP   COMMITMENT OFFENSE: PC 187, MURDER,

FIRST DEGREE   SENTENCE: 30 YEARS TO LIFE

INITIAL HEARING DATE: MARCH 5, 2020

Inmate Reilly has been scheduled for an INITIAL parole hearing on March 5, 2020. He remains housed in the Sensitive Needs Yard (SNY) at Valley View State Prison. Inmate Reilly has been employed in Prison Industries as Leadman on the construction crew since 2012. Per his most recent Work Supervisor's Report, his performance was rated exceptional. Group and self-help activities within the last five years included Alcoholics Anonymous, Narcotics Anonymous, Victims' Awareness, and Gang Rehabilitation Group. Per the Institutional Gang Investigation unit (IGI), Inmate Reilly completed a formal debriefing process in June 2018 and should be considered an inactive member of the Oaktown Boys. Following his debriefing, Inmate Reilly was classified as SNY due to concerns for his safety.

Inmate Reilly has incurred several rules violations during his incarceration, including Mutual Combat (1989, 1990, 1991, 1995, 1997, 2000); Possession of an Inmate Manufactured Weapon (1990, 1991, 2003); Promoting Gang Activity (1995); Possession of Inmate Manufactured Alcohol (1998, 2005); Use of a Controlled Substance (2006); and Possession of a Cellular Telephone (2008, 2010, 2016). He has remained disciplinary-free for the last three years.

Should he be found suitable for parole, Inmate Reilly reported his plan to reside in transitional housing at New Hope in San Francisco, California. He is awaiting letters of support from counselors at New Hope and his daughter, Emily Rockwell, with whom he has been in recent contact.

Inmate Reilly is scheduled for a pre-hearing psychological evaluation on January 2, 2020.

REPORT PREPARED BY: Correctional Counselor, Edwin Lacy, Jr.
cc: Belinda Jett, Attorney-at-Law

CHAPTER FIFTEEN

Will knocked for a third time, rapping his knuckles against the heavy oak door and shaking the holiday wreath hung at the center. *The nicest set of doors in Fog Harbor*, JB had muttered the first time they'd visited. *Cost more than my first car.*

Will leaned in and listened for footsteps, voices, any signs of life. But the house kept its secrets well hidden. The only sounds came from the winter wrens in the bordering forest and the occasional hum of a passing car. Will couldn't see a thing through the beveled glass inlays and the windows offered no help either, their curtains pulled tight.

James' SUV sat in the driveway, the hood cold to Will's touch and still wet from the early morning rain. Next to it, a set of fresh tire tracks that left him unsettled. Someone else had been here.

Will pressed his face against the car's tinted windows, leaving his breath on the glass. The empty seats came as a relief until he spotted the two boosters in the back. A stuffed whale carelessly tossed between them, probably days ago when life still made sense for the McMillan family. He thought of the two boys and the trip they'd taken with their father. How unfair life could be with its twists and turns and loop-the-loops. Its sudden, hard stop.

All this time, Will had been waiting for a sound. But when it came, he wished it hadn't. A groan like that meant he'd arrived too late. Something bad had already happened.

He slid his Glock from its holster as he moved toward the rear of the house, staying close to the manicured hedges. At the corner, he posted up and risked a quick glance, cataloguing the McMillans' backyard in a single mental snapshot. Leaves rustled across the pool cover and onto the stone deck, where the boys' toy trucks had been left haphazard. A swing set swayed in the wind as if pushed by an unseen hand. The orange flame from a firepit stretched itself toward the sky. And in the grass nearby, a fire poker.

Will turned the corner, keeping his gun ready, and approached the poker. It lay still and heavy as the wind blew around it, but to Will it pulsed with life.

Will followed the trail of blood from the poker to the deck. Fat drops that led him like breadcrumbs to the sliding glass door. It had been left open, and a few wet leaves had blown across the threshold and into the living room, where the carpet had been spotted bright red.

From somewhere inside the house, a door shut. A soft sound, but final somehow. Like the closing of a coffin.

The acrid smell of fear and booze bit at Will's nose, its source the five empty beer bottles stacked on an end table. In the far corner, a Christmas tree, its lights dark. The presents beneath it a cruel reminder of what would never be. As he crept past the leather sofa, the television screen eyed him blankly. It knew what he didn't. Whose blood? And where had they gone?

Will continued into the foyer, pausing at the hallway closet. He flung it open so fast, a stack of towels tumbled to the floor, and he gritted his teeth to keep from crying out. He kicked the towels and took another look inside to find winter coats hung on the rack, swinging slightly. A perfect hiding place. Sucking in a breath, he pushed them back, sweeping his gun across the closet bottom. Nothing but muddy shoes and boxes and one of those fancy vacuums that cost Will's monthly rent. He'd all but moved on, when he realized.

The biggest box sat at the right corner of the closet, its flaps slightly opened. Will nudged it the rest of the way, peering inside.

Just as he'd thought. The box contained at least fifty smaller boxes. Packaged cell phones. Will held one in his hand to test its weight. Still full.

A whisper of a noise, delicate as the swish of a knife through the air, brought him back to the foyer and beyond. To Bonnie's closed office door, where the trail ended, the doorknob slick with blood.

As Will struggled to swallow, he recognized his fear. It had been a while since he'd felt afraid. Since he'd moved to Fog Harbor, his nerves had grown fat and happy without the need to look over his shoulder anymore. But now they buzzed beneath his skin like lean live wires.

Taking a position alongside, Will tapped on the bottom of the door with his boot. "Fog Harbor Police. Show yourself."

In the stillness that followed, he readied himself. For what he might find. For what might be done to him. What he might have to do. *Fear is your partner*, his dad had told him, his first day on patrol. *Let it have your back.* But his dad hadn't said fear could be an enemy, too. Could make you do things blindly, stupidly. Things you'd regret forever.

Will twisted the knob and kicked the door open, scanning the room for threats: Bookshelf, posters, chairs, desk.

Desk. In the slim space beneath the mahogany beast, a pair of hands trembled, sticky with blood.

"Come out now." Will's voice matched the beating of his heart, fierce and steady as a pounding hammer.

"Don't shoot," James whimpered, as he crawled from under the desk and curled onto the floor, moaning. "I thought you were him."

One side of his face had already begun to swell. Blood wept from a split in the skin above his eye. More blood fell from his fat lip.

"Who?" Will asked, crouching alongside him. He kept his eyes up, his gun too. "Is there someone else here?"

James groaned again, only answering one of Will's questions. "I think he's gone."

"And the boys?"

"With their grandma. Thank God." He touched his fingers to his wounds. They came back freshly red and shaking. "How bad is it?"

"I've seen worse. What happened?"

"I'm in trouble, Detective. Big trouble."

"Is this about the money you stole from Drake?"

James began to sob. Will took that as a *no*.

When it came to a skinned knee or a black eye or a fire poker to the head, a frozen bag of peas had always been the best medicine. Will's brother, Ben, had taught him that. He fished one out of the McMillans' freezer, while James rearranged his broken pieces at the kitchen table. He'd stopped crying at least.

"Want to tell me what the hell happened here?" Will asked, wrapping said miracle peas in a dish towel.

James took the ice pack and pressed it to his head. "Do I have to?"

"Judging by the looks of you, I'm the best friend you've got right now. But I can't help you if I don't know what you've gotten yourself into."

"Debt." One syllable that sounded a lot like *death*. "Gambling debt."

Will pulled out a chair and sat across from James. Interrogation time. "I'm sorry to hear that." He'd made a split-second decision to play Good Cop. For now. "With everything else you're going through, that must be hard. Have you always been a gambler?"

James' laugh scraped from his throat, sharp-edged. "Ironically, no. Not until we moved back here. They'd built the Lucky Elk by then. It's an Indian casino a couple miles north of here."

Will knew it well. It was anything but lucky. He and JB had worked at least five robberies there in the last two months. Not counting the money given up willingly by sorry suckers in search of their next heater. "I've been there a few times. Lost a couple hundred myself."

"Well, that puts you about twenty thousand ahead of me."

Will held his *you've got to be kidding me* cards close to the vest. He figured that sum amounted to half of James' yearly salary. No wonder the guy had a cache of phones in his closet. "Is that why you stole Drake's book money?"

James lowered the ice pack, his left eye swollen shut. He'd have a hell of a lot of explaining to do when his mother-in-law showed up. "I didn't think he'd figure it out, and he was giving it to charity anyway."

Will nodded. "And the phones?"

"What phones?"

"C'mon, James. I opened the closet. I saw your stash. Those will get you a pretty penny behind bars. And don't tell me they're Christmas gifts for your nieces."

"Don't have any nieces." James leaned back in his chair and plopped the bag back on his forehead, covering both eyes now. Sweet green peas and a busted lip. That's all Will could see. "I'm not gonna lie to you. I thought about selling them. A smartphone goes for a thousand bucks in the joint. Desperate times, you know? But I couldn't go through with it. Not with Bonnie working there too. It was too risky."

Will didn't believe a word. He'd once arrested a bankrupt professional poker player for taking a bat to his parents' heads in their Pacific Heights mansion. That guy had looked him right in the face and claimed he'd been asleep upstairs the whole time. The things a man would do for money. Smuggling cell phones was the least of it.

"So, this beat-down is about what you owe the casino then?"

"Not exactly. I thought I could make my money back with a football bet. It was supposed to be a sure thing. But then, Belichick benched Brady in the fourth, so they didn't cover the spread. Next thing you know, I'm down another twenty grand. And I've got a bookie named Lyle Adams on my ass."

"And bookies need to get paid."

"Yeah, in blood or money, I guess. I gave him all I have. And he beat the shit out of me anyway." James grimaced, lifting his shirt and revealing a patchwork of bruises across his abdomen. "He wants the life insurance money. I tried to tell him I don't even have it yet."

"Jesus. Are you sure you don't want to go to the hospital?"

"Can't. He told me not to breathe a word or I might end up like Bonnie. I'm all the boys have left."

Even Bad Cop couldn't argue with that. Will knew the ache of growing up with just one parent. The gut punch of Mother's Day. The ghost that clung to his father like stale cigar smoke. "Why'd you tell *me* then?"

"For my wife. It's for her. I just feel so…" James' good eye welled again. "Guilty."

"So this guy, Lyle, you think he killed your wife? Because just yesterday you were pointing the finger at Drake Devere. And then we found this."

Will slid his phone across the table, the note magnified on the screen. James lowered the bag and held it up close, studying it.

"What is it?"

"You tell me. We found it in your wife's car."

"I've never seen it before. Bonnie didn't mention it."

"We don't think she saw it. Her prints weren't on the note."

James tossed the bag of peas in the sink and sighed. "All I know is Bonnie did nothing wrong. That note just proves it. Whatever happened to her, I'm to blame. One way or the other."

Probably right, Will thought to himself. "Don't be too hard on yourself, man. We'll find out who did it, and we'll make him pay."

*

Will sat in James' driveway. He cranked the radio as loud as he could stand it and shut his eyes. Otherwise, he'd fall dead asleep. A hard reset. That's what he needed. Eight hours of dreamless slumber. But a few long blinks would have to do for now.

Before he headed back to the station, he dialed Petey's cell. Every ring jabbed at him like a crooked finger, accusing. He had one brother left—hell, one family member—who still claimed him, and he'd blown it. When he'd finally reached Dan the Bailout Man on the drive over to James' house, the secretary had informed him the money had already been posted. Petey was a free man.

"Thanks for nothin', big brother."

"I'm sorry, Petey. I got caught up in that murder case. You know how it is."

"Yeah. Story of our lives, right? Dad was always caught up in a case. Then, Ben. Now you. Don't worry. I took care of it."

"Who posted it?" Will felt like a kid again, that same hollow pit in his stomach every time he'd covered for Petey. Every time Petey had gotten caught, anyway. Every time he'd watched his dad take a belt to Petey's bare butt. Those lashes had stung Will like they were meant for him instead. "Please don't say it was that scumbag Bertolucci."

"Vinnie's not a scumbag. He's a personal banker."

"You mean loan shark. So yeah, scumbag."

"Well, he's there when I need him. Which is more than I can say for—"

"Hey, Petey. I gotta call you back."

Will raced from the truck to catch the slip of paper that had blown in a gust of wind from beneath the windshield wiper of James' SUV. He finally tracked it down, pinning it under his boot.

He slipped a pair of latex gloves from his back pocket, grateful for another of his father's lessons. Always be prepared to encounter evidence. After he'd gloved up, he bent down and retrieved the note.

Now you know what happens when you do the wrong thing.

Neatly drawn in the bottom right corner a symbol he recognized. Only the Oaktown Boys could make a tree look as if it had been drawn by the devil himself.

Will waited for JB inside the forensics lab, the box marked with Bonnie's name placed on the table before him.

"This better be good, City Boy. Traffic was a bitch."

"Traffic?" Will shook his head. He lifted the lid and removed the plastic bag marked VEHICLE. "The station is a block from here."

JB stretched a pair of latex gloves over his stubby fingers. "That's about a block further than these legs want to go. Besides, the place is crawling with reporters. Worse than ants at a picnic. I had to park in Chief Flack's spot."

"Good luck with that. Isn't she giving a press conference at four?" Will opened the bag and began to arrange the contents in front of them. "To discuss the *s* word."

JB checked his watch. Shrugged, smirked. "She'll probably walk."

"So how'd it go with the judge? Did you get that warrant?"

"Does a donkey have a shadow?"

"Uh…"

"Of course I got it. Me and Judge Purcell go way back. She's got a little thing for me."

Will had heard that story. Apparently, JB had the hots for the judge way back when. Somewhere in between wives two and three. But the romance fizzled the moment he opened his mouth. Will's theory, anyway.

He examined the items one by one, as JB looked on. The refuse of Bonnie's life. A baseball cap. A thermos. Two matchbox cars. Five half-crumpled gas receipts. A McDonald's to-go order. Her *Vertigo* movie ticket. Three crayons. And various drawings, done by a child's hand and paperclipped in the center, probably by the lab.

"Want to tell me what you're lookin' for?"

Will slid the clip aside and flipped through the drawings, his anticipation building even as his hope dwindled. Maybe he'd been wrong. But, what if? What if.

Between a stick family portrait and a ripped page from a coloring book, Will found it. He laid the small scrap before JB, smug.

JB squinted at it, his face a blank. "A Christmas tree? A marijuana leaf? Is this like that ink blot test?"

Will bit his tongue and pulled up the image of the note they'd found in Bonnie's car. The ripped edges lined up perfectly. "Oaktown Boys. Ever heard of them?"

"Damn, I'm good. I told you the husband had guilt written all over him." JB gave a self-satisfied smile while Will drove them the block back to the station. Though their pace amounted to more of a crawl. His partner had been correct on one thing; every reporter within a three-hundred-mile radius had shown up here with a news van and an attitude. Brake lights in front, blaring horns behind, they'd moved about ten feet in the last five minutes.

"Were you even listening?" Will asked. As promised, he'd told JB the whole story. Every sordid detail. James' embezzlement of Drake's book money. Drake's theft of the rolling pins. The mysterious bookie. The cell phones. "Setting aside his airtight alibi, what makes you think James killed Bonnie?"

"I never said he killed her. I said he looked guilty. Two totally different things. He's covering one lie with another. I know Lyle Adams. The guy's a local deadbeat for sure. Dumb as a box of rocks. Ain't no way Lyle murdered Bonnie McMillan without leaving something behind."

"I agree." Will couldn't believe it when the words left his mouth. But there's a first time for everything. "You want to know how I know?"

"Not particularly."

"Lyle's in jail in Brookings, Oregon. Has been since Thanksgiving. Apparently, he pummeled the Sheriff's son in a bar fight."

"Like I said, box of rocks."

"Alright. So that leaves us with the Oaktown Boys, the Vulture, and our theater mystery man."

JB chuckled. "Don't forget about the Easter Bunny."

CHAPTER SIXTEEN

Olivia chose the lesser of two evils; a booth in the back, as far from the bar as she could manage. Even if that table happened to be adjacent to Hickory Pit's Lovers' Lane, a length of the redwood wall carved floor to ceiling with the initials of high school sweethearts hell-bent on forever.

Olivia found the wormhole in the wood that marked the spot where she and Erik had immortalized their ill-fated love affair. She should've known better. Because that very same day he'd driven her up to Willow Wood, the abandoned psychiatric hospital on the outskirts of town, and told her he wanted to be her first. When your boyfriend asks you to lose your virginity in a rat-infested nuthouse, odds are he might not be your soul mate. Every time she'd returned to the Pit, she'd thought of taking a knife to his carving, replacing it with a big, fat X, but the past had a life of its own. Who was she to snuff it out? Besides, it reminded her of how far she'd come. How much she had to lose.

She ran her hand across it like a touchstone, wishing she'd ordered whiskey with her Coke. Something to appease the butterflies in her stomach that had only multiplied when Emily had shown her Chief Flack's press release. They'd sat dumbfounded in the prison parking lot, replaying the four o'clock press conference on Emily's phone. Laura and Bonnie, both dead by the same hand. A shadowy person of interest outside the theater. Olivia's plan to shake down Em about their dad—*Recent contact? Debriefing?*—dissipated in the horror of it all. It would have to wait.

Eerie, isn't it? Bartender Jane had said, gesturing to the empty restaurant as she retrieved Olivia's drink. Usually, by five o'clock, the place was stacked wall to wall with customers. Tonight, only a few regulars filled the booths, but the bar seemed as crowded as ever with out-of-town reporters and local folks who counted alcohol as the best medicine.

Olivia fidgeted with the loose button on her sweater. Despite her sister's best efforts to convince her otherwise, she hadn't bothered to change out of her work clothes, but *Deck* wouldn't notice. *Deck* wouldn't care. *Deck* had his own problems. Like the two murders he had to solve. She'd started calling him Deck in her head now, but not in front of Emily or Leah. They'd try to twist it into something else. Like a date, or a crush, or a prospect. Something it most definitely wasn't.

Yep, a little splash of Jack would've hit the spot. But she needed a clear head to handle Deck with his mussed hair and his clever comebacks and his serial-killer questions. Chief Flack hadn't said those words, but she saw them shifting between the lines like a shadow at the dark end of an alley.

"Hey, Liv." Olivia stared at her hands on the table, wishing he would disappear. Wishing he hadn't co-opted the nickname reserved for Em and her mother. Just Em now. "Why are you hidin' out back here, beautiful?"

She focused on the curve of Graham's biceps—her favorite part of him—on display beneath his obnoxious one-size-too-small T-shirt. If only she liked the rest of him as much.

"Hi, Graham."

The front door opened, and half of FHPD's day watch filed in, joining Graham's rookie partner, Jessica Milner, at the bar. Jessie caught her looking and gave her a knowing smile that said she'd read her mind. Waterboarding would've been preferable to being stuck with Graham in a patrol car all day. "I'm meeting someone."

He sat across from her anyway. "You hear the news?"

"Yeah. It's awful." She chose as few words as possible so as not to encourage him.

"I was there, you know. This morning. Good thing I was, too. They needed an ID on the body." Like a heat-seeking missile, his hand moved toward her own. Panicked, she snatched it back into her lap before he could grab ahold. "You need to be careful, Liv. There's a sicko running around here. Why don't you stay with me tonight?"

"I don't think that's a good idea."

"Well, I can sleep over at your house. As long as Emily doesn't mind."

Olivia shook her head. "Definitely not."

"Definitely not, she doesn't mind. Or definitely not—"

"Definitely not a good idea."

Graham frowned, thumbing his ridiculous mustache. *It makes me look French, am I right? Sophistiqué.* That's what he'd told her the day after he'd shaved the small rectangular patch above his lip. "Am I missing something here? I thought you and me, we had a thing."

Olivia often wondered about timing. The way life came down to split seconds, missed stoplights, forgotten keys. A moment too late or a moment too soon. It didn't seem fair she'd been the one sent home early from school that day with a stomachache. The one to open the door of their dumpy one-bedroom at the Double Rock. The one to see her father standing over a dead woman, a knife in his hand. To see he hadn't been alone.

But as Deck approached the booth, she said a silent prayer of gratitude to the universe. Because sometimes bad timing could ride in like a knight in a light blue button-down to save you when you needed it most.

"Doctor Rockwell…" Deck cleared his throat, announcing himself. "I don't want to interrupt, but—"

"Then don't, buddy." Graham bristled, his fists clenched. He didn't bother to look behind him, keeping his eyes fixed on Olivia.

"My lady and I are having an AB conversation, and you can C your way out."

With a wry smile, Deck raised his brows at Olivia.

"I'm sorry, Graham," she said. "Detective Decker and I—"

"Detective Decker?" Graham hopped up and extended his hand. "Sorry, man. I didn't see you there. We were just talking about you. How you needed my help making that ID this morning. This is my girlfriend, Olivia Rockwell. She's the chief psychologist over at Crescent Bay."

"Lucky man." Deck still hadn't stopped grinning. When Olivia caught a glimpse of her face in the mirror behind the bar, it confirmed what she already knew. Her cheeks flamed redder than the checkered tablecloths.

"The luckiest. Beauty and brains. It's a rare—"

"Graham." She smacked her palm against the table, and several heads at the bar turned. "Can you give us a minute, Detective?"

"Sure. Take all the time you need." He pointed at the register up front. "I'll go ahead and order. Can I get you anything?"

She'd intended to have a salad. With her luck, she'd leave with a sweater stained with pit grease and barbecue sauce, but, if she couldn't drown her butterflies with alcohol, maybe she could ply them with comfort food.

"Number five, please. The spareribs with the coleslaw and cornbread. And a side of mac and cheese."

"Yes, ma'am." Olivia heard him laughing as he walked away.

CHAPTER SEVENTEEN

Will chuckled, watching Olivia wipe at a spot of barbecue sauce on her sweater. They'd cleaned ten spareribs between them, the bones stacked in a neat pile in the center basket. Smarty Pants took her food seriously. Will could respect that.

Olivia looked up at him and back to the stain, no better now than when she'd started dabbing. But she seemed more relaxed here, outside of the prison. More Olivia than Dr. Rockwell. "Those ribs were worth a ruined sweater. I'd forgotten how much I like this place."

"Because it's a cop hangout? Or in spite of?"

Her half-smile told him the answer. By the time Will had returned with their food, Olivia had been alone in the booth, but he'd seen Graham at the bar, slapping backs, chugging beers, and flirting way too loudly with the badge bunnies. His jealous eyes never wandered far from the back booth. Like two planets orbiting the sun. Or an idiot making an ass of himself. Still, even Graham hadn't been stupid enough to bring his weapon into a bar, the way Will and Ben had that night at Aces High.

"So, you and Officer Bauer, huh? When's the wedding?"

"Very funny, Deck. He's not my… you know. Not anymore. He's just a friend."

"It's none of my business. But, you and him? How did that happen?"

"You're right. It's none of your business." Her dimple softened the sting. "But let's just say Fog Harbor isn't exactly teeming with eligible bachelors. He wasn't always so…"

"Awful?"

She shook her head. "At the time, he seemed nice enough."

"For a guy with Hitler's mustache and hair that doesn't move." Will watched Graham settle himself onto a barstool. He spun away from the eager, raven-haired bartender, stopping his turn with a boot to the footrest. He parked himself in that spot, alternately glaring at Will and scrutinizing his cell phone screen.

Will felt sick. He knew that look too. Different from the look women gave him, it rankled no less. A storm cloud glower thick with judgment that meant his past had caught up to him once more. "What exactly did you tell him about me?"

"Nothing. Well, not nothing. Just that we'd planned to meet here to discuss a case, and I'd talk to him later."

"You didn't say anything then? About me?"

"I hardly know you." But she knew the one thing he'd tried to outrun. Sure, JB knew and Lieutenant Wheeler and Chief Flack, but so far he'd managed to avoid the lynch mob of cowboy cops who considered him a traitor and weren't shy about telling him just that.

"You know about my brother, though. Don't deny it."

She took a careful sip of her soda, avoiding his eyes. "I would never tell anyone that. Certainly not Graham. But he's bound to find out. And if Graham knows, the whole force will soon enough."

Will glanced over at the bar where Graham's brooding had reached a crescendo. He tossed back a shot, slammed the glass on the counter, and stormed out in such a hurry he didn't see the chair in his path. He tripped, stutter-stepped, cursed, then flung the offending chair to the side of the table like a rag doll. Will half expected him to punch its cheap wooden face.

"I still don't get it. You and him."

Olivia studied Will with uncertainty, the way that stray cat did sometimes. Like she couldn't decide whether to bolt or hiss. Then, his knee brushed hers beneath the table and she flinched. "You didn't ask me here to discuss my dating life, did you, Detective? Because that would be a short and uninteresting conversation."

The entire meal they'd been Deck and Olivia. Now, he'd been relegated back to Detective. Fine. He could be all business. "You're right, Doctor. We're here to talk about Drake. He knew both victims. He interacted with them regularly at the prison. I think there's a chance he could be involved in these murders."

"By those criteria, you'll need to investigate half of the inmates at Crescent Bay. I hope there's more to your theory than that."

"Well, you tell me. You were the one reading *Bird of Prey* and taking notes. Surely it didn't slip past you that Drake's main character kills women from death row. It doesn't take a psychologist to figure out the guy's still got major issues."

Olivia stiffened. "Drake is a troubled man. At his core, he's fragile, vulnerable. A little boy, abandoned. He protects that part of himself at all costs. By any means necessary. With a mask of rage and manipulation and a grandiose sense of himself. Yes, he knew both victims, and he wrote a twisted book about murdering women. But Crescent Bay is a fortress even for someone as cunning as him. I'd say the possibility of an inmate getting out of his cell and past the guards and the fences and the security cameras is about as likely as Drake winning the Pulitzer."

She wanted to put him in his place. To win the point with her bleeding heart and her doctorate degree. To convince him of something she didn't believe herself, not entirely.

"Back at the library, you asked why I had a signed copy of that book. You might know Drake better than anyone, but you don't know everything. I bet he never told you about the short story he sent to the cops, bragging about those girls he murdered in San Francisco. Or the detective who worked the case for two years before he finally found a way to put that asshole in cuffs. Or the taunting letters he sends that same detective every February third."

With Olivia sufficiently silenced, Will delivered his own shot across the bow. "That detective is me. In case you were wondering."

CHAPTER EIGHTEEN

"Wait up."

Olivia did the exact opposite. She'd stormed out of the Hickory Pit without knowing why. Well, she knew why, but it pained her to admit it. She hated being wrong. Hated being scolded by Mr. Wise Guy. Mostly, she hated feeling like a professional failure. After all, she had no husband, no kids, no hobbies. No real life to speak of. She was the job. She liked to think she'd gotten damn good at it.

It shouldn't have bothered her what Deck thought, but it did. Boy, did it ever. Hearing him spout things Drake had never told her left her reeling. What else had she missed? Even the sound of Deck's boots approaching on the pavement nettled her.

"Jesus, Rockwell. Are you a speed walker?"

"When the situation calls for it."

"Look, I'm a jackass. I'll admit it. I don't blame you for leaving."

"Well, that's a relief." She reached her car just in time and flung open the door. But she didn't get in. She just stood there, emanating heat.

"And you can tear out of this parking lot like a bat out of hell if you want. You can never speak to me again. But, take this with you. Please."

He handed her a plain manila folder, unmarked.

"What is it?" she asked, laying it on her hood. She wanted to look inside but he wanted that too. So, she refrained. Left it there, unopened.

"I know I said I asked you here to pick your brain about Drake, and that's true. But, with what happened this morning, the second body, I thought you might be inclined to help."

"Help? Help *you*, you mean?" The nerve of this guy.

"I know. I blew it. But yes, help."

"Help with what, exactly?"

Will's eyes darted across the parking lot. He lowered his voice. "I don't know if you heard but we might have the *s* word on our hands."

"The *s* word?"

"My partner, JB, says it's bad karma to say it out loud. The guy's a nut but sometimes he's right. I heard you helped out with a couple of those kinds of cases in San Francisco. I read about your special commendation."

"I don't do that anymore."

"Why not? It seemed like you were pretty good at it."

"Until I wasn't." She held the folder out to him, imploring him to take it. Her thoughts unfolding like a horizonless highway. It's scary how fast the mind can travel.

CHAPTER NINETEEN

Will stared at the manila folder in Olivia's hand. He hadn't been prepared for that. For a *no*. Not for this. Will had done his homework. Olivia had profiled the Russian Hill Rapist right down to his occupation—streetcar driver. She had been good at this.

"C'mon, we're on the same team here. We both work with sickos."

Olivia looked skeptical. Offended even. Will felt like an oaf again. Who says the word sicko to a psychologist? *This guy*, apparently. Petey was right. He'd become the job. Just like their dad. He'd forgotten how to talk to anybody who didn't wear a badge. Which explained why they were standing out here in the freezing cold in the first place. "Okay, okay. It's a little different. You want to help them. I want to see them rot behind bars. But, still."

"I don't think that's true." When she returned the folder to the hood of her car, Will took it as a small sign of encouragement. "You want justice. So do I. Sometimes justice means letting a man free, if he's changed. Sometimes it means helping him change. Why do you work with *sickos* anyway?"

"Family business. You?"

Behind her eyes, he saw a familiar pain he wished he could soothe. "Same."

Will pointed to the folder and backed away, while he was still ahead. "Just take a look. Tell me what you think. Off the record. One justice seeker to another."

*

Will flashed his badge to the officers stationed outside the entrance to Gallows' Lane, and they waved him through. Since he'd left Olivia at the Hickory Pit, the fog had descended like a dream, white and gossamery. But here, among the redwoods, the dream turned dark. Sinister giants, their trunks appeared with no warning as his truck rumbled up the dirt road toward Laura Ricci's house.

As he passed the tree where he'd discovered Laura's corpse, Will told himself to get a grip. But the meeting with Olivia had left him unsettled. He couldn't pinpoint the shifting feeling in his gut. After all, he was no shrink. Still, it rattled him like a minor earthquake, subtle and terrifying.

The first house on the left, JB had told him in the message. *I'll be there at 7 with the warrant. Don't make me wait.* Will parked facing Laura's house and shook his head. His dash clock read 7:15. No sign of JB.

In the scrutinous glare of his headlights, the house seemed to draw back further into the woods, into the fog, shrinking away from him and exciting the part of him that liked to give chase. So, he left the truck running, zipped up his jacket, and cracked the door, shining his flashlight into the trees around him. The thin beam didn't go far, the fog rising up like a wall to meet it.

According to the bank statement JB had emailed him, Laura had been in dire financial straits since the fire, and it showed in the sagging porch that creaked under his weight; the peeling white paint; the old beater of a car in the driveway. Leaned against a nearby redwood, Will spotted part of an ornate wooden sign, RICCI'S RESTAU written in red paint. The rest of it gone in the fire, he supposed. JB had told him the insurance company ruled the fire suspicious, leaving Laura to clean up the mess. Slinging slop in the prison chow hall, she couldn't have been happy.

Will expected the house to be empty. Laura's parents had died years ago; she had no siblings. The houses nearby had been so long abandoned the road had grown over. As if the forest had reclaimed the land for itself. But Will obeyed protocol anyway, steering clear of the door. He'd wait for JB and the search warrant. In his head, he heard Olivia's voice. *You're one to talk.* Alright, so he followed the rules. The important ones anyway. It hit him then. Like an unexpected tap on the shoulder. Olivia unnerved him because she reminded him of himself.

Will swept his flashlight across the porch. Moisture from the fog had begun to settle on the windowsills, on the wooden swing suspended from chains so red with rust they appeared blood-covered. He glanced back toward the road, hopeful he'd see JB's lights, but the fog had swallowed it whole, leaving him completely alone.

Anxious for a distraction, Will approached the picture window adjacent to the door and shined his beam inside. Sofa, television, fireplace. A silhouette darted through it all, heading for the back.

Will held his breath, certain he must be wrong. Just a misfire of leftover adrenaline from this never-ending war of a day. But when he heard the yawn of the back door, he drew his gun and took off toward the sound around the side of the house to where the weeds grew tall enough to smack him in the face. He spit them out and stomped them down, lifting his knees as he ran. When he rounded the corner, he nearly tripped on a discarded tire, barely clearing it in a hurried leap. A man sprinted just out of his reach into the woods, scattering leaves behind him as he ran.

"Stop. Police!"

Will kept his light trained on the path in front of him, listening for the man's footsteps in the foliage as he followed. But the leaves weren't leaves at all, they were crisp one-hundred dollar bills. He tracked them like footprints, even as the redwoods worked against him. The fog too. Obscuring. Misleading. Disorienting. Until the money trail stopped and Will stood breathless in a small clearing.

A flicker of movement behind a tree trunk. He dropped his flashlight as he spun toward it, launching himself onto the man's back and pinning him to the ground.

"Don't move."

Cast in the flashlight's shadows, Will struggled to see the face, the frothing mouth, the body grappling beneath him, wrestling to get free. One flail of the man's arm and his gun took flight, landing somewhere in the abyss of the forest.

Will bore down hard, heard the satisfying crunch of his fist connecting with something breakable. The man went limp just long enough for Will to seize his left hand with his own and slammed it into the dirt. Then, his right. "I said, don't move."

Will sucked in a few ragged breaths, wishing he had a set of cuffs. But he'd expected this to be a routine search. Nothing more.

He came up on his knees and secured the man's hands behind his back, holding them there with his own. Maybe, just maybe, if he moved fast enough he could reach his cell in his pocket.

But then, he heard a familiar voice. "Fog Harbor Police, show yourself!"

A light flickered through the fog.

Time played its tricks, slowing down, speeding up. It seemed to happen all at once.

Will looked down at the man he'd straddled, at the tattoo on his neck. Oaktown Boys.

JB charged through the tree cover, his gun raised. "Hands up," he yelled, pointing the barrel at Will.

"It's me. Your partner."

The man beneath him saw an opening. A brief lapse in concentration. Will felt it too late. Along with a solid elbow to the jaw that knocked him on his ass and left him seeing stars. He reached out as the man's legs rustled past him, his hands grasping nothing but the cold night air.

Blue and red. Blue and red. The lights from the three police cruisers out front washed Laura's walls in the color of disaster. Will stood in the living room, jaw aching, ego bruised. His brain, still a little stunned. JB paced nearby, sucking on the end of a Marlboro.

"You really didn't recognize me?" he asked JB, not for the first time.

"I told you, City Boy. The fog was so thick I couldn't see a damn thing. For a minute there, I thought you two were just a couple feral pigs wrestlin' in the mud."

Will sighed, long and heavy. "How much money did they recover?"

"They're still counting it. Last I heard, at least thirty thousand. And that's just what he dropped in the woods. We got another fifteen in the go-bag we found."

Under Laura's sofa, they'd discovered a duffel packed and ready with a Glock, cash, and a fake passport. Another duffel sat opened in the living room, a few stacks of cash strewn about. Will figured he'd interrupted the thief mid-pilfer. "What does a dining hall supervisor need a go-bag for?"

"I reckon it's got something to do with your Oak Tree Boys."

"Oaktown, JB. Oaktown. I think you're right. Laura got herself involved in something so dangerous she needed a gun and a back-up plan."

"Maybe James wasn't the only one trafficking cell phones."

"It's definitely worth looking into." Will rubbed his jaw, wincing when he heard a disconcerting pop. "Where were you, anyway? You said seven."

"You sound like my ex-wife."

"Which one?"

JB chuckled, then coughed, expelling a puff of white smoke. "I had to swing by Forensics. They're still working on the tire tracks from the crime scene. But they got some info on those footprints. Size ten work boot. Brand, Correct-Tex. It's clear as day on the print. I figured you'd want to know."

"Correct-Tex." Will pulled out his phone and typed the brand into the search bar, clicking on the first result. "As in, 'we supply work boots ideal for inmate and detainee use.' I wonder what size Drake wears."

"Only one way to find out. What do you say we swing by the prison in the morning and see if we can find our Cinderella?"

CHAPTER TWENTY

Olivia didn't drive home. Not yet. She imagined Emily there, curled up on the sofa in the light of the Christmas tree, watching reality television and sipping a glass of red wine. If she showed up now, she'd face the firing squad of questions. From a girl who thought sailing in Bora Bora with the Bachelor counted as a real date.

Instead, she headed to her thinking place. The bluff overlooking Little Gull lighthouse. She had perspective out here, even if she couldn't tell where the black sky ended and the ocean began. Even if the fog had grown thick as smoke. Like the North Star, the lighthouse beacon shimmered through it all, promising you could still find your way.

As a girl, she'd read about the ghost of Little Gull, a Yurok woman who had thrown herself onto the rocks from this very bluff, when she'd fallen in love with a fur trapper who had frozen to death in the harsh winter. Legend said you could hear her wailing in the cries of the gulls that lined the shore.

The manila folder had remained unopened, a safe distance away on the passenger seat as she'd driven here, but it beckoned to her now. One look wouldn't hurt. She could return it to Deck tomorrow and say nothing. She fingered the tab, daring herself. Her curiosity had always been her downfall. That, and unavailable men.

Exhibit A: Her father. It didn't get much more unavailable than a life term behind bars.

With the exception of Exhibit B: Erik, who spent his summer internship sleeping his way through the paralegals at a prestigious law firm in San Francisco.

Which had somehow led her to Exhibit C: Graham. The antithesis of unavailable. He'd latched on like an octopus arm and now she couldn't get rid of him. She cringed thinking of the text he'd sent her from the bar, with a link attached, the ugliness of that single capitalized word. *Have you seen this? He's a SNITCH!*

Olivia cut the engine but left the keys in the ignition, flicking on the interior light. It spotlighted the file as she brought it to her lap and splayed it open, surveying its contents. No different than one of Dr. Clancy's autopsy cases.

She always started with the pictures of the scene, laid side by side, with the feeling she got beneath the disgust, beneath the urge to look away. That was the thing about a photo; it didn't judge. It simply showed. If you looked long enough it might give away its secrets.

Olivia tried to disconnect. She'd always been good at it. You can't therapize murderers without a strong compartmentalization game. But no matter how hard she tried, she still saw Bonnie, laughing in the hallway. Laura, proudly cooking up a feast for the prison's Thanksgiving staff dinner. Her eyes welled up before she realized the first secret the pictures told her wasn't a secret at all. The victims knew each other. They knew their killer as well. Olivia felt certain of that. The scenes were organized. No prints left behind. The bodies moved and placed so they'd be easy to find. Bonnie's, right outside her own memorial, for God's sake. Like he's showing off, making a statement. Bonnie had been more important to him psychologically since he'd held onto her body for days. Clothing askew on both women, but no clear evidence of sexual assault. Possible staging, she thought, turning to the close-ups.

She gasped. It had been too dark in the drainpipe and she'd been too frantic to see much of the garrote around Bonnie's neck.

But here, she saw it all, just as Dr. Clancy had photographed it. The denim blue, the CDCR stamp. Both garrotes the same.

Olivia snapped the folder shut, Deck's voice clear as a bell. *I think there's a chance he could be involved in these murders.*

As she sat there, her nerves rattling, Deck's business card fluttered to her feet, landing face up on the floorboard. She picked it up, studied it, turned it over. Found herself wishing he'd written something there.

She focused on the gleaming light of Little Gull, opened the file, and began again.

Disoriented, she sat straight up, banging her knee on the underside of the dash. The folder slid across her lap, threatening to spill its contents between the seat and the console. Mouth dry, heart racing, she rubbed her sleepy eyes and peered out the windshield and into the dark.

The thin beam of a flashlight illuminated the wooden staircase which led from the bluff to the small rocky beach below. Three shadowy figures moved down the steps, their drunken laughter grating against the stillness of the night.

"Oooo… Oooo… The ghost of Little Gull is right behind—"

"Shut up, Emily. You're freaking me out."

Olivia tensed, listened harder. Surely, this wasn't *her* Emily.

"Relax, Shauna." A man's voice. "She's just teasing. I think."

"C'mon. We'll show you where she hit the rocks."

Panicked, Olivia tugged on her jacket. She grabbed her phone, clicked the flashlight app, and opened the door, following the sound of their voices and the roiling water at high tide. When she reached the bottom of the staircase, she shined her light down the beach.

"Emily Jane Rockwell!"

"Oh, shit." An exaggerated whisper. "It's my sister."

Olivia trudged across the wet sand, avoiding the drowned creatures she knew to be sea kelp. At night, everything looked alien. Including Emily.

Her sister's curls moved wildly across her face, her cheeks whipped raw from the wind. She tried to hide behind Shauna, then collapsed to her knees in a fit of giggles.

"We just came to see the lighthouse. I'll drive the girls back. I've only had one beer."

Olivia had been so laser-focused on her sister, she hadn't noticed this third person, his jacket down at his feet, his shirt untucked and half-unbuttoned. "Hank? What are you—"

"Don't freak out, Liv. Shauna came over and we were totally sad about Laura and Bonnie so we watched *The Bachelor* and then we got mad because Matt eliminated Kelsey and we decided to drive to the Hickory Pit to find you, and then Hank was there and we started talking about the lighthouse and the ghost and how he'd never been out here at night and neither had Shauna, so…" Breathless, she shrugged. "Just don't freak out."

"Are you kidding me? You're what, forty? Fifty?" Olivia fired the questions at Hank, wishing they were poison-tipped arrows. He didn't look at her, focusing his attention on doing up his shirt buttons. "You realize my sister is twenty-five. And… how old are you, Shauna?"

"Twenty-three." The words squeaked out of her bright red mouth. She and Emily huddled together, looking as if Olivia had stolen their balloons and popped them with a straight pin. Sorry, kiddos. That's what big sisters are for.

"I get it. You're pissed. But don't you think you're overreactin' a tad? Your sister's an adult. So is Shauna. Nothin' happened. No harm, no foul."

"We're leaving. Now. Both of you." Olivia pointed at the stairs, and Emily and Shauna stumbled toward them, arms linked. After they'd begun the ascent to the bluff, she turned back to Hank. Flashing a contrite smile, he put on his jacket.

"I'm sorry, Doc. It really was just a little harmless fun. The girls seemed pretty upset about Laura and that press release. I was too. I wanted to cheer us all up. By the way, I'm only thirty-nine. Hardly a dirty old man."

"If I ever see you talking to Emily again, I'll report you for sexual harassment."

"Sexual harassment? Of Emily? Talkin' hardly qualifies for—"

"Of me and a lot of other women at Crescent Bay. All those little shoulder grabs and arm pats and creepy compliments. Just remember, Drake didn't call you Handsy Hank for nothing."

Olivia's chest flamed hot as she stormed away from him. She stopped at the base of the stairs, still fuming. But unsettled, too. She took in a deep breath and told herself to suck it up.

As the waves flung themselves against the rocks, the sudden scream of a gull pierced the night.

"Have you lost your mind?" Olivia asked, eyeing Emily in the rearview mirror.

Shauna had already fallen asleep in the backseat, snoring as her head lolled against the window. She looked younger than twenty-three. Not old enough to have a bachelor's degree in psychology. Certainly not old enough to work part-time at Crescent Bay as the Changes group facilitator.

"There's a murderer—maybe even a serial killer—in Fog Harbor targeting women who work at the prison. The second body turned up this morning. And you think now's a good time to get drunk and go tell ghost stories at the lighthouse with a guy twice your age who you hardly know."

"He's not *twice* my age and he's *not* a serial killer."

"Oh really. I'm sure that's exactly what some poor woman said about Ted Bundy, too. The guy is a total creep. They call him Handsy Hank."

"I know. We felt sorry for him. He was at the bar hitting on Jane and getting nowhere, and we were sad and bored and drunk. Thanks for killing my buzz, by the way." Sister warfare wasn't fair at all. Because Emily knew all Olivia's soft spots. Like the way she worried one of them would turn to be a part-time drunk like their mother. "How was your date? We thought you might still be there."

"It wasn't a date, and don't change the subject."

"Must've crashed and burned if you were out here. That, or you really like him."

Flustered, Olivia started the car, suddenly anxious to be anywhere but here. "Seatbelt, please." She forced herself to breathe. To reverse slowly and carefully. "Did Hank try anything with you?"

"No!" Emily clasped her hand across her mouth as Shauna stirred. She started again, in a whisper. "Of course not. I think he's got a thing for Shauna, though. She can be kind of a tease when she's been drinking. Actually, she can be a tease even when she's not drinking. It was her idea to dare him to go skinny-dipping."

Olivia shook her head at her sister. But she'd already faced away, staring out the window as Hank climbed the stairs, hangdog. He raised his eyes when he reached the top, stared at her for a moment. Until she looked away. "Then I guess it's a good thing I got here when I did. When are you going to start acting like a grownup, Em?"

"Maybe when you start treating me like one. I want to make my own mistakes."

"Like getting plastered with your work colleagues? Like talking to our loser dad without telling me? *Congratulations.* You're off to a great start."

CHAPTER TWENTY-ONE

"I hate this place," JB said, as the control officer checked their IDs and buzzed them through the main gate and into Crescent Bay State Prison.

Will sensed a change in the air today. A tension, taut as a tripwire. Even the guards' eyes darted at them as they passed. Like they had something to hide. Back at the turnoff on Pine Grove Road, there had been at least half a dozen media vans parked in the ditch, reporters lingering outside, with their microphones at the ready. Sharks circling a story. The same way they'd done with him, camped out on the doorstep of his building in Noe Valley—the night before the trial, the night of, the night after—waiting for the money shot.

"It's not high on my list either," Will admitted, inhaling the rank aroma of men who'd lost hope. He could pick them out as they walked the long hallway, shuffling along with no sense of purpose or direction. He wondered if his brother had fared any better at Valley View. The only time he'd visited, Ben had refused to see him, and he'd been the one traipsing back to his car, head hung low. Until he'd gotten good and angry.

"Smells worse than my college frat house." JB pointed up ahead. "Thank God. We're almost there."

It had been Will's idea to skip the formal interrogation and to meet Drake in the warden's office instead. *Let's get him thinking he's not a suspect. That we're here picking his brain as an expert. He'll eat that right up.* Maybe he didn't have a degree from Stanford, or the fancy extra letters after his name, or an attaboy from the FBI, but he knew Drake's weakness. The thing he adored above all else: himself.

Warden Blevins had relocated the office between the chapel and the Education Department, when he'd taken the reins a few years back. Before that, the warden presided over Crescent Bay from the outside. From the row of administrative offices, where you didn't have to clear the control booth or assault your nose with prison stench. The warden had told Will the move brought him closer to the people he served. Which sounded like a load of political bullshit, especially with the fancy key card lock on the door. The only one like it as far as Will could see.

Warden Blevins stood inside waiting for them. He reminded Will of a pencil, tall and thin and ordinary. The in-between kind of kid who would've mostly been ignored. "Good morning, Detectives. Control let me know you were on the way. Devere's already in place."

"What did you tell him?" Will asked.

"Nothing. Exactly as you asked me to." The warden squinted at Will's face, where the bruise on his jaw had turned a lovely blend of day-after blue and purple.

"Let him marinate for a minute," JB said. "We'll check out the security footage and that rules infraction you said our victim wrote yesterday."

"Whatever you'd like." He led them down a corridor, past a nondescript door with a familiar female officer stationed outside. Will did a double-take before he remembered. Maryann Murdock had a twin—*Morgan? Mia? Melody?* Melody. That sounded right. A twin who worked as a correctional officer. He guessed Drake sat behind the door she guarded, stewing. The longer, the better.

"As I told your partner yesterday, our security cameras have been glitching lately. Every time it rains, we get static in B and C Block. Drake's got a single cell over in C—C22—so I'm afraid the cameras won't tell you much. But you're welcome to look. I already pulled last night's footage for you."

Warden Blevins pointed to the desk, to a single photocopied page. "That's the 115 Laura typed up. I haven't had a chance to do much with it yet. She requested Drake be unassigned from the kitchen."

JB scrolled through the footage, grumbling to himself, as Will paced behind him. He felt like a prizefighter waiting for a rematch. Even though he'd won the last go-round, it hadn't felt like a knockout since slippery Drake had managed to bob and weave his way around the death penalty.

"You tryin' to wear a hole in the floor?" JB patted the seat next to him. "Why don't you put that energy to use? You're makin' me nervous."

Will obliged, flopping into the chair with a sigh. The cameras showed a steady image of the C Block hallway, cells C20 through C30 on either side. "Get to the early morning footage. Chet said she'd been dead a few hours at most."

When the ticker reached 4:00 a.m., JB hit play. They stared at the screen till Will's eyes began to blur. Till JB cursed under his breath.

"Nothing," he said. "Not an officer. Not a rat. Not even a goddamn cockroach."

At 4:45 a.m., the screen flickered in and out a few times until it went to static. JB kept scrolling until the image returned. 5:57 a.m. Just in time for 6 a.m. count. Drake had been there, grinning like the Cheshire cat.

"The footage I watched from early Thursday morning was similar. Except the picture went out around midnight and came back around 4 a.m. No sign of anything suspicious. If he did it, he had help."

JB shook his head. "If he did it, he had the timing of an atomic clock."

"Well, he certainly had the motive." Will read aloud from the document Laura had signed. "'Devere reported to work late on 12/16… was previously counseled about failing to report to his work assignment on 12/2, 12/3, and 12/11. When I tried to address Devere's behavior, he became belligerent and argumentative. I repeatedly told him to return to his cell… called me a "fat bitch" in front of other inmates. Devere has created a hostile work environment… fear for my safety… request that he be reassigned from the kitchen immediately.'"

JB hoisted himself from the chair with a groan and summoned Will to follow. "So you say this guy's a psychopath, huh?"

Will didn't hold back his sly grin. Knowing Drake waited in the other room, he figured he probably wouldn't smile for the rest of the day. Best to enjoy it. "Does a donkey have a shadow?"

"Touché, City Boy. Touché."

Warden Blevins led them back to the nondescript door, where Melody Murdock nodded at them.

"He's all yours," the warden said. "Officer Murdock will be right outside if you need anything. Have fun."

Fun? Will couldn't remember when he last had fun. Testifying against your own brother in a murder case has a way of sucking the fun from your life. His fun tank had been bone-dry for years now. Until last night's dinner with Olivia. That had been fun. For the split second it lasted.

Will lingered in the doorway and let JB lead the way into the office. He wanted to watch the scene play out, to study Drake's reactions from a distance. To catalogue his movements like a scientist examining a spider in a glass box.

One desk, large and plain and barren, stanchioned in the center of the room. Drake already seated behind it in the standard blue jumpsuit, his hands shackled in front of him, steady and waiting.

As Will looked on, Drake tracked JB to the first chair. The second chair remained empty.

A pair of eyes met Will's. Shifty and glinting. But the life in them existed only on the surface. Pinpricks of light darting across a deep, dead lake. If someone asked him to point to evil, Will would pick those eyes out of a lineup.

He stepped inside and shut the door behind him. Game time.

"You must be here about the murders." Drake spoke before Will. Before introductions. Before he'd even had time to sit down. "Took you long enough. The whole prison has been talking about me. How I snuck out of this shithole and offed those ladies. It's about time you came to hear it from the horse's mouth."

Will kept his face a blank slate. As usual, Drake had surprised him, left him riding shotgun when he should've been in the driver's seat. Time to think fast, recover quick. But his mind felt slow, burdened. He wished he'd taken JB up on that third cup of coffee.

"I suppose you want to confess then," Will said. "Detective Benson and I are happy to oblige."

Drake's laugh went right through him, an icepick to the heart. "Confess? Where's the fun in that? Besides, I'm as much a victim as anybody."

"You? A victim?" JB scoffed. "How's that?"

"Well, Pops, let me tell ya. Somebody stole my royalties. My hard-earned money. And the women at the shelter depend on me. I haven't told anybody out of respect for Ms. McMillan. Especially since I figure it was her scheming husband who did it. But now, somebody's spreading lies about me."

"Are they lies?" Will asked. "It's not such a stretch. You wrote a book about it."

"Ah. You read it. Did you leave me a review?"

"Yeah. One word." Will's anger throbbed beneath his skin. *Wannabe.*

"That's not what Heather Hoffman told me. She's a reporter for the *Fog Harbor Gazette*. They want to do a feature about me when the second book comes out."

"If it ever comes out. Bonnie's dead. And everybody else sees you for what you really are. A talentless hack."

"Well, think whatever you want to. But if I needed Bonnie so badly, why did I kill her? It blows your ridiculous premise out of the water, Detective."

Will scowled at him, still catching up. Was that a confession or a denial?

"What's your theory, then?" JB asked. "Enlighten us."

Drake kicked back in his chair, flung a greasy strand of hair from his eyes with one dramatic head whip, and grinned. "You're smart, Pops. A helluva lot smarter than your partner here. Ask the expert. That's brilliant. Do I get a finder's fee if I help bag this guy?"

"Of course," Will said. "You get to stay here in these fabulous digs and eat three meals a day and watch free cable TV every day for the rest of your life."

"Don't listen to my partner. He's just jealous." JB leaned in conspiratorially, and Will wondered if he'd underestimated the old guy. "He's an aspiring writer. Go figure. Listen, Drake. You help us. We help you. You know, I have an old friend at a big-bank movie studio in LA. Maybe he'd be willing to take a look at your book. See if it merits the big screen."

"Alright. I'll bite. Benicio del Toro. That's who I want for Hawk."

JB slapped his knee. "Loved that guy in *The Usual Suspects*. Sounds like you've got some Hollywood instincts, man. I'll be sure to let my friend know."

Surely, a sophisticated con man like Drake would see right through his partner's BS. "So, what can I help you with, Detective? Means? Motive? A criminal profile?"

"What's this?" Will slid a photograph of the garrote across the table.

"Looks like a homemade weapon. The kind you'd use to strangle somebody. What do they call it again?" He puzzled for a moment. "A garrote! That's right. I researched those when I was writing *Bird of Prey*. Never used one though. I didn't see the need. Too impersonal. I liked the feel of—"

"Do you recognize it?" Will interrupted. He wouldn't let Drake get off on reliving his crimes the way he'd done the first time. When Drake had finally confessed, he'd spent a solid twelve hours detailing exactly how he'd raped and strangled each victim. Right down to the delicate snap of the hyoid bone.

"I didn't make it, if that's what you're getting at. But I can guess what it's made from. Looks to me like a jumpsuit like this one and a set of rolling pin handles."

"Like the ones you stole from the kitchen, you mean?"

JB flashed his palm at Will to settle him. "Easy, partner. I thought you said that particular rules infraction was adjudicated not guilty. Don't go harassin' the poor man. You know what I'm curious about, Drake. If you wanted to murder somebody outside these prison walls, like your character, Hawk, do you think you could do it? Get past the cameras and the fences and the guards?"

"Purely hypothetical, right?"

"Just two fishin' buddies shootin' the shit."

"Well, there ain't much I can't do. You can ask Detective Decker about that. The cameras are easy. Everybody knows there's blind spots, and the damn things don't work a lick in the rain. I wouldn't even bother with the fences. I'd find a tunnel or dig one myself. Like those two renegades who escaped from Clinton Correctional a few years back. That's what Hawk does in the book. The guards… now that one's tricky 'cause those bastards are everywhere. But that's kind of the best thing about them. All you need is one in your pocket and you're good to go."

JB nodded, impressed. "So you're saying it's not that hard then?"

"I didn't say that. It's a lot like writing a novel. It all depends on how motivated you are. I'll tell you what I see here. Somebody is pretty damn motivated to see me take the fall."

"And who might that be?" JB asked. "Who should we be looking at?"

"The list is long, my friend. Tommy Rigsby, for one. That guy knows I snitched on him to the goon squad. He told me once that he'd see me leave prison in a body bag. James McMillan. For obvious reasons. Ole Handsy Hank Wickersham. Hell, I'll bet the warden would like to see the state stick a needle in my arm too."

"The warden?" Will asked.

A knock at the door, and Warden Blevins poked his head inside. "I'm sorry to interrupt, Detectives, but it seems we overlooked a priority ducat. Drake's got his mandatory TB test down at the medical clinic. Can't be rescheduled."

He stepped the rest of the way in, followed closely by Officer Murdock. Stone-faced, she motioned for Drake to come forward.

"Wait." Will stood too, crowding the small room. "I want to see his boots."

"His what?" Warden Blevins asked.

"Your boots," Will repeated to Drake. "Let's see 'em."

Drake looked smug as he returned to the chair, leaned back, and lifted his right foot. It landed on the desk with a thump. "Correct-Tex," he said. "Like half the inmates in this joint."

"Size?"

"*Big.*"

"Not your ego, asshole. The boots."

Warden Blevins groaned. "Tell him your shoe size, Devere."

"Ten. Wanna know the color of my underwear too, Decker?" Drake made his way toward the door, escorted by Officer Murdock. She pushed him ahead, jostling with him when he slowed to face Will. "Or I guess you could just ask your mom. She's seen them a few times."

The insult bounced off Will's armor made thick by years of working patrol in downtown San Francisco. But he still relished the grunt Drake made as Officer Murdock shoved him into the corridor. He stumbled forward and into the wall.

"We're going to need those boots," Will told the warden.

Drake spit out a laugh. "For what? You makin' a shrine?"

"I'm making a murder case."

"Hmph. Good luck with that."

Warden Blevins nodded at Officer Murdock.

"Take 'em off, Devere." With a hint of pleasure in her hard-as-nails voice, she unlaced the boots. Drake kicked them off, mad-dogging Will and JB. "Keep moving," she told him, with a push to the back for good measure.

"Don't go leavin' the state, though," JB called after him, chuckling as he collected the boots. "We'll be back."

Warden Blevins waited until Drake disappeared out the main door and into the hallway. "We'll get you the lists you wanted of all the officers on duty in C Block on the nights of the murders and the inmate workers assigned to the kitchen under Laura's supervision. I'll have my secretary fax that over to the station."

"TB test?" Will asked. "That really couldn't wait?"

"Prison regulations, Detective. I apologize. You will be happy to know we tossed Devere's house while he was in here, and Christmas came early. We found a little something you might be interested in."

Will waited, expectantly, as the warden simpered.

"Are we in a goddamn Nancy Drew novel?" JB muttered. "Lay it on us, Warden."

"I always did like Nancy. A real spitfire." Warden Blevins smacked JB on the shoulder, grinning. "It's a cell phone. And it's all yours as soon as IGI takes a crack at it."

"IGI?" JB asked, puzzling.

"Institutional Gang Investigators, Detective. Our goon squad, as we affectionately call them."

"What's that noise?" Will pushed past the warden and toward the sudden raised voices coming from the hall. In prison, yelling can mean a lot of things. An inmate getting called out. A fight. A shanking. A breakdown. A nightmare. A staff assault. A riot. Whatever it is, it's never good. Will knew that much.

He flung open the door and ran in the direction of the commotion, through the raucous group of inmates who had already gathered to watch the show.

Officer Murdock pinned Drake to the wall, striking him in the flank with her baton. He spun around, grabbing for it, as she reached for her body alarm. Next to them, another fight had kicked off between two Latino inmates. They rolled on the floor, fists flying. The alarm sounded. It meant stop. But nobody did.

Will grabbed for his gun at his waist before he remembered he didn't have it. He wasn't allowed to. He'd left it, as always, at the guard tower.

A woman cried out. He looked up and saw her caught, frozen in the middle of the fray.

"Olivia!"

CHAPTER TWENTY-TWO

Olivia couldn't hear a thing. Only the snare drum of her heartbeat and the white noise of panic above it. Morrie was marooned in his wheelchair on the side of the runway. Stuck like a sputtered-out jalopy, his eyes panicked. Olivia ran toward him, dodging the fists and flying elbows of the Oaktown Boys and their rivals, Los Diabolitos.

"Are you okay?" she asked, her voice high and breathy.

He nodded his head up and down so fast Olivia feared he'd pull a muscle. She pushed Morrie ahead until they reached a wall of men. With nowhere to go, she backed him up against the wall and stood in front of him, trying to make herself invisible.

Something wet splattered against her hand, and she cried out once more as splash of blood ran like a river down her thumb and spotted the folder she carried. The inmate nearest her wore the same color all over his battered face. He struggled to his knees, flailing his fists like he could still win, then went down in a heap.

As Olivia cowered, her day unwound like a spool of thread, back to the beginning when she'd been up before daybreak to return Shauna to her car at the Hickory Pit with a stern warning. Then, to the prison with Emily, who'd made the entire ride in silence. The long, tense walk up the runway to the MHU, where she'd learned Hank had conveniently called in sick. A couple of grin-and-bear-it meetings she couldn't reschedule. And finally, to Drake. He'd shown up again unexpected and dropped a bomb. All of it led here. To this. Her punishment doled out by the universe.

Because she'd planned to tell Deck he'd gotten it all wrong. She'd walked down here just for that reason, savoring her rightness. Now, she watched Deck push his way to her, skirting the melee even as it grew, spreading down the runway like a wildfire racing through dry grass.

"Pepper spray!" someone yelled.

Olivia felt the instant burn in her eyes. Her throat closed, and she covered her nose and mouth with her sweater, gasping. Morrie had already done the same, tugging his blanket over his face. Her knees weakened, and she leaned into the wall next to him, fearing she'd go down hard. End up flat on her belly like an inmate. But a hand latched itself to her forearm, an arm wrapped around her shoulders, and she collapsed against it.

Through the blur of fiery tears, she saw Deck's face. His jaw the color of eggplant.

"I got you," he said.

Olivia stuck her face under the cold water again, keeping it there as long as she could hold her breath. A swollen-eyed, red-faced crazy lady blinked back at her in the mirror. She dabbed at her cheeks with a paper towel, straightened her ponytail, and reevaluated. At least she'd moved one rung down the crazy ladder.

"You okay in there?" Deck asked through the door.

"Wonderful. Never been better." Her voice scratched her raw throat.

"I figured as much. Sure you don't need any help?"

She sighed and opened it. "I don't think there's any help for this."

"It's really not that bad." Deck gestured down the hallway, where at least twenty inmates had been cuffed and seated on the ground. Twice as many officers tended to them, getting their names and statements. "You should see those guys."

"Is Morrie okay?"

"Who?"

"The man in the wheelchair." Olivia scanned the crowd for him. Found him at the periphery being examined by a nurse. She didn't question her relief. Just let it flood in, not wanting to admit to herself how much Morrie reminded her of her father.

Olivia spotted Warden Blevins parting the sea of officers to get to her. He took her aside, his features arranging themselves into a practiced look of concern. "Are you alright, Doctor? I heard you were caught up in the middle of this nonsense."

"I'm okay. Just a little shaken up. What happened?"

"Drake Devere nearly started a riot. That's what happened."

"Drake?"

"Some of the inmates reported hearing him arguing with Officer Murdock. Next thing you know, he went for her baton, and that kicked off the whole mess." He glanced over his shoulder, leaned in close, and lowered his voice. "This is exactly why I asked you to keep an eye on him."

Olivia stepped back. Glaring at him through her swollen eyes. "I'm not sure what you had in mind, Warden. I'm a psychologist, not a correctional officer. And I'm certainly not a part of the IGI."

As she spoke, Olivia spotted them, the Institutional Gang Investigators, talking with Tommy Rigsby, who had a swollen nose and a cut above one eye to go with his pepper-sprayed face. He kept his bloodied lips shut tight as a clam.

"Why don't you schedule an extra session with Drake? Get him gabbing."

"That seems…" Olivia tried to find another word but came up empty, and she didn't dare mention Drake's early morning visit. "Unethical. Don't you think?"

"Doctor Rockwell, the safety and security of the institution is at stake. I'm not asking you to break any rules. Just give him what he's always wanted. Attention."

Olivia watched him go, her mouth hung slightly open, dumb-founded. She clenched her fists, studied her hands. The spot of blood long gone now, swirled down the drain. But something gnawed at her. When she realized, she hurried toward Deck.

"Do you have my folder?" she asked, panicked. She couldn't remember when it had fallen from her hand. She imagined an inmate rifling through it, passing her profile of the Fog Harbor killer around the chow hall like a tawdry magazine. She imagined it landing, somehow, on the warden's desk. "My folder?" she asked again, more urgent this time.

Olivia vaguely recognized the older man who held it out to her, grinning. She grabbed at it, clung to it like a life raft. The little spot of blood spatter permanent now. "You mean this thing? He read it."

"You what?"

Deck took a quick jump back from her. Like she might bite.

"I told him not to. But City Boy don't listen."

"I didn't read it, I swear. Not even a peek. This lying codger is my partner, by the way. Jimmy Benson. Some people call him JB. I won't repeat what I call him."

"Pleasure is all mine." JB took her hand, and she realized why she'd recognized him. His photo adorned the Hickory Pit Hall of Fame Wall, as one of three Fog Harbor residents to complete the seventy-two-ounce steak challenge. "Will tells me you're a big deal around here. That you've done some criminal profiling. For the FBI, no less."

"I didn't say you were a big deal. I mean, not that you're *not* a big deal. But—"

"Can we maybe sit down somewhere?" Olivia asked, suddenly feeling woozy. Before she knew it, Will had his hands on her again, steadying her. He guided her across the hall and into the warden's office, where they filed into a small room off the main corridor.

Her skin felt white-hot beneath his and impossibly cold when he released her, helping her settle into a folding chair.

"Your first time?" JB asked. "Gettin' pepper-sprayed, I mean."

Olivia nodded, watching Deck lean against the desk opposite her. He rolled his eyes.

"I remember my first time," JB said fondly. "Back in LA in the nineties when the department first got wise to it. We had to take a spray right to the face and fend off an attack by our trainer. Like we needed to know how it feels. Ain't never made sense to me. Are they gonna shoot us too? Anyway, there were guys rollin' on the floor, howlin' like dogs. But I made the worst mistake. Took a shower right after. That spray went straight down to my crotch. And let me tell you—"

"I don't think Olivia wants to hear this story."

"'Course she does. See, it's makin' her feel better. Look at that smile on her face. Watch and learn, City Boy. Watch and learn."

Olivia laughed, mostly to get under Deck's skin. The huff of his exasperated breath told her it had done the trick. Anyway, JB had a point. Smiling eased the sting, loosened the knots in her neck. "I'll bet they called you 'balls of fire,'" she said.

"Please don't encourage him."

"Actually, no." JB slapped his knee, guffawing. "But my third ex-wife did."

Olivia held the folder with the profile she'd made close to her chest like a shield. She knew about adrenaline. How it rushed in, swirling and roiling in her blood. How it rushed out and swept everything clean, leaving her exhausted. As she looked at Deck, at his expectant eyes, she wondered if the whole week had finally caught up to her.

"Are you sure you feel up to this?" Deck asked. "We can do it another time."

"I'm fine. Completely fine." Maybe if she said it often enough, loud enough, she'd believe it.

"Later today, even. I can meet you somewhere."

"It's alright. *Really.*"

"Take a hint, City Boy." His voice ratcheted up an octave. "She's just not that into you."

"Well, you would know," Deck shot back. "With four ex-wives you're bound to be an expert." But his cheeks gave him away, turning a rosy pink.

Embarrassed for him, Olivia cleared her throat, bringing their attention back to her. She laid the folder on the desk and opened it. "I reviewed all of the information you gave me."

"And?"

As Deck peered down at her notes, she quickly hid them beneath a crime scene photo. The picture of Bonnie dead in the drainpipe. Ugly as it was, she preferred it to the two words—the name—she'd scrawled at the top of her notes. She shouldn't have written it down.

"I think you're way off base about Drake. He doesn't fit the profile. Or rather, the profile doesn't fit him."

"Please enlighten us then, Doctor."

Olivia rolled her eyes at Deck but let it slide. The poor guy had to deal with JB's constant ragging. Besides, she liked the way he said it. The way he looked at her, daring her to prove him wrong.

"The most obvious thing is the abnormally short or absent refractory period."

JB contorted his face. "The whoosy-whatzit?"

"The length of time between kills," Deck said, not even cracking a smile.

"Exactly. When Drake was operating in the community, he followed the pattern of a typical serial killer, with years lapsing between kills and an apparent return to normalcy in between episodes of extreme violence. This killer seems to be a different breed. More like a spree killer, where there is no cooling off. At the very least, this behavior is entirely inconsistent with Drake's."

"What about the UCLA study?"

Olivia blinked back her astonishment at the question. Deck had gone and surprised her again.

"It only proves my point. The researchers used mathematical analysis to test the hypothesis that serial killing arises from the simultaneous firing of neurons in the brain. When enough neurons fire, the serial killer reaches a threshold beyond which he can no longer control his urge to kill. Once those neurons fire, they need a break before they can fire again. History tells us Drake's neurons don't fire this fast."

JB's head whipped between them, and he threw up his hands. "Neurons? Mathematical analysis? Where the hell am I? Because I'm pretty sure I just time-traveled back to ninth grade science class. Next thing you know, you'll be asking me to recite the periodic table and use a Bunsen burner."

Deck barely glanced at his partner, keeping his eyes locked on her. She didn't dare look away. That would mean surrender. "But wasn't the whole study inspired by The Butcher of Rostov?" he asked. "He had a similar MO. Successive kills in short bursts. Like a spree. Maybe Drake's just getting it out of his system, being locked up all this time. Patterns can change, right?"

"Two murders does not a pattern make. But that's not all. Your killer is hands-off, relying on a garrote to strangle both victims. Drake *always* used his hands. That was essential for him. The feeling of closeness, of possession. Ted Bundy talked about it, about wanting to feel the last breath leave the body. Same for Drake. It was a turn-on for him."

JB shook his head in disgust. "Now there's a guy you can bring home to meet the parents."

"I'd say the garrote implies a physically weaker suspect, especially since there was no obvious bruising on the victims' backs. A stronger perpetrator would use a knee to the back for leverage. A weaker perp would turn his or her back to the victim and rely on their entire body. Not to mention, Drake is a rapist. It was the only real evidence he ever left behind. Chet's report indicates no clear evidence of sexual assault. I'd guess the victims were posed—clothing torn, leggings pulled down—to make you suspect sex was the motive. And with the materials used to make the garrote, maybe even to make you suspect Drake."

Deck twisted his mouth like he tasted something bitter. "I'm not saying I agree. But, if you're right, then what is the motive?"

Olivia squirmed, flashed a nervous smile. "That's an excellent question, Detective."

"Sounds like you don't have an answer."

"I have an answer. A guess, anyway. But I'm not sure you're going to like it."

Deck smiled back, smug. Not nervous at all. "Try me."

"It seems the killer or killers—I'm not sure you can assume it's the work of a single perpetrator—want to make a statement. That's why they held onto Bonnie's body. And left it near the church where it wouldn't be missed. I would guess the killer was watching that day. Maybe even attending the vigil, wanting to witness the impact. Or to be sure the impact would be felt by as many people as possible."

"But that doesn't fit with the Ricci murder. Laura was found hours after she'd been killed and in a remote location. No big statement there."

"The killer already has our attention. The location was remote, but obvious. Near her home and easily discovered. With footprints this time. Correct-Tex brand footprints. Everybody who works at the prison knows that brand. They sponsor our staff Thanksgiving dinner."

Deck hoisted himself from his perch on the desk and paced to the other side of the room. When he turned to face her, eyes burning, she felt the sting. "Are you saying this guy wants to be caught?"

"I'm saying whoever is doing this wants *someone* to be caught. You have to consider the possibility that Drake is right. He's being set up."

Deck's bitter laugh broke the silence.

"You can't actually believe that."

"You asked me what I thought, and I told you. What you do with it is up to you."

"Oh, I can think of a few things I'd like to do with it." He snatched the folder from the desk and waved it precariously above the trash can, as JB grimaced, wide-eyed.

Olivia watched her notes drop like blades of shattered glass to the waiting mouth of the trash can and onto the floor beside it. She heard Drake's hypnotic voice in her head, what he'd told her just this morning. He could lie with ease, but this time, Olivia knew without a doubt, he'd been telling the truth. Because she'd seen it with her own eyes.

I can't name names but I figured out who might be settin' me up, and it's big, Doc. It's big. About two weeks ago, I'd wandered into the chapel to do some writing. I was on a roll. Words pourin' out like a river. Some real flow, self-actualized type shit. But then my pen ran out. I know I shouldn't have done it, but I snuck into the chaplain's office, snagged a couple of those fancy ink pens he's got. That's when I heard voices. I saw things I wasn't supposed to see.

"Well, ain't that somethin'," JB muttered, as Deck's mouth hung slightly open. They both stared at the page that had landed on JB's loafered foot. At the heading—SUSPECTS—she'd underlined twice, punctuated with a question mark. At the single name she'd written there.

CHAPTER TWENTY-THREE

Still sore from the tussle last night, Will's body protested as he hurried to grab the page before Olivia could snatch it back and tell him he was out of his mind, that he hadn't read the warden's name clear as day on her suspect list. With a groan, he grabbed the nearest corner of the sheet, tugging it across JB's shoe toward him. It didn't budge an inch in his direction, and he knew why. But he didn't dare look up at her. Those eyes would do him in and he'd let go. Then she'd win, and he'd look even more foolish than he did already, tossing her notes into the trash like a petulant teenager.

"Let go," she hissed.

"You let go." He tugged harder and harder until he heard an ominous rip.

JB guffawed, as Will cursed, stumbled back, nearly lost his balance. In his hand, a tiny scrap of paper. He stood, steadied himself, and tossed it, watching as it fluttered into the trash can, landing between a coffee cup and a used napkin, somewhere in the general vicinity of his self-respect. A laugh clunked from his throat, dead on arrival.

"I told you to let go." Olivia mocked him from across the room, holding out the nearly intact page in her hand like a trophy.

"She did tell you to let go," JB echoed.

Will sighed. "I assume you're also going to tell me I didn't see what I think I did."

"You saw something?" Just as he feared, she halved the sheet and halved it again, tucking it into her pants pocket with a smirk. "What did you see?"

Will hustled out the door and into the hallway, leaving Dr. Smarty Pants and her fiery green eyes behind him. He waited there, trying to make sense of it all. Of Drake and the melee that morning. Of Olivia's profile and the name she'd written. Of the tension between them, a dynamite fuse about to blow the rust right off his world-weary heart. But most of all, he tried to make sense of the desperate urge he felt to push her up against the wall and kiss her mouth raw.

Will stayed two steps ahead of JB as they traversed the sidewalk outside the prison gates and headed back to the car. He wished he'd come alone. No witnesses. Because he knew exactly what awaited him. He'd never live this one down. He needed no further proof than JB's uncharacteristic silence.

As soon as he shut the door, Will cranked the engine and turned to him. "Don't say a word."

"Wasn't gonna."

"Good."

JB fiddled with the radio, cranking up "I'll Be Home For Christmas." To Will's horror, he began to sing along.

"You sound like the stray cat living in my garage."

JB belted out the chorus, complete with Broadway-inspired hand gestures.

"Please make it stop."

He finished with a small bow, as the announcer's baritone voice filled the car. "Next up, a children's classic we all love. Good ole 'Frosty The Snow—'"

Will cut the radio.

"Alright, no Frosty. Guess that means you want to talk then. You didn't tell me you had yourself a crush, City Boy. You keep surprising me."

"Well, that makes two of us. Since I didn't realize you had connections in Hollywood."

"You liked that, huh? I told ya. Detective of the Year right here. You don't earn that without gettin' a gold star in interrogation. I'm a man of the people. They open up to me. Like that pretty lady doctor did after you stormed out. She thinks you're a real asshole. The kind of asshole she'd like to see naked."

"She did not say that."

"Hmph."

"Did she?"

With a click of JB's finger, Jimmy Durante cut in halfway through "Frosty The Snowman." "Always thought this was a sad one. I mean, did the damn snowman really have to say goodbye? Couldn't the kids have put him in a walk-in fridge or something?"

"So, what *did* Olivia say about me?"

JB smiled, shook his head, pitying. "Exactly what I thought. You've got yourself a full-fledged schoolboy crush. Don't worry, I didn't tell her you let the bad guy get away last night. But I did mention you got clocked in the head real good. Told her that might explain why you were actin' a fool in there."

Will drove the rest of the way seething as he endured JB's impromptu Christmas concert. Midway through "Little Drummer Boy," their phones dinged simultaneously, mercifully.

"It's from the chief," JB said. "You'll never believe it. That theater creep came to the station and agreed to talk."

"Do we have a name?"

"Yeah. And it ain't the first time we've heard it today."

Will pulled the car to a sudden stop in the parking lot. "Warden Blevins?"

"Nah. Sergeant Hank Wickersham. Or as your psychopath buddy, Drake, likes to call him, Handsy Hank."

An unsmiling Chief Flack met them outside the interrogation room and followed them into the adjacent office located behind the one-way mirror.

Hank sat straight as a board, tapping his foot like his life depended on it. His eyes darted everywhere but the mirror. Will didn't blame him one bit. Even though he did the interrogating, that glass pane always made him feel like a lab rat caught in a maze.

"So what do we know about this guy?" Will asked the chief.

"Sergeant Hank Wickersham. Never married, no kids. Works in the Mental Health Unit at Crescent Bay. He accepted a transfer and moved here from Studio City a few months ago. I talked to the warden down at the Los Angeles Women's Institution and apparently the guy was walked off grounds after they caught him with a female inmate in a janitorial closet in a state of undress. Said he was showing her how to mix the chemicals for mopping the floors when the bucket spilled on his pants. Hers too."

"Jeez. Desperate times." JB peered through the mirror, leaving a spot where his nose bumped the glass. "He's not a bad-looking guy. Surely he could've found a broad in the free world to mop his floors. If you know what I'm sayin'."

Chief Flack groaned. "Does anybody ever know what you're saying?"

"Not usually," Will answered for him. After the morning he'd had, he relished the chance to get a few jabs in at his partner. The chief's encouraging laugh sweetened the deal, the cherry on top. "And if they do, they wish they didn't. I speak from experience."

"Alright, how are you boys gonna play it?"

"City Boy's the bad cop," JB said. "Comes natural to him."

*

"Let's go over your story one more time," Will prompted.

Hank slumped down further in the hard metal chair. As if he wanted to disappear beneath it. The power of the interrogation room—small, sparse, and soundproof—still amazed Will. You stick most guilty guys in there for a while, with just two chairs and a desk, and they'll start singing like canaries to get out. Not Drake, of course. Drake relished it. Being center stage. Two detectives captive to his show.

But Hank was no psychopath. When they'd first begun, the tremor in his voice gave that away. Now, he looked beaten down and on the verge of tears.

"I've already told you exactly what happened. I didn't do anything wrong."

"My partner's old and cranky and forgetful." Will nodded at JB, cramped in the corner, pretending to take notes. His watch read ten past noon, so the scribbles on that pad were more than likely a lunch order. "Humor us, Sergeant. Then we'll get you out of here and on your way home. I promise."

Will learned best under duress. Interrogation 101 at the kitchen table with his father as the bad cop and the belt as the looming death sentence for missing curfew. *Don't look to the left*, Ben had told him. *He'll think you're lying*.

"Like I said, I got pretty drunk that night. Feeling sorry for myself, I guess. Fog Harbor is depressing in the winter. The rain, the cold. Nothing like Studio City. I used to do comedy down there on the weekends. Like a side gig. Now, my only audience are the crazies in the MHU."

Hank made an unconvincing attempt to smile. Instead, his face looked pained and tired.

"Half the time, they're laughing at the voices in their own heads. Anyway, I drove out to the Hickory Pit around nine. Met up with a couple folks from Crescent Bay. I stayed there till closing."

"And what time was that again?"

"One or one thirty. I can't say for sure. I know I should have called a taxi but I didn't have far to go. I was headed home, and I saw the theater all lit up. *Vertigo* on the marquee. It's one of my all-time favorites. The ticket taker had gone home for the night, and it was pouring cats and dogs, so I just let myself in through the side door and found a seat. That's when I spotted Bonnie a few rows ahead of me."

"And you say she didn't recognize you?"

"I don't think so. If she did, she didn't say. It was pitch black in the theater and I had pulled the hood of my jacket over my face. To be honest, I didn't want her to see me. I don't think she liked me too much."

"What makes you say that?"

Hank eyed the door with longing. Like he'd been lost in the desert for days and saw a pool of crystal-clear water up ahead. If only he could make it there.

"Did you flirt with her or something?" JB asked. "Maybe get a little too touchy-feely?"

"So, I guess you heard then. One of the inmates started it. The nickname. Handsy. And it stuck. A lot of the ladies avoided me after that, as you can imagine. Bonnie included."

"Are you?" Will asked. "*Handsy?*"

"I'm just a friendly guy. I don't mean anything by it."

Will nodded sympathetically. He'd been saving this one. His ace in the hole. The way his father had always done with him and his brothers. *I smell beer. You boys been drinkin'?* or, *Is that lipstick on your collar, Petey?* or, *Your teacher told me I signed that report card. Sure as hell don't remember a C in Algebra.*

"Is that what happened at your last job? Just got a little too friendly?"

"Jesus Christ. You know about that? Am I a suspect or something?"

As a boy, Will had always reacted the same way. His stomach bottoming out, his mind blank. Sheer panic.

"We're not saying that. But you're the last person we know who saw Bonnie alive. And we've got to turn every stone."

"Ever heard of Diana Holden?"

Of course he had—who hadn't heard of Diabolical Diana?—but Will only shrugged. "Holden. Sounds vaguely familiar."

JB whistled low under his breath. "She's a real looker."

"Yeah. A looker who played me like a fiddle. Told me I was the nicest, funniest fella she'd met in the joint. Said she was lonely. Next thing you know we're in the closet with our pants down."

"They didn't axe you for that?" JB asked. "Man, I'm in the wrong line of work."

"State job. They just move you along to another one. You've practically got to kill somebody to get fired." A rash crept up Hank's neck. He laid his head in his hands. "Bad choice of words," he mumbled.

"Where were you early Tuesday morning? Between 4 and 6 a.m.?"

"I didn't kill Laura either, if that's what you're asking."

Will raised his eyebrows expectantly, his question unanswered.

"I was dead asleep. Probably still hungover."

"Anyone who can vouch for that?"

Hank sighed. "Not unless my pillow can talk."

"I guess that means you're single. But they call you Handsy. What inmate did you say started that?"

"I *didn't* say. God, I hate that guy. If I was gonna kill anybody…" Will sat, stone-faced, as Hank's words trailed off. Olivia's voice's nagging in his head. *He's being set up.* "Drake Devere is always stirring up trouble. You know what really gets me? The guy offed five women, right? And he's got all these ladies at Crescent Bay championing him."

"What do you mean?" Will asked.

"Well, Bonnie for starters. She helped him publish that novel. Olivia Rockwell, the chief psych. She's always telling me to cut him some slack when he shows up without a ducat, demanding a therapy session. Leah, Shauna, Dawn... all the gals who work over in the MHU. It's like he's a fucking rock star."

Will could relate to Hank's clenched fists. To the set of his jaw. To the palpable sense of unfairness emanating from his pores. Drake had gotten off easy pleading to a life-without-parole sentence. He should've been at San Quentin on death row, waiting for his one-way ticket to hell. Instead, he'd spent the last few years writing books about murder and telling Olivia his problems.

"You ever think about doing anything to him?" JB asked. "Getting even, so to speak."

"Every goddamn day. But the last time, the warden really laid into me. Made it clear Devere is not to be messed with. Unless he's the one doing the messing."

"Did he give you a reason?" Will asked.

"Some bullshit about Devere being a celebrity now. We don't want him blabbing to the media about harassment. That kind of thing."

Will raised his eyebrows at JB before he took a breath and continued. "You have any tattoos?"

"None I want to tell you about."

"Gang stuff?"

"Hell, no. Do I look like a gang member?"

"Then what is it?"

Hank stood up and loosened his belt, dropped his pants before Will could stop him.

"Easy there," JB said. "Keep all your bits covered."

He stretched the waistband of his boxers down to reveal MOM in a heart, smack-dab on the center of his right butt cheek. "Anything else you'd like to see?"

"Must've been three sheets to the wind that night," JB muttered. "I love my mom too, but jeez."

Will took a breath, tried to restore some decorum. "Tell us again what happened after you left the theater."

"I remember it was raining, so I hightailed it outta there. That must've been when you saw me on camera. I got in my truck and drove home."

"No stops?"

"Not a one."

"Anybody who can vouch for your whereabouts that night?"

"There were a few folks down at the Hickory Pit that might remember me being there. The Murdock twins stuck around till closing. Emily Rockwell. Shauna Ambrose."

"Rockwell, you said?" JB repeated, with a pointed glance at Will.

"Yeah. Her sister, Olivia, is the one I mentioned. Drake's shrink. She's a real ballbuster. A couple of the COs from the MHU were there too. But after I left I didn't see anyone."

"Except Bonnie?" Will asked.

"Right. *Bonnie.* Guess you can't talk to her, huh?"

JB hopped up, mouthed *starving* to Will. Then he turned to Hank, unmoved. "If we could talk to the dead, Sergeant Wickersham, we'd be the best damn detectives this side of Eureka."

JB reached for the trash can and spit out a wad of chewed granola bar. His upper lip curled back in disgust, he studied the wrapper and Will with suspicion. "Chocolate chip cookie, my ass. Don't you have any real food?"

"I've got a bag of almonds."

"Salted or unsalted?"

"Un."

"Might as well eat my notes." He flung the small pad of paper on his desk. "Can you believe that guy? Gettin' it on with Diabolical Diana. I mean, she's hot. But not *that* hot. Not overlook-the-dismemberment hot."

A quick Google search produced a mug shot and a myriad of articles about the woman who'd stabbed and dismembered her three children, burying their remains in the backyard, because they'd gotten on her boyfriend's last nerve.

"Do you believe him about that night?"

JB shrugged. "Seems like your run-of-the-mill creep with a mommy tattoo on his ass, but I say we check out his story."

"What about the warden?"

"What about him?" JB asked, hiding the beginnings of a smartass grin with a nibble on the Health-Zone Chocolate Chip Dream.

"His name keeps coming up."

"Sure does, City Boy. But I thought you ripped that one to shreds, so to speak."

Will pointed at the half-eaten bar in JB's hand. "And I thought you'd rather eat your notes. Guess we're allowed to change our minds."

"You gonna tell Doctor Rockwell that? 'Cause I can bet ya this Puke-Zone Chocolate Shit Dream tastes a helluva lot better than humble pie."

Lieutenant Wheeler cleared his throat from across the room and walked toward them, carrying a red Santa hat in one hand and the UBO in another. "How are you lovebirds gettin' along?"

Mouth full, JB chuckled. "I'm not his type. He prefers—"

"Fine," Will said.

The lieutenant laid the evidence bag on Will's desk, the wheelchair footrest inside. "I heard back from Forensics on your, uh—what'd ya call it, JB?"

"UBO."

"That's right. Your UBO. Anyway, Forensics tracked down that serial number. It's an old model Golden Driver. Sold and distributed to healthcare facilities all over the US in the late nineties, including in our very own Fog Harbor."

"Do we know where?" Will asked.

"Sure do. Fog Harbor General, Willow Wood Psychiatric Hospital – but it's been closed for years now – Sundown Nursing Home, and good ole Crescent Bay State Prison."

Will examined the footrest through the heavy plastic. "Looks pretty worn. Maybe bought secondhand."

Lieutenant Wheeler nodded. "Hey, before I forget…" He opened the red hat and held it out to them. "Secret Santa for the staff party on Monday. Pick a name."

JB stuck his hand in first and ogled his selection. "You think it would be poor form to get the chief a vibrator?"

CHAPTER TWENTY-FOUR

The sight of Emily's curls bobbing toward her office, the consternation on her face, quieted Olivia's nerves in a way she couldn't explain. Even big sisters needed soothing sometimes. Even big sisters like Olivia.

"I'm sorry about last night. And about Dad," Emily said, before she'd gotten both feet inside the door. Olivia surrendered to the waiting arms of her sister, inhaling the smell of mint tooth polish. "Why didn't you come find me? Are you okay?"

"I'm fine." Olivia let go first. She left the dad bit alone. Too many listening ears around here. "I didn't want to bother you. I'm sure whatever you heard sounded a lot worse than it really was."

"They're calling it a riot."

Olivia sighed. "*Exactly.*"

"Your face is all red and puffy. Morrie was right, you did get pepper-sprayed."

"Wouldn't be the first time." Olivia laughed it off to ease her worry. She'd warned her sister before about talking to Morrie. Em never understood the fine line between friendly chitchat and overfamiliarity. "Probably won't be the last. What did Morrie say?"

"He said you rescued him like a knight in shining armor."

"More like a shrink in a sweater set."

Emily's eyes danced, alight with mischief. "You know what else he said?"

Olivia groaned and slumped back into her chair. She had no doubt it had to do with Deck. The singsong in Em's voice reminded her of high school—*Olivia and Erik sittin' in a tree*—confirmed it.

"He told me some detective came and saved you, practically carried you out on his shoulders. It wouldn't happen to be the same detective who asked you out to the Hickory Pit last night, would it?"

"First of all, nobody got carried. And second, he didn't ask me out. It was a work thing. Trust me, I'm not his type. And he's certainly not mine."

"So you've thought about it then?"

Olivia busied herself rearranging perfectly stacked piles of patient notes on her desk and replaying the conversation she'd had with JB after Deck left in a huff. *You know somethin' funny*, he'd said. *I met my first wife in fifth grade science class. Couldn't stop pullin' on her braids, and she couldn't stop kickin' my shins. We hated each other somethin' awful till I hauled off and kissed her. Think about it.*

"No. I have not thought about it. Not for one second."

"Mm-hm." Emily stepped around the desk, leaning over her to Olivia's keyboard. "What does he look like, anyway? This *Will Decker*. Is he on Facebook?"

Olivia grabbed the keyboard, holding it just out of Emily's reach, as Leah cracked the door to the office, already laughing.

"He looks like a detective," Olivia said.

Leah grinned at Emily. "Yeah. A ruggedly handsome one."

"I knew it!" Em celebrated Olivia's utter humiliation in the tradition of little sisters everywhere, with a ceremonious high five to Leah. "He's gotten under your skin."

"You two are…"

"Absolutely right?" Emily suggested. "Brilliant? Spot on?"

Then, Leah chimed in. "One thousand percent accurate?"

"*Impossible*. I was going to say impossible."

*

Deck did not have a Facebook page. Olivia confirmed it for herself after she'd ousted Emily and Leah and holed up in her office, waiting for the effects of her mid-morning pepper spray to subside.

She studied the candid photo accompanying the *San Francisco Post* article she'd already read, captured as Detective William Decker left the courthouse after delivering damning testimony in the trial of his brother, Benjamin. *Decker Delivers a Blow to Brother in Blue.* He'd shielded his face from the camera with one hand but they'd caught him from the other side. His face, so cleanly shaven she could see the clench of his jaw. His eyes, focused straight ahead, invisible to her. But she imagined them anyway. She zoomed in closer, leaning in toward the screen.

A knock at the door startled her, and she snapped back in her seat like she'd been burned. She closed the browser with a hurried click and motioned Shauna inside.

"I need to talk to you about something," Shauna said, her eyes already welling with tears. "I messed up."

"Is this about Hank? About last night?"

"No. It's June. I got in trouble today, and I thought maybe you could talk to her about it. She told me I might be fired."

Olivia slid a half-empty box of tissues across the desk. When she'd first accepted the job as chief, she'd been surprised how quickly they disappeared. In a place where tears meant weakness and weakness meant danger, men still cried in her office almost every day. Sometimes against their will. Fighting it and losing, they'd try anyway.

Shauna bit her trembling lip and dabbed at her eyes. "For overfamiliarity."

"Why? What happened?"

"I posted a picture online a couple of weeks ago."

"What sort of picture?"

"Me and this guy."

"What guy?" Olivia wondered how this girl could lead a group of twenty-five inmates toward *Accountability and Action*—the Changes motto—when getting her to talk felt a lot like Em's work pulling teeth. No wonder June, her supervisor for the Changes group, had laid into her.

"An inmate." Shauna sniffled, looked down. "Drake Devere."

Stunned, Olivia let the silence do its work.

"He told me Heather Hoffman planned to interview him for the *Gazette* and asked if we could take a photo together underneath the Changes banner. To show her how hard he'd been working on himself in the group. He wanted me to post it online and tag a bunch of book bloggers and talk show hosts. I didn't think it was a big deal."

"How did you take the photo?" Olivia asked. Funny how fast the churning in her stomach returned. As dependable as the tides.

"With a phone."

"A cell phone?"

Shauna nodded, as her voice squeaked, "His."

"So Drake had a cell phone? You know that's illegal, right?" Another hysterical nod. "Do you know how he got it?"

"Of course not! June asked me the same thing. Like I'd smuggled it in here. I didn't really think much of it at the time. I figured maybe he'd gotten permission. As part of his writing and all. You must think I'm stupid, too. That's what June thinks. Stupid little girl fresh out of college."

"You're not stupid. Just naive. Remember, Drake is a seasoned criminal. He's sophisticated. He knows what he's doing. When I first started here, I made mistakes too. Still do."

"You do?" Shauna brightened. "Like what?"

"Like getting a face full of pepper spray this morning, for one thing. Believing things I shouldn't have. Some of these guys could sell ice to an Eskimo. Now, I trust but verify."

Shauna laughed. A delicate titter, more breath than sound. Breakable. "Drake did tell me one thing, though, that I didn't tell June. I feel bad getting him in trouble."

"*Don't.* The safety of the staff—your safety—is the most important thing. If Drake poses a threat to you or anyone—"

"No. It's nothing like that. Just something he said."

Olivia nodded, encouraging. Though really, she'd rather not know. Her brain had filled to the brim with Drake and Deck and two dead women.

"When he pulled out the phone after group, I freaked. I told him to put it away before June saw. Or worse. Warden Blevins had stopped by that day to talk to June about expanding the program, and they'd gone into the office to chat. But Drake acted like it was no big deal. I said, 'Aren't you afraid of getting in trouble? What if the warden catches you?' and he laughed and said, 'I'll ask him to join in the shot. A selfie with the warden. That'd be a real hoot.'"

"Did the warden see him with the phone?"

Shauna's pieces held together, stronger now. She stopped crying. "I don't think so. We snapped the pic, he emailed it to me, and then he stuck it back in his boot. The whole thing took about twenty seconds."

"How did June find out about the photo?"

"I have no idea. But during the facilitator training, she warned us she could sweep our social media at any time. Just to make sure we're maintaining confidentiality and all. She said not to come back to group until further notice."

"Okay. I'll talk to June. Maybe she'll reconsider."

Olivia patted Shauna on the shoulder as she left—*poor girl*— knowing too well some mistakes didn't come out in the wash. Further notice meant never.

*

Though the door to June's office stood open, Olivia knocked anyway. Best not to poke the bear. And June had the reputation of an old grizzly. As hardened as any lifer, she'd started at Crescent Bay the day it opened in 1989. The thirty-year service plaque hung on the wall to prove it.

"Did that little smart-mouth send you over here?" June glowered at Olivia from behind her desk. But it didn't last. She popped a handful of chocolate candies in her mouth, chewing them noisily, before she spoke again. "Do you know, she had the nerve to tell me I was overreacting? That I was jealous of her *connection* with the inmates? Her word. Not mine. I should've had that brat walked off grounds."

"May I come in?" Olivia asked, carefully. She dared not breach the threshold without permission. Deference. Deference and chocolate. The tricks to turning a grizzly bear to a teddy.

"Kids these days. I warned her so many times. First, it was the flirty smiles she kept giving the guys during group. Then, she went out and bought Drake's book. Asked him for an autograph. Validation, she called it. Hell, if that guy's ego got any more validated they'd need to add on another wing. I even caught her telling some of the guys where she lived. And this photo. *Good lord*. That was the last straw."

Olivia nodded, setting one cautious foot through the doorway, then the other. June said nothing more. She reached into the jar on her desk—the one Olivia had gifted her for her birthday a few weeks ago—and tossed back another batch of chocolates.

"How did you find out about the photo?" Olivia asked.

June held up a finger as she chewed. When she spoke, her teeth were chocolate brown. "These truffles are delicious, Doctor Rockwell. You always manage to outdo yourself."

Olivia waved her off. "Chocolate is a form of therapy, right?"

"The only kind I believe in. No offense." Never mind that June had a graduate degree in social work. Or that she'd headed up the Changes group for the last ten years. "Now, what did you want to know?"

"The photo? Did you discover it yourself?"

"As if. You know I'm a dinosaur when it comes to all that social media nonsense." She motioned Olivia inside, told her to close the door.

"It was strange how it happened," June said. "Two tips in the same day."

Olivia kept very still, knowing how easily bears spook.

"This morning, bright and early, I get a call from Maryann Murdock down at the library. She said Shauna had taken out her phone at the Hickory Pit last night to show off some photos from the Thanksgiving staff party, and she'd happened to see it. You know, not ten minutes later, Hank Wickersham calls. Says he saw the photo posted online. He seemed pissed. Jealous, if you ask me."

"What did you do?"

"I called IGI, of course. Told 'em they better search Drake's cell. I didn't know for certain but I figured the phone might be his."

"Did they?"

June plucked one more truffle from the jar and dropped it into the waiting cave of her mouth before she answered. "They told me the warden's guys already took care of it."

CHAPTER TWENTY-FIVE

In the corner of the garage, the orange tabby sat licking his front paw like he owned the place. When he spotted Will, he didn't make a break for it. He settled comfortably with all four legs tucked beneath him, staring at Will with one green eye. A cyclops.

"Don't mind me," Will said, wincing as he took a few strikes at the heavy bag. Each punch juddered his sore jaw, stung his swollen knuckles, until he finally dropped his hands to his sides, relenting. "Now what, Cy?"

The cat blinked at him, meowed. "Cy. You like that? You've got a name now."

A long-ago memory of his mother greeting him and his brothers at the door on one of her good days, stirred Will's gut. Between them, they'd carried a bag-of-bones stray dog they'd found in the park. The thin belly in Will's arms. The front legs with Ben, and Petey bringing up the mangy rear, the dog's tail whacking him in the face with sheer joy. Will had heard his mother tell their grumbling father, *It'll be good for them. Give them a little responsibility around here.* To the boys, she'd whispered, *Once you name him, he's yours. Remember that.*

Will shook his head, wishing he could expel the sound of her voice. But his music couldn't drown it, not even when he cranked the old stereo past the red line. After all these years, his mother's leaving still burned inside him. A tiny flicker now, but no less hot, no less suffocating.

The garage closed in around him. Even Cy seemed to sense it, pricking his ears as Will paced the cement floor. All wound up with nowhere to go.

Will had to get out.

He thrust open the garage door, just enough to slip beneath it, and started running. The past nipped at his heels like Max, the dog that, once named, had outlasted his mother and stuck around another seven years. Virginia Decker had been gone—in more ways than one—by that fall.

Will headed for the trail behind the house. It wound through the redwoods and followed the Earl River to the sea. At least that's what the real estate agent had told him, figuring him for a bona fide nature buff. Who else hunkered down in a cabin in the middle of nowhere? Henry David Thoreau, the Unabomber, and a disgraced detective ready to step off the face of the earth.

Will set a fast pace he soon regretted. His lungs ached in the cold air, and his calves burned from sidestepping puddles as he navigated the muddy trail at twilight. He'd never been much for running. Running meant being chased. He'd had his fair share of that growing up in Bernal Heights, the middle-class neighborhood a stone's throw from the Double Rock Projects. A cop's kid, he'd had his share of fighting, too. But fighting—fifth-grade bully or garage heavy bag—felt purposeful. Not like an aimless quest to best your own time running in circles.

Still, Will had to admit it felt good to exhaust himself. To breathe in the clean scent of the salt and the redwoods. To breathe out Drake and JB along with last night's debacle at the Ricci house and the sting of pepper spray.

His legs churned faster as he thought of Olivia, her skin soft and cool beneath his fingers. He listened to the sound of the river, made stronger with a week's worth of rain. The water churned and roiled over the rocks, matching his mood. Maybe running wasn't so bad after all, he thought. Until the first drop of rain landed on his forehead like a wet kiss from the universe.

CHAPTER TWENTY-SIX

Rain had a way of lingering around Fog Harbor in December like an annoying party guest. Always popping up at the least convenient time. Like when Olivia realized she'd forgotten her umbrella under her desk.

With no intention of going back inside, she stood at the prison entrance, drops battering the metal awning above her, and looked out at her car. Emily, already seated safely inside with the engine running. Dry and warm and waiting for her.

Behind her, Olivia heard the warden's voice, exchanging pleasantries with the guards. As silly as it sounded, she wondered if he'd purposefully timed his exit. If he'd followed her. She felt five years old again, imagining him as a monster in her bedroom. The sort that disappeared in the light and came alive in the dark, hunting for her feet if she didn't keep them safely covered.

Olivia had never minded the rain much, but now it seemed menacing. A thinly veiled cover for evil. She didn't turn around. Instead, she made a break for the car, splashing through the parking lot, and diving inside.

As she brushed the rain from her clothing, Olivia expected a wisecrack from Emily. The water pooled on her seat, dripped onto the console. But Em stayed quiet even as Olivia put the car in drive and pulled away, the warden small and harmless as a mouse in her rearview.

When Olivia finally looked over at Emily, her sister's face tightened with worry.

"Did you hear about Shauna?" she asked. "That old biddy, June, fired her. Over a stupid picture."

Olivia nodded. "A picture with an inmate. A high-profile inmate at that. Taken on a cell phone he wasn't supposed to have."

"It figures you would take June's side."

"I'm not taking sides. I feel bad for Shauna, but she broke the rules, Em."

"Dad always said the worst crimes are committed by people who only know how to follow the rules. By blind obedience. The ones who break the rules are artists, like me."

Olivia groaned, feeling the kick of those words like a punch to the stomach. "Are we really having this argument now, too? Dad is a criminal. Of course he would say that. And since when are you writing him a support letter?"

"Since he asked me to. I was going to tell you eventually. He's really trying now. He debriefed from the gang."

"Yeah. Now that he's up for parole. Convenient timing, if you ask me."

Emily sighed and rested her head against the rain-streaked window. She ran her finger on the foggy glass, spelling out her name. Finally, as they neared the turn for home, they both spoke at once.

"I know you want to give him a chance—"

"I want to give him a chance—"

"But," Olivia continued, "just be careful. You never lived with him. You don't really know what he's like."

"Because you never tell me. You don't talk about him. Ever."

Olivia shrugged. She planned to keep it that way.

CHAPTER TWENTY-SEVEN

"Idiot."

Directed at himself, Will repeated the insult out loud as he ran toward the faint glow of a light up ahead. It felt like a fight now, the rain a worthy opponent, wearing him down with its single-mindedness, its sheer tenacity. The rain reminded him of his father—relentless—which only made him run faster, until a bolt of lightning struck in the distance and he nearly slid off the trail in the mud.

The last time they'd spoken, inside the courthouse, on the day Will testified, his father wouldn't let up, cornering him in the bathroom and pelting him with the kind of words that leave marks on your soul. *Traitor. Snitch. Backstabber. You're not a Decker anymore.*

The memory lashed at him like the rain, zipped through him like the lightning, but he kept moving, leaving the trail and scrambling up the hill, toward the promise of shelter.

As the light came closer into view, so did its source. A two-story house with a picket fence and a wraparound porch, a lantern-style lamp affixed to the wall near the back door. Will imagined the place belonged to a kindly old woman who would take him in and offer him a towel and a steaming cup of coffee.

He sloshed through the backyard and onto the front porch, where he tripped over a pair of muddy running shoes. He tried to catch his fall with a quick grab onto the railing. Instead, he landed on his ass and came away with a fistful of holiday garland.

Breathing raggedly, he hauled himself to his feet and stood under the cover of the roof. In the window, he barely recognized himself. His hair plastered to his forehead, his shirt soaked through and clinging to his chest.

He rang the bell.

As he waited, already shivering, another lightning flash illuminated the sky. This storm seemed different. Angrier. Vengeful. Will thought of the fritzing cameras at Crescent Bay. Of C Block and cell 22. He wondered if Drake had been returned there after the riot.

He rang the bell again, more desperate this time, and cupped his hands around his eyes to peer inside the window to the pitch-black entryway.

"Idiot," he said again, preparing himself to leave the safety of the porch. To walk down to the main road. Maybe he could find a ride.

But then, a name caught his eye. Etched on the mailbox hung near the doorway and written in fancy cursive: ROCKWELL. Will cursed under his breath, then again out loud, when a pair of headlights fixed him in place by the front door.

CHAPTER TWENTY-EIGHT

Emily grabbed for her and Olivia shrieked at the unexpected sight of a man on her porch, dripping wet and staring wide-eyed into the headlights like a wild animal. Slowly she took him in.

Chestnut hair, dark eyes to match.

White T-shirt, transparent with rain, clinging. Muscles beneath like whipcord. Taut and lean and exposed.

Shorts, waterlogged. Shoes, caked with dirt.

He raised a tentative hand and waved. Then, crossed his arms over his chest, quivering in the cold.

"Deck?" Olivia whispered. "What the…"

She cut the engine, leaving him in darkness, and sat there, bewildered, as the rain beat on.

"That's your detective? He looks…"

Lost. Confused. Wet.

"Sexy," Em teased.

Okay, that too.

Olivia flung open the door and ran headlong into the downpour. Only ten or so steps to the porch but she made it in five, laughing as Emily struggled to open her umbrella.

When she turned to Deck, he shrugged and gave her a sheepish smile. His lips glistened with rainwater. She wished JB had never mentioned them. Because she couldn't get the thought out of her mind.

"You're probably wondering what I'm doing on your front porch."

"Did you run here?" she asked. Then, before he could answer, "Do you live close by?"

Emily sucked in a breath as she hauled herself up the stairs and collapsed into the chair near the door. "I think what Olivia means to say is, *Come in, Detective*. She'll get you all warmed up. I mean, dried off." She extended her hand, grinning. "I'm Emily, by the way. The little sister."

Olivia felt relieved when Deck kicked off his shoes and followed Emily inside. With his back to her, he couldn't see her blush.

"So, yes and no. To answer your questions."

Olivia blinked at Deck as he ran a towel through his hair, rubbing it dry. A small puddle had formed on the kitchen floor beneath him.

"Yes, I did run here. And no, it wasn't that close. I'm renting one of the old cabins on Wolver Hollow Road, and I got caught in the rain. I saw your porch light. Well, I didn't realize it was *your* porch light—yours and Emily's—but..."

Deck wrung out the bottom of his T-shirt with the towel, revealing a sliver of skin. Then, he tossed the towel on the puddle, stood atop it in his socks, and dried his legs. Olivia peered over his shoulder into the living room, but Em had vanished. Probably eavesdropping, taking notes to torture her with later.

"We should get those clothes off you." Her brain, one critical step behind her mouth. "That came out wrong."

"I figured." Deck laughed, and so did Olivia. She felt certain she heard Em giggling behind her bedroom door. She would never, *ever* live this down.

"What I meant was, I think I can find something for you to change into. Then I'll toss those in the dryer, if you'd like."

Deck hesitated, giving her a moment to watch a lingering drop of rainwater snake a trail down his neck toward the collar of his T-shirt and disappear beneath the thin fabric.

"I don't want to intrude," he said, finally. "Especially after this morning."

"After you ripped my notes, you mean?"

"I was going to say, 'made an ass of myself.' But yes. That."

Olivia smirked, settling into the easy back-and-forth. Banter, she could handle. Deck, dripping wet, clothes plastered to his hard-earned body, not so much. "Well, in that case, I like your description better. Let's stick with that."

"Fine by me. As long as the record reflects I rescued you from death by pepper spray first."

"Fair enough. Though I'm certain I would've managed alright. I'm no damsel in distress."

"And I'm no Prince Charming."

"You can say that again."

Olivia spun away, victorious, to retrieve another towel from the stack on the table. Emily had dropped them there before her convenient departure. "Prince Charming would never leave home without—"

The sight of Deck's glistening bare chest, when she turned back toward him, stopped her from finishing the rest. He held the soaked remains of his T-shirt out to her, grinning shamelessly.

"You were saying?"

Groaning, she shoved the towel at him and pushed past into the living room where she could breathe again. She felt his eyes on her but she didn't dare turn around. Instead, she pointed off the hallway to the first open door.

"You can change in there, Prince Smart Ass. Just give me a minute to find something befitting of your royal blood."

CHAPTER TWENTY-NINE

Will balled his wet clothes in a towel and searched out the dusty dresser mirror tucked among boxes in the corner of the room. The dresser itself had been shoved into the opposite corner, a sunk-in, yellowed mattress and bedframe leaning against it. The whole room was cobwebbed with neglect. The antithesis of buttoned-up, ducks-in-a-row Dr. Smarty Pants.

Through the thick film of dust, Will catalogued his new look with the exact amount of humiliation he figured Olivia had intended. Possibly, she'd even outdone herself.

One Hickory Pit T-shirt, size medium. The slogan printed beneath the logo: *I Love Pig Butts and I Cannot Lie*, stretched to its limits across his chest.

One pair of sweatpants. STANFORD emblazoned across his backside.

And the pièce de résistance, Christmas socks. With two fuzzy poms stitched to the back of each that tapped at his heels as he walked. He wondered if she'd knitted them herself.

Will stripped the socks from his feet and tossed them onto the floor. He had to draw the line somewhere.

As he ran the last dry towel through his hair once more, he studied the pictures stacked on top of the box nearest him. He recognized a teenage version of Olivia right away, smack-dab in the center between Emily and an older woman he'd guessed to be their mother. They all shared the same eyes, a cool green but fiery all the same.

As he lifted the photograph, the frame's ancient backing came loose, and another photo slipped from within it. Will snuck a glance at the closed door, listened for the sound of voices, before he took it in his hand and flipped it over.

Instantly, it struck him as familiar, though it took a moment to figure out why. Teen Olivia was there, with her kid sister under one arm. Both of them caught mid-laugh. A diesel truck of a man stood beside them, clad in a denim blue jumpsuit, prison-issued. Broad shoulders, arms like boa constrictors, and a beard concealing the lower half of his face. Only his eyes gave away his smile. Behind the three of them, the very same mural—the landscape of Fog Harbor—Will had spotted today when he'd peeked into Crescent Bay's visiting room.

Something else caught Will's attention, pricking his cop whiskers. He squinted down at the photo. *Was that…?*

With a sense of urgency, he searched the room for a lamp, a flashlight, anything. Only one dim bulb remained in the light fixture above, and his eyes had forty years on them now.

"Are you okay in there, Your Highness?" Olivia's voice came from right outside the door.

"Just putting the finishing touches on my outfit." He hoped she couldn't hear his nerves, which seemed to crackle like live wires as he spoke, or his rustling to plug in the desk lamp he'd found toppled on the dresser. "You really know my style."

After waiting a beat for her laughter to subside, he turned the switch and held the photo beneath the light, studying the man's right bicep. He couldn't say for certain, and yet he knew.

That photo was taken at Crescent Bay State Prison.

That man was Olivia's father.

That tattoo belonged to the Oaktown Boys.

"Does this T-shirt make me look fat?" Will emerged from the bedroom with the best fake smile he could manage. He avoided

Olivia's eyes. He knew one of her secrets now. It sat like a hot stone in the pit of his stomach, and he had no clue what to do with it.

Emily burst into uncontrollable laughter. She sank down into the sofa and hid her tearing face behind a snowman throw pillow.

"It's certainly form-fitting." Olivia smirked as she exchanged the bundle of wet clothes in his hands for a steaming mug of coffee. She'd changed too, into jeans and a sweater. Let her hair down. He absolutely did not stare. He reminded himself she couldn't be trusted. The daughter of an Oaktown Boy.

Emily regained her composure long enough to chime in. "Don't worry. You're just big-boned."

"Glad I could give you ladies a laugh this evening." Will found a seat in an oversized armchair, a safe distance from Olivia, and took a careful sip. Next to him, the lights of a small Christmas tree twinkled—Will could smell the fresh-cut cedar—reminding him of home. Not his cabin, of course, but the only place he'd ever considered home: the three-bedroom stucco in Bernal Heights his mother had filled with so much singing and laughing and chocolate chip cookie-making that her depression had been nothing short of a bomb. Her leaving entirely, Hiroshima. "And thanks for the clothes and showing up when you did. It would've been a long walk back home."

"I'll put these in the dryer." Olivia's voice carried, as she disappeared down the hallway. "They should be dry in a few minutes, and I'll give you a ride back home."

"Thank you," Will said again.

"Thank *you*," Emily blurted, once she'd gone. "It's never this exciting around here."

Will thought of scrappy Olivia, with her bold green eyes and her dimple and sexy-as-hell blue jeans. Her doctorate degree, always meeting him toe to toe. Her secret too. "Somehow I doubt that."

"Why do you think I spend most nights at the Hickory Pit?"

"You like pig butts and you cannot—"

"Ha. Ha. Ha. Very funny, Detective."

Will returned her sly grin, but the photo he'd found, the mention of the Hickory Pit, had tripped a switch. Full detective mode. "Hey, since you mentioned the Hickory Pit, did you see Hank Wickersham there the night Bonnie McMillan went missing?"

Emily deflated. "Uh, is this like, on the record or something?"

"Is what on the record?" Olivia appeared in the doorway, eyes on Will, and he wondered if she'd been listening. He quelled the urge to spill everything. To let her help him sort it out.

"I'm just curious what Wickersham is like. He came by the station today and mentioned seeing Emily at the Hickory Pit. I thought she might be able to tell me more about him."

Olivia's face darkened, the ghost of unease pinching her forehead, drawing her mouth into a hard line.

"Do you think he hurt Bonnie and Laura?" Emily asked.

"We're just covering all the bases. Right now, to be honest, there's a few things we know. And a lot more we don't know."

"I thought you already had your prime suspect," Olivia said. "Did someone change your mind?"

"Nobody changes my mind. I go where the evidence takes me. That's all."

Emily cleared her throat, making eyes at both of them. "Hank seems harmless, but I don't know him that well. Maryann and Melody live on the same street as him though, and they're always at the Pit. Shauna too. Hank has a crush on her, I think. They'd be able to tell you more than I can. But go easy on Shauna. She just got fired."

"And the evidence took you to an inmate at a maximum security prison?" Single-minded as a bulldog with a bone.

"It did."

"Are you sure it was the evidence, not something more personal? Sometimes, our history with an individual prevents us from seeing things as they really are. In my professional opinion."

Will thought of the man in the photo. The tattoo. The inmate number stamped on the jumpsuit he'd committed to memory. "Well, Doctor, I can assure you my eyesight is twenty-twenty."

Emily stood and smacked Olivia with a throw pillow, laughing as she retreated down the hallway. "Jeez, you two. Get a room."

Will sat in the passenger seat of Olivia's BMW, a holdover from her big-city days, no doubt, while she drove them toward the cabin on Wolver Hollow. Her fancy car made about as much sense in Fog Harbor as she did.

His T-shirt felt warm from the dryer, shorts too. With the rain drumming steadily against the windshield, Olivia had cranked the defroster to full blast. Maybe that's why his armpits dampened with sweat, as he watched her handle the steering wheel with one hand, massaging the back of her neck with the other. At least his feet were cool, shoved bare into his wet sneakers.

C'mon, Deck. She's a shrink not a double agent. It's just small talk. You can do it.

"Your sister seems nice."

"Em? She's a total brat. But she's twenty-five and stuck here with me. I guess she's allowed to be. After our mom got sick, she floundered a little. Dropped out of Oregon State, became a dental hygienist, took a job at Crescent Bay. She cleans inmates' teeth all day, every day."

"Yikes. That might be my new number one worst job ever."

Olivia laughed, and he soaked it in, even as he doubted it. Finally, he'd done something right. "What was your old number one?"

"There's been a few. I'm always revising the list. Road stop bathroom cleaner, cat food taste tester. Cop with a target on his back."

Olivia went quiet.

He realized it had been too long since he'd talked to anyone about it. The thing that hung around his neck. Noose or badge of honor, he never could decide. "How about the armpit sniffers? They test deodorant."

She wrinkled her nose at him. "Or the criminal profiler who cost the city of Oakland a few million bucks."

"Seriously?"

"As a heart attack. Which, by the way, is exactly what happened to the guy the OPD falsely accused based on my profile. He needed a triple bypass."

"So, that's why you don't do it anymore? Because the cops got it wrong?"

He recognized a familiar weight in the shrug of her shoulders. "Profiling is no more than an educated guess. It can't take the place of good police work."

"I get it now. You agreed to help me because you know what a damn good cop I am."

"Don't flatter yourself." The corner of her mouth twisted upward. "I agreed to help you because you're so far off base you can't even see home plate anymore."

"Alright, alright. But do you really think Warden Blevins is behind this? The guy is a walking toothpick."

"That's the advantage of a garrote though, isn't it? You don't need to be strong enough to overpower your victim. Just crafty enough to get the thing around the neck. I think both women knew who attacked them. Trusted him. Or her. Or them."

Will mulled it over as he directed her past the vacant cabin nearest his own. Its screened porch lit with a single naked bulb that flickered off and on like a blinking eye. "You keep saying that. *Him or her or them.*"

"The first rule of profiling. Don't make assumptions."

"I wouldn't dream of it." But he was making assumptions. Always thinking the worst and hating himself for it. What if Olivia had a dog in this fight? What if she'd intentionally steered him from Drake to Blevins? The Oaktown Boys wouldn't mind getting the warden out of the way.

Crazy, Deck. Look at her.

Olivia rolled her eyes and shook her head at him. He saw how the moonlight caught the raindrops on the window behind her, making it into a starry sky and her into Cassiopeia.

Shit. Don't look at her.

Olivia turned into the driveway, oblivious to Will's silent warring, and pulled alongside his truck. He searched for a reason not to get out.

"Also, don't rule out Wickersham," she said, putting the car in park. He wondered if she felt it too. The rain, a curtain around them. The fine wire stretched between, crackling. "I don't know what you've got on him, but he has issues with women *and* Drake. I caught him at the lighthouse with Shauna and my sister. Drunk and about to go skinny-dipping."

He matched her frown with his own, *skinny-dipping* echoing in his head longer than it should have. "Really? Your sister? She seems smarter than that."

"When she wants to be. But hanging out with Shauna doesn't help. She's the kind of girl who'll get herself walked off prison grounds one day for something. And Hank is the kind of guy to help her do it."

"Alright. I won't rule him out." And he hadn't. No matter what JB thought.

Olivia lowered her head, fidgeted with her hands. "Or Drake," she added, reluctantly. "Maryann told me he'd researched homemade weapons, and he had a close relationship with both victims."

"But I thought you said he didn't fit the profile. The refractory period, the UCLA study. Remember?" He raised his eyebrows, teasing her.

"Profiling isn't science. It's like matchmaking. You get a feel for people. What they're like, how they'll act in certain situations."

He nodded at her, building up his courage. "If I tell you something…"

"My lips are sealed." He couldn't stop his gaze from going there. Rosy and kissable. He felt guilty for pushing but he needed to know. "You already know how ethical I am."

"These murders could be gang-related."

In the silence, he heard her swallow. He recognized the sound. The effort to keep the past down as far as she could stuff it. "A prison gang?"

"Oaktown Boys. Their symbol has turned up a few times. First, in Bonnie's car. Then, at James' house. Now, at Laura's. One of their guys was there last night. That's how I got this." He touched the bruise on his jaw carefully. As carefully as he studied her eyes. Doing both ached in exactly the same way. A dull throb behind his breastbone.

She looked away, at her hands in her lap. Barely smiled. "And here I was thinking JB hit you."

With the wipers off, Will could just make out the door to the cabin. A beam of light glowed from the hole in the garage siding. He wished he hadn't said anything. Had never seen that photo at all. Had simply enjoyed the ride with a beautiful woman.

"Do you want to come in?" He blurted it out, practically spit it. For no reason he could explain. It sat there between them. A raw hunk of his heart. Disgusting.

"I can't."

He reached for the handle, ready for the assault of the wind and rain in his face. To put him out of his misery. Or rather, smack-dab into the middle of it. He hoped Cy had stuck around at least. He needed a warm body to talk to, and a one-eyed cat would do just fine.

Her fingertips, ice-cold on his forearm, started a small fire inside him.

"Wait."

CHAPTER THIRTY

Olivia stared at the hand on Deck's arm. Her hand, she realized. His skin, fever-hot beneath it. But how did it get there? Why was it *still* there?

"The Oaktown Boys…" She returned the offending hand to her lap. Told it to stay put.

"You know them, right?"

"Well, I work in a prison. So, yes. I had the mandatory gang training when I took the job. The Oaktown Boys are a white supremacist motorcycle gang, primarily in Northern California. Their symbol is the oak tree, a warped version of the one used to represent the city of Oakland. Most of them have tattoos. Like the old guy in the wheelchair I tried to help today. Morrie Mulvaney. He's former Oaktown."

Deck just nodded at her, probably calculating the ridiculous number of words she'd just spoken without taking a single breath. Still, she kept going. Better to give him a little something, the way she did with her curious patients.

"Plus, I grew up in San Francisco. In the Double Rock."

"Double Rock, huh? I'm from Bernal Heights."

Olivia wondered if it was a detective thing—the way he seemed to look into her, not at her—or a Will Decker thing. Either way, she needed it to stop. Because she preferred her past stay right where she'd put it. In a dark, dank hole—no sunlight, no air—where she hoped it would wither and die.

"You know the Double Rock, then. I can't believe the place is still standing. It's not exactly something I'm proud of."

"Why?" Deck's face twisted in genuine confusion. "Look at you now. My mom always said it's not where you start out but where you end up."

"I suppose. But I don't go around telling people, especially at the prison. If my patients knew, they'd think we have something in common." Which they did, of course. The same twisted roots. Thick as redwoods, persistent as weeds she'd spent a lifetime trying to chop back.

Deck nodded again. Like a therapist would. The *keep talking* nod. The oldest trick in the book. She wasn't about to fall victim to her own techniques.

"Was your dad around?" he asked. "As a kid, I mean."

"Here and there." She tried not to squirm. But the car felt too small. Deck's presence, too large. Her secrets, too easily uncovered. "You know, Drake mentioned the Oaktown Boys. About seeing something they were involved in. He's had a beef with them for a while, with this guy Riggs."

"Do you think they could be involved? In your professional opinion." Her words parroted back to her made her blush. Especially now. When she was being anything but professional. Lying by omission. To a detective. To the first man she'd ever wanted to tell the truth to—all of it.

"From what I know of the Oaktown Boys, they hold a grudge, and they don't think twice about collateral damage, so it's certainly a possibility."

Another flash of lightning whipped across the sky, and she shuddered. She didn't believe in signs, only desperate people needing to see them. To make meaning in a world where fathers did the unspeakable. Where mothers drank away their sorrows. Where love seemed a cruel joke. Still, as the sky lit an eerie yellow, she wondered.

"They're extremely dangerous," she said. "Not that you don't already know that, but…"

After a pause that seemed to extend for an eternity, he turned to her, grinning. "Are you worried about me, Doctor?"

"JB, actually. It would be a shame if he had to start over with a new partner at his age."

"He'd probably prefer it. Speaking of the old codger, did he say anything about me after I left this morning?"

She leaned in until the warmth radiated off his skin onto her own. He smelled like rain and sweat and dryer sheets. "Wouldn't you like to know?"

Olivia sped home down the rain-slicked road, cutting a path through the fog, a sick dread twisting her gut. As she'd watched Deck pause and wave from his porch, it had come to her. And now that awful thought made her foot heavy with urgency.

She zipped past the SPEED LIMIT 45 sign, going well over sixty. The patrol car's dark nose perfectly camouflaged by the forest, the fog. The inky night.

When she saw it, she cursed, tapped the brakes.

Too late.

It swung out behind her, lights flashing. Siren like a scream.

No choice but to pull to the side of the road. Her tires sank and slipped a little in the swampy shoulder. She peeked up into the rearview, glanced in her side mirror. Still, she couldn't see beyond the bright lights of the patrol car. Couldn't hear above the throb of her heartbeat.

It could be him. Though she'd told Deck not to make assumptions, her imagination drew a man. Though she'd told Deck that Drake didn't fit the profile, the man had slick dark hair, like wet crow feathers. Two beady yellow eyes, like a bird of prey. A makeshift garrote—CDCR blue—ready in his hand.

Knuckles sharp against the window, and she jumped.

"What in the hell, Liv? You need to slow down."

Her mouth dry, her tongue a useless slab, she cracked the window.

"Graham?" she squeaked. "I thought you got off at two this afternoon."

"I'm doing extra duty on account of the stepped-up patrols. Keepin' an eye on folks out here. It's a good thing, too. Did you know you were doing sixty-seven in a forty-five?"

"No," she lied. "I must've been daydreaming."

"Daydreaming, huh? Alright." With a sudden laugh, he smacked the side of the car. "Only if it was about me."

She tried to smile.

"So, where you comin' from?"

"Just dropping off a friend."

Graham leaned down, shining a flashlight at her. At the empty interior.

"He's not here," she said, too slow to bite her tongue.

"*He?* Hope it's not that Decker fella. The one who snitched on his own—"

A truck sliced the wet air, spraying Graham with rain from the pavement. Not a single strand of his hair moved. Deck had been right about that. She remembered what it felt like under her fingers. Stiff and sticky.

He raised his middle finger at the truck's taillights. "Asshole."

"Are you going to write me a ticket or not?"

"That depends."

Olivia bristled. "On what exactly?"

"What are you gonna do for me?" He paused, looked at her, his eyes narrow slits. "I'm just kidding. Of course I won't write you a ticket. I know you said you need some space, and I respect that. But we're still friends, right?"

She nodded begrudgingly, considering the alternative. She certainly didn't need Graham Bauer as an enemy.

"Maybe friends who sleep over sometimes?"

"Don't push it. And for the record, we only did that once."

"Well, *for the record*, we didn't really sleep." He laughed like he'd just delivered the punchline to the best joke he'd ever heard. And she asked herself again how she'd ended up in bed with him. Tequila. Lots of tequila. That, and loneliness. Though she kept it well hidden, it festered like a blister on her heart.

"Just be careful, alright? We've got a serial killer on the loose." He paused, flashed her a brazen grin. "I've always wanted to say that."

"Congratulations, Graham. Your mother must be so proud."

"Thank—" The squeak of her window, then sweet silence.

"So?" Em perked up, as the door shut behind her. "What happened with your detective?" But Olivia didn't have time. She didn't bother to take off her shoes or strip out of her raincoat. She went straight for it. Stopped cold when she got there, suddenly afraid to go in.

Her mother's bedroom had been long neglected. She had insisted on packing it up alone, intent on having it all hauled away to the dump. But when the time came to get rid of her mother's belongings, she'd gotten stuck, unable to cut the last cord that tethered her to the past. So, it had stayed exactly as Olivia had left it, accumulating dust and accommodating spiders.

She stepped inside, shivering. The room at least five degrees colder than the rest of the house. A flick of the light, and she scanned the room. Past the discarded Christmas socks to the row of boxes on the left.

"What're you doing?" Emily asked from the doorway.

"He knows about Dad."

"Who?"

"Deck. Uh, Detective Decker."

"So?"

Olivia groaned in frustration, grabbing for the framed photo set atop the nearest box, a stack of loose photos beneath it. "Did you take these out?"

Emily grimaced. "Maybe."

"When?"

"A few months ago, when Dad wrote. I was feeling nostalgic."

The backing of the frame felt loose beneath her fingers, and the picture she'd hidden inside it slipped right out. The shot caller for the Oaktown Boys—otherwise known as Dad—mocked her with that grin, that blatant tattoo, those thick arms that had scooped her up and carried her away when she'd felt as small and terrified as a rabbit. She remembered it clear as that picture. He'd left red smears on her dress.

"Is it really that big of a deal?" Emily asked.

"Yes, it is. You wouldn't understand." She pushed past her sister and up the stairs, slamming the door behind her. Illogical, she knew. Totally irrational. But she couldn't help feeling as if she'd just been caught with a bloody knife in her hands.

CHAPTER THIRTY-ONE

Will subjected himself to an ice-cold shower first thing, watching as the water swirled down the drain. With it, the urge to grab a fistful Olivia's hair and press his mouth to hers. Because that would be a mistake. A colossal fuck-up. Keep it professional. Keep it simple. He'd learned that much from Amy. When they'd met, she'd been fresh out of the academy, a rookie cop. He'd been a hotshot first-year detective. Then, he'd turned into a pariah, and she'd exited stage left.

As Will toweled off for the second time that night, his cell rang.

"Hey, partner, what's up?"

A basketball game blared in the background. Chewing noises right in his ear. "Did you get the email from Forensics?"

"Hang on. I haven't checked." He hit the speakerphone, scrolling through his email, leaving a few drops of water on the screen. "I just got out of the shower."

"Well, it came in over an hour ago. What the hell are you doin'? A steam and a facial?"

"Bubble bath."

"Figures."

Will opened the email, subject line: TIRE TRACKS. He scanned the text as JB talked.

"Looks like they found a match in the Tire Tread Guide. It's a Michelin Road All-Terrain Truck Tire."

Will murmured his agreement, anxious to get off the phone. After the night he'd had, JB's antics were the last thing he needed.

"Aren't you gonna ask me why I'm calling?"

Will made an exasperated face at himself in the mirror. "I thought you'd already told me."

"Do you honestly think I'd call in the middle of Duke versus Carolina, with a full tub of popcorn—real butter—to tell you to check your email?"

"Why are you calling, JB?"

"Ha! I thought you'd never ask. This is good, City Boy. You might want to take a seat on the john."

"Sitting." Only because JB had already worn him out.

"I called over to the prison. Apparently, they have a fleet of work trucks they store off-site, a little ways down Pine Grove Road. Guess what kind of tires they put on those babies?"

Will headed for the garage. In one hand, he carried his laptop. In the other, the five-pound sack of Tasty Whiskers he'd picked up that afternoon from the grocery mart downtown, along with a litter box. He poured a handful of kibble into an old pie tin and watched as the smell reached Cy's nose. It twitched a few times before he opened his eye and sauntered over, giving Will a pointed look, as if to say, *it's about damn time.*

Will signed in and opened up the Fog Harbor Police database. He typed the inmate number he'd committed to memory.

As he pored over the file, the rain beat on, and his thoughts drifted to Olivia. How she'd leaned in to his space, daring him. How she'd smelled like fresh air and salt water. It seemed inevitable. Someday, he'd be stupid enough to kiss her.

NAME: MARTIN REILLY (aka Mad Dog)

ADDRESS: 164 LARKSPUR LANE, APT "E"

SAN FRANCISCO, CA

DOB: 11/5/63   AGE: 29   SEX: M   RACE: CAUCASIAN

TYPE REPORT: PRE-CONVICTION

DEFENSE ATTORNEY: PAULUS   PROSECUTOR: O'LEARY

PRESENT OFFENSES:

COUNT 1 PC 187 (MURDER), FIRST DEGREE

COUNT 2 PC 209 (KIDNAP)

COUNT 3 PC 12022(b) ARMED WITH DEADLY WEAPON, NOT FIREARM

CIRCUMSTANCES OF THE OFFENSE:

ON MAY 3, 1992, AROUND 1 P.M., SAN FRANCISCO POLICE OFFICERS RESPONDED TO REPORTS OF A WOMAN SCREAMING IN APARTMENT E OF THE DOUBLE ROCK PROJECTS IN SAN FRANCISCO.

UPON ARRIVAL, OFFICERS LOCATED THE VICTIM, TINA SOLOMON (AGE 28), LYING FACE UP ON THE FLOOR OF THE LIVING ROOM, BLEEDING FROM THE NECK AND CHEST. SHE WAS UNRESPONSIVE. OFFICERS RECOGNIZED SOLOMON AS A KEY WITNESS IN THE UPCOMING MURDER TRIAL OF OAKTOWN BOYS GANG MEMBER, CHRISTOPHER

"BABY FACE" DESOTO. SHE WAS TRANSPORTED TO SAN FRANCISCO GENERAL HOSPITAL WHERE SHE WAS PRONOUNCED DEAD ON ARRIVAL. AUTOPSY RESULTS INDICATED A FATAL SLICING WOUND TO THE NECK WHICH SEVERED THE CAROTID ARTERY. DEFENSE WOUNDS WERE FOUND ON THE VICTIM'S HANDS AND FOREARMS.

A WITNESS INFORMED POLICE THE DEFENDANT HAD FLED THE APARTMENT A FEW MINUTES BEFORE POLICE ARRIVED, CARRYING HIS DAUGHTER, "OR" (AGE 8). OFFICERS LOCATED THE DEFENDANT IN A NEIGHBORING APARTMENT. AFTER A BRIEF STANDOFF, HE SUR-RENDERED TO POLICE. "OR" WAS TAKEN INTO PROTECTIVE CUSTODY BY THE DEPARTMENT OF CHILD AND FAMILY SERVICES. ACTING ON AN ANONYMOUS TIP, THE MURDER WEAPON WAS RECOVERED DAYS LATER UNDER A SEWER GRATE IN THE TENDERLOIN DISTRICT.

MARTIN "MAD DOG" REILLY IS WELL KNOWN TO SFPD AS A HIGH-RANKING MEMBER OF THE OAKTOWN BOYS. THE SERIOUS NATURE OF THE CRIME AND REILLY'S GANG INVOLVEMENT MAKE HIM A POOR CANDIDATE FOR PROBATION.

RECOMMENDATION: PROBATION DENIED, STATE PRISON

CHAPTER THIRTY-TWO

Shauna Ambrose stumbled from the Hickory Pit through the cobwebs of fog toward her sunshine-yellow Mini Cooper. The parking lot spun like a tilt-a-whirl as she careened through it, staggering. Her polka-dot umbrella wobbled over her head. Every bit of her, soaked.

She should've left hours ago. With the Murdock twins or that rookie CO. Whatever his name was. But she'd never known when to say when. Now, her brain felt fuzzy, filled with cotton balls. Cotton balls soaked in vodka and laced with bad decisions. Like flirting with Hank. To her, it meant one thing. She'd always liked to be noticed, desired. To him, it meant something else entirely. The distance between, as vast and slippery and dangerous as the rocks at high tide.

When he'd put his hand on her thigh and his mouth on her ear, inviting her into the men's room, she'd panicked. *I'll meet you there*, she'd told him, with a wink. But the moment he'd disappeared inside, she'd tucked her phone in her pocket and made a run for it. Her heart thrashing like a caged bird in her chest.

Shauna looked back over her shoulder—no one, thank God—and nearly lost her balance. The umbrella tumbled from her hand and skittered across the lot, blown by a gust of wind and another and another until it was lost in the fog. She didn't know why she ran, only that it seemed necessary to put as much distance as she could between herself and Hank. Between herself and this whole rotten day.

Locked safely inside her car, she felt better now. Wet and freezing, but better. Almost giddy. She giggled, burped, then giggled
again, searching her purse for her iPod. She needed "All I Want
For Christmas Is You," and she needed it now. That song was the
epitome of happiness, the antidote to everything gone wrong.

As she pawed through her things, her woozy head floated away
like a runaway balloon. But the feeling didn't last. The balloon
popped and shriveled as a palm smacked on the window beside
her. Hank's face through the rain-streaked glass. Mouth open,
teeth bared. Eyes wild.

"You're drunk," he yelled. "You shouldn't be driving." Then,
when she jerked the car into reverse, "You're crazy, Shauna!"

All true, sadly. Maybe her parents had been right when they'd
told her to pick a new major. Anything but psychology. Then,
to pick a new job. Anywhere but the prison. When she'd moved
in with her grandmother in Fog Harbor, they'd probably taken
bets on how long it would last. How long till she'd run back to
San Francisco with her tail between her legs. Now, she'd have
to tell them they'd been right all along. She'd have to start over,
toss out her college dreams of saving the world one sad soul at a
time. Probably they'd make her get a desk job like her mother,
answering phones for important people and watching the seconds
of her life tick by.

With a sob, Shauna floored it, hurtling through the empty lot
and ignoring the vicious scrape as she bottomed out at the dip
near the exit. In her rearview, Hank flailed like a fish out of water.
Flopping in the cold rain.

The windshield wipers worked double time. Even so, she could
barely see the road in front of her. In the fog, the world revealed
itself too slowly. The double yellow line seemed to blur in and out
of her vision. Her thoughts swam in circles.

Most of all, she regretted telling Dr. Rockwell about Drake.
She shouldn't have blamed him for the photo, shouldn't have

told on him about the phone. At least she'd kept the one thing to herself. Well, mostly. The thing she'd seen today in the chapel. She'd tried to put it out of her mind completely. She'd have to, or else. But the memory lodged at the back of her brain, sharp and penetrating as an icepick.

Anyway, the photo with Drake meant nothing. Hardly *over-familiarity*—not even a real word, by the way. It's not like she'd straddled him in the kitchen storeroom or smuggled in cocaine. Hank had done worse, and look at him. A sergeant.

The car drifted to the left.

Headlights blinded her. A horn blared.

She jerked the wheel to the right and skidded off the road, her front end colliding with the sign she'd passed hundreds of times: PRISON AREA: DO NOT PICK UP HITCHHIKERS. It crunched against the hood, the metal pole yielding, bending toward the ground in surrender.

Panic rose up in her throat, a hot bile, and she cracked the door. Vomited right there in the ditch with the rain pouring.

Her thoughts kept swimming. She'd already been fired. Now what? Arrested for DUI? With the patrols stepped up, the cops would be here any minute to put her in handcuffs and stick her in the cage in the back, not much different than Drake. She wouldn't let that happen. She could still make it to her grandmother's house. Still salvage this day.

Breathing hard, she hoisted her purse onto her lap. The iPod had been there all along. She found the song she'd been looking for and cranked the volume, drowning out the rain. Then, slowly, cautiously, she reversed, singing to herself.

See how careful she could be. How responsible. Only ten miles to home, and she'd keep it between the lines the whole way.

Two miles past the turnoff for Crescent Bay, she took a left onto the decommissioned highway. The Mini rumbled over the neglected asphalt, her teeth juddering with every pothole. But miraculously, the rain slowed. Then stopped completely. She couldn't help but give herself credit.

If you can change your mind, you can change your world. That's what she'd written on the whiteboard the first day she'd set foot in the prison to teach Changes. She'd been good at it, too. The inmates had told her so, Drake included. Because she didn't judge them. She saw inside, right down to the core of the apple. To the lost little boys—men, now—who sat in her classroom searching for the understanding the world had never given them. Even Drake had told her she got it. Understood him better than Dr. Rockwell. Maybe she didn't need a Ph.D. after all.

With that thought sprouting wings, she felt better. She even smiled. But it only lasted for a single beat of her heart.

She cried out, slammed her brakes, skidded to a stop, as a dark creature glided across the road, its black body half-hidden in the low-hanging fog. It stopped, waited. Right in front of her.

As she inched the car closer, it didn't move.

Not a creature at all. A wheelchair. But where had it come from? Who?

Her thoughts stopped swimming in circles. It's a test. A sign. A gift from the universe. I'm a helper. That's what I do. I help. Someone clearly needed help.

The wheelchair rocked slightly in the wind, empty and curiously dry. It looked old, well used. One of the footrests missing.

As Shauna put the car in park and stepped out into the night, she'd never been so brave.

CHAPTER THIRTY-THREE

"I'm worried about Shauna."

The first words out of Emily's mouth that morning hit Olivia like a bowling ball. She'd skipped breakfast and avoided the kitchen entirely, not wanting to face Em.

"You know how she's glued to her phone, right?"

Olivia turned on the radio as she pulled out of their driveway. The rain had ended, at least for now. The sky, a muted gray-blue. She glanced back at the porch, at the handful of garland drowned on the step, and smiled to herself, remembering Deck standing there, dripping wet. It felt like years since last night. "You mean, like someone else I know."

"Whatever." But Emily didn't deny it. The local station's classic Christmas carols played in the background, the exuberant sleigh bells an eerie contrast to the grim new world around them. A world where women they knew were being picked off one by one. "She hasn't returned any of my calls or texts. Not since yesterday night, after you left to drive Detective Decker home. I hardly slept at all thinking about it."

"I'm sure she's fine. She's probably just upset. Maybe she doesn't feel like talking." Like me, Olivia thought.

"But what if she's not? What if…" Emily didn't say it out loud. Thank God.

"Did you see this?" Emily directed Olivia to her phone's screen. *Correctional Officer Hank Wickersham Identified as Person of Interest, Released without Charges.*

"Can we stop by Shauna's grandma's house to check on her? It's practically on the way."

Olivia knew the Ambrose house. Not counting Adele's long-windedness, it meant at least a twenty-minute detour. Which meant she'd be late for the 8 a.m. all-staff MHU meeting. Technically *her* meeting.

"Of course. But let's make it quick."

Route 187—an unfortunate number for a highway, especially one snaking its way past prison gates—had been decommissioned in the nineties in favor of the nearby interstate. By now, the forest had begun to reclaim it. The relentless winter rains took bites of the asphalt, and grass pushed its way through the cracks of what remained. Olivia remembered making the trek out here as a wide-eyed teenager, her friends drunk on cheap booze. Her, on freedom.

Only a few houses remained occupied. The rest had fallen to ruin, ready to be swallowed in time by the wild grass, the river, and the redwoods. The Ambrose house stood at the end of the long straightaway, a ROAD ENDS HERE sign near the mailbox.

But they never made it that far.

A few hundred yards up ahead, lights flashed, painting the horizon in swashes of color. A barricade marked POLICE stopped her from going any farther.

Emily's "oh my God, oh my God, oh my God" beat in Olivia's brain as she steered the car to the shoulder.

"Wait." She reached for Emily's arm. But her little sister skirted out of her reach, flung open the door and ran straight into the eye of the storm. Big sister followed.

A gloved hand stopped them both at the barricade. It belonged to Officer Bullock, otherwise known as Bulldog to his colleagues. Graham had used the nickname a few times, and Olivia had never needed an explanation. The thick jowls, the underbite, and the short, stocky frame. The clipped voice telling her to hold up. She half expected him to growl.

"Can't let you go through here, ma'am."

She nodded at him, catching her reflection in his mirrored sunglasses.

"That's my friend's car," Emily said, pointing over Officer Bullock's head to Shauna's yellow Mini Cooper, stock-still in the center of the asphalt about thirty yards from the barricade. The driver's door gaped open.

Frantic, Olivia scanned the ground for a body bag but saw nothing. No ambulance either. She lifted her gaze to the officers on the periphery. They combed through the thick plant cover where the road met the forest.

JB stood among them, smoking a cigarette. He raised his hand to wave at her. Then he tossed the butt to the ground, stamped it out, and collected it, depositing it in his coat pocket. He disappeared into the redwoods.

"Can you please tell us what's happening?" Emily begged. "Is she… is she dead?"

Bulldog answered with the hard set of his jaw.

Emily's bottom lip trembled, the same way it had since she'd turned two years old. *A little tremor before the big one*, their father had teased. Olivia put her arm around Emily and considered retreating to the car. She could call Deck from there, find out what had happened. But the big sister in her couldn't let this particular asshole slide.

"C'mon," she told Emily, guiding her around the barricade. "We're going to look for Detective Decker."

"Ma'am, no one gave you permission to do that." Bulldog strutted toward her, faster than she'd given him credit for. "You need to go back the way you came unless you'd like to spend the morning in jail."

"I know that detective." She pointed at the spot where she'd last seen JB. "I'm working with him and his partner."

"Yeah. Sure you are. And I'm Columbo." Bulldog grabbed her by the upper arm, squeezing his fat fingers into her flesh. He spun her in the other direction and gave her a little push. The part of her that belonged to her father—hot-tempered and defiant—dug in her heels.

"Don't push my sister." Emily's tears stopped, her lip stiffened. "She's a doctor."

Bulldog removed his sunglasses, squinting at her. "Hey, aren't you Bauer's girlfriend?"

Olivia sighed. Would it ever end?

"It's okay, Bullock. I'll take care of this troublemaker." The voice came from behind her and her stomach clenched. Still, facing Deck would be better than leaving in handcuffs. She had no choice when she felt his hand brush her shoulder.

"Trying to get yourself arrested again?" He barely smiled, the circles under his eyes as dark as her own.

"Em was worried about Shauna. She hasn't heard from her since last night."

"She texted me a few times from the Hickory Pit," Emily interjected.

"We were going to drive out to her house, but…"

Emily whimpered. "Is Shauna okay?"

Deck glanced behind him at the Mini and shrugged. "Honestly, we don't know. Her grandmother said she never came home last night. A neighbor found the car abandoned out here on the way to work this morning. Her purse was left on the passenger seat, and we found her phone a few feet in front of the car. Unfortunately, it landed in a pothole and got very wet. The team's been searching the woods for about two hours. There's no sign of her."

Dread and fear pooled in her gut, but she felt a small comfort when she met Deck's eyes. The little flecks of gold in them caught the sunlight, and she looked away before he saw too much of her. He already knew too much.

"Can I take a look at those messages, Emily?"

*

Olivia stood front and center in the MHU conference room. Fifteen pairs of eyes stared back at her, expectantly, waiting for her to tell them what to do. To be the chief. Only Leah knew Olivia had never wanted the job. After the Oakland Police Department profiling debacle, she'd hoped to blend in for a while. To lay low. But when she'd interviewed for a staff psychologist job at Crescent Bay, Warden Blevins had insisted she'd be a better fit as chief. The position had been vacant for nearly two years since Vernon Hale had retired. *You seem like a natural leader*, the warden had cooed. *You certainly know the population.*

She'd been flattered, proudly telling him about her research at Stanford, even her work with the FBI, but looking back now, she wondered if she'd been way off base. If he'd meant it differently. Her personal knowledge of criminals. Knowledge so personal, in fact, it flowed in her blood; fifty percent of her DNA.

"Alright, everyone. Let's get started." The remaining chatter quieted, then stopped completely. The spotlight on her. "I sent out today's agenda last Thursday. But with the current circumstances, I think it's best if we take some time to process everything that's happened."

One of the interns, Jenny Li, raised an eager hand. "I heard Shauna Ambrose is missing? Is that true?"

A few gasps, a few nods. But mostly stunned silence. "Who did you hear that from?"

"All the officers are talking about it. Melody said she saw her out last night at the Hickory Pit. That Shauna was fired yesterday for posting pictures of Drake online. And then, she got drunk and made out with—"

"This isn't the place for gossip."

Jenny's supervisor, Dr. Stanley, jumped to her feet, ready for a fight. Olivia knew why. She'd wanted the chief job. Had lobbied for it for months. "But if Shauna is missing that makes three. All from the prison. All women. Then this morning, I see a report that Hank Wickersham turned himself in to police as that person of interest from the theater. Yet, he's still allowed to come to work. We have the right to know what's going on."

"Carrie, I understand you're concerned about our safety. We all are, myself included. I wish I had more to tell you. It seems Hank was released without charges. The administration is cooperating fully with the investigation and—"

"Sounds like a line to me."

Leah glared at Carrie. "What do you expect Olivia to do about it? She's a psychologist, not a cop."

"Yeah. Well, she's Devere's psychologist. We've all heard the rumors about him and Bonnie. No wonder she had those fancy boots last year. Probably money she stole from Drake. And then fighting with Laura the day before she was murdered. Have you even asked him if he was involved?"

Olivia began to question why she'd come to work at all today. Why she'd listened to a sniffling Emily and made the turn toward the prison. This didn't feel like a distraction. It felt like a slap in the face. Her chest tightened as she surveyed her staff. *Do you know there's an actual word for a group of psychologists?* Emily had teased her once, laughing so hard she'd barely gotten the word out. *A complex. That explains a lot.*

At the edge of this restless complex, leaning casually against the wall, Warden Blevins watched her. Like a roach slipping in through a crack in the wall, he'd come in so quietly she hadn't noticed.

"I don't think my sessions with Drake are relevant to this meeting. Just like all of you, I adhere strictly to the ethics code and the rules of the institution, which require me to notify Warden Blevins if there is a threat to our safety or security."

She observed the warden's face. At this distance, she couldn't tell the difference between his smirk and his scowl. *Unless that threat is the warden himself.*

CHAPTER THIRTY-FOUR

"These tracks look mighty similar." JB pointed to the tire impressions in the mud just off the road, beyond a set of footprints. "You wanna bet they're a match for the Michelins? And how about those babies? Correct-Tex?"

"Yep. But no body."

"Not yet." The words thudded from JB's mouth, heavy and foreboding as stones laid upon a grave.

Will stood near the yellow evidence markers, trying to see the scene the way the bad guy had. *Or girl*, he heard Olivia caution in his head. He wondered when in the last four days her voice had taken up residence there along with the rest of her. Had it really only been five days?

From here, a small clearing in the redwoods, he had an obstructed view of the road. Its fissures and craters like the surface of an alien moon. The ground yielded, soft beneath his feet, and he let himself sink in, thinking.

"So, our perp is here in the truck, waiting for Shauna presumably. She can't see the vehicle from the road, so why does she stop?"

"She knows him. Maybe he flags her down."

"Then why hide the truck back here in the woods? He wants the element of surprise. Maybe he used a ruse or a partner. Something to draw her in."

Will thought of Drake. Of the way he'd lured his victims deep into Muir Woods, promising to meet them for a picnic. A secluded spot near a waterfall. Then, when they'd hiked to the spot, found his blanket spread beneath a tree, he'd swooped in from behind and captured his prey.

JB nodded his approval. "Not bad. I'll make a detective out of you yet. But I'm still thinking these murders are a one-man show."

"What do you say we head over to the prison?" Will asked. "Talk to the kitchen staff about Laura. Find out exactly why Shauna got fired. Maybe even pay our buddy Drake a visit."

He hoped they'd run into Olivia too. But he would never say that out loud. It had been hard enough this morning, keeping his hands to himself. When they'd wanted to punch Bullock right between the eyes. To linger on her shoulder.

"A visit to Crescent Bay?" JB swooned. Clutching his chest, he batted his eyelashes. "Oh, City Boy. Don't threaten me with a good time."

"What do ya think?" JB asked, from his seat at a table in the Crescent Bay dining hall. "Two Michelin stars?"

Like most things in prison, the tables were metal and bolted to the dingy tile floor. Four seats—also metal, also bolted—surrounded each one. A dismal shade of brown, the walls provided the perfect backdrop for the meals served here. One heaping spoonful of bad decisions. A side of hopelessness. A stale slice of regret. It might've been the saddest place at Crescent Bay, and it made Will's chest ache to think of Ben eating his meals on a cold, hard slab of steel like this one each day.

"Why not three?" Will asked.

"I deducted a half-star for the plastic sporks."

Will chuckled. "Fair enough. But we can't have you shanking your neighbor because he didn't pass the salt."

"And another half for the hired help." JB nodded toward the kitchen. As the lunch hour approached, the din had only grown louder, Will's nerves juddering with every clanging pot. Every dropped dish. "I can't trust a chef who calls himself Cannibal."

JB had finally met a pie he didn't like. His piece sat on a paper plate, untouched. The whipped cream melted.

Luis "Cannibal" Delgado, inmate leadman in the kitchen, had told them exactly nothing about Laura or Drake or the Oaktown Boys. Just said *no comment* and offered them a slice of day-old pie like a goddamn politician. Same as the others—Corey Coleman, Morris "Tiny" Jones, and Scott Guthrie. "Seems like the feeling was mutual."

"Here comes our last shot," JB muttered. "Let's hope this guy lives up to his nickname."

A shifty-eyed, dark-skinned man slunk toward them. He claimed one of the two remaining seats at the table and smiled broadly. An odd contrast to the scar that wormed its way from the edge of his mouth down his neck. "Cannibal says you want to talk to me."

"Are you Michael LaRue?" Will asked.

"Sure am. But folks around here call me Squeak."

"Alright. Squeak it is, then." Will extended his hand before he caught sight of Squeak's, covered in flour. Too late now. "You might have heard we're investigating a couple of homicides."

"Yep, sure did. Ms. Ricci was just about the best supervisor I ever had in the joint. And I've had a few. Ms. McMillan taught me how to read poetry. Both real nice ladies. Didn't deserve to go out like that, if you ask me."

Squeak said it all—already long-winded compared to the others—without taking his eyes from JB's pie. He glared at it like the pumpkin filling had personally offended him.

"Are you okay?" Will asked.

Squeak mulled it over. "Well, that depends. Somethin' wrong with that pie?"

Will watched JB's throat constrict.

"'Cause I made it myself. From scratch. I won the Crescent Bay Bake Off three years runnin' now. Got the recipe from my mama. Best pumpkin pie you'll ever taste. I personally guarantee it."

"JB, why don't you give it a taste?" Will didn't even try not to be smug, his own pie carefully discarded in the trash two inmates ago. "Pumpkin is your favorite, isn't it?"

"Sure. I was just saving it." With the precision of a surgeon, he lifted the spork and extracted the tiniest sliver of pie. "Did Cannibal help?"

"He's leadman. He's got his hands in everything around here."

JB raised the spork to his mouth, grimacing, and took the bite. Trying not to laugh, Will watched Squeak, as Squeak watched JB.

"Well, I'll be damned, Squeak. It's delicious." JB licked his lips and shoveled in another piece. "My compliments to the baker."

"Thank you, sir. Now, what can I help you with?"

JB dabbed at a spot of whipped cream on his chin. "My partner and I were hopin' you might be able to point us in the right direction. You see, we've been chasin' our tails on these murders. The only thing we can come up with is this place. Crescent Bay. Do you know if Ms. Ricci got herself caught up in any shady business?"

An animal caught at a watering hole, Squeak looked ready to bolt. "You see this scar?" he asked. "Oaktown Boys cut me up somethin' good my first year in the joint when I told on 'em for slicin' up my cellie. Since then, I keep my head down and my mouth shut."

"But you make a damn good pie." JB tap-tap-tapped his finger on the plate, collecting the last bits of crust.

"That I do. Lord willing, if the parole board sees fit, I'll be making pies out there. At my own bakery. I want to call it Squeak's Sweets."

Will locked eyes with JB. Nodded his head ever so slightly.

"What if we could bend the ear of those commissioners?" JB asked. "Make Squeak's Sweets a reality."

"I'd say, I'm listening."

Ten minutes and a whole lot of bullshit promises later, Squeak leaned forward, whispered, "We order a lot of flour."

JB frowned. "I don't get it. *Flour?*"

"I think Squeak is saying Laura made some special orders."

"That's exactly what I'm sayin'."

"For who?"

"That there is above my pay grade." Squeak stood up and wiped his hands on his jumpsuit, leaving white palm prints on the sides of his thighs. "But I will tell you this – you best be careful. When it comes to money, ain't no lines some folks won't cross."

As Squeak backpedaled toward the kitchen, JB called out to him. "Think I could get another piece of that pie?"

"Sure thing, Detective. One Squeak special comin' right up."

After he'd retreated behind the swinging door with a wave and a grin, JB turned to the officer stationed at the exit. "What's he in for?"

"Mike LaRue? Poisoned his grandmother."

One hour and an intriguing conversation with June Chatham later, JB still hadn't forgotten about that pie.

"I feel feverish." He splashed his face in the visitors' bathroom, as Will washed his hands. "Do I look pale to you?"

"It's the middle of winter in Fog Harbor. Your skin hasn't seen the sun in weeks. What do you expect?"

"I don't know, City Boy. My stomach's cramping. It looks a little swollen." He turned to the side and patted his belly. "Doesn't it?"

"Are you asking me if those pants make you look fat?" Will grinned at himself in the mirror, studying his raccoon eyes, rubbing his day-old stubble that hid the bruise on his jaw. In these godawful fluorescent lights, he looked more like a street bum than a detective. "Or if you're about to become Squeak's second victim?"

"You're enjoying this, aren't you?"

Will shrugged, turning away from his own reflection before it got any worse. "Maybe a little."

"Alright then, you have your fun. But if I drop dead…"

"I'll be sure to let everyone know you went out doing what you loved. What you were best at."

"Being a damn good cop. Ain't that the truth."

JB puffed his chest and pushed open the door, strutting back onto the main prison thoroughfare, good as new. Will waited until he'd gone to deliver his punchline to the vagrant in the mirror.

"Stuffing your face."

Will let JB go on ahead. Glancing down at his watch, he decided he'd meet him at the Mental Health Unit. The warden had assured them Drake would be busy in therapy with Olivia until 10:30 a.m. anyway. Will could think of worse things than lying on her couch. He'd taken enough introductory psych classes at San Francisco State to know they had a word for that. *Erotic transference*.

He peered in through the window of the library toward the circulation desk. Maryann's head rested in her hand, her elbow propping it up as she gazed downward, flipping the page of a book. At the table, Morrie read aloud from a law book while another inmate took notes.

Maryann looked up when the door clicked shut behind him. She lowered her copy of *Wuthering Heights* and took a sip of tea from a mug that bore the face of a dog with glasses, a tiny book between his paws. "Well, hello there, Detective."

As he approached the desk, she frowned and lowered her voice. "Any news about Shauna?"

"Why? What have you heard?"

"That she's missing? That maybe—*God forbid*—the Seaside Strangler struck again."

"Seaside Strangler?" JB would absolutely lose his shit. "Where did you hear that name?"

She twittered, her cheeks flushing. "Oh, I... well, I just made it up. A strangler in a town by the sea. It fits, doesn't it?"

Will raised his eyebrows, cocked his head at her.

"Remember, I watch a lot of—"

"*Forensic Files.* Yeah, I remember. Did you know Shauna well?"

Behind her thick lenses, Maryann's eyes darted to the inmate table, where Morrie and the others sat stiffly. When she spoke, Will had to lean in to hear her. "That girl wasn't cut out for this place. When they aren't, you can tell right away. They get too comfortable too fast. They forget where they are."

"June said you told her about the picture Shauna posted. How did you find it?"

Maryann beckoned him behind the counter and into the small office. He did a double take at the stuffed white poodle seated beside her desk. "I can't bear to leave my Luna at home, so Melody had her made for me. Doesn't she look real? Just like my little princess."

Will made noises of polite agreement as he shut the door behind him. "So, how did you find that photo?"

"I didn't. I'm not much for social media. Seems like a popularity contest if you ask me. And I was never real good at those. But Shauna was constantly posting pictures and tweeting. Anyway, she showed me and Melody the photo herself. At the Hickory Pit. She was pretty tipsy at the time."

"What did she say about it?"

Grimacing, Maryann wrung her hands together. "I don't want to get her in any more trouble."

"I think we're beyond that now. If you know something, you need to tell me. *Now.*"

Maryann reached for the stuffed dog and clutched it to her chest, strangling its soft body. "She said Drake had asked her to take the photo with a cell phone he had. He wanted her to post it online to drum up some publicity for his book. I didn't tell June the rest of it. I figured what I'd already said would be enough. I did it for her. For Shauna. I was worried about her. A girl like that… well, the Vulture eats girls like that for breakfast."

"Spit it out, Maryann. What else did she say?"

"Drake asked her to get intimate, if you know what I mean? She told him no, and he cursed at her. Called her a tease, which, if you ask me, isn't so far from the truth."

"When?"

Maryann's chin quivered. "One week ago."

"Does anyone else know?"

She lowered her eyes. "Just me and Melody."

Will had to hurry. Drake's therapy session ended in exactly eight minutes. As he hoofed it down the hallway, running on fumes, he tried to remember the last time a case had worked him over like this one. Dead ends, unanswered questions. Suspicions he couldn't pin down careened like lawn chairs in the tornado of his thoughts. At the center of it all, Drake Devere.

"Stay away from Olivia."

Will spun around, his guard up. Ready.

On either side of the red lines, a few inmates loitered, talking and laughing and leaning against the wall like kids with hall passes. Yesterday, after the skirmish in the hallway, Warden Blevins had put the whole place on lockdown, but today it was back to business as usual. Inmates going to work, to the yard, moving as they pleased with more freedom than Will thought fair. Only one of them met his eyes.

Morrie shuffled his wheelchair down the newly buffed concrete toward Will, a stack of books balanced on his lap. The crepe-paper skin and the clouded blue irises couldn't hide the criminal he'd once been. Hard and hot-blooded, that man swam just beneath the surface, darting from the light, hiding in the shadows. But Will saw him for what he was.

"Did you say something to me?"

"Not a word, Detective. Not a word."

CHAPTER THIRTY-FIVE

Olivia nodded, listened. Seethed.

In his quest to keep an eye on Drake, Warden Blevins had crossed the line. He'd gotten Drake to her office under the pretense she'd requested to meet with him. *The warden said you wanted to see me?* he'd asked, his dark eyes glinting and eager. *To talk about yesterday. The incident with Officer Murdock, the riot.*

She'd thought of turning him away—shouldn't he be in Administrative Segregation?—and storming right down to the warden's office and telling him he'd gone too far. But her curiosity had her pinned. She couldn't let him leave. Not with Shauna missing, and the whole prison talking.

Midway through the session, just as Drake had gotten down to the nitty-gritty, JB appeared outside her window. He didn't approach the door. Just sat at the end of the bench, waiting. Half listening, she shifted in her seat to get a better view of the unit. Hank had come in late this morning, pale-faced and sullen. Without a single lame joke, he sat himself quietly in position, hunched over the desk, still as a piece of driftwood. She craned her neck a little to see past him.

"Then that bitch Murdock started roughing me up."

Drake had a way of jolting her back, dizzyingly fast.

"Sorry for the language, but hey, if the shoe fits…"

"So Officer Murdock got physical with you for no reason?"

"I'm sure she'll come up with some bogus story about how I mouthed off. But she's the one who got out of line. Told me she believed the rumors, thought I killed Bonnie and Laura. She said, 'You're gonna fry for it, Devere.'"

Olivia looked at Drake with skepticism. She'd read the pending rules violation report, where Melody had claimed Drake cursed at her and swung his elbow, striking her on the shoulder.

"What're they gonna think now that Shauna's missing?" he asked her. "That asshole Decker is going to be on me like white on rice."

"Did you ask Shauna to take a photo of you?"

Drake hung his head, pouted. "Just one time. But she didn't have a problem with it. She wanted to do it. She was a fan of my work."

"Sounds like something the old Drake would say. Taking advantage. Using a woman as a means to an end."

"When you put it like that, Doc… You think I hurt Shauna, don't you?"

"It sounds like you feel everyone is against you. Even me."

Movement outside the window caught Olivia's attention. Deck had joined JB on the bench. He looked worried, but his face softened when he saw her watching. He raised his hand in a brief wave.

"It sure seems like you are. You got two cops outside, licking their chops. What am I supposed to think?"

"Well, they might be waiting to speak with you. Shauna was fired yesterday. They know about your picture, your phone."

"Or maybe they're here to warn you," he said, with a shrug. As if her words had glanced off his armor. As if his words didn't press a blade to her neck.

"Warn me?"

"Think about it. Bonnie. Laura. And now Shauna. I'm the common denominator. It stands to reason the next victim might be you."

"Next victim?" She sounded like a broken record, echoing Drake. Felt like one too. Something dark and awful scratching away inside her brain. "How do you know there will be a next?"

"I told you. Someone is setting me up. Doesn't this remind you of anything? Hell, I'd sue the bastard for copyright if I knew who."

A shiver zipped up her spine, thinking of Drake's book. Of the last chapter, the fourth victim: Lacey Lawson, Hawk's therapist.

The moment Drake stepped out of Olivia's office, the air felt lighter. Some patients were like that. They brought their own atmosphere.

JB corralled him before he'd made it far, and directed him to one of the unused offices at the back of the unit. Olivia slumped in her chair, exhausted.

"You okay?" Deck asked from the doorway. She let herself look at him. Really look. Not like this morning when she'd ducked away from his gaze. "It seemed kind of intense there at the end."

"Yeah. Well, that's Drake." Under the shadow of his stubble, she could still see the bruise on his jaw. The angles of his face familiar to her somehow. Maybe it was knowing he'd held the photo of her, Em, and their father, and kept it as sacred as a secret of his own. "Wait a minute. Were you lip-reading?"

He smirked at her. "Did you know lip-reading is admissible in court?"

"You're unbelievable."

"I'll take that as a compliment."

She thought he might leave when he glanced toward the office where JB and Drake had disappeared. Instead, he came inside and planted himself in her patient chair.

"Have you heard anything about Shauna?" she asked.

"Nothing. The entire police force is looking for her." He reached behind him and gave the door a little push. It clicked shut. "You know it probably won't end well, right?"

She nodded, but it took effort to swallow the truth. "Em's going to lose it. Shauna's the first real friend she's had in a while. When she came back here, she left a lot in Corvallis. I think she always planned to go back. Like this was temporary."

"For you too, huh?"

"I thought so. At first. But I like it here. It's slower. Less complicated. Or, it used to be."

"I know what you mean. My mom used to say that even if you win the rat race—"

"Wait. Let me guess. *You're still a rat?*"

His easy laugh was a salve, and she lost herself for a moment. Got too relaxed. Said the very next thing that came to mind, no filter.

"You quote your mom a lot."

In an instant, his face changed. She'd learned to study the faces in that chair. To know when she'd pushed too far, or not far enough.

"What did she think of you joining the old family business?"

Then, just as quickly, his face changed again. Whatever lay behind his eyes, he'd buried it deep. "Am I paying for this, Doctor?"

"In my defense, you did voluntarily place your butt in the hot seat. Once you sit there, everything's fair game."

Behind Deck, JB's face appeared in the window. He quietly cracked the door.

"Well, then I'd better relocate my butt—"

"Good lord, City Boy. Sounds like I got here just in time. This is how you impress a lady? By talking about your keister? No wonder you're single as a slice of Kraft cheese."

Deck didn't turn around, didn't acknowledge him. He made an exasperated face at Olivia, and she laughed.

"Can we go do our jobs now?" Deck asked, shaking his head.

JB shrugged, rolled his eyes. "That's exactly what I came down here to find out."

Olivia spotted Leah across the hall, wrapping up the Understanding Schizophrenia group, and she went to wait for her there, taking a seat on the bench outside. Since the vampire incident with Drake, Greg Petowski had insisted on affixing a handmade wooden cross on the door during their daily meetings. Greg had carved it himself in the hobby shop, with a loop of twine stapled to the back so he could hang it around the doorknob.

The group filed out, Greg at the rear, teeth clenched. He moved with purpose, unhooking the cross and holding it in one hand as he extended his finger, the nail long and yellow, toward the office at the back of the MHU.

"Bloodsucker! Demon! Liar! Infidel!" Greg spit out the insults rapid-fire, as if each one was a silver bullet aimed at Drake's heart. "You promised me garlic," he yelled. "Months ago, you promised."

He tossed the wooden cross onto the floor, and it landed with a thud beneath the bench. He watched as Olivia picked it up, offered it back to him. Agitated, Greg shook his head and began to pace.

"I need garlic. It keeps me safe. Safer than that thing!"

A methodical Hank plodded over to them from behind the desk. He drew his pepper spray, readied his alarm, and Greg collapsed in tears, folding to the ground like a crumpled question mark.

Leah waved Hank off, but he loomed over Greg, a towering statue about to topple. "Wait," Olivia said. "Take it easy. He's just afraid."

Hank stopped and stared at them, then slowly lowered his hands as if Olivia's words had traveled a long way to reach him.

She and Leah both crouched near Greg, well out of his reach. In the MHU, you could never be too careful. With the angry ones, the suspicious ones. Even with the fearful ones.

"Greg, what's going on?" Leah asked. "Let us help you."

"Drake... promised... me... garlic... from... the... chow hall... if..." Every word, punctuated with a sob.

"If what?" Olivia felt eyes on her as she spoke. Carrie, Jenny, the whole MHU watching her. Judging. *She's Devere's psycholo-*

gist... And Deck, over her shoulder. He must've left Drake in the office with JB.

Olivia thought of poking holes in Greg's logic. If Drake was really a vampire, he certainly wouldn't be handling garlic. He wouldn't be in this place at all. But she'd watched Leah try and fail, try and fail. Reasoning with Greg always proved futile. And messy. Like the time he'd barricaded himself in her office and dissected every red ink pen, convinced they contained blood to feed the undead. The red stains on Leah's tile floor never did come out.

"If what?" she repeated, as calm as she could manage.

"I can't tell you! But I did it. I did it!" Greg reared back and struck his head on the wall. Again. And again. And—

"Hank!" Olivia yelled, pressing her own alarm. "Restrain him."

Stunned, Greg barely resisted when Hank finally moved in. He weakly flailed one arm that glanced off Hank's shoulder. Hank rolled Greg to his stomach and secured him in cuffs, as a small group of officers filed in to help.

"Hold on," Deck said, as Hank hauled Greg to his feet and started him walking. "Let me talk to him."

"Step aside, Detective. This here's Crescent Bay turf. Now, I understand you've gotten the go-ahead to speak with Devere. You already know I don't give a rat's ass about him. Or Petowski, for that matter. But I don't think the warden would take too kindly to you randomly interrogating our inmates, and I've gotta keep the boss happy."

Unfazed, Deck trailed behind them. "I can get your garlic," he told Greg, without a trace of derision. "My partner and I just made a friend in the kitchen. Whatever you need, it's yours."

Hank pushed Greg forward toward the therapeutic module—a glorified cage—near the entrance, but he dug his heels in, craned his head back to Deck.

"Six cloves. For a necklace. Like Sam in *The Lost Boys*."

"Done."

One firm shove and Greg stumbled into the cage. "Sit down and shut up," Hank told him.

Greg folded himself onto the small metal seat as Hank slid the lock into place, glowering. "You're getting a write-up, Petowski. Assault on staff and resisting a peace officer."

"Aw, c'mon, Sarge. That ain't like you."

"Keep testing me, and I'll make it worse. I'll have you transferred down south. I hear they've got a lot of vampires at that maximum security facility in LA."

Olivia caught Deck's eyes, the mischievous glint there. When she raised her brows at him, he mirrored her with a subtle nod. Game on.

"Assault? Really, Hank?" She sidled up to him, drawing his attention, leading him toward the main desk and away from the cage. "He hardly touched you. Cut the poor guy some slack. After all, you do have a mutual enemy. How about we call it *behavior that could incite violence*? Leah and I will help you write it."

Hearing her name, Leah nodded. "Absolutely. We're a team here. We know you've had a rough few days."

With Hank and Leah busy at the desk, Olivia turned back to the cage, where Greg stood calmly, peering out. Deck had vanished.

Olivia spotted him in the back office with JB, both of them leaning back in their seats as Drake spoke. She knew that look, a watch and wait. Because sometimes, if you gave an inmate enough rope, he'd hang himself.

"Gonna get my garlic," Greg whispered to her, a small smile playing at the corners of his mouth.

After a quick glance over her shoulder, she approached the therapeutic module. "So you told the detective what you did for Drake?"

Greg nodded, sticking out his slim chest. "He said I was *extremely* helpful. That I'm gonna get my garlic."

As Olivia walked away, she looked once more at Drake, framed in the office window. His hair, jet black. His skin, pale and shimmery under the fluorescent light. His metaphorical teeth, sharp as razors. A dark thought came to her. She didn't speak it aloud.

You're going to need it, Petowski.

CHAPTER THIRTY-SIX

Will watched Devere with silent satisfaction, knowing he held Greg's admission like an ace in his pocket.

"I'm telling ya, Detectives. You're barking up the wrong tree here. Did you check the cameras? I was snug as a bug in my cell all night."

"Well, you should've been in Ad Seg." Will already knew what the cameras showed. And more importantly, what they didn't. Devere had been escorted back to his single cell at 8 p.m., with Officer Singletary securing the lock. Between 10 p.m. and 4:30 this morning, the cameras on C Block had gone dark. Warden Blevins assured them he'd stepped up bed checks, that Devere had slept through the night. "How did you weasel out of that one?"

"Blevins thought it was too much of a security risk. I've got a lot of enemies in the hole. Best to keep me up here. Above ground."

"I'm fairly certain you've got a few enemies up here, too," JB said.

"Yeah. I'm looking at 'em."

Will readied his ace, prepared to play it. "Are you sure you've never had any garrote-making materials? Extra jumpsuits? The rolling pins? You must've done some research for the book, right? To make it authentic. Doesn't Hawk use a garrote?"

"Hawk uses a very specific type of weapon. It's highly specialized. I wouldn't expect you'd be familiar with it. It's called a cutter garrote, and it's made of heavy-duty wire. None of that namby-pamby cloth your wannabe's been using."

"A cutter garrote?" JB whistled. "That's an old military weapon. American OSS. Used during World War II. If you knew what you were doin', turned your body to your enemy just so, you could hoist him up, and…" JB made a slicing motion across his neck, complete with the sickening sound effect.

"That's right," Devere said. "Maryann told me it would be a perfect weapon for Hawk. He's former special forces."

"Just like you, huh?" Will rolled his eyes.

"I could've been in the military. Could've been a cop, too. But I didn't want some asshole barking orders at me. Drake Devere doesn't do chain of command. The buck stops right here."

Will placed his bets and laid his ace on the table. "So if somebody told me you had the hook-up on extra jumpsuits from the laundry—let's say a few extra jumpsuits identical to the ones used to make the garrotes found wrapped around the necks of Bonnie and Laura—they'd be lying?"

Devere flashed a solid poker face, for which Will had to give him credit. "I'd say somebody was yanking your chain. They probably heard about the murder weapons and told you a little story. You fell for it, Detective. Hook, line, and uh… garlic?"

Will left JB at the control booth and raced back to the MHU, paper bag in hand, courtesy of Squeak.

He stood outside the door, waving through the small window until Olivia spotted him from the main desk. Relieved, he held up the bag and smiled back at her. He'd been certain he'd have to deal with Wickersham. Which seemed a monumental ask for a day that started with another missing woman.

Olivia left Leah and Hank at the desk and walked toward him, her eyes brightening. That look alone, that single dimple, made the trip back worth it.

With the door unlocked, she cracked it open, leaving a sliver of shared space between them. He leaned into its warmth, wanting to be closer.

"Can you make sure your vampire hunter gets this? I got the okay from his unit officer."

She accepted the bag, held it up to her wrinkled nose. "A man of your word, I see."

"Thanks for your help with that, by the way." Will nodded toward the desk, where Hank had poked his head up, watching them intently. From the look of the messages he'd read on Emily's phone, he had a feeling he'd be seeing Hank again today. Real soon. No wonder the guy looked green around the gills. "We make a good team."

"I suppose we do."

"But you're still wrong about Drake," he said. "And I can prove it."

"Oh yeah?"

"Yeah. Extra jumpsuits from the laundry. That's the price Greg paid upfront for the garlic. So, how do you explain that with your Drake-as-the-fall-guy scenario, Doctor?"

She stepped back, nonplussed, and he wished he hadn't been such a smartass. "Well, that's unexpected. But as my supervisor used to say, 'It's all grist for the mill.' Profiles can change. Theories too. Just like suspects. I have to admit you surprised me with Greg. He's not the easiest person to communicate with, especially when he decompensates like that. Are you gunning for my job now or what?"

Will maintained his easy smile, but inside he felt another crack. The crisp, clean snap of a stem he heard every time he thought of his mother. That's the way it sounds when your heart breaks a little.

"I patrolled for a few years in the Tenderloin. Saw my share of mental illness down there. Trust me, a guy who believes in vampires is the least of it."

He felt reassured by her laughter. It meant he'd fooled her. Not that he'd lied. He had patrolled the Tenderloin. But by then, he'd already been fluent in crazy.

Will ignored the buzzing of his cell phone. His little brother, Petey, had called a few times since Will had left him hanging two days ago. But right now, he had to focus on dodging the gladiators. That's what JB had christened the group of reporters bold enough to position themselves right outside the station, wielding microphones instead of swords. Flinging questions sharp as arrows. Launching spears from their mouths, some of them barbed.

Is it true there's a third victim?
Another woman missing?
A serial killer?
The phone buzzed again, insistent in Will's hand.

Call me, bro. Dad's worried about you.

As the cameras rolled, JB cleared the way. Will kept his head down. He had no desire to be front-page news again. He followed JB into the station and deleted the text, wishing he could take a blowtorch to it. His dad hadn't earned back the right to worry about him. Not now. Not ever again.

They rounded the corner, and JB groaned, cursed under his breath. Will considered throwing himself to the gladiators. Because Lieutenant Wheeler waited by their desks, and he wasn't alone.

"'Bout time you fellas showed up. The chief wants to talk to the four of you."

"About?" JB asked.

"What do you think, Benson? I'm guessing it has to do with the shit storm that's brewing out there with your double homicide and your missing person. And the lack of… shall we say, *progress*."

Will walked single file to Chief Flack's office, JB in front, Graham Bauer and Jessie Milner behind. Like a march to the guillotine, Will had a bad, bad feeling about this.

"Your phone's blowin' up, dude," Graham told him, as his back pocket buzzed again. "It could be important."

Will said nothing, kept moving. Kept sighting JB's head—his salt-and-pepper buzz cut and the mole in the center of his bald spot—like a sad little bullseye.

"What if it's news on Shauna Ambrose?"

The distance to Chief Flack's door had never felt so long.

"Or it could be the killer. You know, serial killers contact the cops sometimes. They like to taunt us. Liv and I watched a documentary about Dennis Rader. Called himself BTK. What a cocky little shit, leaving messages for the cops. Got himself caught though. So, you might want to—"

"It's not the killer." Will spoke without turning around, his ears grating at the sound of "Liv" coming out of the Neanderthal's mouth.

"Well, Liv says it's pretty common for—"

Will grabbed the phone from his pocket and spun around, making a show of studying it, as Jessie looked on behind him, wide-eyed.

"Oh. Would you look at that? It's your girl, Olivia Rockwell. She wanted me to know she had a great time at the Hickory Pit Tuesday night. On our *date*."

JB guffawed. Jessie's mouth collapsed into a little pink O. Graham simply stood there like an oaf. Until the whole of Will's message reached beyond a thick layer of hair gel and into his pea brain.

"Hey, fuck you, man."

Will knew he'd regret it, but it felt too damn good to take it back. So good, it eased the sting of the real message. Not from Olivia, of course, but Petey.

Word on the street down here is that you got your ass handed to you the other night by Oaktown. Watch your back, bro. You know what happens when you poke the hornet's nest.

Chief Flack ruled from her throne of cheap wood and pleather, sizing up JB and Will with a deep frown. There were only two seats at the chief's desk, and Will started to wish he'd given his to Graham. Helmet Hair and his partner waited in the corner silently.

"Two bodies. One more missing. A whole lot of loose ends. And not a single viable suspect."

"Is that a question?" JB asked.

"I'm not done yet." Chief Flack stood up, paced behind her desk. "I've got local media on my ass. National media too. Now the FBI wants a piece of the action. They were planning to send a task force up here to investigate corruption at Crescent Bay. Apparently, they received a tip linking these crimes to contraband smuggling. Cell phones, drugs, weapons. That sort of thing."

Will nodded vigorously. Figured he'd use his head while he still had it. "It's definitely a possib—"

"Save it for your team, Decker." She gestured to Graham and Jessie. "Gentlemen, meet your new partners, Officers Bauer and Milner."

Graham extended his hand toward JB. It hung in the air for a solid three seconds before he let it drop to his side.

"Our new what? Since when are we the last to know?"

"Listen, Jimmy. I would've called you first, but you were up at Crescent Bay. No cell phones allowed."

"Not legal ones anyway." Will tried to defuse the tension.

"You're both great detectives. But you two are in way over your heads on this one. We're a small-town police department. We're not equipped to handle a serial killer."

"Jesus. Can we please stop saying that goddamned word? We only have two victims. *Two*. Ain't nothin' serial about that." JB let out a long, fiery breath. "You gonna say somethin', City Boy? Or are you in agreement with this bullshit?"

Will weighed his options. But nailing Graham with a throat punch didn't seem like a smart career move. "I don't think we have a choice here."

"You don't." Chief Flack returned to her throne, content with her decree. "Besides, Bauer and Milner are eager to learn. Aren't you?"

"Yes, ma'am." They answered in unison but only Jessie appeared sincere, flashing the chief an eager smile.

JB shook his head. "You two best stop kissin' her ass and start kissin' mine."

"That's all." Chief Flack waved them out. "You've got forty-eight hours to bring me something solid. Or I'll have to turn our evidence over to the Feds."

As soon as the door closed behind them, JB escaped out the side entrance, cigarettes in hand, leaving Will to fend for himself with the knaves.

"Truce?" Graham asked. "We've got to work together on this. To catch this asshole. For Bonnie and Laura and Shauna."

"Fine. *For them*. Just remember, JB and I are the detectives here. We're the experts. We call the shots."

Jessie reached the side entrance first.

"I wouldn't go out there if I were you," Will warned. She stuck her head out the door, coughing as she ran straight into a cloud of JB's smoke. Graham stopped short, blocking the exit.

"Then you best remember to steer clear of my girl."

"I don't think she's your girl anymore. If she ever was."

"That's none of your business. You know, I told her the truth about you, William Decker. Man, you are Internet famous. I googled the shit out of you. Olivia doesn't like snitches any more than I do."

Will studied Graham's face. Thought of how he'd like to rearrange it. Once upon a time, fifteen years younger and a rookie cop, he wouldn't have thought twice. But then he'd seen things that changed him. He'd collected them, buried them at the bottom of the junk drawer of his brain. Bullet holes in a child's bedroom. Blood pooling on the asphalt like melted ice cream. A mother falling to her knees. The protruding handle of a knife, its blade stuck down to the bone. A pair of dark, lifeless eyes that belonged to Rochelle Townes. His brother in prison blues.

"You sure about that?"

He turned around before Graham could answer. Made it halfway down the hall, before he heard his partner let loose.

"Can't a man smoke his goddamned cancer sticks in peace?"

CHAPTER THIRTY-SEVEN

Olivia stopped in the clearing and waited for Emily and Leah to catch up. She poked at the thick grass with her walking stick as another group of volunteers passed her, their neon safety vests disappearing into the redwood grove that bordered Highway 187.

Olivia listened to the river in the distance. The wet whisper of the water unnerved her more than the sudden cries of the gulls. More than the sound of the other volunteers calling Shauna's name. She'd thought she could do this—comb the woods for her sister's missing friend—but she'd been wrong. It reminded her of Bonnie. Of the vigil and the church. The drainpipe. She kept waiting for a scream to split the late afternoon stillness. Like the kind of crack in the ice you fall right through.

"We should head back soon," Olivia said, the moment she spotted the other two. "It's getting dark. I'll bet Baby Chapman's getting hungry."

"I'm fine. Jake's picking up dinner tonight. Trust me, this baby will be well fed." Leah gave a sad smile and patted Olivia's shoulder. "Besides, I can't stop thinking about Shauna and her poor grandma. She must be worried sick. At least I feel useful out here."

Emily walked on ahead of them, her eyes down, searching. As they followed her, the river's voice deepened to a throaty growl, and Olivia began to whisper.

"I've got a bad feeling, Leah."

"Don't say that. Maybe it's not connected with the others. It's possible Shauna just got upset about being fired and ran away. You know how she is."

Was, Olivia thought, hating herself for thinking it. "And left her car in the middle of the road? With the door open? And her phone on the ground in the rain? It doesn't make any sense."

Emily stopped, planted her stick in the muddy ground, and spun toward them. "I can hear you, you know. You're not helping."

"I'm sorry," Olivia said. "I just don't know what to do."

"I don't either. But we have to keep looking. What if we find something out here? What if we find her?"

Olivia nodded. But she didn't agree out loud. Em's optimism—and once, her own—her fatal flaw. Olivia had spent her childhood hanging on their mother's promises. *This year Dad will come home. He'll get a new lawyer, win his appeal.* By the time she'd turned seventeen, her father had exhausted his appeals and her goodwill. Seven-year-old Emily had only begun to buy into their mother's bill of goods. But now, looking back, Olivia understood her mother's desperate clinging to hope, no matter how futile.

They trudged on, occasionally calling out for Shauna, until they reached the swollen riverbank.

Emily pointed to a sandy spot past where the other volunteers had stopped. The rain had washed it out, leaving the refuse of the forest behind. Limbs and leaves and pebbles worn smooth as glass.

"I'm going to look out there. Near the water." Her voice, hollow, easily lost on the wind. Dead as the trunk of the redwood that had toppled nearby in the storm. Her eyes, vacant. Exhausted.

"Go talk to her." Leah gave Olivia a nudge. "She needs her big sister right now."

Emily knelt in the sand, picked up a small gray rock, and hurled it into the churning river. "You think she's dead, don't you?"

"I don't know, Em. I don't know."

Another rock, this one white as bone, went flying. "Do you think it's true the Oaktown Boys had something to do with her going missing?"

Olivia glanced back to Leah, resting against the trunk of the overturned redwood, well out of earshot. "Where did you hear that?"

"Around."

"Around? What does that mean?"

Emily tossed another rock into the waiting mouth of the river. The water moved so fast, it didn't even make a ripple. "Do you think we should ask Dad about it?"

"No."

"I know he's done with all that, but he might have heard something."

"I said no."

Emily stood and brushed the sand from her jeans. In the palm of her hand, she held a red stone. "You don't get to decide for me, Liv. Not about this."

Olivia waited for her sister to throw it to the river, another sacrifice swallowed whole. Instead, she tucked it into her pocket and walked away.

Olivia sat in silence and faked a smile as she waved at Leah. But as soon as they'd turned onto Pine Grove Road in opposite directions, she slammed the brakes, jolting her sister, and piloted the car to the shoulder.

"Alright, spill it."

"What're you talking about?"

"Whatever it is you're hiding about Shauna."

"I'm not hiding anything." Emily's hands twisted in her lap. She'd bitten her polished thumbnail down to the nub, an old habit she'd picked up from their mother. A classic tell.

"You look white as a sheet, and you're biting your nails again."

"Just the one. I can't help it. I'm freaking out."

"I know this last week has been overwhelming. For both of us. But we'll get through it. Just like we did all those years with Dad in prison. And then with Mom. Together."

Olivia recognized her own lies. That she'd run away from it all when she'd married Erik. That she'd left Emily to fend for herself. That in the years she'd been gone to San Francisco, their mother had sunk her own hopes to the bottom of a bottle of cheap wine. That her sister had every right not to trust her.

Emily stared ahead at the darkening road, the looming horizon, and past it. Somewhere Olivia couldn't go. But she knew how lonely it felt to have a secret. "Just tell me, Em. Whatever it is, we'll deal with it."

"I'm scared," she whispered.

"Me too."

"Shauna told me something last night right before she left for the Pit. She made me swear not to tell you. Especially after what happened to Bonnie."

Olivia summoned her inner therapist, the face of practiced neutrality. Inside, she felt like an eight-year-old girl standing in front of a door. A door she should never have opened.

"After June fired her, Shauna got really upset, and she started crying. She wanted to be alone for a minute, to get herself together, before she had to go through the control booth and the gate officers and… well, you know. So, she ran into the chapel."

Olivia wondered if Em could see her heart, her pulse quivering in her neck like a small animal.

"The confessional was open. The chaplain had the afternoon off, I guess. Anyway, she sat in there for a while, just crying. Then, someone came in."

"Who?"

"James."

Olivia had heard the whispers up and down the runway. *Can you believe he's back here already? Cold-hearted, huh? He must be guilty of something.* "Bonnie's James? I'd heard he was back at work, but…"

Emily nodded. "And that creep, Tommy Rigsby. Riggs. They were arguing about money James owed. Something about cell phones he was supposed to smuggle into Crescent Bay. James told Riggs he was done with that, and he threatened to go to the cops. Riggs got right up in James' face and said, 'If you do that, I'll tell the General, and then you're dead.'"

"The General?"

Em nodded again.

"Did she tell anyone else?"

"I doubt it. She was pretty terrified. Who knows what happened at the Pit, though? She can be a real motormouth when she starts drinking. But—"

"We have to tell Detective Decker right away."

Olivia's hand on the shifter, her brain already racing ahead at breakneck speed, Emily stopped her. "There's one more thing."

Another door she wished she could simply walk away from.

"She told me Riggs saw her."

Olivia knocked again on the front door of Deck's cabin. Louder, this time. More desperate.

"I don't think he's in there," Emily said. "But look, he's got a cat."

An orange tabby sidled up to the garage door, flicked its tail at them, and slipped through a small hole in the siding.

"Lieutenant Wheeler said he left the station thirty minutes ago. He must be here."

Olivia headed straight for the garage. She squatted down and peered inside the opening, wondering when she'd lost her damn mind. Somewhere between Deck's derisive grunting at the back of Grateful Heart and his showing up dripping wet on her porch steps.

Inside, she spotted Deck's truck, the cat perched atop the open tailgate. A well-worn heavy bag, anchored to the ceiling, swung slightly in the dim light. As if it had been punched. Hard. Then left to suffer. The bruise on Deck's knuckle and the curve of his biceps made complete sense now.

"Maybe we should just wait in the car." But Olivia ignored her sister and dropped to her stomach, certain she'd find him if she could just see a little farther. She realized then, pressed against the cold, damp ground, that the thing she most needed to tell him didn't have to do with Shauna at all.

When she turned her head away from the light, the inky sky surprised her. Nights came on fast in the winter, the darkness sudden and complete. From around the corner of the house, the wind played tricks on her, whistling and moaning until her heart began to race again.

"Em?" She planted her palms in the dirt and pushed herself up, crouching.

"Yeah?"

"Do you hear that?" The soft, measured padding of boots on grass.

Olivia swallowed, then cursed herself. Certain the lump in her throat, the effort it required, had given them away. She picked up the heaviest rock within her reach and took a few quick steps toward the car, pulling Emily along with her, before a voice stopped them both.

"Don't move."

She didn't know whether to laugh, or cry, or spew a string of expletives. So she simply turned around, hands raised, a stupid grin on her face.

"What are you doing out here?" Deck asked, lowering his Glock. "You scared the hell out of me, creeping around. I thought you two were Oaktown Boys."

Next to her, Emily sucked in a ragged breath. Olivia heard herself gasp too. Like he already knew why they'd come. She

stared at Deck, at his wrapped hands, his sweaty T-shirt. She felt
caught, the words she'd planned to say disappearing the moment
she opened her mouth.

"Who are you supposed to be? Rocky Marciano?"

He laughed. A real laugh, his eyes crinkling at the corners.
She supposed, under the circumstances, it was the best she could
hope for.

CHAPTER THIRTY-EIGHT

Will laid his gun on the tailgate while he made quick work of his hand wraps, discarding them in a pile in the corner. He took a cursory look in the side mirror, his face still flushed from his impromptu match with the heavy bag temporarily known as Graham Bauer. Ran his fingers through his hair. Took a sniff beneath his armpits. Good enough.

Cy blinked his one eye and offered a demure meow. "Hey, don't judge me." Though he felt confident Dr. Smarty Pants was inside his house doing just that. Examining the cabin with a shrink's eye. The boxes tucked into the spare bedroom. The sparse, mismatched furniture he'd picked up at a secondhand store in Healdsburg. It probably said something about his inner workings that he'd left it all behind when he'd sold the condo. Every one of his things contaminated by his old life.

"Can I get you two anything?" he called out as he walked back inside. Not that he had much to offer—tap water, instant coffee, peanut butter, sarcasm. The granola bars JB detested. But judging by the worry he'd caught in Olivia's eyes, even as she'd joked with him, this was no social call.

Emily sat at his kitchen table, biting her thumb. She shook her head and tried to smile, her eyes even more uneasy than her sister's. A bit less practiced in the art of concealment.

"Where's Olivia?" he asked.

"Snooping."

"*Em.*" Olivia appeared in the hallway, looking guilty. And tired. And incredibly beautiful. That too. "I wasn't—"

"Oh, I'm supposed to say she's 'using your bathroom.'"

Will took the seat across from Emily, taking mental inventory of what Olivia might've seen. His unmade bed seemed the worst of it. "The bathroom's the other way."

"I wouldn't snoop. I respect your privacy, Detective." Ouch. So, she knew then, and she wanted him to know she knew. "But have you heard what they say about folks who don't make their beds?"

"They're more efficient?"

"That's what I keep telling her," Emily said. "Only Navy Seals, accountants, and librarians make their beds every day. And Type A psychologists, of course."

Olivia jabbed Emily's shoulder, and she finally laughed. Will realized that had been the whole point the moment Olivia met his gaze over her sister's head.

"I guess there's no news about Shauna." Emily's words, like hands grasping for a lifeline. Her laughter, gone.

"Nothing. JB and I stopped by her grandmother's house this afternoon. Her parents are driving up from San Francisco. We're meeting them in a couple of hours." The worry returned to Emily's face, casting a shadow. "Your text messages were very helpful. We've been able to reconstruct Shauna's movements up until the time she left the bar."

Drunk as a skunk and running from Hank. That's the part Will didn't say. But the Hickory Pit's bartender, Jane Seely, had been clear on that. She'd served Shauna four vodka cranberries and a Blue Moon, thinking Hank would drive her home. After all, they'd been flirting all night. Until Shauna had ghosted him, shooting off in her yellow Mini like a deranged canary. Jane had called 911 to report her DUI at 12:33 a.m.

"That's why we're here." Olivia nodded at Emily. "To help."

Emily opened her mouth, closed it again. Will recognized the reluctance, the fear. He'd worn the same face the night Ben had pulled the trigger. The night he'd decided to talk, thinking he'd had a clue what it would mean.

"Alright. I take it there's something you want to tell me then."

Olivia grabbed the chair nearest her sister and dropped into it with purpose, leaning forward. Her hands wrapped around the red vinyl cushion, holding on for dear life. Those chairs were the best thing he owned. Truth be told, the only reason he'd stopped at that secondhand store in the first place. Four red vintage chairs in the window display—*from Ginny's All-Nite Diner circa 1963*—and an unshakable feeling his mother would've loved them.

"We both have something to tell you. I'll go first."

Will couldn't take his eyes off Olivia. Though he already guessed at what she might say, the simple, brave act of her sitting there, preparing to say it shocked him. He didn't feel worthy. But he wanted to be.

"Our father is Martin Reilly, a shot caller for the Oaktown Boys. He's been in prison for the last twenty-seven years for murder."

CHAPTER THIRTY-NINE

Olivia sized up her opponent, dropped her chin and landed a punishing right cross. She felt feather-light now that the lid had been lifted. Her secret, let out. In twenty-seven years, she'd never breathed those words aloud in one sentence. Father, prison, murder. Her friends at school had figured it out, despite her mother's best efforts. Erik too. Word got around. She became one of the Crescent Bay kids. But she'd never told them herself. She'd put it in a box, labeled it unspeakable, and left it there. Until tonight. A random Thursday and a veritable stranger who already knew more about her than most of Fog Harbor.

She threw a jab, and then another, appreciating the satisfying thwack of her fist on the canvas.

"You're a natural." Deck peeked out from behind the heavy bag braced against his shoulder.

"I may have gone a few rounds before." Though the foam bags at Palo Alto's Juice and Jab, the frou-frou gym near the Stanford campus, probably didn't count.

"I don't doubt it."

"I can see why you like it. I always tell my patients to talk out their anger. But there's something to be said for punching the hell out of an inanimate object."

"It works better when you picture a face." He kept smiling, even after she surprised him with one last punch.

"You're right."

She stepped back, dropped her guard. "Do you think Emily will be okay? I don't know how she'll handle it if Shauna—"

"She'll get through it. She's got you, right?"

Olivia shrugged. Uncertain how much that meant these days. She wondered if all of this could be traced back to her, to her indecision. To the chapel, two weeks ago. If she'd said something then, maybe Bonnie and Laura would still be alive. Shauna would be drunk and laughing with Emily at the Hickory Pit. Not deciding had been the worst decision of all.

"Look, we only just met a week ago. But I can tell you're a helluva shrink. And an even better sister. Emily will be fine. Should we check on her?"

"Nah. Let her rest for a little while." After she'd told Deck what Shauna had witnessed, Emily had nodded off on Deck's sofa. Which Olivia had to admit was deceptively comfortable despite its hideous green upholstery. "I don't think she slept much last night."

"That makes two of us."

"Three," Olivia admitted, hopping up on Deck's tailgate. The cat eyed her from the truck bed, unsure, watching and waiting. Deck joined her there. She liked him close to her—his right hand inches from her left, warmth radiating from his shoulder to hers, the smell of soap and sweat and the coffee he'd brewed for them—but she also wanted him farther, afraid of what it all meant.

"Thanks for telling me about your dad. That can't have been easy."

"Which part, the telling it or the living it?"

"Both. But I meant the telling. I get it, though. Why you keep it a secret. Sometimes, the past is so big and so complicated, it's easier not to explain. It changes how people see you."

"Especially when you work in a prison. With murderers."

The cat made a move, slowly advancing toward Deck and purposefully skirting the perimeter, out of Olivia's reach. Ears pricked, tail low. "I assume your prime suspect, Warden Blevins, knows?"

She rolled her eyes, meaning *yes*. Guilt, her old friend, gnawed at her still. She'd forced Em to fess up, but she'd kept quiet about what she'd seen with her own eyes. What Drake had seen too, apparently. Accusing the warden felt too risky, and she didn't need a target on her back.

"You never did say why you wrote his name on your profile." Deck spoke casually, not even looking at her but rather at the cat who'd made its way onto his thigh. Two paws on, two off. But Olivia could spot an interrogation a mile away, albeit a friendly one. Her job was part interrogation, after all.

"Did you know Blevins grew up in Oakland? He worked at San Quentin as a CO on death row for ten years before he got this job. He's old school. Not as progressive as some of the younger wardens. But his reputation is impeccable."

"I'm guessing he didn't tell you all that."

"He didn't have to. Look him up online. He's got a lot to lose. Anybody who threatens that, well… I treated a guy who shot a man over fifty cents, so…"

"Are you saying Devere is a threat to the warden?"

She reached over, ignored the little spark that ignited when her arm brushed Deck's, and let the cat sniff her hand.

"C'mon, Detective. I can't do all the work for you."

He laughed warmly. But leaned back, away from her touch. "This is Cy, by the way. He's a free spirit. Likes Tasty Whiskers and warm places. Hates eighties hard rock. That's why I wear the headphones now, why I didn't hear you drive up earlier."

"Cy? As in Cyclops?"

"Yep. It's not too obvious, is it?"

"It's perfect." Cy rubbed his head against her hand, encouraging her to scratch the spot behind his ear. "But you know, once you name him, there's no going back. He's yours."

CHAPTER FORTY

Will stared at Olivia too long. But he couldn't help it. She'd surprised him with that one, a piece of wisdom straight from the mouth of Virginia Decker. Maybe that's why she felt so familiar. She reminded him of the good parts of his mother. The parts her depression had eventually leeched and corroded like battery acid. Until she didn't work right anymore.

"My mom used to say that. Or she said it once. When we found our dog, Max."

Cy jumped down, done with them, and strutted to his bed in the corner. Will had upgraded his suite from a pile of old towels to a box with a blanket tucked inside it. He circled a few times before settling in.

"And was she right?"

Will sat up, nodded, careful to avoid Olivia's bare forearm. Touching her felt like putting his hand too close to a hot stove. Yet he desperately wanted to do it anyway. Which confirmed it. He'd lost his damn mind. Somewhere between her charging right into his crime scene and her telling him to take off his wet clothes.

Glancing sidelong at Olivia, he inched his hand to the right until his pinky rested against hers. Watched the contact register on her face. She didn't move. Like him, she seemed to be holding her breath, fighting the inevitable. He turned his head slowly to look at her, the way teenage Will would have, every move achingly precise. One mile to every inch of skin.

When their eyes met, he felt pulled toward her, sucked right into her goddamn gravitational field, even as he questioned his own sanity. Just when he'd made up his mind to go ahead and kiss her already, she slid off the tailgate.

"We should probably head back inside. You have to meet JB, right? And I have to get home. Will you call if you hear anything about Shauna?"

The wind knocked out of him, it took a second. "Uh, yeah. Of course." And another before he realized she'd been flustered too. He'd flustered Dr. Smarty Pants. He fully intended to do it again. Better, next time. "Hey, Olivia…"

She paused at the door, looked over her shoulder toward him.

"Be careful, okay? Whoever this guy *or girl* is…" The corner of her mouth lifted, showing her dimple. "It's obvious they have a very specific victim pool. You and Emily are in it."

He left out the other part that had been gnawing at the back of his brain since he'd reread Drake's disturbing book. The fourth victim, Dr. Lacey Lawson, decapitated along with the rest. His blood simmered at the thought of Devere writing those words, getting away with his sick fantasies.

She cocked her head, teasing him. "Now who's worried?"

"Is that allowed?"

But when she answered, her voice came out matter-of-fact. "Only if I'm allowed to worry about you too."

Will mulled over his regrets. One, he'd let Chief Flack steamroll him into his worst nightmare. Worse even than partnering with Jimmy Wise-Ass Benson. Two, he'd let JB take the wheel as they drove the route Shauna had taken last night. Three, he'd nearly kissed Olivia. Four, he hadn't. At least he'd finally gotten her number. Even if it was strictly business.

"What do you make of our new teammates?" JB spun out of the Hickory Pit and headed toward Pine Grove Road, kicking up gravel behind them into the cold Fog Harbor night.

Will said nothing, buckling his seatbelt.

"That good, huh?" JB reached over and gave Will's arm a conciliatory pat, the car veering in the same direction until he jerked the wheel, righting it again.

"Just trying to stay alive over here. This isn't your Camaro, remember?"

"Puh-lease. My Camaro would eat this Crown Vic for breakfast. Besides, I'm just having a little fun. I haven't totaled one of these babies since 1994."

"Not helping." Will gripped the door as JB veered into the turn. "So, where *are* the two stooges?"

JB chuckled and revved the engine as they rumbled in the direction of the prison. "I gave them a job. Remember our UBO? I told them they need to figure out exactly where it came from and when."

"That sounds like the proverbial needle in the haystack."

"Exactly. Should keep 'em busy for—oh, I don't know—the next couple years."

A few minutes later, Will pointed up ahead, to the sign illuminated in the headlights, the pole leaning forward so it nearly touched the grass. "Hey, look at that. Just like the caller said."

JB eased off the road and into the ditch, and they got out to examine it up close.

"She hit it, alright," JB said, looking on while Will touched the streak of yellow paint that had transferred onto the metal. "It explains the cracked headlight and the scrape to the front end of the Mini."

"Did you find out what happened with the DUI call?"

"Never located her. Then the lazy ass went off duty."

"That makes no sense. Jane said she told the dispatcher exactly who to look for and that she lived with her grandmother off of 187. What kind of moron cop couldn't figure that out?"

JB gave Will's back a congratulatory slap he feared was anything but. "The kind of moron we've got on our team now, buddy. Officer Graham Bauer."

"Man, I hate this part of the job."

JB hung his head as they sat in the car outside the Ambroses' old Victorian, the light blue paint peeling as if the house had decided to shed its skin. In the front yard, an inappropriately jolly plastic Santa grinned at them. Will wished he could cover its face. He knew Christmas for the Ambrose family would never be the same. Grandma Adele's Cadillac collected leaves in the driveway. Next to it, a shiny rental car with Arizona plates.

Shauna's parents had arrived, and Will had nothing to tell them. Still, he cracked the door anyway, resigned.

"Let's sit for a minute." JB reached across the console and into the glove compartment, retrieving a package of Twinkies.

"Never figured you for a softie." Will shut the door, grateful for a moment's reprieve. One more minute until he had to face Glenda and Paul Ambrose, their devastated eyes. Their expectations.

JB shrugged. "That's the thing about being a cop. It'll harden your heart to stone before it turns it to mush again."

"Give me one of those." Will didn't wait for JB's permission. Just grabbed the snack cake and ate it in two bites.

"Oh, Jesus. Now we're in trouble. City Boy's eating real sugar."

"I didn't have a chance to grab dinner. Olivia came over and—"

JB paused, mid-chew. "Hold up. Is that how you found out about Shauna's little secret? The throwdown between Riggs and McMillan? *Olivia* told you."

Will cursed himself. He should've kept it quiet, but he had to face facts. He needed JB's help. Chief Flack hadn't been wrong. They were both in over their heads.

"Or did she come over for some other reason?" JB wiggled his eyebrows while he washed down the rest of the Twinkie with a swig of soda.

"Just don't say anything, okay? I don't trust anybody at the prison. Not Hank Wickersham. Not James McMillan. Not the COs. Not even the—"

"Holy cow." JB smacked the steering wheel. "Did you kiss her?"

"No. Not that it's any of your business."

"Because she pulled you over to the dark side, man. The Area 51, Bigfoot, second-shooter conspiracy theory dark side. You think the warden's in on this."

"I don't know what I think. The whole case is a mess. But I do know the Oaktown Boys are in the middle of a turf war with Los Diabolitos, the Mexican street gang. And Blevins picked a side." Will pulled his cell phone from his pocket, opened the bookmark on his browser, and handed it to JB. "Read this."

San Francisco Post

"Correctional Lieutenant Hailed as Hero after
Record Contraband Bust"
by Nicola Perido

San Quentin Lieutenant Lester Blevins was honored by California Governor Miriam Zaruba with the 2017 Medal of Valor at a ceremony in San Francisco this weekend. According to Zaruba, Blevins was instrumental in exposing a sophisticated criminal enterprise involving inmates affiliated with the Los Diabolitos street gang. According to prison officials, members of Los Diabolitos conspired with five correctional officers over the course of several years to smuggle cellular telephones into the institution. Blevins was described as a hero, after he intercepted a drone delivery of wire cutters, a machete, and one thousand dollars in cash which had been arranged through the illegal use of a cell phone. As the result of Blevins' actions, twenty Los Diabolitos members were arrested both inside and outside prison walls. Information obtained from the confiscated cell phones also yielded a major cocaine seizure at a warehouse in Oakland.

Cellular telephones have been an ongoing problem for many California institutions, as the devices enable inmates to carry out crime from the confines of their cells, including ordering violence on the streets, planning escapes, and dealing narcotics. In the weeks since receiving the award, Blevins was appointed as Warden of Crescent Bay State Prison, a maximum security facility, where cell phone use has become so rampant officers collected over 2,000 contraband devices just last year.

At the Medal of Valor ceremony, Blevins eschewed the term hero. "I grew up on the mean streets of Oakland, not so different than the inmates I supervise. I understand the challenges these men face in reforming their lives, as many of them have never been afforded the opportunity to have a positive male role model. I became a correctional officer both to ensure public safety and to promote an environment of rehabilitation where change and hope can thrive. As Warden, I plan to continue that mission at Crescent Bay State Prison."

CHAPTER FORTY-ONE

Back at home, Olivia slipped into her pajamas and joined Emily on the sofa, with a generous glass of wine and a bowl of Cheerios. The dinner of champions.

"How're you feeling?" she asked, as Emily flipped through the channels, settling on her second-favorite reality show set aboard a luxury yacht. They'd both been quiet on the drive back, lost in their own thoughts. Olivia's as scattered as beach shells.

"Better. I'm glad we talked to Will. I like him."

Olivia shoveled in a heaping bite of cereal, stalling. She remembered Deck next to her on the tailgate, leaning in. His kind, brown eyes asking her a question. A question she hadn't answered. Though she'd desperately wanted to say yes, she'd run away instead.

"It's okay to admit you like him too. I know you do. You told him about Dad. You never tell anyone about Dad."

"I just wanted him to give me my due. To realize I know what I'm talking about. I lived it."

Emily paused the television, her head swiveling toward Olivia. Eyes rolling, hard.

"Okay. You're right. I like him."

"*A lot.*"

"Don't push it." But Olivia couldn't contain the twisted smile she knew gave her away.

Emily hit play, absorbed in an instant by the show's manufactured drama—the yacht's chef crawling into the bunk of the younger chief stewardess, his lower half blurred by the network's censors. Olivia half watched as she downed her wine, hoping it would knock her out, down for the count tonight.

Emily surprised her when she spoke. Her little-sister voice, trying to be brave. "So what now?"

"Now, we wait. We hope Shauna's okay. We don't assume the worst." Though Olivia already had. Every time she pictured Shauna, she saw that same denim blue garrote around her neck. Pictured her ivory skin, gray. Her blue eyes, cold as marbles.

"What about Dad? I still think we should talk to him."

"Let me think about it, okay?" Olivia felt relieved when Emily nodded in agreement. "Most of all, we have to be careful. *You* have to be careful, Em."

"I am careful."

Olivia's eyes rolled. "Says the girl who drove five hundred miles to meet an online catfish in Seattle."

"Oh, come on. You can't seriously hold that against me. I was only eighteen. And that guy's pictures were smokin' hot." Emily chuckled. "So, *he* ended up being a *she*. Who lived in Texas. No harm, no foul."

Olivia remembered it differently. Her panicked mother on the telephone. How helpless she'd felt. Then, hours later, her drunk mother sobbing about Emily being as reckless as their father. Olivia had to call in a favor with the Feds to unmask model Damian Osgood as supermarket clerk Donna Milenchuck.

"Just promise me you'll be alert. Aware of your surroundings. That kind of thing."

"Duh." One glare from Olivia, and she added, "I promise."

Olivia finished the last of her cereal and deposited the bowl in the sink. It could wait until morning. Her eyes heavy, she headed for bed, thinking Emily would follow to her own.

"I guess you're not tired, huh?" Olivia asked. "You must've slept pretty hard on Deck's sofa."

"I wasn't sleeping." Emily shot her a mischievous grin. "I was giving you two some alone time. Hopefully, you didn't waste it."

Olivia sighed and shook her head, but she smiled the whole way to her bedroom.

Olivia looked down at her feet, confused. They were small, clad in the white Keds her dad's friend's son, Termite, had stolen from the mall in San Jose. She knew they were stolen because they didn't come in a box. He'd brought them into the apartment slung over his shoulder in a plastic bag like a badass Santa Claus. She liked Termite—he was seventeen and had a cute smile—but she didn't like stealing. Still, she'd worn them anyway because the bright white canvas made her happy and all the other girls at school jealous.

Olivia felt queasy, like she might upchuck on the steps in front of her. The three floors up to Apartment E in the Double Rock. When she planted her Keds on that first step and gazed around her, she realized: This is a dream.

For one, the Double Rock had never looked this good; no cigarette butts or beer cans. The grass in the courtyard was a vibrant green, the color of life, not that burnt-out brown it actually was. Two, you could only hear birds singing. Not the loud music that usually stabbed at her ears or the couple in Apartment B who never stopped yelling. But most of all, because when she caught her reflection in a window, she looked like a girl of eight years old. Inside, though, she felt old, and she knew things. Things that hadn't happened to her yet.

Olivia knew she had to walk up those stairs and open the door. In every version of her life, she'd done it. Opening that door was inevitable. So, she put one foot in front of the other and before she blinked, she'd arrived at the light blue door with the gold letter E hanging crooked in the center.

Though it was practically summer, the knob felt cold in her sweaty little hand. It turned with ease, giving in to her will. Olivia closed her eyes, knowing exactly what she'd find inside. Her father, standing over Tina. Next to him, Termite. It was safe to think his name in her dream. But she could *never* say it out loud.

Olivia had seen Tina before, hanging around the Double Rock. Tina had pretty hair, long and cherry red, even if her mom said it was as fake as a three-dollar bill. Tina had given her a stick of Big Red bubblegum her mom made her throw out later. Tina carried a fancy purse and had pink toenails and lots of guys liked her.

When Olivia told her eyes to open, something wasn't right. Her father froze there open-mouthed, the knife in his hand, dripping. Termite's face had turned a pale white that matched the walls. But the girl on the ground had strawberry-blonde hair and soft curls that framed her face.

Olivia looked down at her feet to remind herself: This is a dream.

She wore boots now, not Keds. Black designer boots she recognized as Bonnie's. The heels clacked against the tiles as she ran inside, pushed past her father and collapsed to her knees. The floor, slick with blood.

She leaned in, already opening her mouth to scream. As if she already knew.

The girl, not Tina, not Bonnie, not Laura, but Emily. Her little sister, dead.

CHAPTER FORTY-TWO

When the early morning DJ announced, "Just five days till Christmas," Will felt blindsided. The days since Bonnie's body turned up had collapsed together into one never-ending saga of coffee, uncertainty and sleepless nights. No rest in sight, he'd been out the door and on the road by 4 a.m., heading to the station. Better than lying in bed, eyes fixed on the ceiling.

Most of the media vultures hadn't opened their beady little eyes yet. A few stragglers roamed the parking lot, but they looked as exhausted as Will and stayed out of his way.

Inside the nearly empty station, the cubicles where he and JB set up shop were still dark. He shrugged out of his coat, his mind still in a fog.

It took nearly five full seconds for him to notice the box on his desk. Innocent as a stapler and wrapped in brown paper. It had his name, Detective Will Decker, printed on a Christmas tag in black marker. Probably some junior officer getting a jump on the Secret Santa. He picked it up—heavier than he would've guessed—and unwrapped it without thinking.

Will gasped, dropped the box to the floor. He stared down at it and, for a moment, wondered if he'd dreamed it. But it didn't disappear, and he didn't wake up. He spun around to find the office still empty.

He knelt down and examined the box more closely, the dry piece of toast he'd eaten on the way in threatening to come back up. He'd seen worse. But this was personal. Inside lay a seagull. Its head twisted at an unnatural angle, the neck broken. A note had been pinned to its feathered body and signed with the symbol of the Oaktown Boys.

> *Back off, Detective. We'd hate to see your brother leave Valley View in a body bag.*

He flinched when his phone rang, his heart pounding in his ears. He knew he had to reach for it, had to look, had to answer. But he couldn't stop his mind from imagining the worst. The number would belong to Valley View State Prison. The voice, to some apathetic administrator who'd pretend to care Ben had been shanked in the shower, or thrown from the tier, or choked with a bedsheet. Will would have to live with it.

"Will Decker, Homicide."

"Hey, Will. It's JB." He knew then it was the next worst thing. Because JB never called him Will. "I just heard from dispatch. Looks like the lightkeeper found a body down at Little Gull."

Will retrieved the lid, covered the shoebox. Tucked the whole awful thing under his arm. "I'll meet you there. I've gotta make a stop first. Are you sure it's—"

"It's her. Shauna."

The sun still hadn't come up, and Will sat in his truck, reeling. Wishing he could call it a day. The shoebox watched him from the floorboard, guarding its dark secret. He had to admit he had no clue what to do.

Once upon a time, he would've called his dad. When it came to bad news, Captain Henry Decker always had a plan. He knew a guy; he could call in a favor. He could make problems disappear. Even after he'd retired, he kept his finger on the pulse of the city, and his boys—the two he could depend on, anyway—on a tight leash.

It had been nearly two years since Will had dialed the number he knew by heart. His father would be up by now, shaving his face like he did every morning. Preparing the same breakfast he'd been making since the day Mom walked out. Two eggs, sunny side up. Two strips of crispy bacon. One glass of OJ with a nip of vodka that had become more substantial with every passing year. After all the shit they'd put him through—Petey, the black sheep; Ben, the crooked cop; and Will, a full-on Judas—that glass was probably all vodka by now.

Will punched in the area code, then the first three numbers. He thought of what he'd say and what his dad would say back. How his father would blame him like he always did. How he'd hear the booze in his hello from three hundred miles away. How he'd hang up first, like a scared little boy hiding from Daddy's belt.

He mashed the button, deleting the numbers in one fell swoop, and composed a text to Olivia instead.

His finger hovered for a moment, the reality of the morning still sinking in. Again, he glanced at the box, confirming its existence. Real.

He took a breath. Pressed send.

CHAPTER FORTY-THREE

Are you awake?

Olivia almost laughed when the text bubble appeared on her screen at 4:45 a.m. The wine had done the trick, put her right to sleep. But that dream—that nightmare—had dragged her to the surface way too fast, leaving her sick and gasping. Like a diver with the bends, she still hadn't recovered.

Yep. I'm awake.

If you could call it that.
Deck's reply came back in an instant.

Is Emily?

Two words, innocent in their own right. Together, they made her skin cold. She sat up and put on her sweatshirt. It didn't help.

I doubt it.

Meet outside in ten minutes.

Olivia's hands trembled as she opened the search browser and typed *Shauna Ambrose*. She couldn't wait ten minutes. Couldn't stomach the thought of Em curled in bed, oblivious.

The results told her nothing she didn't already know. She felt reassured but her dream-self lingered in the dark, mute with panic.

Shoving her worry into a cobwebbed corner of her mind, Olivia tugged on a pair of blue jeans, pulled her hair into a ponytail, and splashed cold water on her face until she felt halfway human again.

She padded down the dark hallway, somehow much darker than her bedroom, and stopped outside Emily's door, waiting for her eyes to adjust. When she took the knob in her hand, she almost cried out. It reminded her of the one on the dream door, cold but yielding to her touch.

It opened effortlessly. Emily's bed unmade, and empty.

For one horrified second, Olivia stood there like always, frozen. Taking in the shard of moonlight on Em's comforter. Her painting of Little Gull, finished now and resting against the wall, another blank canvas on the easel. On her dresser, displayed adjacent to the snow globe, the smooth red rock she'd taken from the river.

She hurried out and down the hallway, searching. The guest bath, empty. Kitchen light, off. Mom's old room, cold and musty.

Tears welled in her eyes, but she fought them off like she always did, wondering if this was how it felt to be a parent. This roller coaster of panic and relief. It certainly explained her mother's perpetual need to be a little bit tipsy. Ever since Olivia had come back here, she couldn't shake the fear that clung to her like a shadow. No wonder she'd had that dream.

"Thank God," she heard herself whisper.

Emily lay on the sofa, still in last night's clothes, her head propped on a sofa cushion.

Olivia covered her with the throw and took one last look, before she put on her coat and boots and went outside to wait for Deck. The thought gnawing like it always did.

Em is all I have left.

*

Deck's headlights approached down the long, straight road. As he neared the house, a deer bounded across the highway and disappeared into the forest, heading for parts unknown. Olivia envied that. The ease of escape. Because when he turned into the driveway, and she finally met his eyes, she saw a heaviness there that threatened to drop the ground out from under her.

He cut the engine and climbed out. Already dressed for work, she noticed, in a white button-down and gray slacks. His gun, holstered on his belt and that badge—the talisman her father had feared and loathed in equal parts—glinting in her porch light. He stepped closer to her.

"Olivia…"

She couldn't remember ever hearing him say her name aloud. She liked it, but not like this. It clunked out, hollow. A bell with no ringer.

"I didn't want you or Emily to hear it on the news. Someone found a body at the beach."

Olivia's knees felt wobbly. She didn't trust them. "Is it Shauna?"

"I haven't been out there yet. JB called me at the station. He seemed convinced it's her."

"Does her grandma know? Her parents?"

"Not yet."

Olivia nodded. She bore it like she always did. Like a soldier. But inside, she felt her heart break again, a jagged little fissure that branched out from the big one, the crack that had been there for twenty-seven years. Her heart had been broken before she'd even learned to ride a bicycle. Before she'd lost all her baby teeth.

Deck didn't ask permission when he wiped a tear from her cheek. His touch, a salve, though his fingers felt cold against her skin. She stuttered forward, then back, unsure what to do next. But he seemed certain, pulling her into his arms.

She'd imagined it, him holding her. Still, it shocked her how good it felt. To lean into the solid wall of his chest. To feel the steady push and pull of his breathing. To let someone else bear the weight of her burden even for a moment.

When he released her, she heard him sigh. A tremulous breath that made her wonder if that embrace had been just as much for him as for her. A salve for his burden, too.

"Are you okay?" she asked. "I mean, is there something else?"

He looked at her for a long time before he answered. Even as his eyes welled, she recognized the hesitation, that need to soldier on, no different than her own.

"No. And yes."

CHAPTER FORTY-FOUR

Will drove to Little Gull on autopilot, his mind traveling elsewhere. To the shoebox on the floorboard. To Valley View. To Olivia's porch and her arms around his waist. He'd wanted her touch, needed it even, but not like that. Not with her tears wetting his shirt and the hurt in her eyes when he'd told her about Shauna. Then he'd felt guilty as hell when she'd proven what he'd already suspected. She could see right through his bullshit, could tell he'd been about to lose it himself.

Will parked in the lot on the bluff, between JB's blue Camaro—a wedding present from his second ex—and Chet's old pickup. A couple of patrol cars had already arrived. Will felt certain the media vans weren't far behind. Those vultures could smell death for miles.

The lighthouse beacon pricked the still-dark sky. No trace of fog this morning. Even so, he couldn't spot the horizon from here. As he walked to the wooden staircase, he tried to preserve the moment. Before. The ocean air, the waves kissing the rocks, the salt grass swaying in the light wind. After, he knew this beach would be ruined for him forever. Just another hazard of the job.

JB waited on the bottom step, holding a large flashlight, while Chet moved carefully above him. Will quietly groaned when he spotted the rest of their so-called team, Graham and Jessie, further down the beach.

"'Bout time you showed up," JB grumbled, as Will ducked under the crime scene tape strung from one side of the railing to the other. "You stuck me out here with Tweedledum and Dumber."

Chet paused before snapping a photograph to cast a disapproving glance at JB over his shoulder.

"Not you, Doc. Those two nincompoops."

"Milner's not so bad." Will watched Jessie work, scanning the sand with her flashlight. Meanwhile, Graham worked on his pouty face. "Anyway, I'm sorry. There was something I had to do."

He ignored JB's quizzical expression and finally forced himself to look at the blonde hair strewn on the step like seaweed. The head lolling forward. The hands, already bagged. "Catch me up."

"Well, it's definitely our girl, Shauna Ambrose. She's got that triple piercing in her ears her mom told us about and the butterfly ankle tattoo. Doc, you want to tell him the rest?"

"She's been dead about twenty-four hours. Probably killed shortly after she abandoned her car. Same as the others. Manual strangulation. Minimal sea lice activity, no other insects. She's probably been out here a couple hours at most."

Chet didn't even look up, just rattled off the facts with the kind of stoicism Will didn't envy but recognized. By the time he'd retired, his father had been that way too. Practiced in the dirty business of death. Barely blinking as he uttered phrases like *circling the drain* to describe the condition of a victim to his buddies.

"The garrote?" Will asked.

"Identical. And her pants were pulled down to her knees. Underwear, too. But we did—"

JB cleared his throat, the obnoxious rattle stopping Chet mid-sentence, as Graham and Jessie headed back up the beach within earshot. Jessie carried a few items in her gloved hands. Graham carried nothing but a single used beer can and a chip on his shoulder, visible even from here.

"Found a couple of beer cans and a few cigarette butts." His face half in shadow, Will couldn't read Graham's expression, but he sounded like a man who'd just traipsed a cold beachfront picking up trash. "No footprints. The garbage cans were empty."

"Bag them up for the lab," JB said. "Then head on back to the station. Keep working on that UBO. We'll finish up here."

Jessie started up the hill, alongside the stairs. But Graham stayed put, fixed like an anchor in the sand.

"That's it?" he asked. "Chief Flack said—"

"I don't give a rat's ass what Chief Flack said. Out here, Decker and I are in charge. You're both way too green to be working a case like this anyway. Your best bet is to stay out of our way."

"Whatever you say, *Grandpa*." Graham dropped the beer can he'd collected onto the beach and kicked it, sending it skittering up into the salt grass. He followed Jessie up the hill, huffing and muttering under his breath.

Will stifled a grin, relishing the distraction as much as JB's putting that punk in his place. "What's gotten into you, Gramps?"

"Shoddy police work, that's what. Bauer and Milner heard the call over the radio. Thank God Chet and I got here when we did. Bauer almost lost our smoking gun messing around with the body. Trying to look at her hands."

"Her hands?"

Chet stopped working, nodded. "With her being dead over twenty-four hours, she's in full rigor mortis. Officer Bauer spotted something clenched between her fingers, and he thought he'd just reach right in there and grab it. Break the case and be the hero. Milner tried to stop him. We walked up just in time."

Will shook his head, though it didn't surprise him. He'd worked with plenty of cowboy cops. Guys ready to write their own rules just to break them. "So, what's with her hands then?" he asked.

JB pointed the flashlight back at the body. Shauna's slender arms dead-ended into plastic bags, tightly rubber-banded at her wrists. Beneath the bags, he imagined her fingers, delicate as a bird's bones. Just as cold and stiff as the gull in that shoebox.

"This one fought back. She took something from that asshole that's gonna lead us right to him."

"Are you going to make me guess?"

JB offered a smirk, nothing more.

"Hair," Chet said, finally. "She got a handful of hair."

Will paused at the bottom of the stairs—bare since they'd carted the body away—and looked toward the beach, desolate and gray now even with the sun strong-arming its way over the horizon. He'd been right. Ruined.

"How do you think she got down there?" JB asked.

As Will had watched Chet's crew struggle to lug the stretcher up the steps and to the van, he'd wondered the same.

"Let's walk," he told JB, pointing the hundred or so yards to the drainpipe. His cop clairvoyance pushed him forward like an unseen hand. Past four sets of Graham and Jessie's footprints and the jellyfish left stranded at low tide.

Will stopped and pointed to the stone path that ran from the steps to near the pipe's entrance, leaving only five or so feet of uncharted sand. "What if our perp used the wheelchair, same as we suspected with Bonnie, to transport the victim here via the pipe? Then, he wheeled her along the path to the steps. Dropped her there and headed back the same way."

"Only one way to test that theory. Since the dynamic duo didn't walk out that far."

"That's assuming the wind didn't blow it all away." But already, he could see the tracks. Two deep indentations, the width of a wheelchair, that spanned the length of soft sand between the pipe's entrance and the path. Footprints too, though they were hardly discernible. Just holes, sunk deep.

Will jogged ahead and snapped several photos on his cell. When JB caught up to him, he slapped Will's back as he caught his breath. "Hot damn, City Boy. You're finally starting to pull your weight around here."

Inside, Will's own weight felt too much to bear. Only Olivia had been able to budge the stone that laid upon his chest. As soon as he'd driven away, leaving her waving half-heartedly in the rearview, it had sunk back into place, pinching his lungs shut. But, he played along, sighing and rolling his eyes. "Better mine than yours."

JB laughed, then coughed, hacking up a glob of spit he deposited on the shoreline. He rested against one of the larger rocks, rubbing his right knee. "Careful what you wish for. I might need you to carry me back."

"Shit's gonna really hit the fan now," JB said, as they neared the top of the stairs. "Once the media gets wind we've got a third victim, the *s* word will be plastered everywhere."

Already, Will spotted several media vans parked outside the roped-off periphery of the parking lot. The reporters called out to them—"Hey, Detective! What's going on? Can I get a statement?"—as they walked. He recognized one of them from the crime beat in San Francisco and quickly looked away.

"I'll give 'em a statement." JB surreptitiously extended his middle finger.

Will batted his hand down. "Careful. Or you'll turn into the story. *Rogue cop makes obscene gesture toward female reporter.* Trust me on this one. It's not just Fog Harbor media out there. You're not in Kansas anymore."

"Well, wherever the hell I am, I hope they serve breakfast, because some of us didn't take our time lollygagging out to the crime scene. Some of us didn't even get a damn drop of caffeine."

JB peered into the cab of Will's truck, eyeing the paper cup in the center console, the coffee long gone cold.

"Are those doughnuts?" he asked, pointing to the shoebox on the floorboard.

Will said a silent prayer of thanks he'd remembered to lock his door, imagining JB's horrified gasp at finding a strangled seagull, not a glazed dozen. He'd planned to toss it in the nearest dumpster as soon as he left there—he couldn't wait to be rid of it. "I'll get you doughnuts on the way. We need to head over to the Ambrose house. Then get back to the station, put a rush on the DNA."

"I've got a plan for that." JB headed toward his Camaro, a new bounce in his step. "Did I ever tell you my fourth ex-wife works in the crime lab?"

"And that's a good thing?"

"She owes me big-time. I let her keep the dog." He lowered his head, his own eyes drooping like an old hound. "Damn, if Princess wasn't the best friend I ever had."

CHAPTER FORTY-FIVE

Olivia knew it wouldn't help, that Em wouldn't be able to stand the sight of food after she heard the news, but she made her sister's favorite breakfast anyway. French toast with cinnamon and two eggs scrambled. It gave her something to do, somewhere to put her mind other than the dark places. The cobwebbed corners and shadowy nooks where her worst fears multiplied. Where Deck said things like, *Someone found a body at the beach* and *The Oaktown Boys threatened me*. Showed her things, too. A dead seagull, its filmy yellow eye fixed on her in judgment. But worst, he'd asked things of her, things she'd agreed to but regretted now in the petal-pink light of the morning.

"Liv?" Still in last night's clothes, Emily stood at the kitchen's entrance, already shell-shocked. The bomb hadn't even been dropped yet. "What's going on? Why did you make French toast?"

"Sit down, Em."

"You're scaring me." But her sister did as she was told, taking her place at the table. Just as she had the morning Olivia had found their mother lying impossibly still in her bed. She'd tried to protect Emily from the fallout to make up for all the times she hadn't been there. This was no different.

"Are you hungry?"

Olivia didn't wait for an answer. She took the plate that had been warming in the oven, and placed it on the table with a fork and knife. Her sister stared at it as if she'd just served her a heap of arsenic.

"Detective Decker came by the house this morning. The lightkeeper found a body near Little Gull."

Emily looked up at her, horrified, then pushed the plate across the table. It slid off the edge and clattered against the floor, leaving a sticky mess of toast and syrup and eggs and broken wedding china. "I can't believe you didn't wake me up. You let me sleep! My friend is dead and you let me sleep."

Olivia moved toward her, her arms extending, but Emily had already fled with the table knife in her hand. She ran from the kitchen and into her room.

"Emily! Wait."

The door slammed in Olivia's face but she pushed it back open, her chest aching when she spotted her sister kneeling near the wall, thrusting the knife's dull edge into the canvas. Her painting of Little Gull destroyed, stabbed clean through.

"Why?" Emily wailed. A question for which Olivia had never had an answer, though she pretended to on a daily basis. She'd sat through eight years of schooling. Spent her alimony. Stayed up until her eyes twitched reading Freud. Because she'd wanted that and only that. To know why.

Olivia held her sister, let her cry. Her own tears she kept dammed. Safely walled behind her eyes. This morning, with Deck, was the first time she'd cried in years. Since long before her mother's funeral, when Erik had moved out the last of his things. But Deck couldn't have known that when he'd reached for her, he'd caught her so off guard she'd lowered her wall, letting tears spill over and making a stupid promise she had to keep.

"I hate French toast," Emily said, when her crying finally slowed. She sat back against the wall, wiping her eyes on her shirtsleeve, yesterday's mascara smudged beneath them.

"I thought it was your favorite."

"It was. It used to be."

The ache in Olivia's chest deepened. Like an axe driven through the middle of her breastbone. She'd been a fool to think Emily would forget.

"Do you even remember the last time you made it?" Emily asked her, already accusing.

In her mind, she traveled back two years. Olivia wearing a black dress she'd bought at Neiman's in San Francisco. It seemed too fancy for the Grateful Heart Chapel. "Of course."

After Emily called in sick and crawled into her bed, Olivia lied to her, telling her sister she had to report to work at the prison. That the warden had scheduled a meeting to discuss his concerns about Drake. She hated to leave Emily but she saw no other choice. She didn't want Em to know what she was doing. She didn't want anyone to know.

"I'll take the rest of the day off. Be back in an hour. Call my office number or Leah's if you need anything."

Twenty minutes later, Olivia made her way through the prison control booth on autopilot, mindlessly displaying her ID badge and exchanging a chit for the MHU key, though she didn't plan on visiting her office. She needed a spot away from prying eyes. Still, she wondered if Hank would show his face. According to Deck, he'd been the last one to see Shauna alive. But Olivia didn't buy him as the killer, mostly because of the staged nature of the first two scenes, the pretend sexual assaults. She had Hank figured for the kind of guy who would take what he wanted if he wanted it bad enough.

Olivia entered the main prison and stared down the runway. She'd never seen it so empty. No signs of life in either direction. Just those shiny floors, polished by men with nothing but time. The officer at the booth had told her the warden had just issued a mandatory lockdown—necessary movement only—after the administration had gotten word about the discovery at Little Gull.

The eerie clap of her flats down the quiet hallway unnerved her but emboldened her too. She'd rather it this way. No one saw her while she waited outside the administration office, slipping in behind a member of the free staff and into the office left vacant since Teresa Gunderson's departure on long-term disability leave three months ago. She scrawled a quick IN USE on the whiteboard hanging from the door and closed herself inside.

Olivia logged onto the computer and navigated through the Institutional Directory until she located Edwin Lacy, Jr., her father's correctional counselor.

She moved with purpose, not allowing herself to stop and think as she dialed the number. As it rang and rang and rang. Because she'd already made up her mind the moment Deck had pleaded with her. Not with his words, but his eyes.

"Edwin Lacy. How can I help?"

Olivia considered that question and the warm voice that delivered it. It came with the familiar prod of guilt. "Good morning, Mr. Lacy. My name is Belinda Jett, and I'm an attorney here in San Francisco. I'd like you to locate an inmate on your caseload for me. His name is Martin Reilly, inmate number 22CMY2. I need to speak to him immediately about his upcoming parole hearing."

"You're Reilly's attorney, ma'am?"

"Yes, sir." She held her breath, hoping she'd managed to sound as confident and demanding as any other lawyer.

"Alrighty. The inmates on SNY were just released for breakfast, so it'll be a few minutes before I can locate him and transfer the call to the attorney visiting booth. Should I buzz you back?"

Now that she'd finally done it, she couldn't imagine hanging up and waiting for the shrill sound of her past to zip down the phone line and into the office. To shatter the tomb-like quiet. "I'll hold."

Olivia thought of the last time she'd spoken to her father. She'd been sitting cross-legged on the floor in her studio apartment in Palo Alto, the phone receiver tucked against her shoulder, highlighting her Victimology textbook, when he'd delivered the news about his transfer to Valley View. *I'll only be an hour's drive away*, he'd said, hopeful. *I'd be real happy to see you. I'll bet you're all grown up.* He'd wanted her to be excited but she'd only felt a strange concoction of resentment and dread. Turns out she'd preferred him three hundred miles away. Still did, to be honest.

"Hello? Ms. Jett? This is Martin Reilly. Please don't tell me they postponed the hearing."

Ten years had passed, an eternity really, but her dad's deep baritone turned her into a little girl again. She drew in a breath.

"Are you alone?" she asked. "Just say yes or no."

"Of course. Attorney–client privilege. Mr. Lacy's got me in the booth. I thought I'd be meetin' you in person though. My case is pretty complicated, and I'm real nervous about the psych eval. I've never talked about my crime."

"This isn't your attorney. It's Olivia."

"Olivia? *My* Olivia?"

"Calm down, Dad." The word felt strange and heavy on her tongue. Practically foreign.

"I'm just… it's… it's just damn good to hear your voice. You sound so professional. I read all about your award from the FBI a few years back. Saw it in the *Post*. I was showin' it around the dayroom like a proud papa. I'm so glad Em convinced you to give me a chance to explain. To tell you who I am now. I tried callin' you a few weeks back at the prison. Left a message. I've been wanting to talk to you about—"

Whatever came next, Olivia couldn't bear it. She couldn't go back there. To that nightmare in Apartment E that hadn't been a nightmare at all. But her real life. "She didn't. Em doesn't know. I'm not calling to talk about the past."

"Oh." The silence had a sound. The low drone of disappointment. "Well, are you okay? Is Emily? I heard about those murders up there in Fog Harbor. It's all over the news. Is it true those ladies worked at the prison?"

"Yes, they did. We're both fine." Olivia tried to imagine her father as a patient. She tried to keep her distance. Tried to ease them both into it, this awkward dance. "Have you heard anything? Any talk on the yard?"

"About the murders? How the hell would I know anything about that?"

His indignation—the way he said *murders* like a thing he couldn't claim—wriggled under her skin, and she lost all pretense. "C'mon, Dad. Or should I call you Mad Dog?"

"I'm not involved in that nonsense anymore. I debriefed, Liv. I'm out of the gang. If anything the Oaktown's got a target on my back."

"How did you get a cell phone then?"

"What?"

"You didn't leave that message for me from a prison phone. You couldn't have." The Inmate Calling Service, GTL, required prepayment, and Olivia wouldn't have spent a dime to hear her father's BS.

"I called from Mr. Lacy's office. You can ask him. Give me the benefit of the doubt, alright? I thought, you being a shrink and all, you'd believe I could change. But I guess all that bleeding heart mumbo-jumbo doesn't apply to me."

"I believe people can change. I'm just not sure you're one of them. I've seen your C-file. You're still breaking the rules."

"That was three years ago. That cell phone wasn't even mine."

"Sure. Haven't heard that one before. Let me guess. It belonged to your cellie." With her bitter arrows lodged in his chest, her father sighed like he'd admitted defeat, and Olivia let go of the breath she'd been holding. She'd gone so far off track she'd forgotten about Deck completely.

"I have a favor to ask. That's why I called. I think we can agree you owe me that much at least." He offered no protest, so she plowed ahead. "Do you know Ben Decker?"

"The dirty cop?"

Olivia winced. "Yes. He's in SNY, like you."

"Obviously. A cop, specially one like him, wouldn't last a day on the mainline."

"So you know him?"

"I wouldn't say that. I mostly keep to myself. This place is nothin' but sex offenders and gang dropouts like me." At least he didn't use words like *chomos* and *snitches* like the old Mad Dog would have. Maybe that *was* progress. "Anyway, what about him?"

"Is Oaktown going after him?"

"I told ya. I ain't Oaktown no more."

It was Olivia's turn to sigh in frustration. "Would you just keep your ear to the ground? Word at Crescent Bay is that Oaktown might want to take him out to settle a score."

"That's askin' a lot, Liv. Who's this guy to you anyway? Please don't tell me he's your boyfriend. That you got yourself involved with some cowboy cop. You always did know how to pick 'em. I told you not to marry that Ziegler boy. That one time you brought him to meet me, he could barely look me in the eye."

"Really? You want to lecture me about my choices? You weren't there for me or Emily or Mom. You chose Oaktown over your family. I think I turned out pretty well, all things considered."

Her father cleared his throat expectantly.

"No, he's not my boyfriend. Not that it's any of your business. Are you going to help me or not?"

"I did hear a rumor, now that you mention it. Good ole Inmate. com." Olivia rolled her eyes. *Inmate.com.* There was the prison slang she'd expected from him. In the past twenty-seven years, he'd surely become fluent. "They say he's got to pay to stay, if you catch my drift."

"I don't speak inmate, so…"

"Give me a break. You work at a prison. You know what it means."

Olivia squirmed. The last time she'd heard the phrase, one of her patients had ended up dead on the exercise yard with ten puncture wounds to his neck. He couldn't afford to pay; he couldn't stay.

"Who does he pay?"

"He lets a couple of the Oaktown dropouts use his canteen account."

She felt sick. "You?"

"Hell, no. Look, I'll keep an eye out. But I'm not fightin' anybody for him. I'm too old for that shit, and I want to get out of this place someday. Have a chance to do it better. To make things right. To tell you exactly what happened that day back at the Double Rock. I'd like the opportunity to be your dad again. If you'll let me."

Those words tugged at her heart but Olivia held firm. She'd had too much time to mull over the past. Not only the murder but all of it. The empty promises. The times she'd cowered in the closet with her teddy bear while he'd raged, high on meth and Jack Daniel's. The nights her mother crawled in bed with her and cried them both to sleep. "Those are just words, Dad. You have to earn my trust, and it won't be easy."

"I'm counting on it."

After Olivia hung up the phone, she sat there for a moment, stunned. That she'd done it. That he'd been different than she'd expected, different than she'd remembered. That a long-frozen part of her had started to thaw. Which is exactly why it felt necessary to admonish herself out loud. Him too.

"Don't you get your hopes up."

Olivia logged off the computer. She straightened the phone and the keyboard and tucked the mouse back into the top drawer. She left no trace, peeking through the cracked door before she exited Teresa's office and headed back to the runway which appeared as long and empty as when she'd left it. A deserted road to nowhere.

She hoofed it in the direction of the control booth, hoping to get in and out of the prison unseen. She couldn't face anyone today. Not after this morning and its cruel surprises. Shauna's lifeless body and Deck's broken bird and Emily's wailing.

As Olivia neared the exit, she readied her ID badge, glancing down to remove it from the small plastic sleeve she wore on a lanyard around her neck. When she looked up, two identical frames emerged from the control booth. She gave a tentative wave, as Maryann and Melody approached blank-faced. Neither woman smiled, which confirmed they already knew the worst of it.

Just before Olivia had left the house, the breaking news of the discovery at Little Gull had interrupted *Good Morning San Francisco*. She'd muted the TV in a hurry, before Emily could hear it, and watched as the camera panned the beach at Crescent Bay, its pristine beauty marred by the garish yellow of the crime scene tape. By now, the whole town would have been clued in to the headline plastered at the bottom of the screen: *Fog Harbor Serial Killer Strikes Again, Another Local Woman Found Dead*.

"Have you heard?" Melody asked, coming to a stop right in front of Olivia. Sure-footed, she rested her hands on her duty belt, as Maryann rocked from one foot to the other, her own hands hidden in her pockets.

Olivia nodded at them grimly.

"We couldn't believe it," Maryann said. "Another one. And to think, we just saw Shauna at the Hickory Pit. It's like an episode of *Forensic Files*. I don't think I'll be watching that show anymore."

Melody considered her sister with skepticism. "That's a likely story. Should've stopped a long time ago, if you ask me. Keeps her up every night, jumping at all the little noises. Thinking it's some crazed lunatic with a bone saw and lye."

Twittering, Maryann shook her head. "Not *every* night. And Olivia understands. It's just fascinating what some people can hide. Like this guy, the Seaside Strangler—"

"That's what Maryann calls him," Melody explained, as Olivia's eyes ping-ponged between them. "I still think it's the Vulture myself."

"*Anyhoo...* the Seaside Strangler must be a regular wolf in sheep's clothing. With everyone on such high alert after Bonnie, it's a wonder he's been able to carry out these attacks without getting caught. He must be very clever."

Melody coughed, a short and sudden burst that reddened her face and quieted her sister. "I'm surprised to see you here. I know Emily and Shauna were friends. She must be taking it hard."

"Yeah. I was actually on my way home. I just popped in to check on a few patients."

Olivia didn't feel good about lying. But she'd learned to keep whole parts of herself tucked away for safekeeping, not so different than the perps on Maryann's TV show. But she gave herself a pass. Impersonating an attorney and fibbing to her colleagues seemed small potatoes compared to burying bodies.

"I thought about calling in sick, too," Melody said. "Usually, one of us stays home with Mom, but I needed the overtime. Those damn medical bills don't pay themselves."

"How is your mother?" Olivia asked, letting her eyes wander to the exit. She felt desperate to leave this place. To get back to Em.

The sisters gave a synchronized shrug, with Maryann speaking for them, her eyes flat behind her glasses. "Sad to say, but she's got one foot in the grave. She never did recover after she broke her hip last summer."

"I'm sorry to hear that. She's lucky to have you both. Now, if you'll excuse me..."

Olivia prepared to make a break for it. Already, she could imagine herself giving the exit door a push. Could feel the cold air stinging her skin, could smell the redwoods, their branches waving her on as she fled.

"Should we ask her?" Maryann nudged Melody.

"Ask me what?"

Maryann leaned in conspiratorially. "Well, we were thinking of organizing a little something in honor of Shauna, Laura, and Bonnie. Nothing too elaborate. Just a small staff get-together after Bonnie's funeral on Sunday to share stories and memories. Would you want to help us set up?"

A flash of Grateful Heart Chapel and the scream that sent her running. She didn't know how she would sit through the funeral, much less what came after. "Do you have a venue?"

Maryann laughed. "A venue? You make it sound so formal. We were going to have it at our house since Melody and I finally fixed the place up a little."

"Your mom is okay with that?"

"Oh, she'll be out cold the whole time. Our stepdad, Ken, always did say she could sleep through anything."

CHAPTER FORTY-SIX

After JB had pled his case to ex-wife number four, Tammy Benson, she sighed and laid a pitying hand on Will's shoulder. "Jimmy goes through partners like he goes through underwear. I'll say a prayer for you, Will Decker."

"Thanks. I need it."

"Hey, you're supposed to be on my side, City Boy. Bros before—"

Tammy smacked JB's arm, momentarily silencing him. A rare and illustrious feat, as far as Will could tell. "And you wonder why I left you."

It didn't last long. "C'mon, Tam. Everybody knows I left you. I can't be with a woman who doesn't respect me."

She rolled her eyes. "Get ready for a life of celibacy then, Father Benson."

"I've got no problems in that department. I'll have you know, the offers keep rolling in."

Tammy's laugh—a single, discordant note—and the way she watched and waited for JB's reaction told Will two things. She'd pronounced JB full of bullshit a long time ago. And she wanted him back anyway. He wanted her too, judging by the way his gaze lingered on her cleavage, just visible beneath her lab coat.

"That may be true, but I'll bet you don't get many repeat customers."

"You never had any complaints."

When they locked eyes, Will wondered if Tammy was about to demand a do-over. Right here, right now in the lobby of the Del

Norte County crime lab. He cleared his throat, tapped his watch. "I don't want to interrupt this reunion, but…"

"Will you do it, Tam? When Chet sends it over, just bump it to the front of the pile. He should be done with the autopsy by this afternoon."

"I can't make any promises. I'm just a lab tech in Fog Harbor." She paused, waiting for JB to pout. "But I know a gal at the San Francisco County lab who owes me a favor. They've got that fancy new rapid DNA machine down there on loan from the FBI."

JB pumped his fist in the air and leaned toward Tammy's cheek, lips puckered. She pushed him away half-heartedly, her manicured fingers grazing his chest. "It's not for you, you big nincompoop. It's for that young girl and the other two victims. For all of us Fog Harbor women. I can't even take Princess for a walk anymore without looking over my shoulder."

JB winced. "How is my girl? Does she miss her daddy?"

Tammy slipped her cell from her back pocket and scrolled through her photos until she found the right one. She shielded the screen from JB, so only Will could see. He had to bite the inside of his cheek to keep from laughing.

In the photo, JB dozed in a recliner, his head drooping. A black Dachshund laid belly-up across his chest, his small, furry head just beneath JB's chin.

"He's a big teddy bear." Tammy cast a flirty glance at JB. "And don't let him tell you otherwise."

JB didn't say a word until Will had steered the car back on the road, pointed in the direction of Crescent Bay State Prison.

"Breathe a word about that picture and I'll make your life a living hell."

"And that's different how?" Will chuckled, grateful for a distraction. Leave it to JB to make him feel better with a threat of eternal damnation. "Seems like Tammy's still hung up on you. Why'd you two call it quits?"

JB shook his head. "If you have to ask, you're not as smart as you look, City Boy. And to be honest, you don't even look that smart."

Will figured why, or he had a good guess. But it hurt to admit it, to say it out loud. His father was no different, his badge driving a bitter wedge between him and anyone who tried to get too close. *You don't have a job. You are the job*, Will had heard his mother say once, right before she'd dissolved into a puddle of tears.

"Did she eat all your doughnuts? Scratch your Camaro? Interrupt you in the middle of the big game? C'mon, why'd you leave her?"

"*She* left me, just like she said. Same as the others. It's the job, man. It gets them every time."

Warden Blevins sat, steely-eyed, behind his desk, his hands steepling beneath his chin. As Will and JB waited at the threshold, he nodded at Leeza, his secretary, allowing them entrance. She ushered them to the two chairs arranged side by side and scurried out. Though the warden showed no sign of surprise, Will felt certain he'd been waiting for them.

"How can I help you today, Detectives? More bad news to deliver?"

Will nodded. "Unfortunately, we discovered the body of Shauna Ambrose this morning. We've notified her grandmother and her parents, and we'll need access to her employment records, same as we did for Bonnie and Laura."

"Of course. I placed the institution on a temporary lockdown this morning as soon as I heard. The inmates are getting restless. Rumors have started to circulate about the nature of the evidence, that it might point to one of their own. In here, any upset of the applecart brings all the bad apples to the top. As you can imagine, we've got a lot of bad apples. Some of them rotten to the core."

JB chuckled. "There's a few of them rotten apples we're particularly interested in."

"Devere, I presume."

"And Tommy Rigsby," JB added. "Goes by Riggs."

"Riggs, huh?" Warden Blevins unfolded his spindly legs and walked to the barred window behind him. The sky gray through the dingy glass. "He's one nasty SOB. Affiliates with Oaktown. How's he mixed up in all this?"

Will cut his eyes at JB, answering for them both. "We'd rather not say. Not yet."

"I understand." But Will didn't miss the slight flare of Warden Blevins' nostrils that suggested the exact opposite of understanding. The warden unlocked the file cabinet behind him, removed a large envelope, and laid it on the center of his desk, a small bulge protruding from its middle. Like a snake that had swallowed a rat. "I'll call over to B Block and have them send Mr. Rigsby right over. In the meantime, you gentlemen may be interested in this."

"I hope it's Devere's confession," JB said. "Or a Reese's Peanut Butter Cup. Either works for me."

Will cast a disapproving glance in his partner's direction.

"What? Don't you know the road to heaven is paved in peanut butter and chocolate?"

"I can't help you there. But IGI did finish their investigation of the phone we recovered from Devere's cell. It's all yours."

After Warden Blevins excused himself to round up Tommy Rigsby, Will slid the envelope toward him and opened it, fishing out a cell phone fancier than his own.

"What should we look at first?" he asked, as JB peered over his shoulder.

"Hell if I know. I've still got a flip phone and an AOL email address."

Will navigated to the photos, the last one taken on Friday, December 6th at 1:30 p.m. "This is the one Shauna posted online."

In it, Drake and Shauna posed by the Changes banner. Devere had one arm around Shauna's shoulder and the other raised, giving the camera a peace sign. He'd written two words at the bottom with one of those photo-editing apps.

Stupid Slut.

"Real nice fella. A true gentleman," JB said, as Will began scrolling through the others, most of them selfies of Devere posing on his bunk with a copy of *Bird of Prey*, smug but unsmiling, in various states of undress. JB punctuated each shirtless photo with a guttural groan.

"Make it stop," he pleaded, as Will neared the end, with only a few photos remaining. All of them taken in mid-November.

The first was a photo of Bonnie standing at her classroom podium, taken at a strange angle, as if the photographer—Devere presumably—had snapped it in secret from his desk. He'd captioned it, *Thieving Whore.*

Laura, bent over and peering into the industrial oven. He recognized her raven hair pulled into a bun, her apron's strings tied in a bow at her back. This one had a caption too. *Greedy Pig.*

JB's breath quickened, matching Will's, as he opened the last photo, the hairs on his neck prickling when he realized. A woman's figure, captured from a distance on the Crescent Bay yard. Her auburn hair, caught by the wind, leaving a trail of flames behind her.

"I'll be damned. Is that…?"

"Olivia." Even as he said her name, Will couldn't tear his eyes from the awful words beneath the photograph, scrawled in angry red strokes. The whole of it gripped him, no different than that broken-necked bird.

Arrogant Bitch.

By the time Warden Blevins returned, pronouncing Tommy Rigsby on his way with an officer escort, Will and JB had combed through the rest of the phone.

In the last two months, Devere had made calls to Heather Hoffman, as well as to several reporters at SFTV, the most popular San Francisco station. Even a few national networks. He'd also created a Facebook page for his main character, Hawk McGee, where Will found a few of the shirtless photos had been posted and commented on by his fans. Each comment more disturbing than the last.

> *R u the author? Impressive.*
> *Smokin' hot.*
> *Innocent man. Framed by the cops.*
> *Marry me, Vulture!*
> *If I have to die, I wouldn't mind if you did it. #chokemeout*

"I don't get it," JB had said. "These women look so normal."

"He's the ultimate bad boy, I guess. Even Charlie Manson had a fiancée."

As the warden loomed from the doorway, Will tossed the phone on the desk, still reeling from that photo of Olivia and what it meant.

"When were you going to tell us about this?" Will asked, pointing to the cell. His outrage spurred him to his feet. "There are photos of the victims on there."

Warden Blevins shrugged, and Will fought the urge to throw a hook, snap one of his pencil ribs in two. "I haven't looked at it myself. But IGI thought it was pretty tame. Compared to some of the other stuff they see."

"Tame? Devere was stalking these women. Taking clandestine photos, calling them obscene names. Then they turn up dead, and we're supposed to believe it's a coincidence?"

"I understand, Detective Decker. But these are the women he interacts with on the daily. As far as I know, only three of them have been murdered."

"So far." Speaking his fears out loud knotted Will's stomach. "Did you even bother to tell Olivia that her photo is on this asshole's phone? I want him moved to a more secure location. Now."

Warden Blevins' pale cheeks reddened, little splotches of fire. "Listen here, Decker. I'm the captain of this ship, and I don't take kindly to you giving me orders. We've already got regular patrols outside Devere's cell every night. The guy's in a maximum security prison. That's razor wire out there. What more do you want from me?"

A few choice words were poised like drawn arrows on the tip of Will's tongue, but he never got the chance to unleash them.

First, the panicked shouting from the main hallway. A scream Will couldn't categorize as male or female, human or animal. Only a living creature fighting like hell to stay that way. The alarm blared. Then, boots on concrete.

Warden Blevins took off in the direction of the noise, Will and JB behind him. As Will ran, the scene materialized, slowly, slowly, slowly. Then, in an instant, shades of red and panicked voices. The sickening, metallic scent he'd grown used to in this job.

A body lay at the bottom of the staircase at the far end of the hallway, surrounded by officers. One of them knelt over the inmate, breathing into his mouth. Another held a handkerchief to his chest, blood seeping through the officer's fingers.

Will swallowed his own vomit. Not at the sight of the blood. Or the fear he felt rise up in him like an old friend. Not even at the dying inmate's face. Which he'd never seen in person but recognized from the mug shot he'd found the night prior on the Internet.

When he trusted himself to speak without upchucking, he turned to JB. "It's Riggs."

What had him sick to his stomach, he'd spotted at the periphery. Three officers surrounded the suspect. The man's frail hands, cuffed behind him and slick with the blood he'd spilled. A shank tossed on the polished concrete. His glasses and his wheelchair, discarded in the fray.

This face Will had seen before. It belonged to Morrie Mulvaney.

JB let out a low whistle as they carted Riggs off in a body bag. "What the hell was that? I tell ya, the Robbery-Homicide Division ain't no picnic but it makes this place look like Disneyland."

Will shushed his partner so he could eavesdrop. They'd hauled Morrie to his feet, and he'd started talking before they'd even finished reading him his rights. As old as he'd looked already, he'd aged ten years in the last fifteen minutes.

"...the right to remain silent. Anything you say can and will be used against you in a court of law. You have—"

"Lord, forgive me," he mumbled. "I had to do it."

"The right to an attorney. If you cannot afford an attorney, one will be appointed for you."

"You think I care about that bullshit? Ain't no attorney can help me now. Not even Atticus Finch."

"You wanna make a statement, Mulvaney?"

Morrie hung his head, grimacing. His own bloody palm prints stained his prison blues. "Like I said, he gave me no choice. I had to do it."

Will turned those words over and over and over in his mind. He wanted to question Morrie himself. But Warden Blevins lurked nearby, his eyes trained on the detectives. Even as Will watched Morrie, he felt the heat of them on his back.

"Who gave you no choice?" the officer asked.

The question lingered unanswered.

"Detective Decker?"

Will turned toward the breathy voice of Warden Blevins' secretary. She smiled, all teeth, despite the chaos and bloodshed around her. That's what happened when you worked in a prison, he supposed: a man getting shanked in the hallway became your new normal. No different than patrolling the streets of San Francisco, where he'd acclimatized to dead junkies with needles in their veins and sixteen-year-old kids firing ghost guns over the color of their jerseys.

"The medical examiner is on the telephone for you. Says it's very important."

Will and JB followed her back to the office. After she'd left them alone, Will put the call on speaker.

"Will Decker, Homicide. You're on speaker, Chet."

"Hey, Deck. Sorry to bug you guys. I just finished up with the victim. I couldn't wait to tell you. There's something you both need to know."

"Give it to us, man," JB said. "We need some good news."

"As we thought, I found several strands of black hair clutched in her right hand that I rushed over to the lab for processing. There was no evidence of vaginal or anal penetration, similar to the first two victims. The garrotes appear identical. Manner of death, consistent with the others."

"C'mon, Doc. The suspense is killin' me."

Will leaned in, saying a silent prayer for something that could salvage this day. Could bring it back from the brink.

"I also found a small amount of bodily fluid on her thigh. I can't say for sure but I'm betting it's semen. Our perp messed up big, times two. We've finally got his DNA."

JB clapped his hands together. "Hot damn. I can't wait to tell the chief. Screw forty-eight hours. We caught us a killer in twenty-four."

CHAPTER FORTY-SEVEN

After Leah called, Olivia locked herself in the bathroom, leaving Em staring at the television, zombie-like. She dropped to her knees over the toilet, desperately wanting to vomit. To puke it all up and flush it away. *It* being her past. *It* being that conversation with her father and whatever he'd planned to tell her about that long-ago night. *It* being the image she couldn't get out of her head now, though she hadn't even seen it for herself. Morrie springing to his feet, spry and determined, his arthritis momentarily forgotten. Poking two deep holes in Riggs' chest with a shiv fashioned from a metal bedpost. Riggs bleeding out before the ambulance had arrived. Apparently, despite the lockdown, Morrie had been given permission to leave his cell for a medical ducat. He'd been waiting at the bottom of the stairs for Riggs and his escort, attacking suddenly before the officer could stop him.

Leah also told her Deck had been there—that's how Leah had found out. He and JB had come to the MHU looking for Olivia. That thought, of all the things sloshing in her gut, finally did it. Guilt rose up in her throat and she heaved until her stomach had emptied.

"Are you okay in there?" Emily asked.

"Fine." Though she could see her face in the mirror, pale as a ghost. "I'll be out in a minute."

A splash of cold water and a few swipes of blush to her cheeks and she returned to the land of the living. She opened the door to find Emily still standing there.

"I know you liked Morrie." Em wrapped an arm around her shoulders, but Olivia shrugged her off, afraid she'd cry again. Since this morning with Deck, her tears had remained dangerously close to the surface.

"It's more than that. I thought he was…" Olivia waved her hands as if she could conjure the right word to sum her dismay. She had no right to feel betrayed. Morrie owed her nothing. But somehow it ached just the same. "I thought he'd changed. After all these years and all the good he's done for other inmates, I actually believed he was a decent guy."

"Oh, Liv. I get you're a shrink and all. But you're not a human lie detector."

Olivia raised her eyebrows at her sister. "Neither are you."

"I have a feeling I know what you're getting at, and you're wrong. Dad is nothing like Morrie. He debriefed. He's got a target on his back now. Taking that kind of risk means something. You'd see that too if you'd just call him and hear him out."

"I did." The words tumbled out of her mouth before she could stop them. Now that she'd said it she realized her sister had one thing right. If she could be so wrong about Morrie—the warden too, for that matter—how could she ever trust herself to let her dad back in her life?

"And?"

"I don't want to discuss it."

Olivia checked the time. Almost noon. She needed to talk to someone who could tell her what Riggs knew, what she'd landed herself in the middle of when she'd seen him and the warden in the chapel. She knew exactly where that someone would be.

James' fancy SUV stood out like a sore thumb at the Hickory Pit, where the vehicles in the parking lot, mostly pickups, proudly bore their scratches, dents, and second paint jobs like badges of honor.

Olivia parked her BMW alongside it. She spotted James in the driver's seat, his prison ID affixed to his pocket, inhaling a barbecue sandwich. As he wiped a drip of sauce from his chin, she marveled at him. How his life went on, cruelly. How it could blow up in your face one day and demand you keep moving, keep breathing, keep eating barbecue sandwiches on your lunchbreak.

In between James' bites, she got out of her car and approached the passenger window. She tried to get his attention with a little wave but he seemed a million miles away. There, but not there.

When she rapped on the window, he flinched, his eyes darting. In one quick motion, he dropped his sandwich and reached beside him. His hand strangled the grip of a gun, as he sized her up, wide-eyed.

Olivia gasped, staggered back.

"Sorry, Olivia." James lowered the passenger window and showed her both his hands, finally looking right at her. His face bore the consequences of his bad decisions – a blackened left eye and a puffy lip. "You scared me. What are you doing here?"

"Why do you have a gun?"

"Why do you think?" His words lashed back like a whip, stinging her, and when she met his red-rimmed eyes, she wished for a do-over. Because when your wife is brutally murdered and you've got two little boys to protect, having a gun at the ready doesn't seem barbaric. It seems reasonable. Prudent even.

She approached the window and lowered her voice. "I apologize. With how crazy it's been around here, I haven't even had a chance to tell you how sorry I am about Bonnie. How are Nathan and Noah doing?"

"As well as can be expected. Bonnie's mom has been a big help."

"What about you?"

He released a long breath and glanced down at the gun again. The grip smeared with barbecue sauce. "I'm still here. That's about all I can say. To tell you the truth, I probably went back to work too early, but I was going stir crazy in that big house."

Olivia had holed up in her office and worked on patient notes the afternoon of her mother's funeral. Needless to say, she understood.

"So, are you here for lunch too, or...?"

She shook her head. "I need to talk to you. Can I get in?"

"Okay."

Though it seemed more question than answer, Olivia opened the door and removed a stuffed whale from the passenger seat. As she climbed inside, she took a quick inventory of the vehicle. The gun, two booster seats, a few gum wrappers and receipts, one half-eaten barbecue sandwich. A black duffel bag squatting toad-like beneath the backseat. Ordinary but ominous somehow.

"I assume you heard about Tommy Rigsby."

"Yeah. I had to get out of there. I mean, the whole place has been teetering on a razor's edge since Bonnie and the riot the other day. But I can't believe Mulvaney would do something like this. I thought he was done with Oaktown. I just saw the guy this morning. He wanted me to proofread an appeal he'd written for another inmate. You know, I even gave him a laudatory chrono for his parole hearing. Said I wouldn't mind having him for a next-door neighbor. Damn was I wrong."

"You weren't the only one. But I'm not so sure the attack was gang-related."

James hadn't taken his eyes from the windshield. Beyond it, road and sky, the same charcoal gray. Olivia watched him blink a few times before he responded. "What else would it be? They're both Oaktown."

"Remember when we took our senior class photo out here? In front of that stupid sign they used to have."

James managed a smile. "We were idiots."

"We really did it though. We made it out. *Anywhere or bust.*" Olivia repeated the tagline the previous owner had carved into a slab of redwood and stanchioned in front of the restaurant. Jane had told her the sign had been removed after a drunk teenager had stolen it, toddled across the road with it, and promptly got himself flattened by a big rig.

"Until we came right back. What the hell is wrong with us?"

They both laughed but it rang hollow to Olivia. As if the sound had traveled a long way. All the way from the past.

"I have to tell you something." She brought them both back to the godawful present. "Shauna saw you arguing with Riggs on Wednesday. Something about cell phones and the General. I'm sure you've heard the rumors. What are you mixed up in? Please tell me all this craziness in Fog Harbor is not over prison contraband."

"Do the cops know you're here?"

"Of course not." And Deck would certainly disapprove. Which up until this morning would've given her more than a smidge of satisfaction. But now, with him already worried about his brother, made her feel even worse. "I'd understand if you smuggled cell phones. You've got a family to take care of, two kids to put through college. Those things go for a few hundred each."

"A thousand, actually." He finally looked at her, his mouth slightly opened. His face still. Caught in his own web. "At least that's what I've heard."

"You do realize I work with criminals too, right? I have a pretty good idea when I'm being lied to. You've got a gun and a duffel bag back there. Like you might be about to make a run for it."

"That bag is chock full of the boys' soccer stuff. I'm taking them to practice later." He glared at her, his voice low and menacing. "Did your dad send you out here? To shake me down? To collect my debt?"

Fear dropped like a hot stone to the pit of Olivia's stomach. She'd gotten so good at keeping her father in a box, tucked away from her new life, that she'd forgotten James knew. They hadn't run in the same circles. But in a graduating class of just over one hundred, word got around.

"Of course not. I don't even talk to him. He's supposedly out of the gang anyway."

James craned his neck to survey the parking lot. He looked right, left, then right again, before he leveled her with his eyes. "Listen close, because I'm only gonna say this one time. Then you're gonna get out of my car and forget you saw me today. My little boys' lives depend on it. I smuggled in phones a few times. I thought it would be an easy way to make a little money. Turns out it wasn't."

"Who else does Riggs deal with? Who's the General?"

"I don't know anything about all that. If you're smart, you don't either. These guys know about you. About your dad. Where you're from. All of it."

Olivia opened her mouth to speak. But the sirens snuffed the words out. Every last one. As the police cars converged, barricading James' SUV, her body went numb. The only sound she heard came through the bullhorn. Like the voice of an angry god. Hard as nails, unforgiving. Ready to unleash a lightning strike.

"Driver, passenger, put your hands where I can see them."

CHAPTER FORTY-EIGHT

Will swerved off the road into the Hickory Pit parking lot, joining the platoon of cop cars already surrounding the SUV that belonged to James McMillan. GED instructor. Widower. Contraband smuggler. Co-conspirator to PC 187.

Will followed JB out, positioning himself behind the driver's door, both of them drawing their weapons. As Graham wielded the bullhorn, Will's heart ricocheted like a stray bullet, pounding against his chest. It hadn't let up since Warden Blevins returned to the office and delivered the news.

Morrie Mulvaney just made a full confession to IGI. He said James McMillan provided him with the weapon this morning. Told him he had to do Riggs or somebody else from Oaktown would do them both.

"Driver, toss the keys out the window and keep your hands outside the vehicle."

A jumble of keys clattered against the pavement.

"Passenger, put both hands out the window."

Two hands, a woman's, emerged, shaking. When Will spotted Olivia's BMW parked alongside the SUV, he cursed under his breath, mouthing her name to JB.

"Slowly, using your right hand, open the door from the outside and step out of the vehicle."

The door swung wide, and Olivia stepped out. Arms raised, her face tight with fear.

"What the—" Graham too lost himself for a moment, forgot who he was supposed to be. Hard-ass, helmet-haired cowboy. For once, Will didn't hold it against him. "Face away from me. Walk backward to the sound of my voice."

Olivia turned, the clumsy pirouette of a ballerina scared shitless.

"Keep walking. Further. *Further*. Drop to your knees."

Follow protocol. Protocol will keep you alive out there. Will let his father's voice drill away inside his head. Without it, he'd have been there in an instant, doing the exact opposite of what he should be doing. Providing cover.

An officer Will didn't recognize bulldozed toward Olivia, grabbing her arm and twisting it behind her. Pushing her down against the concrete, a knee in her back.

"Fuck protocol."

He didn't realize he'd said it out loud, didn't even feel his feet moving, until he heard JB call his name. "Get back here, Deck!"

Too late for that. He pushed past Graham and approached the asshole cop suffocating Olivia, her breath coming in desperate gasps beneath his meaty thigh. "Hey, dude. I got it. You don't need to manhandle her. She's a doctor at the prison."

If he hadn't been so fired up, he would've laughed at himself. He sounded like Chet. *She's kind of a big deal.*

Olivia lifted her head. "It's okay. Just let him—"

The cop palmed her cheek, shoved it back down. "She's in the car with a murder suspect. I don't care if she's the goddamned Queen of England."

"Well, I do. And I outrank you, so move." Will stiff-armed the asshole, cuffing Olivia himself. He knew he'd messed up. That there would be hell to pay later for going rogue, but right now he didn't care.

"Are you okay?" he whispered.

She nodded, and he guided her back to the car, where JB waited, shaking his head in disapproval.

"You can sit in the car," Will told her. "Till it's over. Then we'll get you out of those cuffs."

"Deck?" Her voice cracked. "He's got a gun."

CHAPTER FORTY-NINE

"10-32! 10-32!"

It had been a long time, a lifetime, but Olivia knew that code. She'd heard it before, shouted just like that by a whole firing squad of cops who'd pulled her dad over. A high-risk traffic stop since he had a slew of warrants. The officer at the window must've seen her mother glance down at the door slot, where her dad had concealed a pistol.

She felt the same as she had back then. Out of her own body, watching from above. Later, her lungs and wrists would ache. She'd pick gravel out of her skin. But right now, she felt absolutely nothing. Except confused. The officer who'd kneed her in the back had called James a murder suspect.

They had him now, out of the car and flat on the pavement, his hands secured behind him. As they stood him up, another officer leaned into the cab and retrieved the gun. Which for James' sake, Olivia hoped wasn't stolen like her father's.

James' head dropped to his chest as if he couldn't bear the weight of it all. He said nothing, didn't even look up until they'd reached the patrol car. "Why am I being arrested?"

No one answered him. Instead, Graham shoved him against the car and ordered him to spread his legs, patting down the length of his body and emptying his pockets. When James raised his eyes to hers, she turned away. It felt like staring too long into the sun. Only the sun was her past, her father. And it burned.

"I want to know why I'm in handcuffs. Detective Decker? Is this about the cell phones?"

Olivia realized then Deck had been standing beside her, his hand wrapped around her forearm. In its absence, her skin chilled.

"I'm gonna go talk to James." He opened the rear door of his car. "Do me a favor and sit back here. Don't talk to anyone."

"I didn't do anything. I just—"

He put a finger to his lips, silencing her, and helped her into the backseat, her arms still awkwardly pinned behind her. Her dad had always told her being cuffed up robbed you of your dignity, made you no better than a stray dog carted away to the pound. When Deck shut the door on her, she realized. She got it now.

Jessie had retrieved the duffel bag and placed it on the trunk of Olivia's car, its zipper gaping open obscenely. From its mouth, she withdrew stacks of cash and two more guns and some other things Olivia couldn't see from the confines of her cage.

"Hey! That's not mine!" James struggled futilely against the hands that held him, thrashing as Graham opened the backseat of the patrol car and tried to force him inside. "Ask Olivia! It's not mine!"

A few official heads, Graham's included, turned to look at her, huddled in the backseat. When Graham frowned like she'd done something wrong, she stared right back at him, unafraid. He looked away first, punctuating her already miserable day with a Neanderthal grunt as he gave James one last hard shove into the backseat.

Graham stalked back to the SUV, and a few of the other officers dispersed. Despite the cold, a small crowd had gathered on the deck of the Hickory Pit. Olivia hoped they couldn't see her. She didn't want to end up the talk of Fog Harbor—*did you hear about Olivia Rockwell?*—over beer and ribs.

She wished she could call Emily but she'd left her phone in her car. And her hands had been rendered useless. Obviously. She turned her back to the door and worked the window down a crack, hoping she could hear more clearly, as Deck and JB made their way to the patrol car where James had been sitting, undisturbed, for a few minutes now.

She listened hard for Deck's voice cutting through the clamor. Though when she heard it, she wished she hadn't. "James, you're under arrest for conspiracy to commit murder."

"Of who? I didn't kill my wife. I swear to God I—"

"Of Tommy Rigsby."

Graham opened the back door of the car. A sure sign her bad day was about to get worse. After James had lawyered up, Chief Flack had arrived, summoning Deck and JB to her vehicle. They'd gotten in the backseat at least ten minutes ago and hadn't come out yet.

"Get out." Before she had a chance to swing her legs around, Graham grabbed her arm, jerking her to her feet. "I can't believe no one searched you."

"Jesus, Graham. What's your problem?"

"What's *my* problem? I'd say you're the one with the problem, Liv. Why were you in the car with James McMillan? Are you two... *involved*? Were you helping him abscond?"

"Abscond?" She started to prepare a smart-ass comeback. Something about how she didn't realize he'd been studying for his SATs again. That *abscond* was an awfully big word for a small-town cop.

When he pushed her into the side of the car and ran his hand along her backside, she got the message. Graham meant business. *Fine*, so did she.

"You're supposed to have a female officer search me."

He leaned against her and whispered through gritted teeth. "It's not like I haven't seen it all before. In fact, I seem to remember you liked it when I got a little rough with you."

"You really should have your memory checked." She shrugged out of his grasp and spun toward him. "Now, get off me. Unless you want to explain your behavior to Chief Flack."

"Sheila Flack doesn't tell me how to handle a suspect. And if she has something to say about it, you can tell her to—"

When Olivia raised her eyebrows at him, smirking, he screeched to a halt, as Chief Flack approached over his shoulder, JB and Deck trailing behind.

"Is everything okay here?" she asked.

"Under control, Chief. I was just a little concerned that Detective Decker hadn't searched Doctor Rockwell before placing her in his car. All good now." Graham mumbled something about bagging evidence and slunk away, his tail firmly between his legs. In the exact spot where Olivia wished she could've landed a solid kick. Or three.

"Am I free to go?" She looked past the chief to Deck's brown eyes. They stayed fixed on hers as Chief Flack answered.

"We'd like to take you down to the station to get a full statement. If that's okay with you."

Olivia nodded, knowing that asking her permission counted as a courteous gesture. Really, she had no choice.

CHAPTER FIFTY

Since Will had first met Olivia outside the Grateful Heart Chapel, she'd never been this quiet. But he hadn't pushed either. She'd already been through enough, sitting for at least thirty minutes, marinating in the interrogation room, then talking for another hour to him and JB, with Chief Flack listening in through the two-way mirror. She answered all their questions, calm and practiced. Like a professional.

With no indication she'd been involved in Riggs' murder, Olivia had been released. Not that Will had any doubt. Which explained why he hadn't searched her. Why he hadn't followed protocol in the first place. Well, that's what he'd told Chief Flack anyway. The other part—his massive crush on her—Will kept between himself and the loud-mouthed partner he'd left at the station while he returned Olivia to her car.

Will glanced over at her in the passenger seat. On the surface, she seemed remarkably unrattled. Like still water. But he knew better. He'd seen it for himself. That woman, though, the one he'd held to his chest this morning, had been banished by this one. All heat and ice.

He spoke first. "Just between us, they found DNA on Shauna's body. Hair and semen. Guess we know it's a guy now."

He heard the sharp intake of her breath. Then a confused, "Really?"

"Why do you say it like that?"

She shrugged. "Just strange he'd mess up now. In such a major way. That he'd leave so much evidence behind."

"Maybe he wants to be caught."

"Total TV show BS." She'd come back to life now. "No killer wants to be caught. You know that."

Will immediately thought of Ben. All the lies his brother had told. All the favors he'd called in. All in the interest of getting off scot-free.

"That's not how I meant it," she said, reading his glum face. "But in my opinion, this killer is not stupid or careless. He's calculating. If he left evidence, it's because he's telling you something. He wanted *you* to find it."

"But why?"

Olivia gave him a pointed glance.

"Please spare me the old *set-up Drake* theory again."

"Rumor has it I know Drake pretty well. And I'll bet you he'd never leave his DNA behind. Not after it got him locked up the first time."

"I'll take that bet." Even though her words rang true, he liked to push her buttons. "Winner buys ribs at the Pit."

Reluctantly, she shook his hand. "I talked to my dad, by the way. About Ben."

Her deflection put him right back in his place. With guilt weighing on his shoulders and his voice catching in his throat. "What did he say?"

"He promised to look out for him. For whatever his promises are worth these days."

"I shouldn't have asked you to do that. I just lost my mind when I saw that bird. I mean, if anything happened to Ben I'd blame myself. I know it's not my fault, but…"

The corner of Olivia's mouth lifted ever so slightly. The hint of a smile. "A simple thank you will suffice, Detective."

He smiled back and pressed his luck. "So, how was it talking to your dad after all this time?"

"Surreal." She leaned back and rested her head against the seat, briefly closing her eyes, and he took the opportunity to study the freckles on her cheeks, the flutter of her lashes. "I'm not sure I can ever trust him again. Especially now."

"With what Morrie did, you mean?"

She nodded, her eyes still shut.

"Do you think he's being honest about James?" Will wondered. Though the question had already been asked and answered in the cold, sparse room designed to elicit all manner of truths.

Eyes open now, she turned to him. "I don't know. I don't get it. Morrie was supposed to be one of the good guys. That's exactly why I don't profile anymore."

"You said it yourself. It's not science. People are unpredictable."

"People aren't just unpredictable. They're unknowable. Brownie points for quoting me, though."

Will tried to laugh, but it clunked out, hollow.

He parked the Crown Vic in the empty spot beside Olivia's BMW and followed her out into the late afternoon gloom. Fog and darkness threatening descent.

"Are you sure you're okay to drive home?"

"Fit as a fiddle." She unlocked her car, leaving the open door between them. He watched her scan the parking lot, the same way he did. The after-work crowd had begun to roll in, and the twang of old-time country music wafted from the Pit, along with the smoky aroma of brisket. It made Will long for something he knew he'd never have. A simple life. A life where work stays where you leave it. You don't bring it home with you, rooted in the dark crevices of your mind.

"I'm sorry you got caught in the middle of all this."

"Not your fault. But thanks for… you know…" She shrugged, kicking at the pavement with the toe of her sneaker.

"Violating police procedure? You're welcome."

He stepped around the door and reached to touch her, wrapping his hand around her wrist. "There's only one person around here who gets to cuff you."

No sooner he'd said it, he cursed himself. Could he be any cheesier?

Olivia's muscles tensed beneath his fingers, but she didn't pull away. His heart beat faster and faster as she leaned toward him, so close he could smell the clean scent of her shampoo. He chided himself for letting his eyes wander to her lips, but then he did it again anyway.

"Well…" With a sudden jerk upward, Olivia grabbed his wrist and twisted it from her own, freeing herself. "Don't get used to it."

Will stood there like a bumbling idiot, while she got into the car, retrieving her cell phone from the console.

"You are going straight home, right?"

"Where else would I go, Detective?"

When she winked at him, sending his stomach on a loop-the-loop, that settled it for Will. Olivia had been dead right. People were predictably unpredictable. Her, especially. And as much as it scared the hell out of him, he liked it even more. He liked it a lot.

CHAPTER FIFTY-ONE

Olivia sat in the parking lot of the Hickory Pit long after Deck's taillights had disappeared in the fog. She examined her left wrist. Even now, she could feel the heat of Deck's hand around it more intensely than the cold metal sting of the handcuff. Her face flushed, thinking of how his eyes had lingered on her lips. How badly she'd needed the distraction. How easily she'd lied by omission, with a wink no less. Maybe Morrie hadn't been so far off the mark, when he'd called her more Reilly than Rockwell.

Fittingly, Olivia fired off a text to Emily, telling her she had to make a stop, and another to Leah, asking her to check on Em. Then, she drove into the thick of it, down Pine Grove Road toward the prison, until the wet, white smoke enveloped her.

Something about the fog always unnerved her. As a girl growing up in San Francisco, she'd marveled at how it could disappear the entire Bay Bridge. The Golden Gate too. The fog made its own rules, created its own secret world. It hid things, swallowed them whole, revealing them only when it wanted to. When it was too late to get out of the way.

The Ad Seg officer checked her ID and buzzed her in to the secure unit. When Olivia heard the door grind to a close behind her, she shivered. It felt different here. Airless. Like a prison inside a prison. No wonder one of her patients had told her, *Solitary is where inmates go to die.* Each solid metal door secured the worst of the very bad men who lived at Crescent Bay.

She walked down the line until she found cell 117 and peered through the tiny bulletproof window.

Morrie sat on a mattress, stripped bare of the sheets he might've wrapped around his neck. He wore a white jumpsuit and booties with no laces from which to hang himself. The empty cell devoid of any comforts he could've used to slice his wrists or gouge his eyes.

Olivia turned to the guard on duty. "I need to speak with Mulvaney for a mental health check."

His eyes had that glazed over look. No different than most of the inmates in there. But he mumbled his agreement and sputtered to life. It took another twenty minutes to transfer Morrie by wheelchair down the hallway to a therapeutic module inside another locked room. The prison ran on its own time. Nowhere to go and no hurry to get there.

"You okay in here alone?" the officer asked, dragging a folding chair into the center of the room for her.

Olivia watched Morrie slump, hangdog, onto the small seat inside the cage. He rested his hands on the metal, sticking his fingers through the wire mesh. She half expected them to be dripping blood. But she didn't fear Morrie's hands. Only his words. The things he might tell her.

"I'm fine." She waited to speak again until the officer had left. Until they were alone.

"Why did you come here?" Morrie asked.

"You're on suicide watch. Someone has to check in on you."

"I ain't gonna kill myself. I done lasted this long in here. It'll be thirty-five years come January. What's a few more?"

Olivia's heart deflated. Working at Crescent Bay, she'd come to realize that the absence of hope took a form more dangerous than any weapon. A shape, a sound, a smell. It could end a man's life surer than a shiv to the heart, slower than a blood-letting. "But Morrie, you got a parole grant. I just don't—"

"You know as well as I do, the governor ain't never lettin' me out of here. You looked up my case, right? You saw what I did. Who I did it to."

She gave a solemn nod. Because Bill Jeffries, the man Morrie had taken a knife to at the Thirsty Traveler, happened to be an alcoholic like him. He also happened to be the son of one of San Francisco's most prominent attorneys.

"That parole grant is bullshit. It's window dressing. Like puttin' lipstick on a pig."

"That makes it okay for you to take Tommy Rigsby's life? I thought you'd changed. I thought your gang days were behind you."

Morrie threw his head back, and his bitter laughter echoed in the empty room. There it was, the sound of hopelessness. "You think I shanked Riggs for Oaktown?"

"Then why?"

"Not everything can be put into one of your neat little shrink boxes, Olivia. You don't always get the why."

Olivia had learned that lesson well enough. For the last twenty-seven years, her father's why had always been just beyond her grasp, slipping through her fingers like quicksilver.

"Is this really about James McMillan?"

He shrugged half-heartedly. Like he could barely lift his shoulders.

"It doesn't make any sense. You've always told me no good comes from talking with the cops. That the only good snitch is a dead one. Then you went and gave IGI a full confession. You pointed the finger at James. He's got kids, Morrie. Kids who are already without a mom."

"He ain't innocent. Lord knows, neither was Riggs. I don't feel a thing for that sorry SOB."

Olivia winced. She recognized that line. Morrie had uttered those exact words when the detective had asked him how he felt about putting four holes in Bill Jeffries' chest with his hunting knife.

"You don't mean that."

"Let's just say, I had to choose between hurtin' Riggs and James or watchin' somebody I care about get hurt. That choice ain't no choice at all."

"You always have a choice." Even as she said it, she doubted it. Choosing was a luxury not everyone could afford.

Morrie smacked the wire mesh with his palm. "Exactly! And I made mine. Your daddy saved my life too many times to count. I swore him an oath when you started workin' here, and a man's word is all he's got left in the joint. That and his free will. Can you blame me for exercisin' mine?"

Olivia steadied herself, gripping the cold metal of her chair with both hands. Dread settled over her, a poisonous fog. Though she'd feared something like this, hearing it out loud made her sick to her stomach. "Who threatened you? The warden? The General?"

Morrie shook his head. "If I told ya that, I might as well kill ya myself. This ain't nothin' to mess with, girl."

"Does my dad know?"

"I'm sure word will get around."

"He wouldn't have wanted this." But that, too, she doubted. "Promise me you won't hurt yourself."

Morrie chuckled, and it unsettled her more than his sour cackling. This man, chortling like he could have been anyone's grandpa.

"Ain't no need to promise that. I don't have the stomach for it."

"Then why do they have you on suicide watch?"

Morrie grinned, beckoning her with a crooked finger, and she leaned in toward him. In the flicker of his eyes, she saw all of him. Old and young. Good and bad, too. Just Morrie. "How else were you supposed to get in here to talk to me?"

CHAPTER FIFTY-TWO

Will still had Olivia on his mind when he pushed past a row of squawking reporters, through the station doors, and straight into the hornet's nest.

"How dare you interfere with my case." JB wagged his finger at Graham. "When I got promoted to detective, you were still sticking marbles up your nose."

"Shows what you know, Gramps. I'm pretty sure marbles went out sometime in the 1920s. By the way, you're welcome."

Jessie rolled her eyes as Graham guffawed liked a frat boy.

"Is this a station house or a schoolyard?" Chief Flack poked her head out from her office. "Get to work."

After she'd gone, Graham retreated to his newly assigned cubicle like a scolded puppy.

"Schoolyard," Jessie muttered, earning a laugh from JB. He flopped into his chair and seethed at the blank computer screen.

"That's what happens when you get little kids to do a man's job."

"What the hell is going on?" Will asked. "I leave for twenty minutes, and you're taking names."

"Yeah. Defending your ass. And keeping that nitwit from blowing our whole case sky-high. I caught Tweedledum giving a statement to that tabloid hack, Hoffman."

"*Fog Harbor Gazette*'s Heather Hoffman?"

"The one and only. That broad is ruthless."

Will removed a small paper bag from his jacket and joined JB at his desk. "What makes you say that?"

"Saw it with my own eyes. A couple years back, I arrested her myself. She got caught slashing Suzie Medina's tires."

"Who's Suzie Medina?"

"Exactly. Eliminate the competition." With a few keystrokes, JB pulled up a photo of a young raven-haired reporter who'd won an award for Best Feature at the *Gazette*. "Suzie left town, refused to testify. Hoffman lives another day. She's just waiting for her big break from print into television. This kind of story—the *s* word—well, it might as well stand for salivate. 'Cause that's exactly what she's doing."

"Speaking of…" Will opened the bag from the Stop-and-Shop and angled it in JB's direction. "I got you a little something."

JB made a show. Sniffling, he pretended to wipe tears from his eyes. "What's this for?"

"For having my back."

JB reached in, removed the orange package, and tore it open, taking a bite of the first Reese's cup. He closed his eyes and moaned. "Hell, for one of these I'd let you call yourself lead detective."

"I *am* lead detective."

"There you go, City Boy. That's what you call an affirmation. Keep repeatin' it and who knows what might happen. C'mon, say it with me. 'I am lead detective. I will solve this case. I will make out with Olivia Rockwell.'"

Will huffed out a laugh. "So, why did Graham say you're welcome?"

JB nodded at the flash drive on his desk. "He thinks he found a smoking gun. In exchange for yapping his trap, Hoffman gave him a copy of some cell phone video taken outside the Hickory Pit the night Shauna disappeared. Supposedly, our guy Wickersham is in it."

"And? Have you watched it?"

JB finished the last peanut butter cup and dabbed at the corners of his mouth with a tissue. "Nah. I was waitin' on the lead detective."

*

The video opened on a polka-dot umbrella. It weaved and wobbled through the parking lot in the driving rain.

"That must be Shauna," Will said, as the camera panned out revealing the yellow Mini parked near the edge of the lot. "Looks like our videographer was sitting inside a vehicle facing the main road."

JB nodded. "Here he comes."

The camera shifted focus to Hank, barreling out the front entrance with no umbrella of his own. He shielded his face with his hand, his shirt already plastered to his chest.

Back to Shauna, with a whiplash glance over her shoulder. An almost-fall. The umbrella lost in a gust of wind.

The Mini came to life, headlamps on, as Hank ran toward it. Smacked the window. His mouth like a pike, teeth bared.

"Jeez," JB said. "Somebody needs anger management."

"What's he saying?"

"There's no sound. I can't tell."

"Play it back."

After a few more tries, one in slow motion, they agreed on two words. *Drunk* and *crazy*.

The camera stayed with the Mini as Shauna sped out of the parking lot and onto the main road, nearly taking out her chassis. Then, it panned back slow and steady to the parking lot, where Hank brought it home, waving his arms and dropping to his haunches before the screen went black.

"Weird," JB said.

"Very."

"On the count of three, say why you think it's weird."

Will twisted his mouth at JB. "What are we, five?"

"I just don't want to influence your opinion."

"Bullshit. You want to prove you're a good detective."

"That's like proving gravity, my friend."

"Alright." Will smirked at him. "I'll play. But what if I've got two reasons?"

JB groaned. "Just pick one. In three, two, one—"

They answered simultaneously, JB shouting, "No audio!" like a game show contestant, covering Will's quiet pronouncement.

"The truck."

"What truck?" JB asked, as Will rewound the footage to the methodical pan of the road and the parking lot. He paused the image, tapped the screen. Zoomed in.

"Does that say what I think it does?" he asked.

JB squinted at the still shot. "Looks like the Crescent Bay State Prison emblem there on the side. Might be our guy. Might be a coincidence."

"That seems like a pretty big coincidence. You know, I was gonna say the audio thing too."

"Sure ya were." He leaned back, hands behind his head, preening. "Who makes a video these days without sound? Without their own asinine commentary?"

"That's a good question. *Who does?* Do we know anything about who shot this? How it got to Heather Hoffman?"

"One of us will have to ask Tweedledum."

"Not It," Will answered.

Graham stood up, glaring over the wall of his cubicle. "You know I can hear you."

"We were counting on it," JB said. "So? Got anything to add?"

He stalked over and tossed a flat manila envelope onto JB's desk. Unmarked and nondescript. "Just the envelope she put it in. She said someone emailed her the file at the news desk. Should be enough for you two though. What with your exceptional detective skills and impeccable code of conduct."

Will just smiled. He planned on going a full nine rounds in his garage tonight.

After Graham had left them in peace, he picked up the envelope. Light as a feather and probably empty. Still, he opened it anyway, shaking out any contents.

A single, folded piece of paper fell at his feet.

To: Heather Hoffman <hhoffman@fogharborgazette.net>
From: A Concerned Citizen <Hawk.McGee@pacbell.com>
Date: December 20 1:03 AM PST
Subject: Hickory Pit Footage

See attached.

"Un-fucking-believable."

"You know this guy? Hawk?" JB asked.

Will reached in his drawer, picked up Drake's book, and turned to Chapter One, page one, displaying it for his partner. "He's Drake Devere's main character."

CHAPTER FIFTY-THREE

Olivia stood in front of the locked door of the administration office and checked her watch. Well after six o'clock. Warden Blevins and his staff would be long gone by now.

"Can I help you, Doc?"

Olivia jumped, then laughed at herself. "Melody, you scared me. I just realized I forgot my notebook inside Gunderson's office. Could you unlock it for me?"

"Don't see why not. You just missed Warden Blevins. He left about five minutes ago. He's still real shook up about that stabbing. Damn Riggs and Mulvaney. Can you believe Bonnie's husband was in on it? I always told Maryann there was truth to the gossip. Where there's smoke, ya know?"

Olivia only nodded, surprised the news of her own detainment hadn't yet reached the Crescent Bay rumor mill.

Melody swiped her access key card and allowed her inside. "Go on in. Just be quick about it."

Not ideal, since she had no key to the warden's office and no freaking clue what she'd find there—a name placard that read "The General"?—but at least she'd gotten this far.

She skirted inside and made her way down the dark hallway toward the last door, her heart throbbing in her throat.

One quick glance back.

Hopeful, she tried the knob.

Locked.

Olivia wished she'd thought to bring her purse, but it sat useless in the trunk of her car. She felt certain she'd seen a few stray paperclips in Teresa's office, and she'd left the door unlocked that morning, so she crept toward it feeling as sly as a cat. Until she realized her mistake.

Her father might've called the shots for Oaktown, held up a couple of convenience stores, strong-armed a few law-abiding citizens out of their money, even peddled drugs out of Apartment E. But nobody ever called Martin Reilly a sophisticated criminal. And apparently, the apple didn't fall far. Because the blinking red eye of the camera mounted above the warden's door followed her as she moved.

Olivia heard a voice outside the main door. A man's voice. But not just any man.

She ducked into Teresa's office as Warden Blevins swiped his card, and listened to the sounds of her demise, the mechanical *beep, click* then sharp creak as he pushed the door open the rest of the way.

"I told you not to call me on my state cell. They can trace that shit."

When his heels began to click against the concrete, she ducked beneath the desk, holding her breath until he passed. He fit his key into the lock. For an instant, Olivia went back there, to the Double Rock. To Apartment E and jiggling her key that never fit into the lock but that day, of all days, had slid in with ease.

"I'll be there. Tomorrow at seven."

Then, silence.

She waited, listening and trying to control her breathing. She closed her eyes, scared that even a blink might be too loud.

Finally, Warden Blevins shut his office door. Inserted the key again.

It would be over soon. If she could just hold on.

Beep, click. "Hello? Olivia? Did you get what you— Warden Blevins! Didn't expect to see you here."

"I forgot my car keys on my desk. Won't get very far without those. Were you looking for someone?"

Olivia swallowed her panic in one massive gulp. Climbed out from under Teresa's desk and – just like that day at the Double Rock – she opened the door. But this time, she knew exactly the sort of carnage she'd find.

"I'm here, Melody." She avoided Warden Blevins' avian stare. "I didn't see the notebook. I must've left it at home."

"It seems we're both forgetful today, Doctor Rockwell." He pulled Teresa's door shut behind her. Locked it. Checked it. Checked it again. "You must be as distracted as I am."

Adrenaline carried Olivia past the control booth and through the parking lot. She didn't turn back, though she knew Warden Blevins had followed her out. She suspected his eyes had trailed her long after, all the way to her car. For once, she hoped to be swallowed by the fog. She didn't retrieve her purse from the trunk, didn't check her phone. She fired up the engine and peeled out. Anxious to lose this place. Or better yet, to be lost herself.

Like a rogue wave capable of shifting an island, the entire day had swelled inside her, ready to break. She rolled down the windows, let the cold air stream in, as she kept driving past the turn for home. She knew where she was headed, even if she couldn't admit it to herself. Even if she felt like the worst big sister, running away again.

Her headlamps cut through the tendrils of fog, rising up like steam from the ground, and spotlighted the cabin at the end of Wolver Hollow Road. She moved without thinking. Out of the car, onto the porch step. In front of the door, knocking.

Deck looked surprised to see her standing there. He'd untucked his shirt, undone the first two buttons. In his hand, he held Drake's book. The hawk's golden eye judged her from the cover.

"Is everything okay?" he asked, looking her over.

That wave finally crested, knocking against her heart with indescribable force. She shook her head *no*.

The words in her head went like this. *I need to hit something right now.* But that's not what came out of her mouth. Not at all. Her signals crossed in translation. Before she had time to take it back, he dropped the book to the floor, closed the space between them, and pressed his mouth to hers. Where it turned out she'd wanted it all along.

CHAPTER FIFTY-FOUR

I need you to kiss me right now.

Will had done it a thousand times in his head. How different could it be? But then—

He laced his fingers through her hair.

She grabbed a fistful of his shirt.

He pushed her up against the doorframe.

She gently bit his bottom lip.

He moaned into her mouth.

Play by play, he matched her. Until the rest of the world blurred out of focus, small and insignificant beneath them. Until he stopped thinking entirely.

Until she laid her hand on his chest and pushed him away.

Will collapsed onto the sofa, breathless.

Olivia stood over him, leveling him with those impossibly green eyes. "I'm sorry. We shouldn't have done that."

"Right." He smirked at her. "Bad idea. The worst you've ever had."

"Excuse me? You kissed me first."

"Only because you told me to."

Olivia's cheeks pinked, as she busied her hands, straightening her hair. Will thought about how his own hands had mussed it. How soft it felt tangled around his fingers. He wasn't sorry.

"Oh, I see. So you were just doing me a favor?"

"I do what I can." He shrugged. "Protect and serve, you know?"

She groaned at him but still joined him on the sofa, leaving a safe distance between them. "I need to talk to you about Warden Blevins."

Her matter-of-fact tone crashed him back to earth. Where women went missing and turned up dead. Where sickos put broken-necked birds in boxes and stuck shivs in soft places. Where he'd somehow been anointed as the fixer of it all.

"I overheard him say he's meeting someone tomorrow night. I want to follow him. I think he might be involved in Riggs' death." She paused, took a nervous breath. "I saw them exchange a package in the prison chapel a few weeks ago."

"So that's why you came over? To talk me into some half-baked conspiracy theory?" It didn't matter that he believed it.

"No." She sighed. "Maybe. I thought you'd want to help me."

Will stood up and started pacing. He didn't know what irked him more. That Dr. Smarty Pants had taken a straight pin to his ego. Or that it bothered him as much as it did. "Blevins hasn't committed a crime."

"That we know of."

"You have no idea where he's going."

"Isn't that the whole point?"

"Last time I checked, you're not a cop."

"And *you're* not my father. You don't get to tell me what to do."

Will gritted his teeth and turned away from her. When he looked back, the sofa was empty. The cushions, slightly sunken. Olivia marched toward him and planted her feet, her lips inches from his own. Her eyes dared him to do something about it.

"I'm going anyway," she said.

"Knock yourself out."

Olivia hesitated at the door. She knelt down and retrieved his copy of *Bird of Prey*. In his rush to kiss her, it had fallen awkwardly to the floor, creasing some of the pages.

She cocked her head at him, the corner of her smug mouth tilting upward. "You dropped this."

Fog Harbor Gazette

"Dead Woman's Husband Implicated in Prison
Murder Plot"
by Heather Hoffman

The Fog Harbor Police Department arrested local resident
James McMillan yesterday on multiple criminal charges,
including felony conspiracy to commit murder, and
misdemeanor smuggling of cellular devices into an institution. At the time of his arrest, McMillan was also found
in possession of several stolen firearms and a large amount
of cash. During a search of the family home, authorities
located approximately fifty cellular devices which they
believe McMillan intended to smuggle into Crescent Bay
State Prison (CBSP), where he manages the GED program.
Prison officials suspect McMillan brought the cell phones in
by secreting them in the bottom of his insulated lunch box.

In the hours leading up to his arrest, forty-five-year-
old CBSP inmate Thomas Rigsby was stabbed to death
by another inmate, seventy-year-old Morris "Morrie"
Mulvaney. Though the circumstances of the attack remain
unclear, Mulvaney implicated McMillan as a co-conspirator
in the crime. Sources close to the investigation reported
Rigsby, who had ties to the Oaktown Boys street gang, may
have used McMillan as a mule to smuggle various types of
contraband for lucrative sums.

McMillan's wife, Bonnie, was recently found murdered, the first victim in a string of brutal homicides that has stricken the usually peaceful Fog Harbor community, prompting concerns of a serial killer some have dubbed the Seaside Strangler. Newly minted FHPD detective Graham Bauer issued the following statement: "We don't believe James McMillan had anything to do with his wife's murder or the murders of the other victims. But we're looking into his ties with the Oaktown Boys. The victims' too. Any victimologist will tell you most homicide victims do something stupid—however small—that ends them up dead."

Lester Blevins, Warden of CBSP, declined to comment on recent events, citing an ongoing investigation by the Institutional Gang Investigators (IGI). However, he noted that plans to install a cellular signal blocking system to restrict illegal phone usage had failed as residents living nearby complained of interruptions to their service.

James McMillan has reportedly retained Orillius Van Sant, a prominent San Francisco-based criminal defense attorney. Van Sant could not be reached for comment.

CHAPTER FIFTY-FIVE

Will lay in bed and watched Cy circle a few times before he curled at the foot of the bed, satisfied with the prime real estate he'd selected. When Olivia left last night, he'd heard the poor cat meowing outside in the rain. He'd been feeling especially lonely then.

For hours, he'd tossed and turned, second-guessing himself. Replaying the entire scene. The way she'd fit in his arms, the words she'd said. How he'd screwed it up like usual. All of it, a song on repeat.

Cy still had his good eye open, his head resting on his paws. "I messed up. Didn't I?"

Two blinks which probably meant *yes, you oaf.*

"What was I supposed to say, buddy? Was I really supposed to go traipsing after Blevins when we've got a real killer to worry about?"

Three blinks this time. Which also probably meant *yes, you oaf,* though he had plenty of good reasons to say no. Most importantly, he didn't want Olivia to get hurt.

"God, I'm an idiot."

Two more confirmatory one-eyed blinks from Cy, and Will tossed off the covers, dragging himself out of bed.

He walked to the window. Still raining with no sign of letting up.

"She wouldn't go alone," Will told a purring Cy, rubbing the soft fur on the cat's orange chest. But then he remembered that first day at Grateful Heart, and every day since then, how she'd made a habit of running head first into trouble. Cy rolled over and bit him, leaving two tiny marks on Will's hand. He wholeheartedly agreed with Cy's ruthless assessment. *Of course she would, you numbskull.*

"Any news from Tammy about our DNA?" Will asked when JB arrived at the station, toting the newspaper and his breakfast: coffee and doughnuts, plural. Judging by the powdered sugar on his tie, he'd already had at least one.

"Nothing yet. What about the email address? Did IT have any luck?"

"Not much. It's a dummy account. They traced it to the free Wi-Fi at the Hickory Pit. So, it's basically a crap shoot." Will sighed, thinking of Devere and his stupid book, and its fall to the floor, which brought him back to where the day had started. Olivia. He'd called her three times. All three had gone to voicemail.

"This will cheer you up, City Boy." He tossed the newspaper onto Will's desk. "Chief Flack is going to rip Tweedledum a new one, and I would pay for a front row seat."

Will opened the paper and scanned the top story, searching for Graham's name. "So, he's a detective now?"

"Self-appointed, as far as I'm concerned."

"And a victimologist?" Will remembered how Graham had introduced himself as Olivia's boyfriend at the Hickory Pit. "He appoints himself to all sorts of things apparently."

"I've got a committee I'd like to appoint him to. It meets right now at the end of my fist."

When Graham walked in a few minutes later, JB smacked his fist against his palm and they both chuckled. But Will's laughter came to an abrupt stop as Graham headed straight for his desk.

"What was Olivia doing at your house last night?"

"Excuse me?"

"You heard me."

"How is that any of your business? And what do you care, anyway? Yesterday you acted like you didn't even know her until she was cuffed in the backseat of my car."

"I followed procedure. But I guess total disregard for policy runs in the family."

"Following procedure?" JB interjected. "It looked to me like you were feeling her up, trying to get your rocks off."

The door to the station opened, briefly letting in a raucous chorus of reporters' voices, then closed hard, with Chief Flack appearing on the other side. Her face redder than Will had ever seen it.

"Bauer, I need to see you in my office. Now."

Head hung and mouth shut, Graham shuffled away. When he'd gone a few steps, JB called out, his voice deep and solemn as a knell.

"Dead man walking."

Then, he turned to Will, a sly grin spreading cheek to cheek. "So, Olivia came over. Guess that affirmation worked, huh?"

CHAPTER FIFTY-SIX

Olivia wanted to be anywhere but here, on this barstool at Myrtle's Café, facing Leah's inquisition. Because she couldn't tell her the truth. But she didn't want to lie.

"Are you sure you're alright?" Leah asked, breaking her blueberry scone in two equal-sized pieces. "You sounded pretty shook up last night."

Olivia shrugged, keeping her eyes down as she moved her eggs around her plate. She hadn't taken a single bite.

"Why were you with James anyway?"

"I told you. I just ran into him at the Pit. I realized I hadn't really talked to him since the vigil. Before I knew it, we were surrounded by cop cars, and he was getting arrested."

Leah cocked her head to the side, a sure sign she was about to call Olivia out on her tall tales.

"What aren't you telling me, girl?"

The list seemed endless. You knew you were in trouble when you'd lost count of your secrets. Olivia chose the safest, even though it felt raw. "I kissed that detective."

Leah brightened, smacking Olivia's arm. "I knew you were into him."

"I'm not into him." Another cock of the head. "Okay. I'm a little bit into him. But, I'm pretty sure it was a big mistake. No, it *definitely* was. A colossal screwup."

"Did he say that?"

"He didn't have to. I did it for him. But I'm sure he's thinking it now anyway. We're both professionals."

"What does that have to do with anything?" Leah asked, picking at one half of her scone. She hadn't eaten much either, come to think of it. Not surprising since the whole place felt shrouded in a dark pall. Even Myrtle had seemed off, standing quietly behind the counter, regarding the few customers with a far-off stare.

"He sort of asked me to help with this case."

"The serial killer?"

Olivia cringed, looked around, thinking of JB's superstition. Then she nodded.

"I still don't see what the problem is. Unless you think he's the Seaside Strangler."

"I just don't want to mix business with pleasure, okay?"

"Pleasure, huh? You *are* totally into him."

Olivia had concluded the same, the moment Deck had dropped that book to the floor and made her forget everything but his lips on hers. Until she'd freaked out and messed it up, first by pushing him away, then by asking too much of him. She'd do well to remember the lesson Erik had taught her. Only one person would never let her down. Which explained why she hadn't answered any of Deck's calls. She had to do this alone.

"So, do you think Emily's okay?" Olivia asked.

"She's hanging in there. Em's a tough cookie, like her sister. But not nearly as skilled at changing the subject."

"It's an art that takes years to master. I'd call myself a sensei."

Leah laughed but it didn't reach her worried eyes. "I'd agree. But yeah, she seemed okay last night. It will do her good to go in to work today."

"You think?" She and Emily had argued that morning, after Em had told her she planned on showing up for her usual Saturday shift. But Olivia had relented, guilt-ridden, and driven her sister to Crescent Bay, fighting off a chill when Warden Blevins had raised his hand in a motionless wave to her from the entrance.

Since when did he start working on the weekends? Emily had asked.

I'm not surprised. He's got a lot going on right now. Olivia had gulped down the rest of it—*like running his own criminal enterprise*—and felt the bitterness coat her throat. Maybe that's why she hadn't touched her food.

"It'll help her to get back in a routine," Leah said.

"You're probably right." Olivia half-smiled and forced herself to put the fork to her mouth. Nope, she couldn't do it. "So, have you and Jake reached a consensus on a name? Is it boy band time?"

"Liam or Lily, depending." She rested her hands on her belly and finally took a bite of her scone. "And you *are* a sensei."

At 6 p.m., Olivia cut her lights and parked her mom's old Buick on a dirt side road with a partial view of Warden Blevins' gate. Beyond it, the driveway led up the hill to the two-story rock home that abutted the Earl River. Olivia had been invited there the past two summers for the annual Crescent Bay barbecue. She'd stood in Warden Blevins' picture window, admiring the river as it curled lazily through the redwoods. In the wet winters, it turned into a different beast, unsheathing its claws, scraping up the hillside, and carving out the land. Olivia imagined it now, raging, as the rain drummed against her windshield.

She tugged the hood of her raincoat over her head and hunkered down lower in her seat, waiting. Her mind flitted from one horror to the next, her whole body buzzing. From the prison chapel to the drainpipe to Highway 187 and back again. The nastiness of it all crawled under her skin until she couldn't stand it. She wanted to scream. To shake herself. To let Deck and his lips make her forget again. Not likely, since she'd ignored all his calls and then had the nerve to text him and ask him to lie for her.

Please don't tell Emily where I am. She thinks you're picking me up to discuss the murders.

Thankfully the rain blocked out the sounds of the forest. But after sitting in the pitch black awhile, that unnerved her, too. She'd never hear approaching footsteps. Boots would sink into the soft ground. The rain would drown her screams. At least she'd been smart enough to bring her mother's gun, the old snub-nosed revolver that had spent most of its life collecting dust beneath the bed.

The sudden *beep* of her phone started Olivia's heart racing. She glanced at the reminder on her screen, cursing under her breath.

7:30 p.m. Meet Murdocks for set-up

Olivia had totally forgotten. No way she'd be back in time. Nothing she could do now but text Emily and hope the twins would forgive her.

Can you help Melody and Maryann set up for a staff get-together at their house? I totally spaced. You can take my car. Tell them I'm sorry.

Emily responded right away.

Sure. But you owe me. Their mom is super-weird.

P.S. Don't blow it with the detective.

Olivia's smile sparked then doused when Warden Blevins' gate whirred to life, his white sedan gliding out like a swan in the darkness. She counted to ten and followed.

The warden didn't head back toward town as she hoped, but rather past the Fog Harbor city limit sign, which had been riddled with bullet holes by drunk teenagers looking for a little fun. Tonight, though, those smooth wounds in the metal felt personal. Somehow meant to foretell her future.

Olivia locked onto the taillights—two red eyes cutting through the rain—and gave the warden plenty of room. The road had grown too narrow, too dark to drive without her bright lights, and she didn't want to spook him. A few cars approached on their way to Fog Harbor, but in her rearview, only the rain tracked them mile for mile.

Ten minutes later, the warden turned down a gravel drive into the middle of nowhere. Blindsided by the past, it took all the courage Olivia could summon not to turn back. She'd been here before. A very long time ago. Before she'd realized what it meant.

The rain slowed to a drizzle as she pulled into the ditch. If she trailed him any farther in the car, he'd spot her, so she'd have to go the rest of the way on foot. A handmade sign told her his destination and exactly how long it would take to get there. ROCKY'S SALVAGE YARD ½ MILE. One half mile and one wrong turn straight to hell.

CHAPTER FIFTY-SEVEN

The sign looked exactly as it had back then. A little more weathered, perhaps. Olivia marveled at her mind's tricks. Buried for years, she'd unearthed the memory intact. Perfectly preserved like a fly in amber.

As she trudged up the gravel road in the drizzle, she could almost feel the heat of her mother's fingertips, grabbing her by the chin. Telling her to stay in the car. A few days after they'd moved to Fog Harbor, her mother had driven them to Rocky's, leaving Olivia hunkered in the Buick while she'd disappeared inside the junkyard. She'd returned with a bag of money and the Smith and Wesson revolver, courtesy of the Oaktown Boys.

The past fragmented. Memories scattered like crows as a hand clamped over her mouth. Another pinned her arms.

"Don't make a sound," up against her ear.

She tried to scream—couldn't.

The hands pulled her into the ditch, and she fell against the muddy hillside. Moments later, a pack of motorcycles blurred by her, mud spitting from their tires.

She grabbed the biggest stick within arm's reach and scrambled to her feet, swinging it wildly at the man in the raincoat.

When the hood fell from his head, she gasped.

"You! What are *you* doing here?"

"What the hell does it look like? I'm obviously saving your ass."

She tossed the stick in Deck's direction, hoping it might graze him just a little. But the wind grabbed it, sending it into the road instead. "I'm doing perfectly fine without you."

"I see that." He gestured to the stick, as he struggled to his feet. "Is that how you were planning to defend yourself?"

Olivia didn't have time to argue. She hurried up the road.

"I'm sorry." It irked her he'd caught up so fast. "You were right. Something's going on with Blevins. I should've agreed to come with you. Especially since you can't spot a tail to save your life."

She stopped, turned to him. Raised her jacket, so he saw the gun tucked at her waist. Her father had taught her how to shoot. Sure, they'd been makeshift targets out behind the Double Rock, and he'd emptied those beer bottles himself first, slurring by the time he'd told her to keep it steady. "I'm not helpless."

Deck didn't answer, just followed her down the road until they'd reached the fenced perimeter of the rust bucket graveyard. Its innards were spotlighted by the motorcycles' headlamps, casting shadows that slunk between the cars and dissolved into blackness.

"What now?" Olivia whispered.

Still, Deck said nothing.

Guns shut people up, her dad had told her once. *All you gotta do is show 'em.*

Olivia didn't like his voice in her head. But about this, he hadn't been as wrong as she'd hoped.

CHAPTER FIFTY-EIGHT

Will didn't like that Olivia had a gun. She didn't have the stomach for it, she'd made that clear when she'd picked up a stick to defend herself, the gun tucked useless in her waistband. If you strapped a gun to your body, you had to be certain you could use it. Not the mechanics, per se. Not the point-aim-fire. But the bit nobody ever talked about. The living with yourself once you'd pulled the trigger. Will fingered the knife scar on his hand and gently pushed the memory away again. It always drifted in and out, like a dead body floating in the water.

"What now?" Olivia asked again, her voice so quiet he wondered if it had come from inside his own head. But she looked at him expectantly.

"Let's get a little closer. I can hear them talking."

Will stayed in the shadows, skirting to the side of the dilapidated metal carport at the main entrance. He crouched down in the wet grass, the weathered shell of an old pickup blocking him from view. A dozen others just like it marked the yard like gravestones. When a gust of wind sent the rusted-out WELCOME sign swaying on its chains, he shivered, the eerie creaking like a scrape to his soul.

Will motioned Olivia over, and they peered through the chain-link fence.

Five men stalked around inside the carport, circling Warden Blevins, their guns drawn. They backed him into a stack of crushed cars, pushed him around a little. Will felt sick as they patted him down. He pulled his own gun from its holster, preparing for the worst.

"Oaktown," Olivia breathed, pointing to her own forearm where the man to the right of the warden bore the tattoo on his sinewy bicep. Will studied his face, what parts he could see beneath his wiry red beard, trying to work out if he'd seen it before.

"I'm clean, gentlemen. No weapons of any kind. I thought you invited me here to talk."

"So talk then, *Warden*." The bearded man had a way of making the job title sound like a dirty word. Like an accusation. He pointed his gun at Blevins' chest.

Another man, small and stocky as a bowling ball, stepped up. Will noticed a tattoo on his neck and a nasty bruise on the bridge of his nose. He wondered if it was the same guy he'd run down at Laura's house. "C'mon, Termite. Go easy on the warden. He ain't built for this shit."

Beside him, Olivia tensed.

"Ain't stopped him so far. I wanna know what he's doin' to solve our problems. Our big fucking problems."

"Rest assured, Termite, your problems are my problems. As of tonight, all our problems have been taken care of."

"That's what you said last time. You know the General don't like liars."

Termite bared his teeth and ran his gun up the warden's chest, dead-ending at the middle of his forehead.

Bolder than Will figured him for, the warden pushed the barrel of the gun down, so that it pointed back at the ground. "I do believe the General likes gifts, though." From inside his jacket, Warden Blevins withdrew a package, wrapped in brown paper.

"It's the least you can do." Termite snatched it from his hand, just as another rush of wind whipped through the junkyard, clanging the sign and whistling through the shell of the truck, straining the last shards of its broken passenger window. Will dropped to the damp ground, pulling Olivia down with him, just as the glass fell from its shaky hold and shattered against the ground.

"What the fuck was that?"

"The wind?" the warden suggested.

"Only one way to find out."

Will didn't need to see the face to understand that voice. Hard as nails. Nails hammered into his own coffin, if he didn't get them the hell out of there and fast.

A bullet sliced the air above their heads.

Will stumbled to his feet, staying low in the tall grass, with a wide-eyed Olivia right behind him. As soon as they reached the gravel road, they ran. Though he suspected no one had followed, Will couldn't shake the feeling of being hunted.

The wind, like breath on his neck.

Every stone crunched beneath his boots, a bullet.

The spitting rain like a spray of blood, wet on his fingertips.

CHAPTER FIFTY-NINE

When they reached her car, Olivia collapsed against Deck, her lungs burning. He held her upright, his frantic breathing matching her own. Then, she'd broken away from him. Two fists against his chest. "*Now* do you believe me?"

"Yes, you proved your point. But we've gotta get out of here. I'll meet you back at your house. You can tell me how wrong I was when we get there."

She nodded, not trusting herself to speak. Too many voices in her head telling her what an idiot she'd been for coming here. Because she'd nearly gotten them killed, even if she had been right about Warden Blevins. Her mother's voice too, trembling, as they'd sped away from this place. The gun stashed beneath the seat, but the bag left on the ground behind them. *We'll fend for ourselves*, her mother had said. And another voice she hadn't heard in twenty-seven years, a name she never let herself speak aloud. Hardly let herself think either. *Termite*. He'd been a boy the last time she'd seen him, standing over Tina's body, scared out of his mind.

That boy is always gettin' into everything, her dad had said. She couldn't remember when. *Like a damn termite*. The nickname had stuck.

"Olivia." Deck shook her a little. "Are you sure you're okay to drive?"

She felt her head bob up and down. Felt him lead her to her door. Felt herself slip into the familiar routine. Seatbelt. Ignition. Gearshift. Go.

The time on the dash clock read 7:50 p.m. As she drove, Deck's lights behind her, it drew her eyes in again and again until it changed. 7:51.

Emily must be at the Murdocks' by now.

Olivia slipped her phone from her pocket and dialed her sister's number, desperate to hear a familiar voice. Em would tease her about Deck or chide her for forgetting her promise to Maryann and Melody. They'd both laugh, even if it came with a twinge of sadness, and the world would feel right again.

But each ring zipped down her spine, unanswered, and the road in front of her seemed to stretch on for miles, leading to nowhere.

CHAPTER SIXTY

"I'm sure she's just busy helping." Deck put a hand on Olivia's shoulder. She'd changed into a sweater and jeans, and her hair had begun to dry. But she still felt chilled and wet. Like the night had crawled inside her. "She probably hasn't looked at her phone."

A flare of panic burned away the cold and set Olivia's blood afire. She shrugged off his soft touch. "Are you kidding? She doesn't go anywhere without her cell. Something's wrong. What if she had an accident? Or the car broke down?"

"Alright." He listened without reacting. A part of her hated how calm he seemed, even though she understood it. He'd had years of practice managing the unmanageable. "Why don't you call Maryann? If she doesn't answer, we'll head over to their house."

When Olivia searched his eyes for comfort, she shivered, her worst fears confirmed. "Deck, do you think…?"

"No. I'm sure she's fine. Now, call Maryann."

Maryann answered on the first ring. "Olivia, what happened? We were worried about you."

"What do you mean? Is Emily there?"

"Emily? No. We thought you'd be here by now. We're all done setting—"

"So you haven't seen Emily?"

"Hold on. Let me ask Mel." Through the white noise of her horror, Olivia heard the sisters chattering. She wanted to shout at them, but she bit the inside of her mouth instead, tasting the metal of her own blood. "Nope. Mel hasn't seen her. Did we get our signals crossed?"

Olivia laid the phone on the table, Maryann still blathering on.

Her training taught her what to expect when the unthinkable happened; the way the body would shut down, all circuits firing and overwhelmed. Still, she thought she'd react differently than she had at eight years old, standing in the doorway of Apartment E, blank-faced and stunned into silence.

She wanted to scream but her mouth wouldn't do it.

She wanted to run but her legs wouldn't work right.

In the blank space of her brain, a single image from that awful dream two nights ago. Down to her bones, it felt real. As real as her own heartbeat throbbing in her ears.

Emily, dead.

CHAPTER SIXTY-ONE

Will had lied to Olivia. The situation called for it, but it didn't make him feel any less guilty or any less worried. Shauna had confided in Emily. Had told her what she'd seen. As much as he suspected Drake, he couldn't deny the connection the victims shared. Oaktown, cell phones, secrets. Crescent Bay State Prison.

Emily could be in danger. Emily could be missing. Could be—he let himself think it for a split second—*dead*. But he'd told Olivia none of that. The exact opposite, in fact. He put his arm around her, reassuring her. He kept reassuring her as she put on her coat. As he helped her into his truck. Finally, he shut up, his windshield wipers the only sound, as they drove toward the heart of Fog Harbor.

They didn't make it far.

Olivia's BMW idled in a ditch off Pine Grove Road, its back end smashed. The bumper, dangling. Parked on the shoulder, a truck marked with a Tyrone's Construction decal and a nasty dent to its front end. A large black man, presumably Tyrone, paced nearby, holding an umbrella, his phone pressed to his ear.

Will said nothing as he pulled over behind one of three police cruisers. He'd already gone into full-on cop mode, turning off the part of himself that wanted to throw up. To run away from Fog Harbor and never look back.

When he asked Olivia to confirm the car was hers, he catalogued her whimper as a yes. "It's just an accident," she said, her voice one-note. "She had an accident."

"Stay inside." He knew she wouldn't listen. Her hand already gripped the door.

Will approached the car cautiously, looking back at the ruts in the mud, where it had crossed into the ditch and come to rest. He produced his badge and identified himself to the female highway patrol officer examining the BMW's interior. Officer Rollins, according to the nameplate pinned to her uniform.

He peered over her shoulder at the leather seats. A cell phone and a small purse, its contents scattered, lay haphazard on the floorboard. Lights on. The gearshift, in park. Will catalogued all these too. Same as the whimper.

"What happened here?" he asked.

"We're not exactly sure." She gestured to the man with the umbrella. "Mr. Watkins told us he was driving northbound on Pine Grove Road with poor visibility due to the rainstorm. He got a call from his wife and briefly looked down at his cell phone. When he glanced up, the car was right there. It didn't appear to be moving. The driver's door was open. Mr. Watkins said he didn't have time to swerve, and he struck the back end of the BMW, which traveled into the ditch. He reported no injuries but we've got an ambulance on the way."

"Where is my sister?" Olivia demanded. "I need to see her."

"Uh, ma'am, it's not safe for you—"

"The other driver?" Will asked. Officer Rollins hesitated, eyeing Olivia with concern. Will catalogued that too. He felt something bad coming but nothing and no one could stop it. "Her sister, Emily, was driving the BMW. Is she okay?"

"Well, that's just it, Detective. We don't know. We can't find her. She's just… gone."

From behind him, Olivia made an awful, soul-scraping sound, and Will turned toward her, compelled. Though he didn't want to see the way that sound looked on her face.

His training taught him what to expect when the unthinkable happened. The way the body would shut down, all circuits firing and overwhelmed. How he had to rise above the biology, staying alert and alive by walling off a vital part of himself. Still, he thought he'd react differently than he had two years ago, watching numbly from the shadows as his brother ended a life.

He wanted to hold her but he feared it would break him. She clung to him anyway.

He wanted to say the right thing but no words came. Except the ones he always said, in his cop voice. "It's going to be okay."

In the blank space of his brain, a single image from that awful night. His brother, sobbing, begging him to lie. Down to his bones, it felt real. As real as Olivia's heartbeat throbbing against his chest.

He'd known it then. He knew it now. Nothing would ever be okay again.

Olivia lay on the couch, glassy-eyed. After she'd found a photo of Emily for the missing person press release, she'd dug through her sister's closet convinced she could figure out what she'd been wearing. *Her white sweater. Her blue raincoat.* She'd finally relented and taken half—*only a half*—of a Valium Will had scrounged up from the medicine cabinet. The bottle's prescription label read Louise Reilly. Olivia's mother, Will figured.

When the doorbell rang, Olivia didn't move, didn't even acknowledge it, so Will opened the door and let Leah inside.

"How is she?" Leah whispered.

Will shook his head. "She thinks it's her fault. That she should've been here."

Leah let out a long breath and peeked around the corner with him. Olivia hadn't moved.

"Thanks for coming," he said. "I have to call my partner and let him know. Get back to the scene. Figure out what the hell happened."

"You already know what happened." Olivia's voice scared him a little. The hollowness of it. Like she'd fallen down a deep, dark well. "The *s* word."

Whatever lie he'd planned to tell her, he never got a chance. His phone buzzed in his pocket.

"Will Decker, Homicide."

"Will." JB sounded shell-shocked, too. As if they'd all been fighting the same endless war. "Tammy's friend from San Francisco came through. We've gotta get down to the lab to meet Tammy ASAP. I'll see you there."

"The DNA?" He heard the quiver in his own voice.

"They've got a match."

CHAPTER SIXTY-TWO

Olivia pretended she was dead. She held her breath until her lungs ached. Beneath the covers, she didn't move. Didn't even blink. Her stare, fixed on the dark figure watching her from the corner of the bedroom. Male or female, she couldn't tell which. But she knew she'd find out soon enough.

The figure stalked her, waiting for the exact right time to strike. To slip the garrote around her neck and pull it tight. She'd claw at it, the way the others did, but her struggle would only make it worse. Like an insect thrashing in a spider's web.

A soft knock at the door stopped her heart. The figure didn't move.

Olivia reached for the Smith and Wesson she'd secreted in the nightstand but the empty drawer gaped back at her. She opened her mouth to scream but it came out as a whimper.

She watched in horror as the door opened. A blade of light from the hallway cut through the shadows, revealing the figure and the garrote.

A coat rack in her temporary suite at Shells-by-the-Sea, Leah and Jake's B&B. Where she'd hung her jacket, her stocking cap, her scarf.

Leah peered inside the bedroom. "Just checking on you."

Olivia smiled weakly. "What time is it?"

"Six in the morning."

"Oh. I forgot where I was for a minute."

Leah nodded, handing her another half of a little blue pill, watching closely as Olivia placed it on her tongue. "Get some more sleep, if you can. I'm heading out with the search team to look for Emily, unless you need me."

Olivia waved her off. But as soon as Leah had closed the door, she sat up, tossed off the covers, and stripped the coat rack bare. Satisfied, she scurried to the bathroom and spat out the Valium she'd cheeked, flushing it down the toilet. Then, she splashed her face with the coldest water she could stand.

For a psychologist who worked in the MHU, where pill-cheeking could be classified as a competitive sport, Leah had trusted her far too easily. She grabbed her phone from the dresser, scanning the Internet, a breaking news article from the *Fog Harbor Gazette* online the top story on all the major outlets. Her chest tightened. Her heart, in a vise.

They didn't think she could handle it. *They* being Leah and Deck. The *something* being Drake Devere's DNA found on Shauna's body, his early morning arrest. Probably with good reason, after she'd snuck out of the B&B last night, driving from the beach to Laura's house to the drainpipe and back again until her eyelids drooped and every passing car had Emily's dead body hidden inside it. Deck had found her at 2 a.m., parked in her thinking spot at Little Gull, listening for ghosts, scrawling suspect names, and staring out at the water. A profiling zombie, with a gun on her lap. The only clear recollection, the liquid brown of his eyes when they'd met hers.

She found her gun in the safe, where someone—*Deck?*—had helped her lock it. Her combination, the usual one, ironic now. Her sister's birthdate. She dressed in a hurry and poked her head out of the Sand Dollar Suite. All clear. Unlike her memories of last night, which were smeared by a benzo haze.

Olivia forced herself to choke down half of a banana nut muffin Leah had left for her. She tucked the Smith and Wesson in her purse and looped her lanyard around her neck, declaring herself cured. This zombie had work to do.

*

Everyone looked at her but no one spoke. Just as well, because she had no acceptable explanation for showing up at the prison. Not with Em missing and presumed dead. They expected her to be with the search volunteers, combing the fields, the beach, the roadways. Or curled in a ball somewhere. Not walking down the runway, heading for Ad Seg, her face pinched with determination.

She'd nearly made it when she heard her name called out down the long, empty hall.

"What are you doing at work?" Warden Blevins strode toward her. His ingratiating voice a stark contrast to the one she'd heard at Willow Wood.

"I need to talk to Drake."

"I'm afraid that's not possible, especially with your sister missing. I'm under strict orders to keep him in isolation. No visitors except for his attorney, if he hires one. With the size of his ego, I wouldn't be surprised if he represents himself."

Olivia kept walking as they spoke, so fast even the warden with his long legs struggled to keep up with her. "You asked me to keep an eye on him. To gain his trust. To get him gabbing. Remember? He told me things. Things he might be inclined to tell other people. Attorneys, reporters. People who wouldn't understand. It would be in the best interest of Crescent Bay and the administration if those things stayed between me and Drake. So, let me talk to him. Five minutes. That's all I need."

Warden Blevins didn't speak until they'd reached the door to Ad Seg. "Those things he told you, I expect a full debrief. This stays between us. No more secrets."

Olivia felt the heat from his gaze before she met his eyes, simmering like black coals behind his wire-rimmed glasses. It was a wonder the lenses hadn't fogged. She felt certain he'd seen the security camera, watched her sneaking around and jiggling his office doorknob.

"Of course."

CHAPTER SIXTY-THREE

Will studied the plastic evidence bag on his desk, trying to make sense of the small tufts of synthetic hair inside. Bits of the white faux fur, stained with mud, had been recovered in the grooves of the BMW's left front tire and the roadway.

"You've been staring at that fuzz since I left." JB returned to his cubicle with two subpar coffees from the machine that had been around longer than him. "What's up, City Boy?"

"Something doesn't feel right."

Delivering those words to Devere's smug face earlier—*You're under arrest for the murder of Shauna Ambrose*—had done nothing for him. Not like the last time. When he'd slapped the cuffs on Devere outside his Modesto apartment, Will had believed he'd finally proved himself. Even after the DA had accepted Drake's plea bargain, life in prison instead of death, he'd felt like a winner. But now, after what he'd witnessed at the salvage yard, after seeing Olivia dead-eyed and desperate, after all the wrong turns and red herrings, he didn't trust Devere's obvious guilt. Didn't trust himself.

"C'mon. Devere's gonna die in prison either way. All we've got to do is get him to talk. We need to find Emily's body, bring her home. That's our angle. That's our bargaining chip."

"So you're sure then? Emily's dead? She's one of his?" The questions had played in his brain all night on repeat.

"She disappears on a rainy night. Leaves her cell and her purse behind. No trace of her anywhere. All signs point to Drake."

"But we haven't found her body."

"Well, Devere's been in Ad Seg since yesterday morning."

"But we know he had help. He must have."

"Nobody is gonna move a body right now, partner."

Will clenched his jaw, breathing through gritted teeth, as JB patted him on the shoulder.

"I know this one's personal. I'm sorry about that. But we're not gonna find Emily sitting in this popsicle stand twiddling our thumbs. Let's go take one more crack at him before he lawyers up like James. You with me?"

"I'm with you." But as Will trailed JB from the station, he couldn't stop seeing his mother's face. Couldn't stop thinking of Drake's first victims, the women in Muir Woods. Of Bonnie, Laura, Shauna. Sometimes, finding someone was worse than letting them stay gone.

CHAPTER SIXTY-FOUR

A wave of nausea nearly bowled Olivia over just looking at Drake. Though she still only half believed it, the big sister in her wanted to pry apart that metal cage and beat him bloody. The professional in her clung stubbornly to her doubts. "You never answered my question. From the other day. Do you remember?"

Drake nodded, one corner of his mouth lifting in a disgusting smile. "You wanted to know how I felt about the families of my victims. About what I'd done."

"And?" She disregarded her revulsion and approached the therapeutic module, where Drake stood, his face practically pressed to the wire mesh. She wanted him to see her up close.

"I wouldn't trade the person I've become. I needed those experiences. A mediocre author writes from imagination. A great author writes from experience. Draws their pen from the well of their own pain. I'm sorry others had to suffer for that, but I can't change the past."

"What a load of crap. I defended you. To the warden. To the cops. How could you do this?"

"You think I'm guilty then, don't you? You think I hurt Bonnie? Laura? Shauna? *Emily*." Olivia couldn't tell if he sounded wounded or smug. But the way he'd said her sister's name, taking his time with all three syllables, made her skin crawl.

"Did you?"

"What do you believe, Doc? That's what I want to know. Your opinion means everything to me."

"They found your DNA on Shauna's body. What am I supposed to think?" Saying it out loud broke her, and she clung to the side of the cage to stay upright. "Please, just tell me. Where is my sister?"

Olivia shook the wire mesh.

"Where is my sister?"

Felt a scream rising in her throat.

"Where is my sister?"

She heard the door burst open behind her. Felt a pair of sturdy arms around her, pulling her backward from the room. Saw a scar on a hand she recognized.

"Get off me." She squirmed out of Deck's grasp, still shaking, terrified and so, so angry. At herself more than anyone. She'd flaked on her promise to help the Murdocks. She'd asked Em to go. She might as well have wrapped the garrote around her sister's neck herself. The image of *that* in her mind's eye—her sister, strangled, her body cold in a ditch somewhere—made her double over.

"What are you doing here?" Deck asked her, in his cop voice.

When she didn't answer, he turned to the guard. "Who let her in?"

"Didn't see. I was on a break."

CHAPTER SIXTY-FIVE

Olivia insisted on waiting outside the room. He could see her through the small window, sitting on the edge of a folding chair they'd brought out for her. Her hands gripped the metal sides, and she leaned forward. No tears. Just a resolute stare that told him she expected answers. Answers Drake had withheld earlier that morning when they'd gone to Crescent Bay to formally arrest him.

Devere didn't look up as Will reminded him of his rights and the ever-present recorder. When Will asked if he still wanted to talk, he mumbled a half-hearted, "Whatever."

"You seem upset." Will paced around the perimeter of the metal cage that held his ungettable get. The once-in-a-lifetime case you never get over. Twice-in-a-lifetime, apparently.

Devere shrugged.

"Is it Doctor Rockwell? Did she upset you?" Still no answer, so Will pushed further. "I get it. She understands you. She's easy to talk to. You opened up to her. It must be hard to see her in pain, especially knowing you're the one who caused it."

Will ran his hand along the wire mesh front of the cage, prompting Drake to raise his eyes. "You know what I don't understand, Devere? If you care so much what she thinks about you, why'd you kill her sister?"

Kill. Will took a necessary risk with that word, hoping it would prod something in Drake. Something human.

"I didn't."

"Okay, so we're going to play that game again? You're as pure as the driven snow. You have no idea how your goddamned semen ended up on a dead girl's leg. You have no clue where Emily Rockwell could be."

"I didn't *kill* Emily."

JB cleared his throat in the profound silence. "So she's alive then?" He cut his eyes at Will.

"Maybe. Maybe not. That's up to you."

Will felt himself teetering at the edge of a cliff. One push and that would end it. Devere would clam up, and they'd lose their chance forever. "Was she alive when you last saw her?"

Devere closed his eyes, and Will tried to imagine the things that went on behind them. But he could only conjure a dark pit with no bottom. An abyss that had never been touched by light. "It wasn't supposed to be Emily. I wanted *her*."

He thrust his head at the small window. At Olivia.

"I was going to take her with me."

The recorder whirred on as Drake confessed. To killing Bonnie.

"I stalked her from outside the theater. Dumped her body in the drainpipe. That bitch was robbing me blind."

To killing Laura.

"Everybody knew she went running before work. She thought she was hot shit now after she got skinny."

To killing Shauna.

"She was drunk that night. Easiest one I ever did. She wouldn't give it up to me like I wanted."

Will stanchioned himself against the wall, just watching, as JB took over the interrogation. Not that Drake required much prompting. A nod here. A *then what happened?* there. He barreled full steam ahead toward the night of Emily's disappearance. It didn't surprise Will. Hearing himself talk was one of Drake's favorite pastimes. But the whole thing didn't sit right.

"Emily is alive. For now. I can take you to her. But I want the death penalty off the table. Again."

Will suddenly came alive, pushing off the wall and stalking toward Devere. "That's never gonna happen. Not on my watch. Not this time. If she's alive, you need to tell us where she is."

Devere sat back, an easy smile stretching across his face. "As far as I see it, Detective, I'm the one with all the power here. Doesn't feel so good, does it? When you're not in charge. You pigs don't like that. Just look at your brother. He couldn't handle it, put a bullet in that woman on his little power trip. You think you're better than me? I know you. We want the *exact* same thing. *Control.*"

"Just to be clear, I don't believe half the bullshit you've been spewing. You haven't told us anything we don't already know. You haven't given up any crime partners, and we know you had help. You haven't told us how you managed to get out of here, or pull any of this off, or why the hell you came back inside. So you can take your offer and shove it."

"Alright. Then Emily dies. If that's how you want it. No skin off my back. I suppose you'd like to be the one to tell Doctor Rockwell."

JB motioned outside. "Can I have a word, partner?"

As soon as the door opened, Olivia sprang to her feet, and Drake shouted, "I'm sorry, Doc. But I didn't kill her. She's still alive!"

Will understood then why he'd had to leave his service weapon at the tower. Because he would've put a few permanent holes in Devere's forehead.

"Oops. Guess I spilled the beans."

CHAPTER SIXTY-SIX

Olivia had never felt more alone. Not even after they'd carted her dad off to prison and her mom got two jobs to support them. Not even after they'd moved to Fog Harbor in the middle of her fifth grade year, and she'd had to make new friends and pretend nobody knew her dad hadn't really drowned on a fishing boat. Not even after her mom left her alone to take care of screaming baby Em, when she went out drinking. Not even then.

She'd nodded at Deck, when he'd told her to sit back down. To wait. But only because the weight of Drake's words had made her legs sandbag heavy. *Emily is alive.*

"What's going on?" she asked, when he finally left JB and stood before her. His eyes as impossibly tired as her own. "Is it true? About Em?"

"We don't know yet. You said yourself he'd never leave his DNA behind. Devere is a con man. I don't trust him. IGI raided his cell and found nothing. Just a bunch of books and his precious writing. We need to verify his story before we react. Certainly before we make any deals. I want you to go home. I promise I'll come by as soon as we wrap up here."

"Deals?"

Will sighed. "He wants the death penalty off the table, in exchange for—"

"For what? For Emily? Does he know where she is?" Olivia saw herself, as if from a great distance. A hysterical woman talking a mile a minute. But she couldn't stop, couldn't slow herself down. "What if she's hurt? What if she's dying? Deck, please."

"Look, it's not my decision to make. We have to talk to the chief and the DA. Even then, I'm just not sure. I know Drake. There's something off about all this. Can't you feel it? I mean, after what we saw…"

"Maybe he's trying to do the right thing for once." She felt herself grasping at straws. *But Emily is alive.* He'd said it.

"Are you kidding? Devere loaned his moral compass to Ted Bundy." He squeezed her shoulder. "Now go home. There's nothing else you can do here."

Olivia crossed her arms, planted her feet firmly on the ground. "I'm not leaving. Not until I find out about Emily."

Olivia let herself in to Deck's garage and found his boxing gloves in a bin in the corner. Cy, cozy in his bed, watched as she put them on.

Deck had won the battle, having JB escort her out to the parking lot. But before, he'd grabbed her hand, slipped his key inside it. "Go hit something," he'd told her.

She started off easy with a jab to the center of the bag. Then, harder and harder still, once she got her rhythm, until she felt her teeth judder. Until the world had narrowed to just her and that bag, and the fierce thud every time she hit it.

When her cell phone rang with a call from an unknown number, it startled her. But she tossed the gloves aside and answered it without thinking.

"It's Dad. Don't hang up."

"How did you get this number? Are you calling from a cell phone? God, Dad. You never learn."

"Liv, I had to. I'm just borrowing it from a friend. I needed to know you were okay. What are the cops saying about Emily?"

Olivia wanted him to suffer, but she couldn't bear the splinter in his voice, threatening to crack right down the middle. "She may be alive. That guy, Drake Devere, was a patient of mine. He said he could take them to her."

"So what are they waiting for?"

"It's complicated, Dad. You know that. Now, stay off the cell phone. I'll call your counselor if there's any news."

He whispered her name so low she strained to hear it. "Be careful. If the General got a guy like Morrie to shank some Oaktown punk, he can get anybody to do anything."

Olivia drew in a breath, shocked by what her father knew. Confused about how he knew it. But the line went dead, and the sound of the heavy bag creaking on its chain gave her no answers.

CHAPTER SIXTY-SEVEN

"What the hell is that?" Chief Flack pointed to the sheet of paper in JB's hand. Will had swiped it, along with a pen, from the Ad Seg control booth. He didn't want to look at it now though, not with his signature penned at the bottom alongside Drake's. It meant nothing, of course. Just an empty gesture. But it disturbed him. The only kind of gesture he'd ever wanted to offer Devere involved his middle finger.

"Well, it's not my Christmas list," JB said, placing it on the desk. "Although I was hoping for a brand new Fenwick rod and reel, if you're buying."

Will narrowed his eyes at his partner and pushed the sheet toward District Attorney Collison. "It's a list of Devere's demands."

Xavier Collison ran a hand through the last wisps of hair on his head and let out a low whistle. Like Drake had just offered him a deal on oceanfront property in Arizona. "Death penalty off the table. On camera with Heather Hoffman. Devere's got balls, as the kids say. What's your gut telling you on this, Detectives?"

Their guts did not agree, hence the long, awkward silence that ensued. Followed by the always-pleasant WTF stare from Chief Flack.

"I think it's bogus. It's too risky. Devere's a psychopath. He's setting us up for something. I just don't know what."

"So we do nothing?" JB asked. "You want to sit on this?"

"I want to do our jobs. We got the confession. If we can figure out who's been helping him, we can leverage that to find Emily."

"How long is that gonna take? She'll be dead by then. We've got nothing to lose."

"I hate to be the one to say it, JB, but she's probably already dead."

"Is that what you told Olivia?"

That hit Will like a sucker punch. Leave it to his partner to hit below the belt.

"Olivia Rockwell, the victim's sister," Chief Flack explained. "She's in full support of proceeding with the deal for obvious reasons."

"And Warden Blevins?"

"He's on board," JB said. "Provided he and two COs of his choosing come with us."

Collison sat back, pondering. "If we find this girl alive, we look damn good." Meaning he'd be assured reelection, Will thought. That's what it always came down to with these guys. Votes not lives. Perception not prudence.

"And if we don't? If something goes wrong? If Devere escapes?"

"Just make damn sure he doesn't. Got it?"

Will's stomach knotted as the district attorney removed a pen from his front pocket. He crossed out the last of Drake's requests for professional editing, cover design and marketing for his sequel to be paid for by Del Norte County. Apparently, the DA drew the line just short of absurdity.

The red ink bled through the cheap notebook paper.

"Tell him we'll do the deal."

Will found Olivia seated on the concrete next to Cy's bed. He'd abandoned it in favor of her lap.

She moved to get up but Will stopped her. Sat down beside her instead.

"You okay?" he asked.

"Not really. But my jab is rock solid."

It took effort, but he smiled at her. "I'm sorry I didn't call you right away when we arrested Devere this morning. I thought it would be best to hold off until we knew more, and you were already so upset and Leah said to wait. It's not an excuse. Just a reason."

When he hung his head, she rested her hand on his knee. "It's a good reason. I get it. I lost it in there today. I know he's a sick man but I never saw this coming. It just didn't fit. But, you were right. I guess this officially puts an end to my profiling career."

"Devere said it was meant to be you he kidnapped. He thought we were getting close to solving it with the DNA and he planned to take you with him. Head up across the border and into Canada."

"Wait—what?" She pushed Cy from her lap, stood up, and started pacing. "That makes no sense."

"Yeah. I know."

"So, why did he come back to the prison then? Why didn't he just run?"

"He won't tell us. I guess he's saving that for the camera. Better ratings."

"The camera?"

Will hoisted himself to his feet, needing to be on solid ground when he delivered the news. "It's another one of his terms. The DA agreed to the deal with Drake."

Olivia hid her face in her hands as he walked toward her.

"When?" she asked, her voice muffled through her fingers.

"Later today. JB's already at the prison. That reporter, Hoffman, will meet us there. Then, we go."

She peeked out at him, her eyes tearing. "I'm going too."

"No, you're not. No way in hell. It's—"

Her hands dropped from her wet face. She put them on her hips, taking a wide stance. Her voice deepened. "It's way too dangerous, Olivia."

"Is that really what I sound like?"

"I need to be there, Deck. She's my sister."

"I'll call you the minute we find her." One at a time, he carefully took her hands in his, surprised when she didn't protest. "I know you've got your hopes up about this, but…"

She tucked herself against his chest, and he couldn't bear to say the rest, so he pressed his lips to her forehead instead.

Olivia let go first, shaking her head as she wiped her eyes. "I don't cry, you know."

"Noted."

"No, *really*. I don't. Ever. Except when I'm around you, apparently."

"Doesn't that go against your shrink code? I thought tears were good for you. They release stress hormones."

She half-smiled. "Says the hard-nosed detective."

"Hey, I want you to see something." He slipped his phone from his pocket and swiped at the screen, showing her the photo he'd taken of the white fibers found on Emily's tire. "What does this look like to you?"

She studied it, zooming in with her fingers. "Fur?"

"It's not fur. It's synthetic."

"Maybe from a stuffed animal, then? Where did you find it?"

"On Emily's tire. I think, whatever it was, she hit it. She ran it over."

Olivia got quiet, and he thought she might cry again. He wondered what that meant. That she only cried with him. He couldn't decide if that was a good thing or a decidedly bad one.

"You think that's why she stopped, don't you? That was the ruse."

He nodded. "I don't cry either. For the record."

"Noted," she parroted, in that same deep voice. She held up his cell phone. "Hey, can I use this? My battery's dead and I need to call Leah and let her know I'm okay."

He watched her for a moment before she shooed him away with her hand.

CHAPTER SIXTY-EIGHT

Olivia pushed the old Buick to its limits, speeding down Pine Grove Road well in excess of the fifty-five miles per hour limit. The manila folder Deck had given her days ago rested beside her, its contents spewing onto the passenger seat. She'd ripped through it like a tornado as soon as she'd left his house.

The synthetic fur. The use of the garrote. The staged sexual assaults. She couldn't believe it had taken her this long to see it hiding in plain sight. But she'd been wrong before and an innocent man had suffered, nearly died. This time she had to be sure.

As she neared the police station, Olivia floored it, the station wagon responding to the hairpin turn with the precision of a drunk elephant. She thrust the gearshift into park and checked the tracking app on her phone, relieved to see the flashing red dot hadn't moved.

Olivia hurried toward the door, where Graham waited outside with the box, just as she'd asked. She forced herself to smile at him. And when he set the box down to wrap her in a hug, she feigned comfort. Even if it meant she had to endure the cloying smell of his body spray and fancy hair gel. The furtive rub of his hand on her lower back.

"Are you sure you're okay?" He kept her prisoner within his muscled forearms.

"I will be. Once Em's safe at home."

"You know I'm here for you, Liv. No matter what happens. We've had a bit of a rough patch, but my feelings haven't changed. I've missed you."

Olivia glanced at the box at his feet. She needed it desperately. "I've missed you too."

"What do you want this for, anyway?" he asked, kicking it with his boot. "IGI told us there's nothing of value. Just a bunch of books and drawings and whatever else that sicko had in his cell."

She reached for his hand, imploring, and he took it, lacing his fingers in hers. "I want to see if I missed anything. I've been beating myself up about this. I should've known."

"It's not your fault, babe. If anybody's to blame, I'd point the finger at that asshole, Decker."

"Detective Decker? Why?"

"Because I don't like the way he looks at you."

She rolled her eyes, the word *babe* still clanging in her ears.

"Well, I *don't*. He's too busy flirting with you to do his god-damned job. I don't trust that guy."

"That's exactly why I needed your help."

He squeezed her hand. "If anyone asks…"

"I never saw you." Olivia reached for the box. As she walked away, the weight of it in her hands felt like victory.

Olivia sped out of town, pulling off the road the first chance she got. The Buick protested, rumbling as she guided it down Gallows' Lane, stopping the car in the shade of the redwood grove, where she wouldn't be seen.

The yellow tape had fallen down in the rainstorm but Olivia knew Laura's body had been propped against that tree when Deck had found her. She still had the crime scene photographs in the folder, tucked beneath the box marked EVIDENCE.

She worked the seal open with her fingers and took a breath. Cast the lid aside and started with the books. At least ten of them. She rifled through the pages, ripped off the covers, peeled back the library labels, and checked the bindings, discarding them on the floorboard in a heap.

Frustrated, she stared at the pile, Drake's own copy of *Bird of Prey* perched atop it.

Next, she flipped through Drake's important papers, finding the medical chrono signed by the prison doctor, diagnosing him with dry eyes. For the last two months, he'd been listening to the library's audiobooks.

As she mulled over that chrono, she knew her hunch was right. Retrieving *Bird of Prey*, she found the passage in the final chapter and read it in a whisper.

"'Hawk lay on his bunk, reliving the kill. It was the sounds he liked best. Lacey's piercing scream. The way she gasped for breath. His own lecherous grunts. He wished he could have recorded it.'"

A mediocre author writes from imagination, Drake had said. *A great author writes from experience.*

Olivia rifled through the box until she reached the bottom. Three plastic cassette tape cases, like the kind she'd decorated back in high school, with hearts and smiley faces: Olivia + Erik, Side A.

These tapes had also been labeled. PROPERTY OF CRESCENT BAY STATE PRISON LIBRARY. The first, titled *Crime and Punishment* by Fyodor Dostoevsky, appeared to be wound halfway through.

She slid it from the case and pushed it into the Buick's tape player. Hoping the ancient thing still worked, she cranked the volume.

White noise like rain falling. Then, a hard click that startled her. Ominous as the cocking of a revolver.

Olivia swallowed, her mouth suddenly bone dry. The trees closed in, hiding their secrets beneath a canopy of shadow and dappled light. She took the Smith and Wesson from her purse and tucked it beside her. Locked the doors, rewound a bit, and tried again.

Small, ragged gasps that went on and on. She gripped the steering wheel, sucking in a breath herself.

A sudden, desperate gulp. Her hands began to tremble.

A wheeze, a gurgle. She jammed her finger against the STOP button, revulsion bubbling up in her throat. She touched her own neck, half expecting to feel the pressure against her windpipe. Then, she rewound the tape, farther this time, and listened once more in shock. To the panicked voice, the struggle, the ugly fight to stay alive. The last sounds Bonnie ever made.

CHAPTER SIXTY-NINE

Drake Devere shuffled out of the side door of the prison to the waiting transport van, Officer Murdock gripping him by the arm. He'd been cuffed exactly as Will had requested. His hands in front, connected by a chain to his ankles. It would take a Houdini to weasel himself out of that predicament. Even so, seeing Devere so close to freedom made Will's stomach churn.

"Listen, Devere. You try anything, and it's game over. I end you. Understand?"

"Are you threatening me, Decker?"

JB pushed Drake toward the open van.

"Those aren't threats. Those are promises. You get one shot at this. No funny business. If Decker doesn't shoot you, I will. Either way, Vulture goes *bye-bye*. Wings clipped. Stuffed like a Thanksgiving turkey. Got it?"

"You should be a writer, Detective Benson. You've got a real gift for metaphors."

With Melody's help, Devere settled himself inside the enclosed backseat, stuck in a cage where he belonged, and Will started a mental countdown.

"Handsy?"

Not even five seconds had passed before Devere spotted his MHU enemy in the driver's seat. Warden Blevins had requested two officers familiar with his nonsense, and Hank Wickersham fit the bill. Given what they knew about Wickersham, Will didn't like it. But the warden had overruled him.

Devere let out a gleeful yelp. "I didn't know you were comin' along for the ride, Handsy. Road trip! This is gonna be fun. Just keep your hands on—"

Will took satisfaction where he could find it, slamming the door in Drake's face.

"Alright, everybody, Devere is secure. Detective Benson, Officer Murdock, and I will ride in the transport van. Ms. Hoffman, you'll follow behind with Warden Blevins and the cameraman in your own vehicle. When we get wherever the hell we're going, Devere stays in cuffs. We clear the scene first, before we move in."

The tension palpable, Will's thoughts turned to Olivia. He had to remind himself of the why.

"Remember, we're taking a big risk here. Our goal is to get Emily home safely."

Because the how burned beneath his skin like a fever, scorching every last one of his cop instincts.

CHAPTER SEVENTY

Olivia rang the bell for the third time. The blinds were drawn, so she pressed her ear against the door and listened for the shuffle of Nancy Murdock's slippers against the hardwood as she scooted herself along the hall in her wheelchair.

Since Nancy had been diagnosed with dementia, she never left the house. And after she'd nearly set it on fire baking a Bundt cake, Maryann and Melody alternated their shifts at the prison to stay home with her. Olivia never understood why they didn't get her a bed at Sundown. Especially after the rumors that their stepfather, Ken, had molested them for years right under their mother's nose. It explained why the girls had never dated, had never really fit in. Trauma could stunt growth. Could change a sapling to a weed, a magnolia bush to oleander.

When no one answered the door, Olivia approached the garage. She stood on tiptoe, peering into the sectioned windows, at the empty space beyond, the dust motes drifting in the afternoon sunlight.

She scanned the room, stumbling back when she saw it.

She had to get inside.

Her pulse pounding, Olivia ran silently around the back of the house and withdrew the Smith and Wesson she'd kept in her waistband. Deck didn't think she could use it. She'd seen that in his eyes. But what did he know?

She smashed the butt against the lowest window, clearing the razor-sharp shards from the sill with the barrel. Then, she hoisted herself inside.

Keeping the gun raised and ready, Olivia made her way through Maryann's bedroom. Her flowery shirts hung neatly in the closet. A stack of books threatened to topple on her nightstand. Her prison ID badge sat on the dresser.

Olivia crept through the living room and into the kitchen. On the table, a Scrabble board, the tiles still arranged as they'd been left. Luna's pink leash hung from the door.

Swallowing her fear, Olivia turned the knob and took the two steps down into the garage.

She lumbered to the corner, dread weighting her legs, to confirm what she'd seen from the window.

Nancy's wheelchair, MURDOCK printed in permanent marker on the back. One of the footrests was missing. The other matched the one Deck had photographed and included in her folder. Next to it, two pairs of Correct-Tex boots. She turned the shoe over, scraped the mud off the sole. Size ten.

The room began a slow, dizzying spin, threatening to put her on her ass. Olivia dropped into the wheelchair to stay upright. She closed her eyes. Took deep breaths, the way she taught her patients. In through the nose, out through the mouth. The gentle humming of the freezer the only sound.

When she opened her eyes, she looked at it. A small piece of blue fabric protruded from its lid.

Olivia's heart throbbed, picturing Emily in her blue raincoat.

She moved toward the freezer, even as she willed herself away. She had to look. She couldn't not.

With effort, the lid creaked open. The light came on. Nancy Murdock stared back at her, her freezer-burned face perfectly preserved and dotted with ice crystals. She wore a blue caftan. The garrote, still looped around her neck.

Olivia retreated, collapsed to the ground, shaking. She might've stayed there forever if her phone hadn't buzzed in her pocket. An alert from the tracking app. The red dot was on the move.

CHAPTER SEVENTY-ONE

"So, where are we headed, Devere?" Hank eased the van through the parking lot, approaching the turn for Pine Grove Road.

"Out of town. You know that old loony bin?"

Will stared out the windshield, glad Devere couldn't see his face, the shock that had surely paled him a little.

"Willow Wood?" Hank asked. "That place is a death trap. Uh—I mean, it's falling apart. The floors have bound to be rotted through by now."

"How you'd get out there, Devere?" Will asked, as the caravan rumbled onto the main road. "Did the Vulture fly?"

Devere cackled. "Hot-wired a prison work truck. But you already knew that, Detective. I assume you got my little home video."

Hank cleared his throat, his face reddening. His knuckles white on the steering wheel.

"Oh Handsy, this is awkward. Did I not get your good side? If you ask me, you delivered an Oscar-worthy performance. Such raw emotion."

"Shut up." JB pounded on the steel mesh, but Devere didn't flinch. He pressed his cheek to the window, and Will watched him smile in the rearview.

"Beautiful day, ain't it, Detective Decker? It reminds me of our anniversary. A rare bit of sunshine in the middle of winter. Just like that day in February, when we first met face to face. We've come a long way together."

"I said, shut your piehole."

"It's okay," Will said. "Let him talk. He can't help it. He's obsessed with me."

"If anyone's obsessed, it's you. Poor thing. The things you did to catch me the first time, the lines you crossed. And look where it got you. All alone here in Fog Harbor. Exiled by your own family. All you've got left is your badge, your cases. Your old-as-dirt partner. And a cat with one eye. It's sad."

Will felt the sudden jolt to his heart, the electricity in his veins but he showed no signs. Just let it course right through him, frying his nerves in self-imposed silence.

"But you know what's sadder? All that effort, and you've only ever caught me because I wanted you to."

"Yeah, well, prison blue is your color. It really brings out the deadness in your eyes. Congratulations on ending up exactly where you wanted to be. You'll have the rest of your life to enjoy it."

When they turned down the road to Willow Wood, Will gripped the door's handle. He couldn't wait to get out of this coffin of a backseat. To be free of the poison that wafted from Drake, making it impossible to breathe.

He looked past Officer Murdock, who'd squeezed herself into the center seat, to JB. But she seemed to believe his worried frown, his *I-told-you-so* sigh was meant for her.

"Don't worry, Detective. He'll be out of your hair in no time."

Willow Wood's redbrick carcass loomed over them. Like most dead things, some of its pieces had been swallowed by the forest. A fallen redwood rested against the roof. Another leaned precariously toward it. Vines fell like hanging rope out of its broken windows, and its crumbling spires cast long shadows on the grass. But the unexpected sunlight glowed through the windows that remained, giving a flicker of life to its ramshackle eyes.

As Will waited for Officers Murdock and Wickersham to escort Devere from the van, he checked his phone. No signal. Go figure.

"Your cat has one eye?" JB muttered.

"That's not the point. Never mind."

"I get it, City Boy. And there ain't no tellin' how he knows. No way that Jack-the-Ripper wannabe had time to pull off these murders and swing by your house. He probably paid off some flunky like McMillan to spy on you. Just don't let him inside your head."

Devere smirked at Will as he shambled toward them. *Too late.*

"In there." Devere pointed into the dark mouth of the lobby. The ornate front doors stood ajar, as if someone inside had expected visitors. "She's in there."

CHAPTER SEVENTY-TWO

Olivia hit redial, speeding down Pine Grove Road, desperately chasing the red dot otherwise known as Will Decker. She could only hope she wasn't too late. That Em was still alive. Deck too.

"You have reached Detective William Decker with the Fog Harbor—"

She looked at the map on her phone again and cursed, realizing where they'd stopped. On the road with no name, where only one vehicle at a time could travel. It carved a path through the towering redwoods. At the end of its twists and turns stood a large, brick building, long abandoned. Hotel developers had purchased the land years ago, but it remained as it had when its doors were shuttered. Beyond it, a stark cliff with a sheer drop into the ocean and a set of stairs down to secluded Willow Beach.

She'd been there before with Erik, that day he'd carved their initials. And she'd run from Willow Wood then. So fast, she'd left her favorite jacket behind. Denim with blue rhinestones on the collar her mom had sewed herself. Probably, it was still inside somewhere, rat-eaten and mildewed. Slung over that old mattress.

With two miles to go, she pressed the accelerator to the floorboard, the Buick straining with the effort. She tried Deck again. No answer.

The turn in sight now, she dialed the station.

"Fog Harbor Police Department, how can I help you?"

"Chief Flack, please. It's an emergency."

"The chief is monitoring an operation. She asked me to hold her calls."

Olivia groaned in frustration. "That's what I'm calling about. Detective Decker's in trouble. I know who—"

The call dropped, the signal lost, as she steered the car onto the road to Willow Wood. The Buick toiled up the dirt path, steam pouring from beneath the hood. Until it finally gave up, dying on the hill.

Olivia thrust open the door.

She imagined Emily huddled in a cold, sunless place. Bound and gagged. Her throat raw from crying. Rope burns on her wrists. She screamed her sister's name.

CHAPTER SEVENTY-THREE

Will breached the threshold, flashlight in one hand, Glock in the other. JB followed with his gun drawn, covering the door.

They waited inside while Officer Murdock guided Devere up the stone steps. Per Will's instructions, Warden Blevins, Heather, and her cameraman lagged at least ten feet behind. Wickersham had been relegated to patrol the outer perimeter.

The brittle bones of the place creaked in protest as they made their way across the lobby, past the nurses' station. Frozen in time, a calendar hung from the wall proclaimed it December 1992. Will's mother had been long gone by then. His father, well on his way to becoming captain.

Behind him, Heather loud-whispered to the cameraman. "Get a shot of that."

She shrugged when he glared at her.

Will stopped at the entrance to a maze of shadowy hallways, paint peeling from the walls like a snake shedding its skin. Door after door after door laid out before them. Some closed, some opened, some halfway in between. To choose felt like a cruel game.

"Which way, Devere?"

Drake lifted his cuffed hands and gestured toward the first long corridor of patient rooms. At its end, an elevator shaft marked with a blood-red sign: CAUTION: OPEN SHAFTWAY.

Beyond the nurses' station, the cold raised goosebumps beneath his jacket. But not only the cold. Dread began to thrash in his stomach. It only got worse the further they went.

They cleared the rooms one by one, and the group filed down the hallway.

"Room 34," Devere said, finally. "That's the one. She's in there."

The door had been left slightly ajar. Its frame so warped Will doubted it would close anyway. He nudged it with his boot, and it barely moved. Staying flush against the wall, his gun ready, he pushed it the rest of the way, moving inside, as JB trained his sights on the hallway ahead.

Will scanned the room, his heart kicking like a frog in his throat.

A skeleton bed frame pushed to one corner.

A broken mirror leaned against a graffitied wall.

A bedpan. The smell of decay.

A ragged teddy bear slumped on the floor, eviscerated. Its stuffing scattered.

A closet door, bolted shut. The sight of that padlock—the newest, shiniest thing in the room—chilled him.

"Where the hell is she, Devere? I told you. No games."

When Drake didn't answer, Will returned to the hallway.

"Where is she?" He shoved Devere against the wall and out of Melody's reach, holding him there with a forearm to his neck. He poked the barrel of the gun into Drake's ribs. "You think you're safe with a camera here? You think my finger won't slip?"

"Careful." A hint of a smile played on Drake's face, even as it reddened with the effort of breathing. "It would be a shame to see you turn into your brother."

From inside the room, JB called Will's name. "Get in here. I think I heard something."

JB tugged at the lock. Then rammed the door with his shoulder. It didn't budge. Will joined him there, pressing his ear to the slim opening in the wood. Past his own breathing and the rapid *rat-tat-tat* in his chest, he thought he heard a strangled whimper.

"Shit. We need a hammer. Or a crow bar. Something."

"There's a Halligan bar in the trunk. That might work," JB said. "I'll radio Hank."

Will headed back toward the door. He couldn't wait to call Olivia, to hear the relief in her voice. But right now, he needed to lay eyes on Drake. Because he couldn't shake the bad feeling that had clung to him from the moment they'd entered this place.

"Looking for this?" Drake's tongue darted from his mouth. In its pink center, a small, silver key. The sort that would fit a shiny new padlock. It snaked back between his teeth like quicksilver, and he swallowed.

Will didn't believe in ghosts. But he sure as hell believed in monsters.

CHAPTER SEVENTY-FOUR

Olivia's lungs burned as she raced up the hill. But she couldn't stop. Wouldn't. Every time she thought of slowing, she pictured Emily's face. *Baby Emily, with her cherub cheeks. Her perfect tiny fingers latched onto Olivia's thumb.*

Her legs ached. *Little girl Em. Her curls and mischievous smile. Her making a mess of the wall with her paint set.*

The incline grew steeper, the path more treacherous.

She stumbled over an exposed root, breaking her fall with her hands. *Emily in her hand-me-down prom dress, her cap and gown, her fuzzy pink slippers.* She plucked a fat thorn from her palm, and kept going.

Finally, she spotted the spires of Willow Wood, extending their crooked limbs into the sky. As she reached the courtyard, she looked up in wonder, enchanted and terrified.

It looks like a haunted castle, she'd once told Erik, gaping.

I'm gonna lock you up in the dungeon, he'd teased, grabbing her from behind.

Olivia stopped, gasped. Reached for her gun.

A hand on the ground, still as a stump, the rest of the body hidden behind the prison van, its tires slashed. Keeping her eyes up, Olivia moved around the back of the vehicle.

Hank lay there, face down. She hurried to him, rolled him to his side. His bulletproof police vest still intact, his gun missing. A wire garrote had been pulled tight around his throat. So tight it had cut through his flesh. His eyeballs bulged, blood red from the strain.

Terror coursed like ice water in her veins, and she froze. Eight years old again and waiting for her father to scoop her up and carry her away.

But then, she spotted the woman, familiar yet strange, slinking toward the side of the building, a gun in her hand. Their eyes met.

She wasn't eight years old anymore.

They both started running.

CHAPTER SEVENTY-FIVE

Will heard Olivia's voice, frantic and screaming his name. Impossible.

"Deck!"

She materialized, specter white, at one end of the long hallway. She darted toward him, pointing past him to the elevator shaft. The door stood open, like the portal to another world.

"Maryann!"

Devere smiled, baring his teeth.

Face to face with that wicked grin, the last puzzle piece slid into place for Will. A stuffed white dog on the library desk. Maryann sobbing at the drainpipe, researching garrotes and telling him about *Forensic Files*.

A steel canister hit the floor. From nowhere and everywhere an earth-shattering explosion.

CHAPTER SEVENTY-SIX

Olivia's ears rang.

She struggled to open her eyes.

Found herself lying on the floor, her whole world upended.

Through the dissipating smoke, she saw the video camera, discarded on the hardwood. It whirred on, oblivious. Its operator God knows where. Heather, bleeding from a gash on her head.

Olivia squinted through the haze at Maryann, as she dragged a stumbling Drake toward the elevator shaft, firing gunshots over her shoulder.

Melody followed alongside them, ducking around the corner. Unleashing a hail of bullets. Her face distorted by the smoke. Warped by something else Olivia recognized. Feared. But couldn't name.

Warden Blevins rose to his knees and drew his own weapon. He pulled the trigger, and Melody slumped to the ground.

Olivia raised her head and waited for him to fire again, to put Drake down. But instead, the warden turned and scrambled inside one of the rooms.

Maryann struggled on toward the shaft with Drake. JB on his radio, Deck in pursuit; he discharged one shot, then another. Both pinging off the metal shaft doors.

"Stop!" he yelled. As if his voice had the power of a bullet.

Olivia had just pushed herself to her feet when Maryann let loose another canister. It rattled down the hall like a ghost in chains.

The world blew up again.

CHAPTER SEVENTY-SEVEN

Damn flash bang grenade. Will couldn't see. Couldn't breathe either. Couldn't hear a goddamned thing. A sitting duck, he crouched low and clung to the wall, waiting for the smoke to clear. For the ringing in his ears to let up.

The first thing he saw: Melody. Her head twisted awkwardly. Blood seeped from a wound in her stomach. A quick scan of her body, and his heart raced faster. No gun. No keys to her cuffs.

Devere had made it to the elevator shaft. Maryann too. Will fired at them again as Devere pushed the door open, and they scurried down a ladder and dropped out of sight.

"I'm going out the front," JB yelled, as Will ran down the hallway. He peered into the shaft. Dark and graffitied and cluttered with debris, it looked like the gateway to hell. The ladder lay useless at the bottom.

He didn't have time to second-guess it. Just stepped over the side and plummeted straight into the pit.

Relief came first, stopped short by a white-hot pain searing through his foot.

He leaned down to examine it, picked it up. The exposed nail on a rotted baseboard had gone right through his sole.

He gritted his teeth, yelled. Yanked his foot out. Kept moving. Out of the shaft and into the pitch-black basement.

Will hobbled in the dark, listening for footsteps. For breathing. For signs of life. Anything would've been better than absolute silence. Better than the feeling he'd messed it up beyond saving.

Except the clinking of another flash bang launched in his direction. He dropped to the ground, hands over his head, as it exploded. The only sound now, a dull throb behind his eyes.

A blade of light cut a swath through the dark. In that moment, strangely, he thought of Ben. Of that dream he always had that wasn't a dream at all. His Glock, like a viper in his hand. Alive and writhing. Hungry. How easy it would be to pull the trigger. To make a mistake. The line between life and death, between wrong and right, between him and his brother, razor-thin.

"Easy. It's me, partner." Backlit by the sun, JB stood at the door leading out. The smoke escaped around him, dissipating into the blue winter sky. Will lowered his gun and sprinted up the stairs, his foot throbbing.

"Where are they?"

"Heading for the cliffs. Olivia took off after them."

"Was she armed?"

JB shrugged.

"Shit." Will started to run. He knew he'd pay for it later when the adrenaline wore off, but right now, he had to find Olivia. Foot or no foot. Hell, he'd have a found a way to get there on two bloody stumps.

As they raced through the courtyard, Will heard the approaching sirens. His heart deflated, flattened.

"Where's Hank?" he asked, sucking in a breath of bitter-cold air.

"Dead."

CHAPTER SEVENTY-EIGHT

As soon as Olivia reached the tree cover, she stopped running.

She couldn't catch them, not this way.

She closed her eyes and chased a memory instead. Clinging to Erik's hand, they'd walked into the redwood grove in the summer haze. He'd laughed at her when she'd gasped at the rusty sign peering out at them from the overgrowth: SHORTCUT TO WILLOW BEACH.

The shortcut. It had to be here. The path would lead her straight to the cliff. The sand and rock pools below.

She scanned the trees until she spotted the sign overturned in the dirt, entombed in the thick weeds. The Smith and Wesson in her hand, she took off down the path that had long since grown over with neglect.

She weaved between the trees' long, slim bodies. Dodged the smaller branches that whipped against her face. Hurdled the thick roots tangled like arms on the forest floor.

The salt air filled her aching lungs. A gull screamed overhead. The first signs. She was close.

At the edge of the grove, the two paths converged. She took cover behind a tree trunk, peeping out to listen for the rustle of the underbrush. The ragged breathing, not her own. She readied herself.

Still, it scared the hell out of her to lay eyes on Drake, free of his handcuffs, his face red with exertion.

Behind him, Maryann lay in the dirt, grabbing at her foot. "Don't leave me! Please!"

Drake never looked back, never slowed down. He sprinted straight for Olivia, firing at her as he ran. She ducked behind the trunk, the bullets whizzing by her and dead-ending in the belly of an ancient redwood.

As he darted past, she stepped out, intent on giving chase.

"Let him go." Maryann struggled to her feet and pointed her own gun at Olivia.

"Or what? Are you really going to shoot me? You're a librarian." Though she looked anything but. The sweat and wind stood her short hair on end, giving her a set of horns. The sunlight cast strange shadows on her face. Her eyes, two dark holes. Her mouth, a wound.

"Not anymore."

"Where's Emily?"

Maryann kept her gun trained on Olivia. "It was supposed to be you, you know. Drake wanted someone high-profile, someone people really cared about. That way, when he said you were still alive, he figured it would be easy to convince the cops to let him out to lead you there. We didn't realize it was Emily in the car. Not until she'd gotten out. But we couldn't very well stop then. I figured Drake would be pissed off, the way he was when we lost that footrest from the wheelchair. But he was happy. Overjoyed. He said it was perfect. That between Detective Decker being out for revenge and you wanting Emily back, there was no way he wasn't walking out of Crescent Bay. And damn, he was right."

"So this was the plan you agreed to? Him running off, leaving you behind?"

Maryann fired a shot in the air, and Olivia winced. "He loved me. He warned me that we might have to make sacrifices for each other. But he's everything a man should be. Gentle and brutal, all at the same time. He said that I understand him. Even better than you."

"And you've watched *Forensic Files*?" Olivia laughed, hysterical. "He just wanted to screw you. Did he give you his semen too? To plant on Shauna's body. Real romantic."

"Shut up, bitch." Maryann scowled at her. "Emily's dead, you know. She didn't go quietly. She bleated like a poor little lamb. But don't worry. We got it all on tape. I'm sure the cops will let you listen to it, so you can—"

Olivia's mind went blank. An empty slate with two words writ large. *My sister!*

She raised the revolver, white-hot heat coursing through her blood. She understood then, the murderers she counseled at Crescent Bay. How they'd given in to the impulse for total destruction. The need to inflict their own pain on somebody else.

She pointed the barrel at center mass. The vital bits, her dad had called them. The thought of her father, the blood on his hands and the wreckage he'd left behind him, changed her mind.

Olivia redirected the gun, aiming at Maryann's kneecap, and pulled the trigger again and again. Again.

Nothing happened.

CHAPTER SEVENTY-NINE

JB huffed and wheezed as they lumbered toward the redwoods that lined the cliffside.

"How much farther?"

Cracks of gunfire had spooked the gulls that took to the skies, wheeling into the clouds. It propelled Will forward.

Every step, a shooting pain.

Every step, an indictment. If he'd become the job, then he should've at least been damn good at it. Better than this. Smarter.

Under the tree canopy, the sun disappeared. The air, cold and wet and heavy with secrets. It reminded him of Muir Woods, where a hiker and his border collie had unearthed the intact femur of Drake's first victim.

"You okay back there?" he yelled, listening for the sound of JB's boots on the soft ground. The frantic noises of his labored breathing. But he couldn't stop to wait for him.

Will smelled the ocean, that loamy brine, before he spotted Olivia. Her back to him, her auburn hair wild and whipping, as she fired an empty gun.

His fault. He'd unloaded her Smith and Wesson last night, when she'd been out of her mind with worry. He'd helped her lock it in the safe and taken every bullet with him. Stuck them in the drawer of his nightstand and felt like a hero, thinking he'd done the right thing.

"I'm going to enjoy this." Maryann laughed wickedly, her own weapon raised and pointed at Olivia's heart.

Will aimed his Glock. This time he didn't hesitate. He just fired.

CHAPTER EIGHTY

"Are you okay?" Deck asked.

Olivia didn't answer. She wasn't sure.

She watched as the firemen worked with single-minded focus, snapping the padlock from the door with a set of bolt cutters. The catch gave way, but Olivia didn't rush in as she'd thought she would.

Until right then, it hadn't been real. Not when she'd stared into the blank eye of Maryann's gun, anticipating the shot that would end her. Or when she'd watched Maryann slump to the ground with a bullet hole in her head. Not even when Deck had run on without her, tracking Drake to the sea.

But now, it hit her. An earthquake to the soul. Emily could be—might be—dead. Maryann had said so.

Deck pushed the door the rest of the way. She had no choice now but to look.

Bound and gagged and blindfolded, her strawberry-blonde curls crusted with blood, Emily's body lay balled at the back of the closet.

Olivia touched her sister's hands—cold, so cold—and whispered her name like a prayer, watching desperately for the rise and fall of her chest.

San Francisco Post

"Vulture Escapes Crescent Bay State Prison, Leaves a Trail of Bodies Behind Him"
by Lillie Ferraro

Drake Devere, otherwise known as the Vulture, escaped police custody two days ago during a planned rescue operation at the former Willow Wood State Hospital. Devere had promised authorities he would lead them to Emily Rockwell, who had been missing since Saturday. Conspiring with two female accomplices who worked at Crescent Bay State Prison (CBSP), Devere managed to free himself and flee from authorities in a small fishing craft near Willow Beach. Correctional officer Hank Wickersham and cameraman Joey Marcello were pronounced dead at the scene. Both men sustained fatal injuries. Maryann Murdock was shot and killed by police during the incident, while her sister Melody sustained a gunshot wound to the stomach, attempting to aid in Devere's escape. Rockwell, who was discovered alive after nearly twenty-four hours in captivity, is also receiving medical treatment.

Police Chief Sheila Flack confirmed Melody Murdock, a CBSP correctional officer, was placed under arrest for multiple counts of first-degree murder and kidnapping at Fog Harbor General Hospital, where her condition is listed as guarded. Murdock and her twin sister, Maryann, are believed to have masterminded the recent attacks on local women at the behest of Devere. The body of an additional victim, Nancy Murdock, the twins' mother, was discovered strangled in their Fog Harbor home. Additional charges in the deaths of Wickersham and Marcello are pending. Devere remains at large, along with an unknown accomplice who police believe aided his escape. Authorities believe the suspects are armed and dangerous and may have fled up the coast and into Canada.

Though the Fog Harbor Police Department has been widely criticized for their handling of the rescue operation, CBSP Warden, Lester Blevins, was praised for his heroics during the exchange of gunfire. Governor Miriam Zaruba lauded Blevins, telling reporters, "Without his quick thinking in taking down the suspect, Melody Murdock, there is no doubt she would have escaped as well, likely injuring or killing other law enforcement personnel. He is nothing short of a hero."

Fog Harbor Gazette's Heather Hoffman, who sustained minor injuries in the attack, obtained video footage of the botched operation, which was seized by law enforcement officials pending further investigation. Hoffman announced plans to release a first-person account of Devere's escape in her television debut on *Good Morning, San Francisco,* this weekend.

CHAPTER EIGHTY-ONE

Olivia's eyes opened, closed, opened again. Her lids heavy, as she watched the twinkle of white lights on a tabletop Christmas tree. She pulled the cheap blanket up to her chin, leaving her feet cold, and repositioned herself in the chair near her sister's bed.

"Merry Christmas, Em."

Still half asleep, Emily blinked a few times before she spoke. Her eyes, ringed like a raccoon's. "Typical dysfunctional Rockwell family Christmas."

Olivia laughed, nodding. As girls, their Christmases had been spent in the austere visiting room at Crescent Bay State Prison, eating their holiday feast from a vending machine and looking into their father's eyes, lifeless as an unshaken snow globe. Em didn't know about the Christmases before. In Apartment E, there never seemed to be enough money for presents, and they had no chimney for Santa to shimmy down. By afternoon, her dad had passed out on the sofa, drunk or high or both, and her mom's eyes would get misty. But at midnight, the whole neighborhood gathered in the courtyard at the Double Rock to shoot their pistols in the air and watch Termite's dad, Freddie "Three Fingers" Colvin, pop wheelies on his Yamaha. When he leaned back, rising onto his rear tire, and the crowd erupted, Olivia almost believed in some kind of warped Christmas magic.

"How's your head?"

Emily rubbed the back of her head, her mild skull fracture swathed in gauze. "Feels like I've been clocked by a psychopath wielding a blunt object. Oh, wait."

"Not funny."

But if anyone could find humor in being kidnapped, Em could. The only bright spot for Olivia, her sister's amnesia. All Emily recalled about her ordeal could be summed in a few sentences she'd recited for Deck and JB and the FBI. Fugitive Task Force.

I hit something in the road. And then Maryann came running up, yelling for the dog, telling me I'd run Luna over. When I got out of the car, I realized it was a stuffed animal. The one Maryann kept on her desk in the library. I started to say something and next thing I know, I woke up bound and gagged and freezing my butt off in the dark, thinking they'd stuck an axe in my head.

"When do you think I'll get out of here?" Emily asked, scooting over to make room for Olivia. She patted the mattress and Olivia winced at the sight of the rope burns on her wrists. "This place is depressing. I mean, who puts a bedpan next to a Christmas tree?"

"The doctor said tomorrow. They want to do another CT scan just to be sure."

Olivia climbed in the warm spot next to her sister, leaned her head against her shoulder. After a few minutes of hospital silence—the mechanical beeps, the squeaking wheels on tile, the occasional moan—she felt certain Em had fallen asleep.

"Hey, Liv? You awake?"

"Yeah."

When Emily spoke, she sounded so small. Like she'd hidden in the smallest, darkest corner inside herself. "You know how I said I didn't remember anything from the Murdocks' basement?"

Olivia nodded, bile rising in her throat. She couldn't recall when she'd last eaten. A barbecue sandwich Deck had brought her last night, maybe. She hoped it wouldn't come back up.

"That wasn't exactly true."

"Okay." It wasn't okay. Not at all. But the shrink in Olivia took over, knew what to say. The big sister in her knew what to leave unsaid.

"I do remember something. But I'm not sure if it's real or if I dreamed it. Maryann took the blindfold off for a little while. She told me I looked scared and let me hold Luna. She said Luna always made her feel better. I didn't realize at first how limp the dog was in my arms. How her little eyes didn't open. I freaked and tried to give her back but Maryann got right in my face. She told me, 'This is what I'm capable of. There's nothing I won't do for him.'"

"Sounds like a bad dream." Olivia held her sister close. She didn't have the heart to tell her, not today. Maybe not ever. The cops had found Luna in the Murdocks' basement, stiff and cold. Her neck, broken.

Olivia draped an extra blanket over her sister, tucking her in, snug as a bug, the way she'd always done when Em was little. She'd resented it back then, being stuck with her kid sister playing Candyland and Barbies, while their mother spent her nights working two jobs or drinking at the Hickory Pit. She'd always wondered why her mom stuck around Fog Harbor, why she didn't kick life-term inmate Martin Reilly to the proverbial curb. But looking at Em, her eyelashes fluttering, she got it now. Her mother had done whatever it took to keep their family afloat, all together on the same patched-up life raft.

When Olivia woke later, in the middle of the night, she felt certain someone had been there. In the room with them. That the hospital door had opened, letting in the light from the hallway. That a long, thin shadow had breached the threshold, followed by the man who cast it.

She knew because he'd left a package near the tabletop tree Leah had brought over yesterday. FROM WARDEN BLEVINS on the front in black ink.

Olivia held it, studied it. The same size, the same dirty brown paper as that package she'd watched pass from his hands to Riggs and to Termite's. Same as the one Laura had unearthed from a sack of flour.

Her stomach flipped as she removed the wrapping. Lifted the lid.

"What is it?" Emily raised her head, her voice groggy.

Olivia frowned, still trying to make sense of it. Of all she'd imagined, never this.

"A fruitcake," she said.

CHAPTER EIGHTY-TWO

"You ready, City Boy?" JB paused in front of the hospital room door. The handwritten name drew Will's eyes in like a magnet. *Murdock, Melody.*

But he thought of her sister, Maryann, instead. Of her dog, Luna. And her books. Her dumpy wardrobe. A perfectly crafted façade. Still, he saw Maryann as a victim. Melody too. Innocent in their own right—like a claw hammer or a butcher knife—but in the wrong hands, a deadly weapon. Devere had wielded the twins without regret. The way he'd always handled women.

"As ready as I'll ever be."

They nodded at the officer out front as they entered, taking their usual positions at the foot of the bed where Melody's legs lay covered by a white thermal blanket.

She looked more herself than she had in the last ten days. The tube had been removed from her nose. Her hair had been combed. Her face, washed. Her eyes regarded them with wary recognition.

"We heard you wanted to talk." Will figured there could only be one reason for that, so it didn't surprise him when her first words croaked out like she'd scraped them up from her throat and spit them.

"That bitch." Melody took a sip of water and started again. "We were supposed to leave together. Me and Drake. That was the plan."

"So what happened?"

Will already knew the answer. He'd seen the letters between the Vulture and his birds of prey. The Osprey, Drake's nickname for Maryann and the Falcon, his nickname for Melody. He'd read enough to realize the depths of their obsession. But not enough to understand it. Not even a post office full of letters could have done that.

"She wanted him for herself. She always had to be the center of attention. Even with our perverted stepdad, Ken. Like it was a competition, who he liked to feel up more. This whole thing was her idea, you know. Hers and Drake's. *She* killed Mom. Not that I would have stopped her."

JB dragged a chair from the corner to the side of Melody's bed and motioned to Will. His foot still ached but he couldn't sit. Every time he let himself relax, he imagined Devere slithering further from his grasp. Like a snake in the underbrush. To hell with doctor's orders, he shook his head and leaned against the wall instead.

"Tell us your side of it," Will said. "Everything you can remember."

JB started the handheld recorder, placing it on Melody's nightstand. She stared at it for a moment, a faraway smile on her face. The seconds ticked by on the counter as she talked.

"I remember it all. Sometimes, I wish I didn't."

Melody told them how Devere had seduced her. First, with kindness. He'd complimented her. Written her little poems. Taken her hand when no one was looking. Then, he'd asked for a few favors—extra helpings from the kitchen, cigarettes, dirty magazines. By the time he'd promised her a new life far from Fog Harbor and they'd armed themselves with flash bang grenades from the prison arsenal and guns from the local bait and tackle store, she'd long been a player in an irresistible game for three. Her opponent, her own sister. Her twin.

"Drake told us he had to look guilty. He selected the victims. We concocted the ruses. He told us how to stage the scene, what evidence to leave behind. What rumors to start at the prison and when. He knew the cameras didn't work in bad weather, that it would look suspicious. So, we waited for the rain. At the end, he'd started to get frustrated. Cranky. That's why we got into a fight in the hallway. Nobody was really taking him seriously as a suspect, even you two. So, he had us make that video at the Hickory Pit, showing the prison truck in the background. He pulled out a few hairs, jacked off into a tube. He played us all like puppets."

Will understood he'd been a puppet, too. His own strings pulled by Drake's skillful hands. That part, out of all of it, rankled him the most.

"Did you love the guy?" JB's mouth twisted after he'd asked her. Like he'd tasted something rotten.

"I'm not stupid. I know what he is. What he's done. But it felt nice being noticed. Being wanted. I didn't realize he was doing the same with my sister. He told me I was special, prettier than her. Smarter too."

"And the murders?" Will asked. "What was your role?"

"Maryann did the killing. She was good at it. A little too good. I should've known right then. We used our mother's wheelchair to move the bodies. At least Mom was useful for something, you know?"

Will didn't let himself feel the shiver up his spine. Later, he'd need a long, hot shower to wash this one off.

"She was a sorry excuse for a mom. She blamed us when our dad left. Blamed us when she couldn't find a man. Then, she blamed us when the one she found couldn't keep his hands to himself. She knew. The whole time, she knew. She just looked the other way."

JB snorted. "So, that's what this was all about? Your mommy issues? Give me a break."

"I wouldn't expect you to understand. But we got tired of it all. Tired of Mom. Tired of Fog Harbor. Tired of the women in this town prancing around like they're on a runway in Paris."

Melody's face reddened as she talked. Her hands curled into her blanket, a death grip.

"He promised us a new life. But he told me we'd split from Maryann once we crossed the Canadian border."

Melody's eyes trailed toward the window, where a light rain had started to fall, tear-streaking the glass.

"So, Canada? That's where he's headed." The fishing boat had been found abandoned days ago on a beach ten miles from Devil's Rock. Three hundred miles from Canada. Far from the razor wire of Crescent Bay.

She shrugged. "I hope you catch him. I'd like to stick the needle in myself."

JB's eyes widened, not for the first time. "Jeez," he muttered.

"What do you know about his accomplice?" Will asked. "Female as well?"

Melody shook her head. "Couldn't tell ya. He wasn't exactly forthcoming."

Will took a breath, readying himself for his last question. For the answer he knew would make him feel like the biggest fool of all.

"Did Devere ever leave the prison?"

Melody's bitter guffaw startled him. "Not once. But he wanted to. Before we did the first one, he told me he wished he could be there. That's when Maryann got the idea for keratoconjunctivitis sicca."

JB made a face. "For *what?*"

"Dry eyes," Will said, as Melody nodded.

"Maryann made Drake a fake medical chrono. He could check out audiobooks from the library. It made perfect sense. He wouldn't be there to witness the life draining from their faces. But he could hear them gasping. Could hear Emily struggling in the basement. Could hear the last breath Bonnie took. We got all of it on tape."

JB opened the glove box as soon as Will started the car. "That was some crazy shit, partner. I need a Twinkie. A foot rub. And a long vacation."

"How about a raise?"

"Hell, yes. That too."

Will noticed the gold band on a certain stubby finger when he accepted the second Twinkie from the package. "Did you run off to Vegas when I wasn't looking?"

"Nah." JB laughed, his cheeks flushing.

Will recognized the look, though he'd never seen it on JB's face. "You look happy, man."

"Tammy and I are givin' it another go. Her and Princess moved back in last night. She asked me to wear my ring again. Just so everybody knows I'm off the market."

"Congratulations." Will extended his cake for a Twinkie toast, but JB wrinkled his nose. Shook his head. Took a whopping bite.

"You keep your Twinkie to yourself, City Boy."

As Will sighed, JB spoke with a mouthful. "Wanna know the best part?"

He waited for the punchline, already rolling his eyes in anticipation.

"I don't have to spring for another goddamned wedding ring."

CHAPTER EIGHTY-THREE

Olivia placed an order—two number fives and a side of mac and cheese—and retreated toward the booth in the back to wait for Deck.

Not for the first time that night, she reminded herself this was not a date. Even though she'd worn her hair down and spent way too long rifling through her closet to pick an outfit. Even though she'd taken a long swig of her beer to quiet the restless butterflies and imagined the way Deck would smile when he saw her.

She had to get a grip. Keep her hands, her lips—and, most importantly, her heart—to herself. Because the alternative led down a dead-end road. To other dead-end things. Like the *l* word. Things with teeth that made wounds that never closed. Nearly losing Em had reminded her of that. JB had been right. Some words should never be said aloud.

"I found your name on the wall."

Olivia jumped, spilling a little foam onto the floor as she plunked down her glass on the table, and turned to Deck. He stood at the site of Erik's meticulous carving, running his finger across the notched wood with a mischievous grin.

"Did you? I'm sure more than one Olivia R. has passed through Fog Harbor."

"But I doubt those Olivia R.'s were named Cutest Couple with Erik Z. by the graduating class of 2002, as seen in the Fog Harbor High yearbook. *Go Sharks!*"

She slid into the booth and took another sip, feeling her cheeks flame. She'd been stupidly proud of that title, relishing it more than her other designation. Most Likely to Succeed. It didn't get more dead-end than that.

"Don't look so surprised. I am a detective."

Something dark passed across Deck's face as he took the seat opposite. His smile dampened, and she felt a stab of pity. Guilt, too. "A good one," she said.

"That's debatable." He took his phone from his pocket, swiped the screen, and displayed an online article to her as evidence. *Former SFPD Detective Botches Serial Murder Case.* "And you should see the comments."

She pushed it away, shaking her head at him. "It's total BS. You were one hundred percent right about Drake. You told the chief it was a bad idea. She should've listened to you. *I* should've listened to you."

"Can I get that in writing?" He laughed a little, all breath. "You know, your profile was spot on. It takes a lot to impress Chief Flack. You were right about the murders. Copycats. Female copycats at that. I totally missed the boat." He paused for a beat, hanging his head. "Literally. And I almost got you killed in the process."

"True. But, you also saved me. It's the ultimate paradox. Like being a wise fool."

"Well, when you put it like that…"

She laughed. "Look, the only thing that really matters is we found Em. And she's gonna be okay. We're already talking about her starting at San Francisco Art College in the spring."

Olivia felt grateful when Deck agreed with her, knowing it wasn't the whole truth. The thought of Drake walking free in the world had kept her awake most nights, her gun within reach on the nightstand. Fully loaded. She'd never make that mistake again.

Even so, she woke up in a cold sweat sometimes, convinced she'd seen him standing in her doorway. All shadow and teeth.

Deck puzzled for a moment, resting his head on his chin. "So you're saying we were both right. And wrong. Does that mean we make a good team? Or a hopeless one?"

"I think it means we're splitting the check, and we need to work on our timing."

He grinned, and she hoped he hadn't read too much into it.

"What about Chief Flack's offer to help out on our cases? Do a little profiling again? JB and I could use your expertise—well, JB could anyway—assuming you learn to follow police commands. Are you in?"

Olivia gulped her beer. She'd known the train was coming when she'd tied herself to the tracks and agreed to this non-date. "On one condition."

"Name it."

She forced herself to look into his eyes so he wouldn't doubt her. Kept her hands clasped in her lap. Ignored the brutal twist of her heart. "We keep things platonic. Just friends."

"Forget it, then. Offer withdrawn. You're fired."

They both laughed. Olivia's clunking from her throat, hollow.

"Kidding." She hated how easily that word rolled off his tongue. "Friends it is."

EPILOGUE

Two Months Later

Even on a dreary Monday in February, Cy had found the sun. He rolled onto his back in a spot of warm light on the walkway, lifting his head when Will pulled his truck into the garage. By the time Will slipped back out the garage door, Cy had righted himself to a dignified position, licking his front paw.

"You hungry, buddy?"

The cat followed him up the steps, waiting not-so-patiently as Will checked the mailbox. His plaintive meows channeled Will's soul. Because he hadn't forgotten the date even if he'd wanted to. It had been there all day, banished to a dark corner of his mind.

As Cy weaved through his legs, Will sorted through the stack. Bills, junk mail. A coupon for ten dollars off ribs at the Pit he planned to put to quick use. Nothing from Devil's Rock, Oregon. Not even a *Happy Anniversary, Decker* postcard. It didn't give him the relief he'd expected. He preferred the predictable Vulture. The one who'd left him staring out at the ocean, gray and churning, where a small motor boat had left its wake. He'd emptied the Glock, but by then the boat had been too far away to hit. As it passed the rock jetty, it had idled, swaying on the waves, and Devere had raised his hand. Will pictured it some nights. The way Devere looked like a fisherman returning home from a journey, celebrating his whopping big catch. One detective, reeled in and writhing. Hooked firmly by the gullet.

Disgusted by the memory, Will tossed the mail on the counter, changed into a pair of shorts and the T-shirt his Secret Santa had given him for Christmas—FHPD printed on one side, CITY BOY on the back—and headed back to the garage, where Cy waited by his bowl.

Will upturned the bag of kibble into the dish. It overflowed as he stared at the large unmarked envelope resting in the cat's bed.

A chill zipped up his spine. It went straight to his heart, and for a split second he swore it stopped, like an old watch someone had forgotten to wind.

He took the envelope with him as he retrieved his gun from the counter. As he searched the garage, the house, the backyard. Satisfied he was alone, he tore it open and removed the book inside. The cover image drawn by the same hand as the first. A bird's talons, dripping red, below the title.

Hawk's Revenge
Book Two in the Bird of Prey Series
by Bestselling Author, Drake Devere

Will flipped through the pages, desperate. As if he expected to find the man himself pressed between the parchment paper. Or the last shred of his dignity, hidden like a petal, carefully preserved. Or a memory he'd boxed up and put away, knowing one day it would claw its way out, slimy and malformed.

He found himself back at the end of the beginning, when he hadn't been so by-the-book, had been more like Ben, making a choice to cross a line. To walk into a bar in Modesto. To order a girl a strong drink and another and another. To walk her out to her car. To ask for her help. Just one little favor.

We have overwhelming evidence on your boyfriend.

We could charge you for obstructing.

All we need is Drake's DNA to put him away forever.

We won't go for the death penalty. I promise.

Will thought about her sometimes, Drake's girlfriend, Isabella Torro. She'd met him the next day with hair from Drake's comb and a cup he'd discarded in the trash. More than enough for a DNA sample.

He studied the dedication meant for him. It had been printed in ink this time for the whole world to see. The ultimate schoolyard call out. As he read, the scar on his hand tingled.

For Will
What you did to me will be done to you ten times over.

How could he have known Isabella would change her mind? That her guilt would turn vile and vengeful. That she'd be there, waiting for him outside the station. That she'd sink a knife into his hand, go for his partner too. That he'd have no choice but to shoot Isabella in self-defense. No choice but to live with it.

Sweat dripped onto the concrete as Will fired another jab-cross into the bag's meaty flesh. He'd exhausted himself, so that when Petey pushed open the garage door and stood there, he could only stare back at him.

"Ain't you gonna say nothin', big brother?"

"What do you want me to say?"

"Ask me why I'm here, for starters. Then, tell me it's been too long. That you're glad to see me. Hell, maybe even give me a man hug."

Will realized then, looking at his brother's eyes which were so much like their dad's, like his own, it had been too long. He was glad—relieved—to see him. It made him feel less alone. And on February 3rd that was no small feat. He wrapped his brother in a sweaty embrace Petey quickly wriggled out of, both of them laughing.

"So, why are you here? Don't tell me you need money. I'm not paying that Bertolucci a single penny."

Petey sighed and slumped onto the tailgate. "I do need money. But it ain't for me. Oaktown's been saying our brother's got to pay to stay, and his canteen account's run dry. Ben's in trouble."

A LETTER FROM ELLERY

Want to keep up to date with my latest releases? Sign up here!

www.bookouture.com/ellery-kane

We promise never to share your email with anyone else, we'll only contact you when there's a new book available, and you can unsubscribe at any time.

Thank you for reading *Watch Her Vanish*! With so many amazing books to choose from, I truly appreciate you taking the time to read the first installment in the Rockwell and Decker series. The town of Fog Harbor and Crescent Bay State Prison are fictional places but are loosely based on my travels as a forensic psychologist in the state of California. Olivia and Will have many more exciting adventures ahead, and I hope you'll continue on this journey with them.

One of my favorite parts about being an author is connecting with readers like you. You can get in touch with me through any of the social media outlets below, including my website and Goodreads page. Also, if you wouldn't mind leaving a review or recommending the Rockwell and Decker series to your favorite readers, I would really appreciate it! Reviews and word-of-mouth recommendations are essential, because they help readers like you discover my books.

Thank you again for your support! I look forward to hearing from you, and I hope to see you around Fog Harbor again soon!

TheLegacyBooks/

@ellerykane

ellerykane.com

ACKNOWLEDGMENTS

First, I owe an immense debt of gratitude to you, my avid readers. Knowing my writing has affected you, inspired you, and even scared you just a little, makes every word worth it! I hope you love Olivia, Will, JB, Emily, and the rest of the Fog Harbor crew as much as I do and will stay tuned for more of their adventures.

Thank you to my family, friends, and work colleagues who have always been there to support me and to encourage me to keep dreaming big! All the best parts of my characters are based on them. Though my mom is no longer with me, she taught me her love for words, and I know she's cheering me on even though I can't see her. Thanks, too, to my dad, who's never been a reader but thinks I'm brilliant anyway.

To my special someone, Gar, who deserves so much more than an acknowledgment or a dedication—though he has both—for the countless hours of plot discussion; for the kick in the butt to keep writing; for the occasional bad review pep talk; and above all else, for guarding my heart like a dragon and believing in my dreams as fiercely as if they were his own.

And finally, a huge thank you to Jessie Botterill for taking a chance on me! Her keen eye and sharp editorial lens have helped shape this book into something fantastic. Like Rockwell and Decker, I think we make a great team, and I feel so lucky to be working with her and the entire Bookouture family!

I have always drawn inspiration for my writing from my day job as a forensic psychologist. We all have a space inside us that we keep hidden from the world, a space we protect at all costs. So many people have allowed me a glimpse inside theirs—dark deeds, memories best unrecalled, pain that cracks from the inside out—without expectation of anything in return. I couldn't have written a single word without them.

Printed in Great Britain
by Amazon

40703543R00235